DREAD AND DESIRE

He began at her throat, at the first appearance of a faint blue vein in her translucent, alabaster skin, which he trailed with his lips until they touched her breasts.

Lacy punched him with the heels of her palms, resisting the exquisite torture he was only beginning. "Oh, God," she groaned. "No, Jesse."

"Yes, Jesse," he countered, sure of himself, sure of her.

And why shouldn't he be? He was the lover who wed her, wasn't he? He was the husband who loved her, wasn't he? Even if her mind could not remember, certainly her body could.

Unless lust itself lied, like everything else. . . .

MIRROR, MIRROR

MIRROR, MIRROR

Donna Julian

AN ONYX BOOK

ONYX
Published by the Penguin Group
Penguin Books USA Inc., 375 Hudson Street,
New York, New York 10014, U.S.A.
Penguin Books Ltd, 27 Wrights Lane,
London W8 5TZ, England
Penguin Books Australia Ltd, Ringwood,
Victoria, Australia
Penguin Books Canada Ltd, 10 Alcorn Avenue,
Toronto, Ontario, Canada M4V 3B2
Penguin Books (N.Z.) Ltd, 182–190 Wairau Road,
Auckland 10, New Zealand

Penguin Books Ltd, Registered Offices:
Harmondsworth, Middlesex, England

First published by Onyx, an imprint of Dutton Signet,
a division of Penguin Books USA Inc.

First Printing, December, 1996
10 9 8 7 6 5 4 3 2 1

Copyright © Donna Julian, 1996
All rights reserved

PUBLISHER'S NOTE
This is a work of fiction. Names, characters, places, and incidents either
are the product of the author's imagination or are used fictitiously,
and any resemblance to actual persons, living or dead, events, or locales
is entirely coincidental.

To the fairest of them all:

My grandmother, Dolly Pritchett,
who taught me that the sweetest
joy is found in family,
and
My mother-in-law, Katie Julian,
who showed me through example
how unconditional love should be.

This is for you, dear ones,
with love and admiration.

Acknowledgments

Every writer should have benefit of friends and experts—very often one and the same—as I did during the creation of this book. The list is long, but then, I am very lucky:

E. J. Cunningham, M.D., who helped me pull off a diabolical plot twist, while telling me jokes and keeping me healthy all at the same time.

Bill Preston, U.S. Federal Marshal, who always has time to answer my questions about how the "system" works. Stay safe.

Jack Atherton, Executive Assistant to the Warden of Lompoc U.S. Federal Penitentiary, for helping me "see" it.

Lindell Ames, son-in-law and honest-to-goodness cowboy, who taught me a whole bunch about guns, and horses, and "get-along-little-dogie."

Jackie Hansard, who polished the coal I mined into the sparkling gem it was intended to be.

Diana Hagan, owner of The Armchair Adventurer Bookstore, and Amy Templer, manager of the Midrivers B. Dalton, who are already talking this one up to the readers.

Susann Batson, Julie Beard, Norma Beishir, Anna Eberhardt, Suzanne Forster, Mary Martin, Bonnie Jeanne Perry, Meryl Sawyer, Bobbie Smith, and Katherine Stone, because they understand the process and help me endure.

Jeanne Beckerle, Barbara Carbray, Julie "Sami" Collins, and Sheila Jackson, because they can't understand, and still they care.

Leah Bassoff for never screaming no matter how great the provocation.

Maureen Walters for convincing me to take on Texas and cowboys. You were right: they are as exciting and sexy as Manhattan and Wall Street executives.

And Audrey LaFehr, whom I can list last because she is so obviously number one with me.

Prologue

She'd come to Dallas in search of proof that would exonerate her in the eyes of the man she loved. The perfect birthday gift for her husband. She frowned. Not that she'd even known the date of his birthday until yesterday. Wouldn't have known that it was this weekend if she hadn't happened to overhear his mother and brother discussing the party they'd planned for him before ...

She shook the rest of the thought away, discarding it along with the threat of depression. Not today. Today she was going to pretend that everything was as it should be; that she and Jesse were the perfect couple just as the mirror had boasted earlier that morning. Correction. As they truly would be once she handed him the envelope tucked away in her purse. The ultimate present!

As she cut a path through the mezzanine of the shopping mall, she smiled at the memory of the two of them caught in a chance moment together in the reflection of the huge, beveled antique mirror that hung in the foyer. For just an instant, he, too, had been mesmerized by the perfection of the two of them standing there together—he so tall and strong and dark; she so fair and slender and delicate by comparison. She'd seen it in his startled dark gaze.

Lifting her chin as she rounded the famous mall fountains, she balled her hands with conscious determination. There remained so much that confused her, so little she understood about her marriage, her husband, their life together before the accident, but she knew one thing for certain. She was going to right all that was wrong between her and her handsome cowboy. Today was the beginning of a new life for the two of them. The questions that still begged answers could be put aside for the next couple of days. At least until after Jesse's party.

Her step quickened with the confident bounce of her stride, she grinned happily. A long black-and-white plastic bag bearing the Saks Fifth Avenue logo contained the gown she'd selected for the Saturday night gala. Now, she was headed for Lord & Taylor's. She had one last purchase to make before the two-hour drive home.

It was a second gift for Jesse; the one she would present publicly at his celebration: a sterling silver belt buckle inlaid with turquoise and jade. An intricately crafted depiction of a rearing stallion and coiled snake. She'd seen it advertised in a magazine the night before and had been delighted to find it available in the Dallas department store.

This morning she'd raced through a fabricated explanation for her sudden trip to Dallas. Talking so fast, she wondered at her ability to keep her words from tripping all over each other; she told Jesse she was consulting a specialist she'd learned of, perfectly mindful of the quantum leap he would make in the wrong direction and praying he wouldn't question her. Contrarily, she'd been hurt by his pointed uncaring. Other than a slightly raised brow, a mocking display of mild surprise that she would trouble herself to such lengths for answers he no longer cared whether or not she ever found out.

She doubted he'd even ask what the doctor had to say, but if he did, well, the only thing spoiled would be the timing. Nothing could diminish the value of the actual gift.

Her grin was wide, expressive of her almost nearly irrepressible joy. She quickened her step, patting the soft leather handbag containing the envelope and the single most significant sheet of paper of her life.

"Shelby!"

She turned, spinning on her heel, surprised at hearing her name called so far from home, but a smile was already in place, and her hand was raised halfway in greeting by the time she met the man's gaze. And then she realized that the person rushing toward her from across the tiled floor was a stranger. The smile withered and her raised hand began to tremble as her heart slammed painfully in her chest. She took a step backward, losing her balance as her ankle twisted beneath her. The man who had called out to her rushed forward to grab her arm and save her from the fall.

"My God, Shel, are you all right? You're as white as paste! I didn't mean to startle you."

She shook her head from side to side, whipping her pale blond hair with her denial. "My name's not Shelby," she said in a strangled whisper. *Then why, God, did I think for a moment it was?* her mind screamed.

PART I

Mirror, Mirror, on the wall,
Who's the fairest of them all?
—*Snow White*

The three FBI agents watched her cross the room and perch a hip on the corner of Bureau Chief Warren Anderson's desk to dangle a long, shapely leg as she examined the documents he'd given her. After a moment she looked up, her blue eyes dancing and her deep, throaty laughter reflecting her satisfaction. "So, it's official. I'm really Lacy James now." She pulled a cashier's check from the manila wallet, tracing the zeros with one of her pearly, lacquered nail tips. "And fiscally very comfortable."

"Spend it wisely, Miss, um, James—"

"Un-uh," she said, wagging a finger in the chief's face. "Never, ever, ever, lecture me about money. I was born with an understanding of the value of the almighty dollar."

Though Warren Anderson didn't like the woman, he couldn't help but admire her. She was as cold and calculating as the man she had helped convict on racketeering, four counts of conspiracy to commit murder, yada, yada, yada; the same man who had been her lover for nearly ten years. She was probably the most beautiful woman he'd ever met. She was self-centered, clever, and ambitious. Most of all, she was a bitch. But she had better instincts for survival than most of his best trained agents. In the year since she'd first appeared in his office to present her terms for the deal she sought—the government's money, connections, and a new identity in exchange for her damning testimony against bad guy Sammy Wyatt—he'd come to know her well.

She was a chameleon. A vamp who could seduce a monk with a simple swipe of her tongue over her sensuous lips or an arched brow and suggestive gleam in her blue eyes. A vulnerable, helpless woman when she turned those same baby blues on a man, turned on that innocent smile that produced a single dimple in her cheek, and twisted a strand of pale corn-silk-blond hair around her finger. Or an intelligent, articulate business-woman with both brains and street savvy to serve her. There were a half-dozen more sides that he'd witnessed personally, and probably more than that, yet Warren Anderson couldn't help but be glad that today was the last he would see of her. With the money, credentials, and a carefully constructed background, she was ready to begin a new life. He only hoped she hadn't made a mistake with the location she'd selected.

"It's not too late to change your mind," he said.

She grinned, ignoring the chief and directing her comment to Frank Mandell, the young, carrot-topped agent. "It suits me, don't you think?" She chuckled as she followed his eyes to the deep vee of her silk blouse. "The *name*, Franky, baby. I look like a Lacy, don't you think?"

"Uh, yes, ma'am."

Lacy almost purred as she gave her head a catlike shake of pleasure, her shimmering mane reminding each man in the room of nights he'd spent with his hands entwined in the silky strands, if only in his dreams.

Scooting off the desk, she faced Warren, who stood in the middle of the room, ready to give the order for her escort to the airport and the awaiting private jet the bureau had chartered for her. Her legs braced wide in spite of her customary tight, short skirt, and her head tossed back, she grinned. "Don't look so worried, Warren, darling." She raised her hand and held up two fingers. "Scout's honor, sweetie, I'm not going to change my mind and come looking for you to relocate me. I'm going to Rooster Corner, Texas, pretend to write my romance novels, and get to know a certain millionaire oilman."

"I did some research on Jesse Pryde, Sh—Lacy. His family may claim to be simple ranchers who got lucky when they struck oil, but Pryde's no hayseed who'll pro-pose marriage just because a beautiful woman crooks her finger."

Lacy grabbed Warren's tie, her gaze locked with his

for a long moment as her fingers slid slowly down its conservative striped pattern before stopping midchest to nimbly unfasten one of his shirt buttons and slip inside. "Ah, but I'm not just *any* beautiful woman, Warren."

His face burning with his flush, he clamped a hand over her wrist, struggling to control the timbre of his voice. "And I'm only giving you warning, Miss James. The bureau won't finance another move if things don't work out the way you've planned."

Her smile was slow and lazy and as seductive as a kiss. "I'm going to miss you, Warren, and I'll worry about you. You're too serious. A man as sexy as you shouldn't be so earnest ... except about the way he makes love to a woman."

Warren turned away, crossing the room in three long strides to circle his desk and claim his chair. Disgust marred his handsome features though Lacy and the other lawmen knew it was self-directed. "Agents Mandell and Waters will take you to the airport. Have a safe trip."

"I'll send you an invitation to the wedding," Lacy said, blowing him a kiss as she picked up her purse and a leather travel bag that clearly didn't belong to the matched set of Gucci luggage the bureau had just purchased for her.

Chief Anderson raised his chin in the direction of the bag. "I thought we agreed you'd take nothing with you from your past life."

Lacy brushed away his concern, unzipping the leather tote at the same time and extracting a porcelain doll that was as blond and blue-eyed as the woman who held her up for his inspection. "Only this. She's the one connection to my past that I won't leave behind."

The bureau chief didn't speak for a long moment. In truth, he was amazed at the doll's uncanny likeness to its owner even down to the distinctive, lone dimple. He shrugged his acquiescence, though he couldn't entirely dispel an uneasiness that he knew was irrational. It was only a doll, after all. Picking up a pen, he dismissed the woman by busying himself with paperwork. "Good luck to you, Miss James."

With a shrug of her shoulders, Lacy placed the doll in the bag once again and turned her attention to the other two men. "My luggage already in the car? Good, then let's get going. The sooner I get to my new home, the sooner Mr. Jesse Pryde will have the pleasure of making my acquaintance."

Chapter One

One week before the shopping trip to Dallas

She stared into the mirror at the face that had once been beautiful. Distorted by bruising, swelling, and scarring, it was almost impossible to reconcile this shattered visage with the perfection of the woman in the photograph on the Texas driver's license she held in her hand. Not that she didn't believe the police when they assured her that she and the woman named Lacy James-Pryde were one and the same. She did. Even through the ruins, evidence of the resemblance existed as well as remnants of the perfection of her features. The pure blue of her eyes, for example, or the straight, narrow bridge of her delicate nose, and the uncompromising bow of her lips.

Yes, the woman called Lacy had once been an incredibly beautiful woman. And the doctors promised she would be again as soon as the residue of their meticulous surgical reparation disappeared.

But it was not for signs of improvement that the woman stared so hard at the reflection in the hand mirror Dr. Peacher had given her. She was searching for recognition; a memory that would connect the name with the face, for in spite of all their assurances, the woman in the hospital bed could not remember ever hearing the name before. In fact, as she had joked, she might well have not existed prior to waking up in the UCLA intensive care unit three weeks before. Apparently, the idea was not particularly funny, for none of the doctors laughed, and she wept after making it.

Her hand began to tremble, subtly at first and then with such ferocity the mirror clattered against the table, then fell to the floor, shattering on impact. She squeezed her eyes shut in an effort to close out her misery and frustration. A sound that was half whimper, half scream slipped through her lips, and she felt her doctor's arms circle her as he pressed her to his chest.

"It's all right, Lacy. You'll remember. In time, it'll all come back to you. Maybe even as soon as tomorrow when your husband arrives."

"And what if it doesn't? What if I never remember anything about who I am, where I come from?" Extracting herself from his embrace, she shoved the table away and slipped from the bed. She winced, grabbing at the bandages that still supported her cracked ribs as she walked stooped and unsteadily to the window. There she stared out at the lawns that had become familiar to her in the weeks since awakening from the coma following the hit-and-run accident.

"Do you realize the only people I know are the doctors and nurses on your staff, Peach? That the only place I can visualize is this hospital? The police have *told* me my name is Lacy. They've *told* me I have a husband and a home in Texas."

She turned to face him, her arms circling her waist as she hugged herself. "I try to see him and our home. I really try, Peach, but there's nothing there. It's all a black, empty void with these vague patches of light my imagination creates because my memory can't. It's almost like a photograph negative—there's a definite impression, just not enough to put together the whole picture."

She began to move around the room, her gait awkward and painful to watch. Yet Dr. Peacher didn't move to help her. He felt her desperation and sensed her need to express it independent of his interference. He knew the cost to her physical strength, but realized as well that the tenuous grip on her control had finally snapped. She had to be allowed to express her fears. Only then could she take the next step of accepting the future no matter how bleak it loomed at the present.

"I'm terrified, Peach. Scared to death! Tomorrow you're going to turn me over to a man who claims to be my husband but who is a virtual stranger to me. I know nothing about this man."

Matt Peacher opened his mouth to interject that in

fact she did know a few things, details gleaned by the police, but she silenced him with a wave.

"Oh, I know what I've been told. We've been married for six months. We live on a ranch. His name is Jesse Pryde and he's filthy rich." At Peach's raised brow, she actually laughed softly under her breath. "Blame Detective Dailey. Those were his words.

"But I don't know about *him,* do I? I don't know if he's soft-spoken like Dr. Ivers or energetic like you. I don't know if we were childhood sweethearts or if our meeting was kismet—a chance meeting of our eyes across a crowded room."

At this Dr. Peacher, who had been leaning against the far wall, his arms folded across his chest, laughed. "Well, now you see, you're wrong. We do know something about you, something we've just this minute learned. We know you're a romantic at heart."

"How is she?" Jesse Pryde asked. "My wife, Lacy."

There was a smooth, dangerous quality to the tall Texan's soft voice that caught a man's attention like aged whiskey or a coiled sidewinder.

Dr. Matthew Peacher's next impression of the man standing in his doorway was that Jesse Pryde could well have posed for one of those "We grow *everything* bigger in Texas" tourist commercials.

The doctor motioned to a chair, claiming his own behind his desk as the man swept his Stetson from his dark head, lowered his tall frame into the chair, and repeated his original question. "How is she?"

"How much were you told on the telephone, Mr. Pryde?"

"Next to nothing, Doctor. Why don't you fill me in."

The specialist who looked more like a high school football linebacker than a thirty-something UCLA staff neurologist referred to a file folder as he spoke to his patient's husband. "Most of the injuries your wife suffered were to the head and face. She sustained a fractured collarbone, a couple cracked ribs, contusions to the chest and belly as well, but the most serious injuries were to the head area," he said, drawing an imaginary circle around his own head with a sweep of his hand.

Jesse swallowed hard at the extensive list of his wife's

injuries. "But the police said on the telephone that her condition is good."

"Yes," the doctor agreed with a brisk nod of his head. "What they didn't tell you is that she has been convalescing for nearly three weeks now. During that time, her condition has been upgraded several times. We were not at all certain she would survive the night when she first arrived."

Jesse's deepset eyes widened with the surprising news. "*Three weeks!* Jesus," he drawled slowly, his amazement evident though quickly changing to bafflement. "Wait just one minute here. There's something I don't understand. Why wasn't I contacted before now?"

"Mrs. Pryde was unconscious for several days after she was brought into the E.R. She had no ID. Don't get me wrong, Mr. Pryde. We knew this was not our typical Jane Doe. Her clothing was designer, her nails manicured, her skin that of a woman who has been pampered, but even knowing that we still couldn't identify her until someone found her purse and turned it in." The doctor held up his hands, smiling with practiced assurance that did not quite reach his eyes.

In fact, his gaze reflected his puzzlement, and Jesse knew he was wondering how it was possible that a woman could disappear for more than three weeks without her husband searching for her. Ignoring the guilt that suddenly twinged in his chest, he asked his next question quickly before the doctor could charge him with his neglect. "But as you said, it's been three weeks. Surely in all that time . . . What aren't you telling me?"

Dr. Peacher opened his mouth to answer, but the jangling of the telephone on the desk behind him checked his response. He held up a finger, reaching for the phone at the same time. "Hold that thought, Mr. Pryde." Then into the mouthpiece, "Yes, Cathy." There was a long pause before he instructed the woman to give him another five minutes.

"You were about to fill in some blanks," Jesse reminded him once he'd replaced the receiver in its cradle.

"The police are here to speak with you, Mr. Pryde. I believe you talked with Detective Larosa yesterday. His partner, Detective Dailey, is with him. They've been investigating the accident and will be able to tell you more

precisely what happened although even they have some
questions they're hoping you can answer. But before you
talk to them, there's something more I need to discuss
with you."

Jesse gripped with white-knuckled intensity the snakeskin ankle of his booted foot that rested on his knee.
"She's been disfigured, hasn't she?"

There was no mistaking the look of disapproval Dr.
Peacher fired his way, and Jesse felt his face heat with
the accusation in the other man's eyes. He shook his
head. "It's not what you think. I don't care for myself.
I was thinking of Lacy. I don't know how badly her face
was damaged, but trust me when I tell you, she is the
most beautiful woman I ever met. You may not have
been able to see that, but you have been treating her
for three weeks. Surely you know by now how important
her looks are to her."

For the first time since their exchange of introductions
thirty minutes before, the doctor smiled, seemingly relieved by Jesse's explanation. "She was banged up pretty
badly, yes, but even with all the cuts and bruising it
wasn't too hard to imagine how pretty your wife is,
Mr. Pryde."

"Call me Jesse, please."

"Okay, Jesse, but I don't want you worrying about
your wife's looks. I called in one of the finest plastic
surgeons in the business to suture the cuts on her face.
She was pretty dismayed the first time she looked into
the mirror, and she still has a way to go before all the
puffiness and discoloration are gone, but except for a
couple of minor scars, I predict she'll be as attractive as
ever in a few more weeks. In the meantime, some artfully applied makeup should camouflage the rest."

"Good," Jesse said, his tone as strained as his patience. He didn't want to be here talking with this doctor. He didn't want to meet with the police. He didn't
care how the accident had happened. He only wanted
to see his wife, to determine for himself that she was in
fact all right. He'd been relieved to hear that her face
hadn't been irreparably damaged. As much as he thought he
hated her for what she'd done to him, he couldn't muster
enough vindictiveness to wish her the kind of anguish
he knew she'd suffer if her incomparable beauty had been

destroyed. The realization that indifference had begun to replace hatred shocked him, but damn if it didn't feel good. Now he could tell her with sincerity how glad he was that she was going to recover fully, hand her the divorce papers, and get back to his life in Texas. He grinned and said more strongly, "I'm really glad to hear that."

Dr. Peacher held up a hand. "That's the good news, Jesse. The bad news is your wife has no idea who she is. In fact, as best as I can determine, she has no memory at all."

Her left arm rested in a sling, though the tips of her swollen fingers trembled as the fingers of her other hand plucked nervously at the sheet covering her legs. Dr. Peacher had been encouraging that morning when he'd announced that her husband was arriving from Texas.

Tears filled her eyes as she remembered the gentle tone of the doctor's voice as he'd squeezed her hand and promised everything was going to be all right. "Who knows, Lacy, just seeing him might be all it takes to jog your memory. If not, at least you now have a name, and you'll be with someone who knows you, loves you, and can fill in the blanks. And I swear to you, eventually, it'll all come back. There won't be any more black void where your memory should be."

If only her husband was like Dr. Peacher, Lacy thought now. If only—

The rest of the thought was lost as a man suddenly appeared in the doorway of her hospital room.

She didn't recognize him, yet she knew for a certainty that this was her husband. The fingers that had plucked at the sheet now curled around the cool cotton fabric, gathering a handful of it into her fist.

He was an imposing figure standing there, staring at her from the doorway as if uncertain whether or not he was welcome to cross the threshold. He carried a gray Stetson in his hand, and Lacy almost wished he'd worn it instead. Then maybe she wouldn't have been able to see how handsome he was and feel so conspicuously ugly by comparison. He smiled, forming deep slashes in his tanned cheeks and softening his otherwise sharply chiseled features. It was not a wide smile, nor even warm, but the tentativeness of it somehow reassured her. Perhaps, in spite of his proud stature, his incredible dark good looks, the expensive cut of his Western suit, he was nervous about their reunion as well. Somehow that possibility made him more human, less godlike.

Though the stitches had been removed from her lips two days before, the wound was still tender and the smile she returned painful. "Hi," she said, ignoring the soreness and hoping to ease the awkward silence between them.

He took a step forward, glancing around at the sterile room as if looking for proof that the battered victim was indeed his wife. "You've had a rough time of it," he said quietly.

Lacy didn't answer at once. She couldn't. She'd hoped she would recognize him; at the very least sense a bond or a feeling of belonging. Instead, she imagined her reaction to be typical of all women when they first caught sight of him or heard his deep, softly modulated drawl. He was sex personified but a stranger all the same.

Her frustration and disappointment were so great she could taste the bitterness and tears filled her eyes. She flinched as they spilled over her lashes, stinging the raw skin in the worst of her facial injuries—a long gash extending from her eyebrow to her cheekbone.

Through her blurred vision, she saw Dr. Peacher enter the room, but as she reached up to dash the humiliating tears from her cheeks, her gaze remained focused on the man she'd been told was named Jesse. "I'm . . . I'm sorry," she said, clearing her throat and starting over. "I didn't mean to cry. I . . . I just wanted so badly to recognize you."

Dr. Peacher came to her side, clasping her uninjured shoulder and giving it a reassuring squeeze. "Patience, Lacy. Don't forget what Dr. Ivers and I have been telling you." Then with a glance at Jesse, he explained, "Dr. Ivers is the psychiatrist Lacy has been working with."

The stranger's thick brows drew together in a sudden frown. "Will she require continued psychiatric care, Doctor?"

"Let's talk about that," Dr. Peacher replied, lowering one hip to the edge of his patient's bed. "Dr. Ivers and I have already discussed Lacy's release with her at length." He glanced at Lacy, winked, then took her hand in his. "Course, for the most part, we talked before we knew who our beautiful Jane Doe here was. Naturally, we assumed she was from around the L.A. area, so we thought we'd be seeing her again on a regular basis after we found her family."

Lacy smiled at her doctor who had become her friend in the weeks since her nightmare had begun. "I'm going to miss you guys, but I'm so glad to have a name and a husband." She looked at the man she knew only as Jesse Pryde. "I know we don't have any children." She blushed slightly. "The doctors tell me I've never been pregnant." The last of her words faded away as she saw Jesse's dark eyes flash with anger. "What's wrong?" she asked, her voice choked to a whisper by her fear.

Jesse ignored the question, looking instead to the physician. "You didn't answer my question. Does Lacy require continued consultation with a psychiatrist?"

"I don't think so. We know the amnesia is a result of physical trauma rather than some sort of psychological stress-induced disorder as is sometimes the case. Think of it just as you do the injuries you can see. Her mind should heal with time. Completely, we believe, though it's impossible to predict how long the process will take.

"I've given Lacy the name of a neurologist in Dallas, but as I told you in my office, your local G.P. should be able to monitor her progress just fine. Unfortunately, we don't have medication or therapy to speed the recovery of one's memory. She's going to have to depend on stimuli provided by her circle of family and friends, and if that doesn't work, time is the only other medicine on the market." Giving her hand a squeeze, he looked from Lacy to Jesse and back again. "So, unless there's something else you need to know right now, I'm going to get out of here and give the two of you some privacy."

"See you later, Peach," Lacy said with a halfhearted smile.

"I'll see you before I leave, Doctor," Jesse said stiffly.

Silence hung heavily between them after the doctor shut the door behind him. For a long moment both husband and wife stared at one another, until Lacy, running a hand over her hair, looked away. "I know how horrid I look. I can't wear makeup yet. My skin's still too tender. They told me they had to cut my hair. I saw my picture on my driver's license yesterday. It was pretty when it was so long, wasn't it?"

"You'll be as beautiful as ever in a few weeks," he

said, though his tone was harsh and at odds with the kindness of his statement.

Lacy cocked her head slightly to the side as she asked, "Yesterday, after they found my purse, one of the nurses remembered reading about you. She looked for a copy of the magazine. She never did find it. Said it was old—a year, maybe—so I guess it was thrown out. Anyway, she told me you're a big-time rancher. I know how busy you must be . . ." When he didn't answer, she lowered her gaze to her fingertips that peaked out from the sling. "Were you worried about me when I disappeared three weeks ago?"

She looked up now, meeting his gaze steadily, though her heart was beating wildly, loudly, threatening to betray how badly she needed the right answer; to hear him tell her how desperate he'd been, how frantic with grief and dread. But somehow—maybe the clue had come in the anger that she'd seen flash briefly in his dark eyes or perhaps from the distance he'd maintained between them—she wasn't surprised by his answer a long moment later.

"You didn't disappear, Lacy. You left me."

Jesse had taken a room in a nearby motel. As he entered it thirty minutes after leaving his wife's side, he tossed his hat onto the table, then flopped down on the king-size bed with a frustrated groan. Why in Sam Hill hadn't he kept his mouth shut? She'd caught him off guard with the question about her disappearance, it was true, but he could have found an evasive answer that would have spared her feelings. Hell, he'd shown crazed bobcats more compassion than he'd just offered her.

Memory of the way she'd flinched, then lowered her head with her apology shamed him. "I'm sorry," she said. "It was good of you to come . . . under the circumstances." Then she looked at him, a grateful smile on her face. "I really do thank you. I won't ask anything more of you except that you tell me where I was going when I, uh, left our home. That'll give me a starting point. Who knows? Maybe all I need is to see some of my things to jog my memory."

The torpor that had begun to settle over his mind three weeks before had cleared in that moment, replaced by an almost debilitating rage. He clenched his jaws until his teeth ached. Long moments had passed before he calmed sufficiently to manage a civil answer. Lacy James-Pryde had been a woman of many faces, but she'd never worn a martyr's mask, and he resented her for pulling it on now without guile. He could deal with deviousness, but how did he handle this?

"I don't know where you were going," he said tightly. "You didn't say. But it doesn't matter. You'll return to our home with me. Once you've regained your health . . . and your memory, we'll decide where to go from there."

Her lips parted in a quivering smile and though she opened her mouth to speak, no words came out.

"Are you all right?" he asked, fear for her suddenly outweighing his anger. Stepping forward, he touched her shoulder, repeating his query. "Lacy, are you okay?"

She nodded briskly, then turned her face away from him. Silence hung in the air between them as heavy, and poignant and redolent, as the perfume she'd always worn. He turned to leave, stopping a few steps away when he heard her say, "I'm fine, Jesse. Just emotional. I'm realizing that despite the trauma of losing my memory I'm a very lucky woman to be married to such an honorable man."

In spite of himself, he glanced over his shoulder. He saw the tear that had slipped from the corner of her eye and fallen to her hand, and damn him if he didn't hate himself more in that moment than he'd ever hated her.

Chapter Two

Four days after her reunion with Jesse, Lacy sat in her hospital room, dressed and ready to leave. She'd watched television for the past hour but would have been hard-pressed to tell anyone what was on. Dr. Peacher surprised her with a tap on her shoulder as she gazed unseeing up at the suspended set.

"Lacy?"

"Oh, Peach, you startled me."

He followed her gaze back to the television where Bob Barker was laughing at one of his contestants' antics. "Both my daughters get totally wrapped up in *The Price Is Right*, too. I guess its the mindlessness of it, huh?"

"Actually, I didn't even realize what was on," Lacy admitted.

Matt Peacher grinned. "Too excited about going home today to think about anything else. Most of my patients feel that way. I'll tell you, it's a good thing I'm as secure as I am. A man could get a complex."

Lacy rewarded his attempt at levity with a chuckle, but her expression quickly sobered. "I wish my husband were as enthusiastic about taking me home as I am to be going."

Dr. Peacher reached behind him for the visitor's chair and pulled it over beside the bed. "You look beautiful, by the way," he said as he sat down. At her deprecating grimace he shook his head. "No, don't dismiss that as just an empty compliment intended to pacify you. You are an uncommon beauty, Mrs. Pryde."

"Thank you," she said softly, turning her gaze to the floor for a long moment before looking back at him. "You've been so good to me. I'm going to miss you."

"I doubt that," he said with a laugh. "No, I think

you're going to be so wrapped up with your life on your family's ranch, you'll soon forget you were ever in a hospital."

"Sometimes, Peach, I hope I never remember who I am."

"Because you're afraid if you do, you'll have to confront the problems that existed between you and Jesse before the accident?"

"If only he would tell me what was wrong between us."

"You know why he hasn't discussed it."

"Yes, Dr. Ivers feels it's best to let me discover my own feelings, recapture my own memories, to let doors and windows open of their own accord instead of forcing them—and that's verbatim. But the fact of the matter is, Jesse cracked that door when he told me that I'd left him. Wouldn't it be better to open it all the way now instead of letting me imagine what demons are peering through it?"

Dr. Peacher took one of her hands in his, giving it a gentle squeeze. "Let me tell you something, Lacy. I don't believe he would be taking you home today if your differences were irreconcilable. I believe he loves you and wants to help you get well so your problems can be worked through."

Tears puddled in her eyes, and she quickly dabbed at their corners with her fingertips, careful not to smudge the makeup one of the nurses had helped her apply.

"Good girl," Dr. Peacher said. "You look too good to let tears mess it all up. Now stand up and let me see that suit you're wearing. A gift from Mr. Pryde, I presume."

Embarrassed, yet pleased, Lacy scooted from the edge of the bed and pivoted gracefully for the doctor's inspection. "It is pretty, isn't it?" she asked, loving the powder-blue silk suit Jesse had instructed the store to deliver to her. "It's a little big. I guess I've lost more weight than I thought since the accident. Jesse says I wore a six before, but I think it kind of hangs."

"Every woman I know would love to have that problem," Matt said with a chuckle.

"How do you like my hair?" she asked, raising a hand to let her fingers trail the short, sleek style.

"Fishing for more compliments, Mrs. Pryde?"

"No," she said with a becoming blush. "Just making sure that I look all right. I want Jesse to be proud of me when he takes me home. Things may have been wrong between us, but I want our homecoming to be good." She sat back down on the edge of the bed, carefully smoothing her skirt beneath her, then clasping her hands in front of her. Her expression was serious suddenly. "Did he tell you that we're flying?"

"No, but I assumed as much. Why? Does the prospect frighten you?"

"Yes, just now when I thought about going to Texas and remembered what he said about flying, I had this peculiar sensation in the pit of my stomach. Do you suppose I'm experiencing my first memory? That I'm remembering my fear of flying?"

"Yes, I would say so. But the question is, how intense is this fear? Will you be able to get on an airplane?"

She didn't answer at once, for she'd spotted her husband standing in the door and knew that she was about to take the first step in mending the tear that had been rent in their marriage. "Yes, Dr. Peacher, I'll be able to fly. I think I'll be able to do anything I have to if Jesse is with me."

An hour later Jesse and Lacy were seated in a limo on the way to the airport. In spite of her excitement and apprehension about her future away from the safe haven her hospital had become, she was trying hard to reassure her husband who seemed every bit as jittery as she. "Do we always travel in such opulence?" she asked with a laugh that was both gentle and teasing.

When Jesse didn't answer right away, she gave herself a good mental kick, certain that she'd offended him. She opened her mouth to apologize, but he smiled just then and met her gaze with his lacquer-black eyes. "You like fancy cars better than me. I usually drive around in a battered old truck."

"Don't tell me," she said, "I probably have a baby-blue sports car."

"You've got the last part right. You drive a sports car, a Mercedes, but it's red." He frowned, then added, "At least you did. The police haven't located your car yet."

"Or any of the things I took with me when I . . . uh, left."

"No," he said, the tension clearly back in his voice and his posture. He'd reached out to lay a hand on her thigh, but he withdrew it now.

Lacy groaned inside, but her defeat was short-lived. They'd separated just before the accident that had claimed her memory. There was no escaping the cold, hard truth of that. On the other hand, they'd loved each other madly once . . . no, not once, only six months before when they'd eloped, according to Jesse, who'd filled in a few statistics for her at her insistence. There would undoubtedly be several walls in this maze she must pass through on her return to happiness, but she'd confront each one, back up, then start out again toward the goal line. "I know you said the police checked motels in the area, but maybe I was staying with a friend or family member. Have you checked with anyone who knew me before our marriage?"

"You didn't have family, Lacy. You were an orphan, and I didn't know your friends. You'd only been in Rooster Corner a few months before we were married."

A muscle in his jaw rippled with barely suppressed anger, but Lacy didn't discourage the conversation. It had to come out, all of it, before they could go forward. "Go on," she said. "Where was I from? Even if I was an orphan, completely without family, surely I had made friends along the way. Was I from California?"

He shook his head. "Oregon."

"So maybe one of my friends from Oregon had moved to L.A., and I was visiting her during our separation. Makes sense, doesn't it?"

"As much sense as any of this, but we won't know what you were doing until you regain your memory. All the speculation in the world isn't going to change that."

She placed a hand on his forearm, felt the powerful bands of muscle tighten, but didn't pull away. "I think you're wrong, Jesse. I think the only way I'm going to remember is by talking about it."

"Okay," he said, his dark eyes flashing now with a passionate mixture of hurt and anger as he grabbed her left hand and held it up before her face. "Then let's talk about where your wedding ring is, Lacy! Try to remember what you did with it! Were you so anxious to be rid of me, you took it off as soon as you left?"

He held her wrist in a painful, viselike grip, but the verbal attack was much more damaging. Tears filled her eyes as she searched first his face, then her own vacant memory for the answer to his query. As the scalding tears spilled over her lashes, she shook her head, wrestling her hand free of his grasp to press it to her chest. "I don't remember, but I know in here, in my heart, that I couldn't have taken off the ring you put on my finger." A shuddering sigh accompanied the last word and a moment later, almost as if an afterthought, she added in a calmer tone, "The police theorize that it was stolen along with my credit cards and cash."

He didn't answer, but after a moment turned an unseeing gaze to the smog-gray day outside the window. "Why don't you try to rest? I can tell you're already tiring. We'll be at the airport soon, but it'll be several hours before we're home, and I doubt you'll be able to relax while we're flying."

She obeyed, closing her eyes and sighing deeply, though her mind refused to unbend. Too many questions roiled through her thoughts demanding answers.

Where had she gone when she'd left her home in Rooster Corner? How had she happened to be standing alone at one a.m. even in such a popular restaurant district, as the police had told her she'd been? Why weren't there any witnesses? Who had hit her, then driven away without even bothering to ascertain whether she was alive or dead?

Through barely parted eyelids, she sneaked a glance at the man seated beside her and realized that was the question that begged an answer more than any of the others.

What could have happened to cause her to run away from this man she had promised only months before to love, honor, and cherish?

Married! A jolt of excitement vibrated from her heart to the pit of her stomach as it had numerous times since their reunion four days before. Even after their daily conversations during which he'd patiently answered her eager queries about their home, his family and staff, their daily routines and those of their neighbors and townfolk, she had difficulty grasping the fact that she was married to him. Not that she wasn't attracted to him. On the contrary. Just being next to him made her almost giddy with joy. She longed to turn right now, lay her head against his chest, listen to his heartbeat, and feel his arms encircle her. Of course, she wouldn't. No matter how vividly he'd painted the picture of their life together before her unexplained defection, he was still hardly more than a stranger.

Oh, she had some facts to go along with his handsome face now. She knew he was thirty-five years old. That she was twenty-eight. She had been told this was the first marriage for both of them and that they lived on his ranch with his mother Rose, his brother Dillon, and his sister-in-law Cybil. R. Davis, his father, had been dead for three years, and though Dillon was the eldest of the two brothers, Jesse was more or less considered the family patriarch.

Lacy had asked a lot of questions about his family and to his credit, he had answered every single one—banal, surface ones such as what each looked like, how long Dillon and Cybil had been married, and so on. His tone might have lacked the eagerness she'd wished to hear; evidence of his enthusiasm to aid her rehabilitation. In fact, he'd replied to each query with an air of detachment, his voice lacking warmth or passion for the subjects they discussed. Nonetheless, he hadn't been as deft at keeping the truth of his deep family pride from his expression. She'd seen emotion sparkle in his eyes when he talked about his mother, the town of Rooster Corner, Texas, and the Southern Star, as their ranch was called. It was obvious that he was a man to whom home and family meant much, and Lacy smiled as she realized she'd learned just what to say to erase the scowl from his brow. "Tell me the history of the Southern Star. How did your family settle in Texas?"

Surprise flashed in his eyes when he looked at her, followed immediately by an expression she couldn't quite read. "We're almost at the airport."

Hurt, Lacy turned her head toward the opposite window, then looked at her husband once again as anger replaced distress. "And then we'll be almost home. After that, you'll insist that I need to rest, or that you have work to do. How long will it be before you stop finding excuses not to talk to me? I mean, *really* talk! I know the doctors told you I need to rediscover myself through experiences, but some things may help me remember. I know you're hurt and angry, but damn it, if you didn't want to help me, you should have left me in the hospital."

Instead of answering, he raised his hand to point out the airport just ahead. "We'll talk on the plane." Then in a kinder tone, "I'll tell you my family history in enough boring detail to take your mind off flying." He offered her a smile as the limousine pulled to a stop outside a hangar, and though the friendliness reflected in his mouth didn't reach his eyes, Lacy's heart quickened. He was tossing her the tiniest of morsels, but she snatched it up as she smiled her acceptance.

Less than thirty minutes later the wheels of Jesse's single engine private plane lifted from the runway, touching down once, twice more before Lacy with her eyes squeezed tightly shut could feel them successfully purchase a hold in the sky. She gripped the arms of the seat Jesse had strapped her into, and she could feel tremors rock her body as she struggled with rising hysteria. "I'm ready to hear your story," she said, spitting the words out. "Please, Jesse, start talking before I start screaming."

She thought he must have turned to look at her and wanted to shout at him to keep his eyes on what he was doing. Then he started talking and almost at once the softness of his deep voice began to soothe her frayed nerves, and she felt herself sink into the velvet folds of its caress.

"We own two thousand acres of some of the choicest land in Texas," he said. "My great-granddaddy, Rooster Cahille, settled there a hundred years ago this coming spring. He said he'd found his little corner of paradise." He stopped then in the telling to smile. "Guess it isn't too hard to figure where the name Rooster Corner came from. There'll be a big celebration to commemorate the anniversary. You were looking forward to it. Even went to Dallas to buy a dress."

He paused a moment, and Lacy knew he expected a comment. "Go on," she whispered in a voice strangled with fear. "Keep talking. Your voice makes me feel safer."

"He—my grandfather—was almost fifty years old when he married a young woman he'd ordered through a mail-order catalogue. According to the family Bible, she was only seventeen when she married him, but she also kept a journal, and she wrote that she loved him at first sight. Her name was Catherine. She bore Rooster thirteen children; ten of them girls, the other three boys. All three of them died, though, before they were weaned, as did the last two girls. The six oldest girls all moved away as soon as they were old enough to marry, but the seventh, Jessica—my grandmother—stayed on. By then, the family had become quite prosperous. They owned most of the businesses in town as well as several thousand acres of surrounding land.

"Jessica was twenty-six when they struck oil on Cahille land. Her daddy was eighty-six by this time and quite senile. Her mother, though still a relatively young woman, claimed to have no head for enterprise, so the business of running the ranch, dealing with the family's holdings in town, and the sudden thrust into a relatively young exploit—the commercialization of black gold—all rested on young Jessie's shoulders.

"She was hardworking and endowed with family pride but she was soon in over her head. Even though they were quite rich by any man's standards, Jessica was almost shamefully frugal." He paused in his narrative to grin then for the first time since their reunion. The taut muscles in his jaws relaxed, easing the lines from his handsome face, and Lacy managed a tight smile in response. "She paid a fair wage to any who worked for her, but she was so stingy, each man and woman did the work of two or even three. So, the whole town and every employee on the Southern Star were amazed when she suddenly hired a law firm in Dallas to represent her interests in town and employed a crew from Houston to oversee the oil rigs. It wasn't like Jessica Cahille to spend the kind of money folks knew these 'foreigners' were charging her, and rumor began to spread that her mind had gone the way of her father's—around the bend.

"She was merely showing good business sense, and

had she been a man, no one would have questioned her motives or her soundness. But the criticism from people whom she'd considered friends hurt her deeply, and Jessie turned her back on those she had once called friends. She had accomplished much in her few short years as manager of one of Texas's most enviable family fortunes, but overnight she changed. She began frequenting a honky-tonk in a neighboring town where most of the oil crews hung out. She was discreet and never left the house until late at night after her mother and the one remaining sister at home were in bed. But it didn't take long for rumors of her behavior to reach her mother.

"Catherine was a gentle, loving woman, but she was also absorbed in her religion, so she issued Jessie an ultimatum. Either give up her men friends at the bar and discard her disgraceful conduct or leave the Southern Star at once.

"There are still a few old people in Rooster Corner who talk about that night; the one and only time our little town ever made headlines in papers not only in major Texas cities but all over the U.S."

"Except for when you were on the cover of that magazine," she reminded him. She had become so caught up in his story, she'd almost managed to forget that they were still sailing ten thousand feet above the earth.

His dark frown was so quick in coming, Lacy immediately regretted her comment, and then the plane seemed to lurch, and a scream bubbled from between her suddenly clenched teeth.

"You're really hung up on that. I don't know why anyone even remembered it let alone mentioned it to you; it had all the significance of a pile of tick shit. I made a mistake by granting the interview in the first place." His voice was tight with emotion that went well past mere anger, and his eyes gleamed like black ice.

Somehow, she was tied to that article. Only a fool would miss that clue, otherwise, why such vehemence at its mere mention?

Lacy let it go. She had no choice. She was trembling so violently now, she could hardly speak. Squeezing her eyes shut, she folded her arms around herself in a pathetically unreassuring hug.

Jesse didn't comment, and in spite of her shattered

Donna Julian

calm, his silence aggravated her. Better than fear, she decided, though not as good as the peace that had settled so sweetly but briefly between them. Irritation at his petulant silence, which had hardly gasped a breath of life, died at once. Lacy groaned inwardly. Okay, so somehow she'd made him mad, and he was determined to demonstrate his ability to sulk. Well, she was going to prove herself good at repairing damage, accident or not. Swallowing hard, she brought the subject back around to his grandmother once again. "Did she leave?"

"Who?" he asked, his tone as cool and bleak as the rain that had begun to pelt the plane as it fell around them.

Although more afraid than ever now that the weather had taken a bad turn, Lacy was determined to try once more to recapture the rapport that existed for a little while at least. "Your grandmother, Jessica Cahille. She was so young. She deserved a little fun and happiness. Surely she didn't let her mother and the rumormongers drive her away."

"Ah, yes, youth, the scapegoat for so many sins," he said, his voice containing so much bitterness and hatred, Lacy's fear momentarily was of him and not the plane.

"She was pregnant," he continued, his tone suddenly as flat and cold as his eyes. "She was too ashamed to tell her mother, and too mad to leave."

"Mad at her mother?" Lacy ventured.

"Angry, yes, but also mad as in crazy. They say something in her snapped when her mother waved the Bible in her face, spouting Scripture about sin and whores. She picked up the poker from the fireplace and began hitting her with it. Her sister, Lizzy, heard the commotion, came into the room, and ran to her mother's aid. Jessie turned on her as well."

Lacy's hand flew to her mouth with the shocking revelation. "Oh, my God. Did they both die?"

Jesse shook his head. "No, they both survived the beating, though Catherine was an invalid after that. Lizzy was only a teenager, and regained her health, but she never married. She lived in the same house on the ranch until she died three years ago. She raised my mother."

"But what happened to Jessica?"

"She left that night. Seven months later, my mother was delivered to the Southern Star doorstep in a basket with a note that said she was Jessica's daughter and that her name was Rose Wolf. She'd been named for the Texas flower, which Jessica had always loved, the note went on to say. The last name was that of her father, whom Jessie had married."

"Did anyone know this man named Wolf?" Lacy asked.

"Oh, yeah. He was an Indian, a roughneck who'd been hired by Jessie's foreman to work on the oil crew. My great-grandmother hired a private detective to search the records in Texas for a marriage license that would validate Jessica's claim that the baby girl left on her doorstep was not a bastard."

"Why? You mean to tell me she was going to refuse to keep the baby if the parents weren't married?"

Jesse shrugged. "I don't know. Probably. Doesn't matter though. The detective found the marriage license."

"What was his name? The Indian, I mean?"

"Joe Wolf."

"And Catherine Cahille let it go at that? She didn't look for your mother or father after determining that they'd married? Didn't she think they should raise the baby?"

"No need. They were both dead by then. The detective had learned that Joe Wolf was killed by Jessie in a bar in San Antone just a few days after she gave birth to his daughter. Witnesses said she walked in carrying the baby in one arm, a handgun in the other. She spotted him sitting at a table in a dark corner with some gal. Walked up to him and stood behind him as he bragged to his date that he'd married big money, and that now that they had a kid, he was going to collect enough money to set him up for the rest of his life. Those watching Jessica said she just raised the gun and shot him in the head. They said she never said a word, and never once stopped rocking the baby in the other arm, even as she turned around and stopped a minute to stare at the crowd that had gathered around her. She raised the gun and warned them all to back off, then walked out of the bar."

"Then she brought the baby to Rooster Corner," Lacy

interjected and at his nod of agreement asked, "But how did Jessica die?"

"Killed herself that same night. Couple of roughnecks found her hanging from a derrick the next morning."

"Oh, my God, that is so sad."

"Yeah, it's not a part of my genealogy I'm particularly proud of, but it's a part of who I am so I guess it's as important as any of the rest."

"It must have been hard for your mother to grow up without her own mama."

"Aunt Lizzy loved her like her own, though I've heard stories about the way the children in school taunted her. She was a half-breed, after all, as well as the daughter of a madwoman."

Tears suddenly burned in Lacy's eyes. Children could be so cruel, she thought, her eyes suddenly widening as she realized she'd been at the brink of her first memory. It was gone now, but hope made her almost giddy. Pressing a balled fist to her lips, she actually giggled. "I'm . . . I'm sorry, Jessie, it's just that I almost had a memory." Laughing again, she shook her head. "I know it sounds crazy. I didn't actually *have* a memory, but it was right there just ready to be recaptured."

Jesse looked almost as excited as she, and she giggled again at the youthful look of expectation on his face. "Oh, Jesse, the doctors were right. All I need to do is be with you, and it'll all come back."

"I hope so, Lacy. For you, I pray you're right."

For you, he'd said. Not *for us.* She tried not to let the implication of his words hurt, but they stung, nevertheless. In a quieter voice, her eyes cast to her lap where her fingers plucked absently at her seat-belt buckle, she said, "Tell me about your father. How did he and your mother meet?"

"I think we've had enough family history for one day," he said.

Lacy searched his face, recalling the smile of just moments before and looking for the reason of his precipitate melancholy. "Oh, please, Jesse. You've taken my mind off my fear. Please tell me about your mother and father."

He didn't answer for a long moment, busying himself instead with the controls, which Lacy recognized as a stall tactic. At last he relented and resumed his narrative. "My father was an oilman from Oklahoma. He came to the Southern Star to talk to the owner about buying the rights to their wells, and instead of gaining what he'd been after, he lost his heart to the beautiful girl who met him at the door."

Lacy was delighted. It was as good as any fairy tale. "And did your mother love him, too?"

Jesse laughed, the first deeply satisfied laughter she'd ever heard from him. "It wasn't love at first sight on her part, no, ma'am. Course you'd have to know my mother to understand that. I don't think she probably loved me or my brother at first sight. She just doesn't give her heart that easily."

Lacy studied her husband's handsome profile, thinking that he should talk of things he loved more often. He looked so handsome when he smiled, the cleft in his strong chin deepening, and his ebony eyes coming to life.

She smiled wistfully, suddenly so peaceful and at ease with the man she had married but still did not remember. "What about you, Jesse? Who did you take after?" She saw his frown and clarified her question. "Did you fall in love with me at first sight, too?"

Even as she asked, she was certain he was not going to answer. After all, the question was forbidden under Dr. Ivers's rules. She never should have asked it, but she'd so wanted him to continue the saga of his family to its completion. She was sure already that she'd loved him at first sight and longed to know if he'd felt the same. And then, though he hadn't said a word, his eyes answered for him, and she was forced to avert her gaze.

Pressing her eyes tightly shut, she almost moaned as his image followed her into the darkness. He was beautiful, yet so sad in that instant, she longed to reach out and lay a hand against his cheek.

She opened her eyes and looked at him once again. She knew what he was thinking, could read his thoughts in the clouds that had filled his eyes. "Never mind. I'll remember, and I swear to you, when I do, when it all comes back to me, we'll find a way to make it right between us ... whatever it was that went so terribly wrong."

She saw the sadness turn to anger and pulled her hand

away almost before she'd reached out. "You're wrong," she said, though he hadn't spoken. "Nothing could be so horrible that we can't fix it. Not if it means saving the love we must have felt for one another on the day we married."

"That's just it, Lacy," he said finally, quietly. "Before you left, you made it pretty clear you never loved me at all."

"How?" she cried.

"Damn it!" He slammed the flat of his hand against the control panel with such force, even the small plane seemed to shudder in response.

"Tell me," she asked in a choked whisper.

"We'd fought. I won't tell you what about. Not yet."

She shook her head. "I don't care. Just tell me what I said that made you believe I never loved you."

" 'I planned it all,' you said. 'It was perfect. A gorgeous guy and a filthy rich family with just enough dirt under their fingernails from all the corpses they'd buried to suit me. Only—' "

" 'Only I didn't plan on being bored to death,' " she finished for him.

He grabbed her wrist, yanking her roughly to him. "Goddamn you, Lacy! You do remember!"

She shook her head in denial, tears pouring from her eyes. "No! I remember that statement, but nothing else! It's weird, but I can even hear myself saying it, Jesse."

The plane glided closer to its destination on autopilot as its two passengers struggled wordlessly with a conflict one of them was endeavoring vehemently to forget and the other was striving desperately to remember.

Chapter Three

Some twenty minutes later the small plane's wheels touched earth, bounced, then connected again, this time staying down.

Lacy kept her eyes shut throughout the landing, opening them only when she felt the plane come to a stop and heard the engine shut down. Jesse's eyes were on her, and she could feel her cheeks catch fire. "Wasn't I always afraid of flying?" she asked defensively.

Jesse busied himself at the controls, then took his time removing his headset and unfastening his seat belt. He reached over to her lap and unbuckled the belt she'd fastened around herself, letting his hands drop to her thighs and rest there. His gaze moved slowly from the flesh of her legs below her short skirt to her hands, and then to her breasts where they lingered for a few seconds. By the time his dark eyes met hers, Lacy was quivering with another forgotten sensation that was oddly wonderful and uncomfortable at the same time.

"What's wrong?" she asked in a strangled whisper.

"Not a thing," he said, shaking his head slowly from side to side and causing a thick shock of black hair to slip from place and fall over his brow. The left corner of his mouth tilted up in a sardonic grin and a muscle ticked in his jaw. "Nothing's wrong. As a matter of fact I was just enjoying the first good memory I've had in some time."

"What? Did I make a fool of myself the last time we flew together?"

"On the contrary, you were extraordinary."

"I wasn't afraid?"

"At first, yes, ma'am, you were. Then you asked if the plane could fly on autopilot."

Lacy's heart was hammering loudly in her chest now,

and her palms were damp, and all because of the way he was looking at her. "Why would I ask that if I was so afraid? Seems to me just the thought of you not being at the controls would have terrified me."

"I thought so too until you showed me what you had in mind," he said.

"And what was that?" she asked, certain by the wicked gleam in his eyes she wasn't going to like his answer.

"That there are ways to occupy yourself so you don't even know you're flying."

"*What* did I do?" she asked, then noticed the way his eyes had dipped down to her breasts again. "Never mind," she said quickly, turning her gaze out the window.

He laughed then, but when Lacy looked at him she saw that the gleam had dimmed from his eyes, and she knew she hadn't imagined the bitterness in his tone. "Don't worry, Lacy. I wasn't going to ask for a rerun."

"Good, because I would have refused."

"Maybe not. Not if I helped you remember how good it was. Seems to me you enjoyed yourself almost as much as I did."

Though Lacy had no memory beyond waking up in an intensive care ward three weeks before, she was suddenly certain she'd never believed in backing down from fighting. Not even those she was bound to lose like the one she was going to start now. Folding her arms over her chest, she turned in the seat so that she faced him fully. "Well, Jesse, you've piqued my curiosity. Tell me all about it. Where were we going, and what exactly did I do that you enjoyed so much?"

She saw the flicker of indecision in his eyes and smiled with satisfaction. "Come on, finish what you started."

He looked away now, a dull flush rising to his face as he stared straight ahead out of the plane's windshield. "Later. My family will be waiting." He reached for the door, but she stopped him with a hand on his arm.

"Let them wait."

"We were on our way to Mexico," he ground out. "We were eloping."

"And? What did I do?"

"You seduced me," he said quickly. Then turning his

dark scowl on her, he added, "You used your fear of flying as the excuse, but it was pretty obvious you were putting insurance on the bargain."

"By that you mean I wanted to make sure you didn't change your mind about tying the knot once we got to Mexico, so I gave you a little quickie reminder of how good I was in the sex department," she said, her voice as soft as the train whistle that trailed it in the distance. A smile slid slowly into place. "Know what I think, Jesse Pryde? I think there's been some terrible mistake. I don't know one darn thing about myself except what you've told me, but in here, in my heart, I know this is all wrong, that I couldn't possibly be your wife."

If she hadn't been so close to crying she would have laughed at the comical expression of incredulity on his face when he whipped his head around to look at her. "*What*? Of course you are. I've got pictures at the house—wait. I've got one of us taken on our wedding day in Acapulco right here in my wallet."

She accepted the picture after he pulled it from its plastic holder, studied it for a few seconds, then passed the photo back. "Yes, I suppose so. Cameras don't lie, do they?" Her hand on the door handle, she shrugged. "Well, shame on me."

"For what?" he asked.

"For marrying a man as mean as you."

In spite of Lacy's delicate condition, which was evidenced by the pain in her eyes as she moved, she opened the door and slipped out to the wing before Jesse could stop her. Remorse for the way he'd treated her knifing through him, he climbed quickly from his side of the plane, hurrying around to help her.

Lacy was already sitting on the edge of the wing, prepared to make the leap to earth. At the sight of him, she pursed her lips and squared her shoulders, determination gleaming in her blue eyes.

Jesse almost laughed. Would have if he hadn't noticed how her legs were trembling, reminding him how fragile she still was since the accident.

She swatted at him as he reached up and circled her waist with his hands. "I don't need your help," she said, though the fear in her eyes spoke more eloquently than the fire in her tone.

Jesse ignored her as he lifted her from the wing and set her down but held fast when she tried to turn away from him. "Lacy, wait."

"No!" she cried, stomping one of her feet in an oddly appealing childlike gesture. "I don't want to listen to anything else! I don't like the game you're playing!"

"I'm not playing a game," Jesse said.

"Aren't you? Dr. Ivers made me promise to let the memories come to me naturally. You agreed to that, too. But you keep changing the rules, giving me bits and pieces of your version of our life together. You're playing blindman's bluff, but I'm the one who's blindfolded. It's not fair, Jesse!"

His hands had moved to her forearms, but he let go of her now though he refused to release her with his eyes. "You're right. I'm sorry. And you were right about what you said in the plane. I have been mean. I promise not to let what happened between us before you left interfere anymore until you've regained your memory."

"See, there you go again! I don't *know* what happened between us. If you're going to keep referring to it, tell me what it is so I can defend myself."

He stared at her for a long moment, then grabbed her elbow, steering her in the direction of the lone hangar they'd parked in front of. "Come on. The Jeep's just around the other side. You can wait there while I get our bags from the plane."

"Not much of an airport here in Rooster Corner, huh?" Lacy said, suddenly relieved by the neutral zone to which their conversation had moved.

"This isn't the airport, though you're right. There isn't much of one there either. A couple of hangars, a mechanic, couple of planes."

"But I thought we were flying to Rooster Corner. If we're not there, where are we?"

"We're on Southern Star land. We put a landing strip and hangar in a couple of years ago. Much more convenient."

"I'm impressed."

You were impressed the last time, too, Jesse thought, though he was proud of himself for not speaking the words out loud. Shutting the door after helping her into the vehicle, he grinned. "You ain't seen nothing yet."

Lacy's answering smile was immediate, and for the first time since his reunion with his wife four days before in the hospital room, Jesse remembered why he'd fallen in love with her.

The Jeep rode easily over the rough dirt road to the house. Every now and then, Lacy was jarred painfully as a wheel hit a pothole squarely. But for the most part, she ignored the aches and pains as she stared curiously around her at the rolling green pasture that was interrupted only by lines of white board fence, an occasional copse of trees, or a small herd of cattle gathered beside a glittering pond. "It's beautiful," she said quietly.

"This is the far west parcel. Another few miles and we'd be in Arkansas," he explained, his eyes never leaving the road before them. "Most of the livestock has been moved to the south for the summer."

"You rotate the cows?" she asked.

Jesse grinned at the enthusiasm in her voice, pleased by her interest, yet surprised, too. "And horses," he said.

"Don't tell me. When I lived here before, I couldn't have cared less about the land or horses or cattle, or anything related to the Southern Star."

"No, ma'am, you weren't too interested."

Lacy suddenly giggled. "Then maybe all I needed was a good knock in the head."

"You said it, I didn't," Jesse replied, laughing with her.

Encouraged by the harmony that might well disappear with the next rut in the road, Lacy laid a hand on her husband's arm. "Could we stop for just a moment, Jesse?" She raised her face to the warm sun and smiled as a gentle breeze tickled her throat and played through her hair. In the distance she'd just glimpsed the faintest outline of a white building and knew it must be the house where she'd lived. Still smiling, she admitted, "I'm suddenly terrified. Could we sit here for a few minutes while I fortify myself?" Looking at him with barely opened eyes, she saw his confusion give way to sympathy, and shut her eyes entirely. "Don't feel sorry for me, Jesse. I don't know much about myself, but I know I'm not a coward. It's just that, well, since I know I left after an argument that must have been terrible, your family can't be happy about my return. I just want a few more minutes before we're forced into a confrontation."

Jesse stopped the Jeep, moved the gearshift into park, then reached for her hand, taking it even though she resisted for a moment. "There won't be a confrontation, Lacy. I promise."

Lacy shrugged as she ran her tongue over her lips. "Oh, I know you've probably warned them, told them to be careful what they say, but it's still going to be awkward, isn't it? I mean, we can't pretend they're going to be glad I'm back, not if I left under such strained circumstances."

"You're welcome, Lacy. No matter what, until your memory returns. You're still my wife."

She felt like a fool when tears filled her eyes, but she couldn't hold them back. She turned her head away, though not quickly enough to keep him from seeing as one splashed onto her thigh. "Here I go," she said, trying for a laugh that was a terrible failure. "Feeling sorry for myself again. Maybe I am a coward after all."

Jesse groaned inwardly, then pulled her against his chest. "No, Lacy, you're not a coward. No one could ever accuse you of being that. It's my fault you're afraid right now. I've done this all wrong. Let my anger and manly pride get in the way of what's important. Your complete recovery is what matters now. I'm sorry I've made it all more difficult for you." Holding her away from him for a moment, he cupped her chin in his hand and tipped her face up to meet his gaze. "Come on now. No more tears. My daddy had a saying: 'If you can't fix what's broken, why waste your time trying? Startin' from scratch makes a whole lot better sense.' "

"Can we do that, Jesse?" she asked. "Can we start from scratch?" She let her eyes rest on the magnificently chiseled planes of his beautiful face. His black eyes below thick brows. The fine patrician nose that looked to have been broken once, marring its perfection in a way that only enhanced the overall picture. The full lips above the deep cleft in his strong chin. She didn't know if she had ever loved this man before, but she knew she could very easily fall in love with him now, if only he could give her a chance.

"For now, Lacy. We can try. That's all I can promise."

It wasn't what she wanted, but it was enough. "Then let's go home."

Chapter Four

As they neared the house, Lacy forced her attention away from the lush, rolling land. Her heart hammering fiercely in her chest, she held her breath as she caught her first full sight of the home where she had lived with her husband and his family.

A red tiled roof capped the sprawling whitewashed stucco structure that adapted itself to the sloping, uneven ground and furled the hills as if a part of them. Swirling wrought iron covered the windows and doorways as well as surrounding the many balconies.

A profusion of trees and flowering plants splashed the otherwise stark simplicity of the structure with color and caused Lacy's breath to catch with the magnificence of the setting. "Oh, it's beautiful," she breathed, her appreciation causing her to forget the inkling of remembrance she'd hoped for with her first glimpse.

"But you don't remember it, do you?" he prodded gently.

She didn't answer for a long moment. When she did, her bitter disappointment was evident in her tone. "No, and I can't understand it! How is that possible? How can I not recall something, *anything* about a place as magnificent as this?" And then she looked at the man beside her; the one she'd been told was her husband. Though instinct was her only guide, she was certain he was the most extraordinary man of her experience. Nonetheless, she couldn't remember him at all.

Apology in her eyes and heavy in her voice, Lacy implored him to forgive her. "I'd hoped I would recognize it at once, Jesse. It's so breathtaking I can't believe that I don't. I'm sorry."

"It's all right, Lacy. Dr. Ivers warned us that it might

take a good deal of time before your memory starts returning. We'll just have to be patient."

The words were right, Lacy thought, only she'd seen the frustration reflected in his dark eyes and knew that patience was a luxury Jesse wasn't prepared to offer her indefinitely. Turning her head away to hide the tears that were suddenly swimming in her eyes, she forced cheer in her tone. "I know, I'm not giving up. The memories will start coming back now that I'm home with my family."

"Of course they will," he said, his tone as chipper and counterfeit as hers.

Lacy surprised herself by chuckling under her breath. She glanced surreptitiously at her husband as he slowed the Jeep and eased onto the paved drive that led to the house, apparently not noticing her amusement. *I don't remember you, Jesse, but I've just learned something invaluable about you. You are a lousy liar.*

As she stood in the doorway, her knees knocking with the rhythm of castanets, Lacy no longer felt like laughing. Jesse had offered his hand as he'd helped her from the Jeep, and she'd not let go of it since.

A pallid shaft of sunshine fell on Lacy from a skylight two stories above, and for just an instant she couldn't help feeling like a specimen under a microscope as two women appeared from a doorway beyond the staircase.

"Welcome home, Lacy," the older woman said, embracing her gently and pecking her cheek. "We're very grateful that you've recovered from your injuries."

Although recognition eluded her, Lacy knew the tall, majestic woman was her mother-in-law. Anyone would have seen the strong likeness between mother and son. Rose Pryde was strikingly handsome, with strong, well-defined features, only Lacy couldn't help but wonder if her dark eyes ever warmed as Jesse's did or if they always looked as cold as black ice.

Lacy's answering smile was abbreviated by the quavering in her lips, and she was grateful when the younger woman who must be Jesse's sister-in-law spoke up, relieving her of the responsibility to say anything.

"You look real good, honey. Not at all the mess we were expectin'. Good gracious that must have been awful having your face cut up the way Jesse said it was. Why, I told Mother Rose right after his phone call that I was surprised the shock from that alone didn't kill you."

Lacy wasn't sure if she was being complimented or insulted, but Jesse saved her from having to respond when he put his arm around her waist and leaned down solicitously to make introductions. "Mother, Cybil, you both remember Lacy, of course, but as I explained on the phone, my wife is at a disadvantage. She's lost her memory, and as I think we can all see, she hasn't remembered either of you."

"That's all right, Jesse," Rose said in her smooth, smoky voice. "We're all prepared to help Lacy in any way we can." She turned her attention to Cybil. "Would you like to show Lacy to her room so she can rest? I'm sure the trip has tired her."

"I am tired," Lacy admitted, "but more than that, I'm curious. Would you mind if Jesse showed me the house before I lie down?"

"Not at all," Rose responded in the same soft tone as her son normally spoke in. Then to Jesse: "We'll wait for you in my rooms. You can help Lacy get comfortable, then join us there."

"Us?" he asked, rudely excluding Cybil by even questioning his mother. "Will Dillon be with you then as well?"

"I'm here now, brother," a deep, resonant voice said from the doorway behind them.

Both Lacy and Jesse turned, but it was to the former he came, gathering her in his arms and picking her up in a tight bear hug. At the involuntary whimper that escaped her lips, he quickly set her down. "I'm sorry, little sister," he growled, though Lacy was already realizing there was no menace in the fierce voice. "You look so good, I forgot you must still be tender from your injuries. Forgive me?"

"Of course," Lacy said, her smile wide for this bear of a man to whom she was instinctively drawn. Like his mother and brother, he was tall and dark, but whereas the others' features were defined in sharp angles, the lines and planes of his face were blurred as if created of wax, then left too close to a hot stove and allowed to soften.

"Damn if it ain't good to have you back home where you belong, girl!" Dillon said warmly, slapping his pants leg with his Stetson and generating great gusts of dust.

"Why, Dillon Pryde, you big, adorable oaf, look what you've done," Cybil drawled, stepping forward and slipping her arm through her husband's. "Come on, now. You go upstairs and change out of those filthy clothes, and let's let Jesse get his wife settled."

Lacy frowned at the tension that suddenly seemed to swirl around them, every bit as tangible as the dust from Dillon's hat. Scanning the faces of those in the room revealed nothing, yet she was certain something had just occurred, something she would have understood if not for the heavy veil shrouding her memory.

"Thank you all for being here to welcome me home. I hope you'll be patient until I remember everything . . . all of you. I will, I know, given time."

"Of course you will," Rose said in her distinctive voice, which Lacy was suddenly finding disconcerting. Rose stepped forward, taking one of Lacy's hands in both of hers. "Perhaps you'll feel well enough to join us for dinner. In the summer we usually dine informally on the patio."

Though unsure whether she'd been chilled by the woman's icy grip on her hand or the cool, black stare of her eyes, Lacy managed an uncertain smile. "I'll look forward to it."

"Come on, then," Jesse said, leading her from the foyer toward the back of the house.

For the next ten minutes they toured the ground level of the hacienda that Jesse explained had been built and decorated by his mother.

The house was a study in contrasts, and Lacy was almost immediately lost in the wonder of discovery and amazement.

From the marble columns and floors in the foyer where little was revealed other than the family's opulent taste and wealth, they stepped into the room Jesse described as the formal living room. Here Lacy thought the essence of Rose Cahille-Pryde had been captured in the eclectic furnishings of Southwest color schemes and patterns, the Native American artifacts, the intricate patterns of mosaic tiles bordering the lower walls, as well as the beautiful hand-woven rugs on the natural wood floors and contemporary paintings hanging above the chairs and sofas.

Though there were at least a dozen rooms on the main level, most were divided simply by arched entrances that were doorless, and yet every room was as individual as the one before it.

Some could only be described as palatial with their satin settees and silk wall hangings even as others were less formally appointed, and therefore warmer and homier.

Lacy decided she liked the kitchen best. She felt an immediate ease as soon as they entered the room with an impossible collaboration of state-of-the-art appliances, dramatic cathedral beamed ceilings, and crude brick floors and whitewashed cement block walls. Her hand trailing the scarred surface of the twelve-foot oak table that filled one end of the room, she listened as Jesse explained that it had been moved from the "old house" where his grandmother had dined with at least eight of her siblings. "You see all the nicks and cuts. I often thought I could almost hear them all banging on it with their spoons and forks. Dillon and I even had a hand at carving a few of the scratches, but nothing compared to what they did," Jesse explained, a happy grin on his face as he reminisced. "My father once suggested having it sanded and revarnished, but my mother would have none of it. She said her Aunt Liz had narrated a cherished memory about every flaw in the surface of that old table."

"Your mother was right. Memories are too sacred to be sanded away."

Jesse looked down at her, silent for a long moment as he leaned against the kitchen wall.

"What are you thinking about?" she asked, disconcerted by the way he was staring at her.

The question seemed to bring him out of the trance he'd slipped into, and he gave a slight shake of his head. "Nothing. Only that you must be getting tired. You've seen most of the rooms on this floor. I skipped the patio on purpose. You'll see it later when we join the family for dinner. Downstairs there's a fitness room, indoor pool, and wine cellar. But why don't we save that for tomorrow? I'll take you upstairs so you can rest for a while."

"Okay," she said, turning away without argument. "Besides, I know you don't want to keep your family waiting." She paused at the staircase to glance over her shoulder in her husband's direction. "I take it your pow-wow is about me."

Jesse didn't argue. "They want to be brought up-to-date. I didn't give them much when I was in California. Promised to catch them up when I got home. Mother said they'd all be here to hear the gory details. No big deal, Lacy. Don't get defensive."

Suddenly almost too tired to drag herself up the stairs, Lacy sighed. "I'm not," she said. Another couple of steps and she added, "Truly. I'm too tired to care what you talk about."

"But you're okay?'

"You mean about not remembering a single thing about the house you say I lived in for more than six months?" She'd been aiming for a wisecrack, something light and airy and very much the Lacy he seemed to expect, but it wasn't there. She stopped midway up the staircase, fighting fatigue and fear and tears. She gripped the ornately scrolled banister of wrought iron with both hands and sank down onto a step. Pressing her face against the cool metal, she squeezed her eyes shut. "Can you imagine how horrible it is to walk through rooms you once *lived* in and not recognize a single stick of furniture?" She asked the question, but reconsidered waiting for an answer as she gave her head a quick shake and pushed herself to her feet. "Don't worry, I'm not trying to worm my way back into your affections by extorting sympathy. It's just weird, that's all."

Jesse didn't answer but his immediate dark scowl revealed his thoughts.

"You're thinking that the Lacy you knew would have done exactly that, aren't you?"

"Lacy, don't—"

"Don't what?"

"Don't start what we can't finish until you remember."

Truly angry with him for the first time since he'd appeared in her hospital doorway four days before, Lacy raced up the remaining steps, stopping only when she reached the landing to turn around and face him, arms akimbo and legs braced wide. "Okay! I won't start anything, but you'd better get some practice masking your feelings, because I'm sick and tired of catching you glaring at me when I can't even defend myself." Without waiting for a response, she turned away and raced down the hall. "Which room is ours?"

"Third door on the left," he called out to her, quickening his pace behind her. "But, Lacy," he said, reaching the doorway just as she pushed it open and stepped inside, "it's not our—"

"Obviously," she said, her gaze sweeping the conspicuously feminine decor of canopy bed draped in billowing mauve silk, peach and rose velvet settee, delicate flower arrangements, and assorted perfume bottles on the dressing table.

"You sometimes chose to sleep in here by yourself," Jesse said, his face flushed red. "Mother thought you would be more comfortable in here until your memory returns."

"How perceptive of her," Lacy said acidly as she stepped into the room, crossing the floor to pick up a blond china doll that had been placed on the settee.

"I'll leave you to rest then," Jesse said. "Your clothes are in the dresser and closet. The bathroom is straight through those louvered doors, and you'll find everything you need if you want to shower. If you need anything else, push that button near the bed. Someone will come."

She felt his eyes on her back for a long moment before she heard him walk away and close the door behind him. Only then did she let the tears come.

For four days she'd ridden the teeter-totter of indecision, vacillating between the hope that she was in fact Lacy James-Pryde if only to be married to the handsome Jesse, and the hope that there was some mistake that would prove him wrong and vindicate her of the unknown crime she'd committed. But she knew the truth now as she held the beautifully crafted baby doll in her hands. For she recognized the face that stared up at her. Only . . .

She heard the door open and spun around, still clasping the doll to her breast. Jesse opened his mouth, then let it close again as if changing his mind, his eyes going from the doll to his wife's face. "You remember her?"

The tears in her eyes pouring over her lashes, and her voice strangling in her throat with her confusion and pain, she could only nod at first. In the mirror on the dresser she caught sight of her reflection and realized that she had the dazed, haunted look of an animal caught in the glare of automobile lights. Cradling the doll, she looked down at her once again and in a choked whisper said, "But her dress was blue, Jesse. Why is she wearing pink?"

Chapter Five

Jesse didn't go immediately to his mother's suite of rooms as he'd promised but detoured into his own bedroom instead. There he sank heavily into the easy chair that faced the window, though he didn't once look out. He covered his eyes with his hands, pressing the palms into the sockets as if to expunge the pitiable vision of his wife standing so lost and confused in her own room as she clutched the doll.

The sharp edge of hatred he'd felt for her when she'd mocked their vows and laughed at his pain nearly a month before had been blunted by compassion for her condition in the hospital. Still, he'd managed to keep a grip on it, not allowing it to totally escape him. He couldn't afford to let her slip back under his skin as she had done seven months before. But the heart-wrenching agony he'd just witnessed had almost succeeded in stripping him of the tenuous grasp of his fury. And that was an accomplishment no one had ever achieved with Jesse Pryde.

He was a proud man; some even called him arrogant. He was a fair man as well, but he never forgot a grievance, and Lacy had grieved him sorely.

He blamed himself for his gullibility, but he *hated* her for her treachery.

Before Lacy, he'd been a man with a strong sense of values, and the things he valued could be listed on three fingers.

The Southern Star.

Family.

God.

In that order.

If he'd bothered to compose a secondary list, women would undoubtedly have been found there right next to tooled leather boots, aged whiskey, a reliable vehicle, and a good horse. They were the luxuries in life that made a man's days and nights easier.

Until Lacy.

No! He wasn't going to think about her anymore. At least, not in the context of what she'd meant to him before . . .

Pushing himself from the chair, he crossed the room in an economy of long strides and pulled open the bathroom door. Only after he'd stepped inside the spacious room did he realize that water was running in the oversized round tub. He didn't have to turn. He caught his wife's startled expression in the mirror and realized that his own gaze was as surprised. "I'm sorry," he muttered, already backing out of the room. "I was just going to rinse some of the grime from my face."

Almost interred in bubbles, Lacy smiled away his embarrassment. "Please, go ahead." Glancing down at herself, she added, "I'm fairly well covered."

"And your equilibrium restored, it looks like," Jesse said, his tone unintentionally containing a measure of sarcasm.

A thin brow arched as she appeared to understand the reason for his anger. "You mean from my upset over the doll?"

"Yes," he said, turning his back to her and twisting the faucet on the sink. Above the sudden noise of rushing water, he raised his voice. "Never imagined you'd get so upset over the color of a doll's dress."

"I know, it was silly, wasn't it, to worry about something so petty. As soon as I calmed down, I realized I had experienced a *real* memory, Jesse, and that I should be grateful for any remnant of recollection." Without warning, she was suddenly laughing. "Do you know that before I saw the doll, I was quite positive you and your family were the ones who'd lost their minds? I was absolutely convinced I had never met any of you before in my life."

"I showed you our wedding picture," he said, turning so that water dripped from his face to his shirt.

"I know, but I had persuaded myself that somehow I'd been confused with another woman who was my look-alike. Don't they say everyone has a twin somewhere?"

Jesse grabbed a towel as he answered, "I guess. But the police found your purse with ID enclosed, remember?"

"I didn't say it was a logical conclusion," she replied, sobering, "only a desperate one. It's so terrifying to have people telling you who you are and not to be able to remember a single iota about any of them or the house you've lived in. I don't think anyone can imagine the panic that keeps welling inside me."

Jesse rubbed his face briskly with the towel, then his forearms and hands before laying it aside. "You're right. I couldn't until I caught a glimpse of it when you were holding that doll."

"I wanted to ask you," Lacy ventured, "where she came from. The doll, I mean. She looks a lot like I must have as a child. Was she a gift from you?"

Jesse shook his head. "No, you had her when you came here to live." Leaning against the sink, he crossed his booted ankles and folded his arms over his chest. "As a matter of fact, I sat on the bed and watched you unpack, and she was the first thing you removed from one of your bags. She was all wrapped up in tissue. I recall being impressed with the care you took with her. Then you held her up and said, 'This is my other self, Jesse. The sweeter part of me.' "

"And from what you've inferred, you soon learned how true that was," Lacy said quietly, her gaze locked with his.

"Enjoy your bath and try to get some rest," Jesse said, pushing himself away from the sink. "I'll send someone to wake you when it's almost time for dinner."

"Jesse!" she called out, and when he stopped, she said, "I know the rules say you're not supposed to answer questions about me, but will you answer one about yourself?"

Reluctantly he turned. "Try me."

"Did you always run away from our fights?"

Just like the woman he remembered on their last day together, she was taunting him. He was glad, grateful she'd reminded him what a bitch she could be. He let a grin slide into place. "We didn't fight," he said, letting his gaze drift purposefully to where the bubbles had parted at the rise of her breasts on the waterline. "We were on one long, perpetual honeymoon. More often in bed making love than not."

"But you said—" She broke off, her face flaming as red as the satin dressing gown she'd hung on the back of the door that led to her room.

"That we had a fight," he finished for her. "Yep, that I did. We had *one* argument, Lacy. The day you left. Before that we never had so much as a cross word between us." His eyes slowly, salaciously roving the curves of her body as if they could be seen beneath the blanket of soap suds, he said, "You were too busy acting the part of loving bride to argue."

Her chin raised just a bit, Lucy surprised him by smiling. "I can believe we never fought, Jesse. I think you would have been much too much fun to love to risk arguing with."

"Nice try, Lace. But there's an old saying I'm rather partial to. 'Fool me once, shame on you. Fool me twice, shame on me.' I won't be giving you another chance to make an ass of me, sweetheart."

"And what about the adage: 'To every story there are two sides'? Can't we call a truce until I've had a chance to remember my side of things?"

She shifted in the water, causing the lavish foam that covered her to separate, revealing too much of her beautiful body.

His own body's responding betrayal caused him to grimace. Using every ounce of control he possessed, he kept his tone even and neutral as he responded, "Sure, Lacy. A truce is exactly what I want."

Without another word, he strode from the room, closing the door behind him. Only then did he acknowledge the swell in his jeans that was evidence of what he really wanted.

"We were about to give up on you," Dillon said when Jesse finally entered the small parlor in his mother's suite. "You get your sweet little bride all settled?"

Jesse's scowl served as a quick warning that his brother's euphemisms for his wife were not welcomed, and the elder Pryde backed off with predictable spinelessness.

Jesse bowed to peck his mother's cheek before apologizing for keeping them waiting so long.

"It's good to have you back home, Jesse. We all missed you," Rose said. Then, "I hope Lacy is settling back in all right."

Jesse claimed the only empty chair in the circle and nodded as he sat down. "I believe she's going to try to sleep before dinner. She's still regaining her strength, which her doctors said might take some time."

"You sound worried about her, hon," Cybil said.

"Of course, he's worried. Lacy is still his wife, and the Prydes take care of their own," Rose said, her tone as cold as ice chips. "Now, may we please let Jesse speak." She turned her attention once again to her youngest and favorite son. "Tell us what you learned from the beginning, son. How did this accident happen?"

Jesse rubbed at the beginnings of scratchy stubble on his jaw with his hand as he struggled with his own fatigue. After a moment he began. "The two detectives I met with said they don't know much. There were no witnesses to the accident. They think she was struck by a car while walking along a wharf in the early morning hours sometime just before one a.m. They described the district she was in as trendy. Lots of restaurants and souvenir shops. In fact, a maitre d' from one of the restaurants remembers her. Said she'd made a reservation for two, but arrived alone and waited for someone who never showed. Confirmed she left a little before one. Unfortunately, the police haven't come up with any witness who saw her walking on the pier after she left. A dock worker who'd apparently gotten drunk and then slept it off in his car claims to have been awakened around that time by a sequence of noises. He *says* he heard an engine revving, followed by squealing tires and a woman's screams. He *says* he shot straight up in the car but still didn't see the actual impact. He thinks he heard the car hit her or maybe what he heard was her body striking the building she was slammed up against but claims he never saw the driver, car, anything except her lying on the pavement."

"You don't sound as if you believe him," Dillon interjected.

"No one believes him. He called 911 from a pay

phone near the accident site, then disappeared. Her wedding ring, watch, and the gold chain she always wore had disappeared as well.

"Then three weeks later, he arrived at the LAPD station with her purse asking if there was a reward. He claimed that he just found it lying between some boxes and trash containers. There was no money, but her credit cards and checkbook had been left undisturbed."

"How did the police deduce that the man who brought her purse in was the same one who had called 911?" Rose asked.

"The voice on the rescue dispatcher's tape matched that of their Good Samaritan."

"Do they think he actually witnessed the accident?" Cybil asked.

Jesse shrugged. "Who knows. He refused to take a lie detector test. The cops threatened to hold him for theft, obstruction of justice, but he's apparently no stranger to law enforcement. Detective Larosa said the guy has an arrest sheet as long as my arm."

"So they may never know what actually happened?" Dillon said with a disbelieving shake of his head.

"They claim they will. Said they don't have any intention of giving up on finding the person who ran her down."

"You mean because the guy left the scene of the accident," Dillon suggested.

"Because they don't believe it was an accident," Jesse said quietly.

"Oh, my," Cybil whispered in a shocked voice. "What kind of company was she keeping out there in California?"

Rose quelled her daughter-in-law with a cold glare, then returned her attention to Jesse. "Why don't they believe it was an accident?"

"Because there were no skid marks near where she was struck. On the other hand, whoever hit her laid tread about forty yards away from her as if starting from a parked position and picking up speed too quickly. It doesn't look like he so much as slowed before he hit her."

No one spoke for a long moment, and Jesse understood that they were each digesting the horror as he had when the homicide detectives had first described the scene to him.

After a while Rose asked, "And what about her prognosis?"

"I don't know all the technical jargon the doctors used, but in a nutshell, they did every test they could think of to determine if there was any brain damage that would prevent her from regaining her memory in full. They found no evidence that there is, but they attempted hypnosis and drug therapy—sodium amitol—with no success."

"Then she might *never* remember?" Cybil asked.

"No, I didn't say that," Jesse said wearily. "Actually, they believe she'll recover fully in time. But for now, they suggest that natural stimuli are the best medicine."

"And what does *that* mean?" Cybil demanded with typical Texan drama.

In spite of his fatigue, Jesse grinned at his sister-in-law's tone. "Only that she needs to be at home, around people she knows."

"Well, I'll certainly do my part to make her feel welcome," Dillon said.

"Of course *you* will!" Cybil cried. "And obviously, in spite of what she did to you, Jesse, you're going to do everything you can to help her, too!" Springing to her feet, she folded her arms across her chest, tilting her head to the side as she looked at her mother-in-law. "And what about you, Mother Rose? Are you going to just let her come back into this house and live here with us like nothin' ever happened?"

"Sit down, Cybil," Rose said, her tone commanding though she hadn't raised it. "And stop carrying on like a banshee. Jesse has brought his wife home to be nurtured by her family as the doctors advised. Until she has regained her health and memory, we will all respect his wishes and treat her with care." Then to Jesse, "Thank you for filling us in on what you've learned. I know this can't have been easy for you, but you've acted with character as I would have expected you to. I'm proud of you, son."

She didn't see the storm that was suddenly roiling in Dillon's eyes, but Jesse did and so did Cybil.

Jesse promised himself to make peace with his elder brother before the night was out.

Cybil was already working on how best to take advantage of the jealous fire in her husband that Mother Rose had once again stoked.

Lacy slept a couple of hours, then bolted upright in bed at the soft rapping on her bedroom door. For just an instant she was disoriented, but her gaze quickly lighted on the doll sitting on the settee, and she fell back against the pillows, calling out to whoever had knocked.

A miniature Hispanic girl, no taller than a child though with the face and full figure of a mature woman, stepped into the room, half bowing as she spoke in stilted English. "Deener, it is een one hour, senora. *Mamacita* Rose, she ask me to tell you to meet the family in the patio. *Comprende?*"

"Yes, thank you," Lacy said, already slipping from the bed. She waited until the tiny woman disappeared back through the door and closed it behind her before going to the closet to select something to wear. Damn it! Why hadn't she remembered to ask how they dressed for dinner? Jesse's mother had said they were informal during the summer. Surely that meant dress as well as location, she reasoned.

She'd intended to dress quickly, beating the others downstairs, but she was soon caught up in the investigation of her extensive wardrobe. There must have been over a hundred dresses hanging in the oversized closet, not to mention a multitude of skirts, blouses, sweaters, and slacks.

Unzipping a plastic bag, she found six furs of different varieties and lengths. Pulling one of the sleeves of an ermine jacket from the bag, she brushed her cheek with its softness as her eyes made another cursory pass over the bright collection of designer togs. Two things were easily apparent, even to her empty head: She liked expensive and she liked it red. Any red. Cardinal, flame, ruby, or claret. Definitely a girl intent on being noticed.

Lacy frowned. Then why, she wondered, had she left so much of her wardrobe behind if she'd intended never to return. She made a mental note to ask Jesse about that as she stuffed the sleek fur sleeve back inside and rezipped the bag.

Returning to her exploration, she discovered that there were rows and rows of shoes on the racks in the rear of the small room and at least three dozen hatboxes on the overhead shelves.

She pulled one from the overhead shelf, raising the lid to peer inside. Had she really ever worn hats? Somehow, she found it difficult to reconcile such frippery with the mental image she had begun to form of herself. In the hospital the nurses had supplied her with more than a dozen fashion magazines, and almost without exception, she'd been attracted to soft, muted tones and simple, tailored designs that suited a casual, relaxed lifestyle.

As she looked in the box at the creation of bows and netting, she clasped a hand over her mouth to stifle a giggle. "Never!" she said, setting the box on the floor and lifting the hat from the box at the same time. Though when she put it on her head, she was surprised at how glamorous she looked.

She tilted her head back and forth, adjusting the veiling several times, then the angle of the hat. "Well," she said at last, "you ain't a bad-looking dame when you're all dolled up, Lacy James-Pryde. Maybe you did like this stuff in your other life."

She was grinning as she took the hat off and replaced it in its container. Tomorrow, she promised, she'd try on more. But for right now, she had to decide on something to wear downstairs to dinner. And she had to decide fast. She'd already wasted too much time.

Ten minutes later, clad in a lipstick-red T-shirt, white linen shorts, and sandals, she stepped from her bedroom. She hurried along the hall, but stopped just short of the landing as she reconsidered the outfit she'd selected. Maybe she should have worn jeans or slacks. Torn with indecision, she stood there, mentally debating with herself. She'd just about decided to go back and change when she heard voices raised in the room behind the door she was standing near. She hadn't intended to eavesdrop, but it was immediately apparent that the voices belonged to Dillon and his wife Cybil, and that she was the topic in debate.

"Oh, give me a break, Cyl," Dillon was saying. "Who do you think you're fooling with this act of yours?"

"It's not an act!" Cybil protested, her voice thick with hurt. "I'm worried about Jesse."

"You're only worried that he'll never look your way with his pretty little wife here again."

"Pretty little wife, my ass. She's pretty all right and dangerous, too. You men may be beguiled by this helpless, 'I just don't know who I am' act she's pullin', but I haven't forgotten how devious and clever she can be."

"So what? You think just because she got caught and you didn't, I don't know that the two of you were cut from the same cloth?" he growled.

"What are you talkin' about, Dillon Pryde? I could never—"

"Couldn't you?" he broke in, apparently frightening or hurting her at the same time, for Lacy heard a muted whimper as he spoke. "Let's face it, Cyl, darlin'. You and Lacy are two of a kind. There's nothing either of you wouldn't do to get what you want. And once upon a time you thought you wanted me. Then you met Jesse and decided you'd made a mistake, only by then Lacy had come into the picture. You hate her because she's beautiful and because she has what you want, but don't go trying to convince me you're better than her, 'cause I ain't buying, baby."

"I'm not like her! She's common trash and not even Texas trash. I come from old money and a distinguished family!"

"Yeah, old money that was used up years ago. As for your eminent family, I wouldn't've cared if you'd been related to that Jones fella who killed all them people a few years back in Rooster Corner, if you'd loved me, Cybil, like you said you did. But you were no different than Lacy. Both of you went trollin' for money and you got what you was after."

"You are so right!" Cybil screeched, obviously teetering on the brink of hysteria. "I got the money I was after. And lucky, lucky me, I got the troll as well."

Lacy gasped at her sister-in-law's cheap shot. Not that

it was especially undeserved. Dillon wasn't exactly a slacker in the meanness department.

With a hand pressed to her mouth, Lacy raced down the hallway, dashing around the corner to the landing, only to be stopped as she crashed headlong into her husband.

Chapter Six

"Whoa," Jesse said, grabbing her arms and holding her back as he bent to eye level with her. "Are you all right?"

"Let me go!" she demanded through clenched teeth.

"Damn it, Lacy, what happened?" Jesse asked, still holding her though she struggled against him.

Her breath competing with the wild pace of her heartbeat, Lacy glared into the handsome face just inches from her own. "Nothing happened, Jesse, except that I just overheard your brother and his wife discussing my lack of virtue, and even though no one will tell me anything directly, I've finally pieced together enough of this puzzle to understand I'm not welcome here. And, buddy, I'm not staying!"

She was livid, her complexion almost as pink as the fuchsia shirt she wore, and Jesse thought she'd never looked more beautiful. Was that because she'd always kept her emotions so well reined? He'd admired her coolness, her air of mystique and unflappable composure. In fact, he thought that, more than her unbelievable beauty, was what had first attracted him to her. Only when they made love did she let the shields down. Then she was animal: untamed, wild, passionate.

She was suddenly as still as death, and Jesse worried that her tantrum might have caused some kind of relapse. "Lacy?" he asked, his voice soft and gentle. "Are you all right?"

He let go of her to wrap his arms around her waist and press her against his chest, but she surprised him by slugging him soundly in the stomach. As he grunted as much with shock as pain, she slipped past him and raced down the stairs.

Jesse recovered quickly and tore after her, reaching

her at the bottom. Grabbing her wrist, he caught her up short and spun her around to face him. "Damn it, Lacy, that's enough! You're not going anywhere!" Grasping her shoulders, he shook her, though mildly so as not to hurt her. "Think about it, honey, you have nowhere to go."

"Oh, don't I!" With a finger pointed at his chest, she jabbed him squarely between his chest muscles, backing him up until he'd allowed her to pin him against the wall. "That's all you know!" *Jab!*

"What do you think I would have done if you hadn't come to the hospital?" *Jab!*

"Do you think they would have just given me a pat on the head, stuck me in a wheelchair, then once we were outside said, 'See ya, Jane Doe. Hope you can take care of yourself till you get your memory back'? No way, buster!" *Jab!*

"They have patient advocates who care for people like me, Mr. Know-it-all. So, I don't need you." *Jab!* "I don't need your brother." *Jab!* "And I don't need—"

Jesse grabbed her hand, clasping the other wrist at the same time. "Okay! Enough! I get your point."

Lacy was panting now with exertion and Jesse saw the color drain from her face. Scooping her up into his arms, he rested his chin on the top of her head so that she wouldn't see his grin.

"Put me down, Jesse. I can walk," she said, though without certitude.

"I'm only taking you to the den so we can talk without the entire household listening in."

"Why? They all know what a bitch I am. They all know you only brought me back here because you're so damned honorable."

He sat her down on the divan, then pulled a chair up, sitting on the edge of the seat as he leaned forward to talk to her. "Look, Lace, I don't know what Dillon and Cybil were saying that you overheard. It doesn't matter. You're my wife, and what anyone else thinks is irrelevant."

Her blue eyes glittering beneath tears that had formed with her anger, she dabbed at the corners with her forefingers, and Jesse saw her struggling to still the trembling of her bottom lip.

"You're still weak, Lacy," he said, his voice low and gentle.

"So what? I can't stay here. I *won't* stay where I'm hated." The tears spilled over her dark lashes now, and her words were as shaky as her quivering lips, but determination still shimmered from her eyes. "I believe I was who you all say I was, Jesse. I know I must have been a class A bitch, and you are apparently a paragon of goodness and fairness, so it's a raw deal for you all the way around, having me back here after the way I treated you ... even though I still don't know exactly what I did, but the bottom line is—"

"The bottom line is you're staying here at the Southern Star until you're well. Then we'll deal with everything that happened between us the way we should have in the first place." Standing up only far enough to reach for a tissue, he wiped the tear stains from her face and grinned. "You may not remember who you are, Lace, but you still want to deal with things you don't like the same way as you did before."

"By running away," she sniffled.

"Yep, but this time, I'm not letting you go."

"Why not? You hate me, remember?"

He did, didn't he? He stared into her eyes as he searched his soul for the answer. He'd hated her enough to kill her before she left. That was why he'd let her go. But now ... now, he wasn't sure. In fact, he, too, was having a hard time reconciling this vulnerable woman who was so easily hurt with the coldhearted bitch he'd married

"I was beginning to think I would be dining alone," Rose Pryde said as both of her sons and their wives exited the house onto the patio from different doorways at the same moment.

"I'm sorry, Mother," Jesse said. "Lacy and I had something that needed to be discussed, but we didn't mean to keep you waiting."

Rose smiled her acceptance of his apology, then arched a dark brow as she noticed the black expression on Dillon's face and the red welt on his wife's cheek. "Is something wrong?"

She'd addressed the question to her eldest son, but it

was Cybil who answered. Her eyes downcast as she slipped into a chair, she said, "We had a disagreement. Nothing important."

A massive black dog almost the size of a small horse lay curled at Rose's feet, his eyes closed as Lacy walked past. Glancing down at the sleeping giant, she registered the sleek ebony coat of fur and wondered absently if he weren't part wolf.

Turning her attention to the rustic charm of the patio, which was almost entirely bordered by foliage, Lacy inhaled deeply. The natural perfume was sweet and heady, and she smiled with the first real glimmer of contentment she'd experienced since her accident. Patting a thick, gnarled branch of a grand old dogwood tree that had been left growing in the middle of the cobbled floor, Lacy noticed that it provided shade for more than two thirds of the dining area. A grape arbor vined across a wooden frame provided shelter from the sun over the remaining space.

She didn't remember the courtyard, but her soul was responding, and she turned quickly on her heel to share her happiness with Jesse.

He was standing only eight or ten feet from her, but involved in what appeared to be a heated discussion with his brother. She felt her face warm and hurriedly looked around for a distraction. She knew Jesse was talking about her and wished he would let it go. After all, he'd promised to leave the past where it belonged until her memory returned in full. Wouldn't it be best to let her start over with the rest of the family as well?

Catching her mother-in-law's gaze on her, she smiled tentatively and crossed the rock floor to join her. "Where do I usually sit, Mrs. Pryde?"

"Across from me to Jesse's right, but please, everyone calls me Mother Rose. You did, too, before you, ah—"

"Ran away," Lacy said, then immediately bit her lip with regret. "I didn't mean that the way it sounded. I wasn't being flippant, really. I just don't want everyone to feel they have to measure their words around me. I know it's awkward, but it'll be so much easier if you'll all just be yourselves."

Jesse stepped up to his wife's side and though he

didn't touch her, she felt a certain intimacy in the way he'd joined her; her ally for the time being at least.

"I was just telling Dillon much the same thing," he said, addressing his remarks to his sister-in-law as well as to his mother. "The doctors asked that we let Lacy regain memories of her life before the accident by herself without influence from us. I agreed, but we've already found out how difficult that's going to be. Things are said, overheard, that are impossible for her to ignore. If we slip, I think it's better if we merely let it go instead of trying to cover it up. It only confuses her."

Cybil lifted a glass of wine that a white-jacketed waiter had placed in front of her. "No problem," she said, "I think we should all bow down and kiss her feet if that'll help. After all, we owe her for breaking up the usual tedium around here." Raising her glass, she winked at her sister-in-law. "You did it with real pizzazz, too, honey. Why, I don't think we've had this much excitement around here since ol' Doc Trajillo—"

"Perhaps you would rather have some coffee instead of more alcohol, dear," Rose interrupted, her tone frigid enough to chill the warm summer air.

"No thanks, Mother darlin'," Cybil said, her tone dripping honey sweetness and her eyes spewing acid. She gave her wild tangled mass of auburn hair a shake. "As always, just being here in the bosom of my lovin' family is quite sobering enough."

"I love the patio," Lacy interjected quickly. "I know you must hate winters when it's too cold to sit out here. Now that I've discovered, ah, rediscovered it, I'll probably spend a lot of time out here." She turned to Jesse as a new thought suddenly struck her. "Did I ever draw or paint?"

Before Jesse could answer, the massive hound that'd been sleeping at his mistress's feet sprang up, his rear quarters bumping the table and rocking it precariously. Everyone grabbed for glasses and plates as they danced with the upset.

Skittering around the chairs that separated him from Lacy, he stopped in front of her, sniffing with gusto even as both Dillon and Jesse moved in a joint effort to catch him by the collar before he could bite her as he had in the past. But the dog surprised them all by sitting down on his back haunches and offering a paw with a meek little yip to emphasize his greeting.

Laughing, Lacy crouched down in front of the dog, accepting the paw and patting his head. He responded with an effusive lick across the side of her face, almost knocking her onto her backside. "Hello, you beautiful big oaf," she said, laughing harder as he seemed to try to crawl onto her lap in an effort to belie his size. "What's his name?" she asked, looking up at her husband and brother-in-law who towered above them, bemused expressions on their faces.

"Thorn," Jesse replied, then to his brother, "Can you believe it?"

"I'm seeing it, but no, I ain't believin' it."

Lacy stood up, giving the dog another affectionate hug before straightening completely. "Don't tell me. I hated dogs in my other life."

"Maybe not all dogs," Jesse said. "But definitely this one. You were terrified of him, and he detested you. Took out after you every time he saw you unless Mother was with him. Then he knew better, but we always laughed about the way he'd sit there, licking his chops and hankering for another bite of your delicious flesh."

"Yep," Dillon agreed, "and the way he'd fix his stare on you." He turned to his wife. "Hey, gal, you remember how you compared him to the temptation of Eve. Said she must have had that same look in her eyes when she was weighing the reward of obedience against the consequence of just one sweet little nibble of that juicy apple."

Lacy was laughing as she stepped past the dog and slipped into the chair her mother-in-law had indicated. Thorn gave a grunt as he pushed himself to his feet, then took a couple of steps and plopped down at the side of Lacy's chair again. "Well, apparently all is forgiven. Maybe this is a classic example of a heart made fonder by absence."

As Dillon and Jesse claimed their seats at the table, Cybil said, "That or he's noticed how skinny you are and decided you'll make a better pet than meal. Heaven knows, that's the only reason he's never showed so much as a passing interest in me."

Lacy glanced down at the enormous animal sitting so

close his hind end actually rested against her leg. "Well, whatever his reason for reform, I'm grateful. His size alone is intimidating. Kind of puts me in mind of a trained bear. Or maybe even the lovesick King Kong. Hardly a thorn, so where did the name come from?"

Every head turned in Rose's direction, and Lacy understood that it was her mother-in-law's explanation to provide. Rather than giving it, though, the woman snapped her fingers, summoning the hound to her side. Then with the slightest of smiles that didn't quite meet her coal-dark eyes, she said, "It's a silly story that's already been worn ragged with repetition."

"Oh, bull, it's a great story," Cybil said, her eyes communicating mild defiance if Lacy was reading the message correctly. "Besides, if Lacy doesn't remember, it's all new to her," she added, turning her attention to her sister-in-law. "Folks are always dropping unwanted animals off at our drive. Usually Luz or Jimmy—you haven't been reacquainted with him yet—or one of the hands takes 'em in. But that one found Mama Rose outside tending to her flowers and it was love at first sight. Mama pretended not to return the affection, always grousing about how he was under her feet every second and carrying on about his long coat attracting everything from burrs to mud. We all kept after her about giving him a name, and she kept protesting, insisting she was going to find him a home somewhere else. It wasn't too hard to see that she enjoyed his adoration, though. So, Jesse named him for her. Called him the thorn in Rose's side. Officially, he's Rose's Thorn."

"Clever," Lacy told her husband with a shy, appreciative smile. Then with another glance at the massive animal, she added, "Still, I think Bear fits him better." She laughed her gaze directed on Cybil now. "And I promise to try not to fall from his good graces."

As dinner was served, conversation continued with ease. Several times, Lacy caught her husband's eyes on her, their opaque darkness unrevealing. Even when he smiled her way every now and then, she couldn't read his thoughts. Was he offering encouragement or merely playing the requisite role of good host?

Lacy spoke little. Her amnesia had, after all, reduced her to a stranger without a history. How could she add to a family discussion about things of which she knew nothing? And yet she was content, encouraged by Jesse, and almost ready to believe whatever it was that had gone on between them, that had driven her to leave, could be gotten past or at least circumvented while they worked to put back the broken pieces of their marriage.

"Did you enjoy your meal?" Rose was asking her.

"Oh, yes, it was wonderful. Especially the salsa. An hour ago I couldn't have said whether or not I liked spicy food, but now I know. Another question asked and answered."

"You've had no memories at all other than of the doll Jesse told us you remembered?" Rose asked.

"No, actually, there was another one," she said slowly, carefully, her eyes on her husband. She wanted to be truthful, but would he appreciate her admitting to remembering a taunt she'd thrown at him on the day she'd left?

"Well, for heaven's sake, Lacy, share it with us," Cybil said, her drawl even more pronounced as her speech began to slur on the fourth glass of wine Lacy had watched her drink.

Lacy shook her head, negating the importance of the memory. "It wasn't much. Just something I said to Jesse the day I left. I recall it, can even hear myself saying it," she said, tilting her head to the side as if listening to the sentence again, "but it still doesn't *feel* like something I would say."

"Well, I for one am confused," Dillon said.

"*Jesse* told me I did, and I remember the words, but it's like someone else was talking." She shook her head again, briskly, dismissing the bothersome subject she wished now she hadn't mentioned. "Never mind. I don't understand it myself, so how could any of you?"

"Ooh, I think it's wonderfully weird!" Cybil said. "And y'all know what they say about the mind playing tricks on us. I'm beginning to think this amnesia thing isn't so bad. I certainly wish I could forget all the hateful things I've ever said."

"Amen to that," Dillon said, his tone heavy with sarcasm. "I sure wouldn't mind forgetting the shit pile of mean things you've said to me either, darlin'."

Jesse stood up quickly as did Rose, and Lacy knew

that they'd done this before. Not that she remembered. It was more an instinctual understanding that Dillon's and Cybil's biting remarks were commonly the signal for the end of the meal.

"I've got some paperwork to attend to," Jesse said to Lacy. "Would you like me to take you back upstairs before I go to my office?"

"You're leaving?" she asked, hating the alarm she heard in her own voice.

"No," he said, a one-sided smile of reassurance appearing for a moment. "My office is here at the house. It's the only one with solid double doors that I can lock when I don't want to be disturbed. Remember, I showed it to you when we toured earlier?"

It was her turn to smile, this time with relief. "Of course. You go ahead. I can find my way upstairs later. I think I'm going to sit out here for a while if that's all right with everyone."

"Fine with me," Cybil said, struggling from her chair and succeeding only after Dillon came around the table to assist her. "I'm going in to watch some TV."

"I always walk Thorn after dinner," Rose said. "Would you join me, Lacy?"

She was pleased by the offer and immediately out of her chair. "I'd love to."

Jesse'd been about ready to leave them, but he hesitated now, provoking a raised brow from his mother.

"Is something wrong?" Rose asked him.

"I was worried about the way Lacy's dressed. She's only wearing sandals, and nothing to protect her legs. It might be better if she waited until tomorrow evening to go with you."

"Nonsense," Rose said, exasperation heavy in her voice. "I know I've always been a stickler about wearing boots and long pants out on the land, but we'll be sticking to the path and Thorn will be with us."

"What are you both talking about?" Lacy asked.

"Snakes," Jesse said.

"Rattlers, primarily," Rose added. "But as I said, Thorn will warn us if we're about to come on one."

Lacy shivered. "I don't think you have to tell me I'm terrified of snakes. I'm pretty sure I just remembered that all by myself."

"That might not be a memory so much as a natural instinct," Rose said, snapping her fingers at the same time as a signal to the big dog who once again sat at Lacy's feet. "Come along, Thorn." Then returning her attention to Lacy, "Most people have an innate aversion to snakes."

"I suppose so," Lacy agreed, wiggling her fingers in farewell to her husband at the same time. "See you later?"

"It may be very late before I'm finished working. The paperwork has piled up while I was away," he said.

Lacy nodded her agreement, valiantly hiding her disappointment before hurrying after her walking companions as they started across the lawn. "You walk every night?" she asked Rose as soon as she'd caught up with her.

"Unless the weather doesn't allow it."

"It's beautiful out here," Lacy said, looking around her at the rolling, verdant terrain.

Rose didn't answer and Lacy lapsed into silence, realizing that this quiet must be a part of the peace her mother-in-law derived from her nightly passages.

Five minutes must have lapsed before the silence was suddenly disrupted by Rose Pryde herself. Her tone though soft was somehow shattering to the peaceful ambience, and even Thorn seemed startled by the sudden intrusion. "You've changed somehow, Lacy."

Lacy shrugged as she plucked at her thumbnail with the fingers of her other hand. "I don't know what you mean. How was I before?"

"You were sharper," Rose declared. "This walk, for instance. You would never have provided me with such an opportunity."

Lacy heard the hatred then, felt the tensile alertness in the woman beside her like that of an animal poised to strike and waiting for precisely the right moment. Her movements had changed as well, becoming brittle, crisp now that all pretense of a casual saunter had been abandoned.

Lacy stopped, tensed and ready, no lamb meekly surrendering to the impending slaughter.

In the west a glorious sunset was beginning to play itself out for its audience of two, but its magnificence was no rival for the contest about to begin between the women.

"Perhaps it was that I was forewarned then. I'm sure you can appreciate the disadvantage you have me at. I don't know who I am, what our relationship is. I don't even know what I will think or feel next, because I have no reference from the past to guide me. Every experience is new until I regain my memory. How could I have known that I should have been wary of a trap?"

Lacy saw meanness then, raw and unmasked, in her mother-in-law's expression. She recoiled even before Rose answered.

"It's all a game. This amnesia. This helpless innocence. You are aware of every calculated move you've ever made, just as you know exactly what your plan is now. Only I'm not going to let you get away with it this time."

Lacy's eyes widened with surprise, but it was surprise at the visceral conviction she heard in her mother-in-law's tone. "You're wrong," she said simply.

"Am I? I think not, but let's play the game by your rules. Let's *pretend* that you have suffered a memory loss. Let's even pretend that I am sympathetic to your plight. That doesn't mean I will allow you to insinuate your way back into our lives. You're here on a temporary basis. If you *choose* not to regain your memory within a reasonable period, then I'll provide you with the inducement to leave anyway. I'll convince Jesse to settle a fair amount on you as part of your divorce. In addition to that, I will give you one million dollars."

"You hate me that much?" Lacy asked, though she could hardly force the words through her chattering teeth. It was a warm, balmy night but still, she was chilled to the core of her being.

The answer was blatantly obvious; Rose ignored the question, instead adding a codicil to her million-dollar offer. "Of course, that's only in exchange for your promise—in writing, certainly—never to darken our doorway again."

"You're crazy," Lacy said though the words were barely audible.

Rose grabbed her wrist, and Lacy cried out with mingled surprise and pain. Thorn growled, baring his teeth, but quieted at once with Rose's command for him to sit. Her attention once again on Lacy, she pinned her with her dark gaze. "One more thing. Don't think you can make Jesse fall in love with you again. He may treat you with kindness, warmth even, but I will be in the background whispering reminders of what you did to him. I won't let him forget, and this time I can't be caught off guard."

"And what if I tell him everything you've said?" Lacy asked, though of course she knew she would never do that.

Rose laughed. "You'd be playing right into my hands, my dear. He wouldn't believe you. You were too convincing as a bitch the day you left for him to really trust anything you could say now. He'd know at once what kind of game you're playing. He learned how hard you worked to create mistrust and friction between us before. He'd know you were up to the same tricks."

She still held Lacy's wrist in a fierce grip, but Lacy twisted her arm free, stepping back out of the other woman's reach. She struggled for words, but her mother-in-law's vehement attack had been too swift in coming, and Lacy's senses reeled. She could not assimilate such hatred. Without another word, she turned away toward the house and a future so bleak, she wondered how she'd face it.

From a darkened room Jesse watched his mother and wife in the distance. Though too far away to read their expressions, their body movements were revealing. He knew that the pretense of a casual walk for camaraderie's sake had been quickly given up. His mother was obviously very angry, and Lacy was not accepting her mother-in-law's diatribe with complacent reserve. He watched as Rose reached out for Lacy's arm, then after a long moment saw his wife twist free of her grasp and turn away to stalk back toward the house. It appeared as though Thorn had decided in favor of the younger woman, though Rose apparently disabused the cur of any such traitorous notions, for he suddenly stopped in his tracks, then returned slowly to his mistress's side.

Jesse muttered an expletive under his breath directed at his mother. All during dinner she had been courteous, even kind to Lacy, asking after her health, offering to make an appointment for her with the family doctor, and even going so far as to suggest that she would drive her so they could have lunch together after her examination. Jesse had been proud of his mother's effort, for it was no secret that Rose Pryde had been ecstatic when her beautiful young daughter-in-law had left the Southern Star for what all believed would be the last time.

He'd intended to talk to Dillon and Cybil after dinner, warn them to be more careful about what they said about his wife in the future when she might overhear, though there'd only been enough time for an abbreviated reminder to his brother. But his mother's friendly caring had appeared example enough for the other two who had also joined in the effort to make Lacy feel welcome.

At the time he'd told himself he only cared that his wife's feelings be spared because of the catastrophic injuries she'd sustained to both mind and body, but as he watched her now, he knew he'd been lying to himself.

She'd held her shoulders squared, her head erect as she marched away from his mother, but after passing a thick copse of trees and glancing back to make sure she was out of sight of the other woman, Lacy gave up the charade. Plainly enervated by the conversation, her shoulders dipped and her head bowed. Dejection taking its toll, she seemed finally to shuffle rather than step, and sympathy nipped at the edges of his heart.

His hands balled at his sides, he squeezed his eyes shut and willed himself to remember the day she'd left, to revive the fury and anguish she'd caused him. If, in spite of his warning, his mother had reminded Lacy of what she'd done, it was nothing less than she deserved, was it?

Chapter Seven

Lacy awakened the following morning teetering on the brink of memories from her past life. She reached for them, struggling to recover what she knew had been clear and sharp in sleep and was now blurred and confused and slipping from her grasp.

Squeezing her eyes shut, she recovered a momentary glimpse of a room. A bedroom. Small, fussy and cluttered, and yet warm and cozy as if someone had carefully filled the tiny space with personal treasures collected over a lifetime. Lacy's heart seemed to leap inside her chest with happy recognition, and she knew that the bedroom had once been hers. But when? As a child? No, it wasn't a little girl's room. Perhaps—

The image began to dim, much like a movie screen fading to black before a scene change, and with its loss profound sadness seeped its way into her heart replacing joy. She willed it away, refusing it prominence as she groped for another recollection.

Nothing came. The other memories that she knew had surfaced in sleep had buried themselves once again in her subconscious. It didn't matter. She'd caught one of them—a memory as bright and silvery and wonderful as an elusive moonbeam—and managed to hold on to it.

Tossing the covers aside, she laughed. Moonbeams! She laughed again. It was a ridiculous, fanciful analogy, but no one could know how exciting it was to realize that the doctors had been right. Her memory was going to return. Maybe slowly ... a dream at a time, but it was going to happen. Then she'd be able to face the terrible wrong she'd done Jesse, and then maybe, just maybe ...

"Maybe nothing," she muttered aloud as the more recent memory of Rose Pryde's cruel words and ominous warning crashed back into the forefront of her thoughts.

"Bitch," she said, though only in a whisper, slipping her bare feet into fuzzy mules and padding across the floor to the bathroom.

As she washed her face and brushed her teeth, the same anger and hurt she'd experienced the night before coursed the length of her back and arms and hammered in her heart. She wrinkled her nose at her reflection in the mirror over the sink. "Idiot. You think Rose is going to be happy to know you've remembered a bedroom you're not even sure was once really yours? Yeah, right. She doesn't even believe your amnesia's for real."

A knock on the door leading to Jesse's bedroom startled her so badly she almost dropped the hairbrush she'd just picked up.

"Lacy?" Jesse called from the other side of the door.

She swallowed nervously and allowed her gaze to slide over her reflection. Hair tousled in sexy disarray and dressed as she was in the floor-length, white satin nightgown she'd found in one of her lingerie drawers, for just an instant she could almost convince herself she was still the unmarred beauty he'd awakened beside in the early months of their marriage. Until she looked at the faint yet evident scars on her freshly scrubbed cheeks. A twinge of self-pity bit at her heart, but only for a brief moment. Raising her chin a fraction of an inch, she met her gaze with defiance and pride. What did she care how she looked to him? Apparently—

He knocked again, and this time, discarding thoughts about her appearance, Lacy called for him to enter.

She turned as the door opened, leaning her hips against the marble countertop and clutching the edges with her hands. "I'm sorry, am I tardy for breakfast, Jesse?" she asked, her tone neither warm nor cool but carefully neutral.

He stared, not answering, and Lacy felt her cheeks heat. His eyes hadn't even found her face but stopped at the clear outline of her breasts straining against the sheer fabric of her gown. She spun around, turning her back on him only to realize the futility as she watched in the mirror and followed his dark eyes as they trailed the length of her. She fought the urge to reach for the bathrobe hanging on the back of the door and then almost laughed at the absurdity of her embarrassment. This was her husband after all. For better or worse. In sickness and in health. Well, she was sick, and she certainly couldn't imagine worse than their present predicament, but neither could she believe that he wasn't seeing anything he hadn't seen before.

She picked up the hairbrush, raising it as she said, "Please, start without me. I'm not hungry."

"I wasn't inquiring about breakfast, Lacy," he said. "Mother and Dillon and I have eaten already. Cybil rarely comes downstairs before noon. Supper's the only meal Mother insists we make a special effort to come together for."

At mention of Rose Pryde, Lacy felt her temper rise. "Then what did you want?" she asked, unable to keep the bitter edge from her voice this time.

"I was waiting for you to get up," he said quietly, evenly, obviously refusing to acknowledge her angry tone. "I thought you might like a tour of the ranch today. When I heard you moving around in here—"

"You thought I wouldn't mind if you just barged in on me." She slammed the brush down on the counter. "After all, I am your wife. This *is* your home. Never mind that I really don't know you from Adam or that you hate me or even that I might be uncomfortable letting you see my face like this ... without ... without makeup and ... oh, forget it."

She put her hands over her face as tears filled her eyes and clogged her throat, choking away her aggravation and leaving misery in its stead.

She didn't hear him move into the room, but suddenly he was behind her and his hands were on her shoulders as he turned her around, then gathered her into his arms. He held her while she wept. Held her tight against his chest. And damn her if she didn't allow herself to believe that maybe she was wrong. *Rose* hated her, no doubt about it, and she'd thought Jesse did as well. But it was possible, wasn't it, that he was merely angry and hurt by the mysterious crime he claimed she'd committed? That as her mind healed so might his heart?

But even as she allowed that new hope, he shattered it in the next instant as he suddenly grasped her arms, practically shoving her away from him. "I apologize, Lace. My mistake. I won't intrude on your privacy again." He turned away, striding quickly from the room. Just outside the doorway, he stopped to add over his shoulder. "I'll wait downstairs. If you decide on the tour, wear jeans and boots, and don't forget your Stetson. Hard to say what's meanest this time of hear. Horseflies or the sun."

Too stunned by the abrupt change in him to answer, Lacy stood frozen until she heard him leave his bedroom moments later. Then the anger ignited by her mother-in-law the night before flared again.

Hotter.

Sharper.

Vengeful.

Angling her head, she stared into blue eyes that glittered with ice. "Another revelation gleaned, Lacy Pryde. You're capable of hating, too."

The frown that had creased Jesse's brow since leaving his wife upstairs more than an hour before deepened when he saw her start down the stairs. Instead of the jeans and boots he'd dictated, she was dressed in a flowered, apple-red cotton shift and high-heeled sandals. And in place of the acrid scowl he'd expected, she wore a smile as sweet as maple syrup.

"I take it you've decided against the tour," he said in his usual soft tone though he wondered how he kept from shouting. He'd wasted the entire morning waiting for her. Silently cursing himself for the goddamned idiot he was, he reached for his hat, which hung on a wall peg. "I'll see you at supper," he told her, already exiting the foyer.

"Jesse, wait," she called, quickening her descent.

"What is it, Lacy?" Rose asked, appearing from the living room. "You've already disrupted Jesse's day. Whatever it is you want, I'm sure I can help you."

Jesse hadn't realized that his mother was nearby, listening and plainly poised to pounce on his unsuspecting wife the moment the opportunity presented itself. He *should* have known. Especially after the scene he'd witnessed last night. Hell, after countless such scenes between the two women in the months that Lacy had lived on Star land. He turned back into the room. He hadn't tolerated her interference before. He certainly wasn't going to allow it now.

"You forget, Mother. I was away for several days. I don't really think another day without me overseeing Southern Star business will wreak too much havoc." He granted her a smile, balm for the sting of his rebuke. Then to his wife, "What is it, Lacy?"

Still maintaining her air of flippant nonchalance, Lacy flicked her wrist at him, leaning seductively on the balustrade at the same time. "Oh, go on, Jesse. Mother Rose is absolutely right. I've kept you long enough from whatever it is you cowboys do out there on the range. After all, I was only going to ask if there's a car I can borrow since the L.A. police haven't found mine yet." Again that honey-sweet smile that made Jesse grind his teeth. "Besides, even without remembering a single iota about any of you Prydes, I think I've pretty much figured out who holds the keys in this family."

Jesse was watching Lacy, though it would have been impossible not to see his mother's complexion darken with her fury. No doubt about it. The accident might have impaired Lacy's memory, but it sure as hell hadn't been able to alter her character. Once a bitch, always a bitch ... and still the only equal to his indomitable mother he'd ever met. Under different circumstances he might have enjoyed the ace his wife had just served her opponent in their ongoing match.

His eyes dipped to the swell of her breasts above the low-cut bodice of her sundress, then moved to the long, shapely legs that only a few scant inches of the short skirt obscured. Clever and beautiful, this woman he'd loved, then hated so quickly the emotions hadn't yet separated themselves.

"No, Lacy. You may not use any of the cars," he said.

Lacy blinked, and he knew his cold tone and unexplained refusal had surprised her. This time he allowed himself a grin, enjoying the satisfaction he'd rarely known in his six-month relationship with her. He turned to his mother. "They're calling for thunderstorms tonight. The boys are moving livestock from the ridge. On second thought, I think I will go help." His gaze involuntarily grazing his wife's seductive figure once again, he added, "Work off some of my pent-up ... frustration."

"Wait," Lacy said.

Jesse ignored her, starting for the back of the house once again.

"I said *wait!*" Lacy almost screamed.

That stopped him, but it was Rose who spoke.

"We don't raise our voices in this home, Lacy."

"Oh, we don't, do we? Well, shame on me. Somehow, though, Mother Rose, I've just got a feeling I've broken every sacred Pryde rule there is at one time or another, and I bet there are hundreds of 'em." She laughed as she slung her purse strap over her shoulder and stepped from the landing onto the marble foyer floor. Jesse had reentered the room in a couple of long strides and now stood facing her alongside his mother. Lacy didn't let the fact that she had to sidestep to slip past them on her way to the front door rattle her. She spoke as she went. "As long as we're on the subject of Pryde rules, and me being a bona fide family member and all, I think I'll just lay down a few of my own, beginning with this one: I won't be bullied. Not by my husband, my mother-in-law, or anyone else. I'm going to town with or without one of your damn cars." Stopping at the front door, she jammed the straw hat she carried onto her head. "And you know what? I'm just willing to bet I won't have to walk far before some little ole farmer comes along and offers me a ride. Either of you care to lay odds?"

Chapter Eight

"**B**ravo!" Cybil called, applauding at the same time from the second-floor landing the moment the door slammed behind Lacy. "Why, I do believe our Lacy is really back! Isn't this fun?"

"Shut up, Cybil," Rose said, immediately dismissing her though gales of laughter trailed along the hallway as Cybil returned to her room.

Rose turned her attention to her son once again, her black eyes shimmering with emotion and her fingers gripping his wrist like talons. "Go after her, son. You cannot allow her to stand out there hooking a ride like a common tramp. As much as it galls me, she is still a Pryde, and I won't have her humiliating us."

Jesse couldn't have cared less about his mother's displeasure. As much as he loved and respected her, he'd always disdained her arrogance. But now was not the time, however, to wrangle with her about meaningless pride. He needed to focus his attention on his wife.

Jesse didn't answer. What was there to say? He didn't intend to let Lacy hitch a ride into town, but neither did he give a damn what their neighbors and friends thought. His motives were far different from his mother's, but now wasn't the time to argue the point. Besides, the tug of war between his mother and wife, with him caught in the middle, was all too familiar. As the saying went: He'd been there, done that.

Twisting his arm from her grasp, he flashed a tight half smile. His stride was long and fast to the door. He paused before stepping outside. "I'll see you at supper."

She muttered something as he pulled the door closed behind him. Something about him and Dillon, and brains between their legs.

The private drive that accessed the highway was both

long and winding, and Jesse quickly gave up the visual search for his wife from the front steps of the house. Digging into his jeans pocket for the keys to his truck, he bounded to the walkway and around the side of the house, his thoughts working as rapidly as his feet.

Why Lacy's sudden desire to go into Rooster Corner? Hell, she'd only been home a day. She couldn't already be so frustrated and desperate to be free of him again, she'd go to outsiders for the answers her mind refused to give.

His conscience immediately refuting that argument, he recalled how he'd left her upstairs in tears. And what about the scene he'd witnessed the night before? It was obvious his mother had inflicted some pretty mean wounds as well. So, why wouldn't Lacy run for help? Even a cornered animal knew to struggle for escape.

Then he remembered the teasing smiles, the daring, almost insolent posture, and the provocative dress.

His brow furrowing and his eyes narrowing, he cursed his stupidity. Lacy hadn't been hurt by Rose or even by him. It was all an act. She might have lost her memory, but she damn sure hadn't lost her ability as an actress.

Make him ashamed.

Make him worry.

Make him crazy with desire.

He'd fallen for it all before. *Well, not this time, baby. Not ever again.*

And she wasn't going anywhere. Not without him, and not until her memory returned. He'd make certain of that, and it had nothing to do with family pride.

He yanked the truck door open and slid behind the steering wheel. But as he stuck the key in the ignition, he paused long enough to blow out a long shuddering breath with his next thought. Maybe he wouldn't wait for her to remember what she'd done to destroy his love. He might just tell his bewitching bride the facts about how she'd sunk her hooks into him, then ripped them out again, tearing his heart out at the same time.

Fuck the doctors and their rules.

Her bravado deflated by the time she reached the highway, Lacy swept her hat from her head and wiped perspiration from her brow with the back of her arm.

She leaned against one of the posts supporting the sign that boasted the entrance to Southern Star land and sighed. "What now, stupid?" she asked aloud. Then silently: *Oh, yeah, you're really going to hitchhike into town . . . and do exactly what? You are a walking, talking blank! Who in the hell do you suppose you're going to talk to?*

She kicked at the grass beneath her feet. "Dumb, dumb, dumb!"

A car approached.

It was heading south judging from the morning sun that shone down on her back, but toward Rooster Corner or in the opposite direction? She didn't even know where the town was.

Dumber than dumb!

She stooped down, pretending to pick a day lily. Maybe the driver wouldn't wonder about a woman standing on the edge of the road all dressed up with somewhere to go and no apparent means of getting there.

The car streaked by.

Her shoulders drooped with relief as she stood up. Okay, but what now?

She looked at the house and wondered if Jesse and Rose were watching her. Miss Independent-*nobody*-tells-me-what-to-do idiot, out here cowering behind a signpost!

A glint of blue caught her eye. She squinted, but only for a second. Then her eyes widened as she recognized her husband's Jeep headed toward her along the private drive.

To her left and over her shoulder, she heard the approach of another vehicle on the highway. No longer undecided, Lacy darted for the edge of the road and stuck out her thumb.

A pickup, battered and gray with primer, screeched to a halt on the far side of the road. "Hey, Miss Lacy, heard you was back," the driver, a red-faced man with long, scraggly, carrot-orange hair, called out to her. "And I might add, lookin' prettier than ever."

Lacy hoped her smile suggested the right amount of friendliness. Obviously the man knew her, but how well and from where? What difference did it make? She needed a ride, and she needed it quick!

She was about to open her mouth to thank him and ask if he and his passenger were headed toward town when Jesse brought his vehicle to a screeching halt less than two feet from her. She was forced to step back to avoid being struck by the door as he flung it open and jumped out. No doubt about it, he was furious. Anger literally flashed in his obsidian-black eyes. So she was stunned when he slipped an arm around her waist and forced a grin at the men in the old truck.

"Hey, Randy, thanks for stoppin'," he said.

"No problem, boss. Looked like the missus needed a ride. Me and Clay couldn't figure that one, but thought we'd better stop, see if we could help before the wrong guy happened along. Can't be too careful these days." The last was offered with an accompanying apologetic smile toward Lacy.

She hardly noticed. At the mention of the name Clay, icy tendrils of fear had spread upward from the pit of her stomach.

Turning her attention to the man seated on the far side of the truck, she stared hard, trying to make out his face. He wore a hat much like Jesse's only his was pulled down low over his brow, and the sharp features of his profile were only silhouetted shadows. It didn't matter. She knew this man. *Recognized* him.

Clay Waters.

The man who'd been hired to kill her.

"Sorry for the bother, boys," Jesse drawled smoothly. "My bride, here, was *pretending* to hitch a ride. Just a game we were playing. I was supposed to get out here and pick her up before someone else came on us. Kinda embarrassing, but nothin' more than crazy fun between newlyweds both old enough to know better."

Damn, lying came easy, Jesse thought. But then there wasn't a Texan born who didn't know the importance of saving face, and most often that meant a little white lie here and there.

He gave Lacy's waist a squeeze, glancing down at her face with a wink and a broad grin. Still playacting . . . and silently begging—as much as he was capable—for her to go along.

She returned his gaze, even his smile, but her face was suddenly as pale and sickly as white ash, and he swore he felt a tremor beneath the arm that held her. "Jesse's right," she began in a voice that was oddly choked and weak. "Just some silliness. Thanks for looking out for me, though." With that, she turned out of his arm and headed in the direction of his Jeep. Jesse watched her for a few seconds, his brow knotted with a perplexed frown. Then he turned back to the two ranch hands who were employed by the Southern Star.

Randy was grinning and saying something to his passenger, hand cupped around one side of his mouth. Both men laughed and though it was difficult, Jesse kept his easy sliding grin in place. "Yuck it up, boys. Beats cryin', which is what I'd be doin' if one of you was the lucky guy married to that sweet package." He gestured over his shoulder with a thumb to where his wife was waiting for him in the Jeep.

Clay waved over the top of the rattle-trap old truck as Randy shifted gears and pulled away from the shoulder with a sputtering start.

Only then did Jesse give up the counterfeit grin and allow his thoughts the sharp detour back to his wife's inexplicable upset. Stalling as he tried to puzzle the pieces of the past few minutes back together, he swept his hat from his head and swabbed perspiration from his brow with the back of his sleeve. No doubt about it, Lacy had been afraid. He recognized fear. Any cowboy worth his salt was tuned in for signs of it.

Could feel it in the way a horse's flesh crawled with the approach of a rattler.

Saw it in the wild-eyed gaze of cattle terrified by signs of a brewing storm.

Even smelled it in the trickle of sweat when it ran down a coward's back once his bluff was called.

And now he'd sensed it in Lacy. Only question was, what the hell had happened to frighten her?

Chapter Nine

Lacy wasn't waiting in the Jeep, and she wasn't just frightened. She was terrified. Absolutely panicked.

Clay Waters had been hired to kill her. She *remembered* that. But who hated her enough to want her dead? And why?

As the questions roiled inside her head, she raced across the lawn toward the house, stopping only once to pull off her high-heeled sandals.

Behind her, she heard Jesse call out to her, telling her to wait, then the engine of his Jeep come to life. Panic grew, swelling inside her chest. She had the uncanny feeling of running for her life and suddenly a sense of déjà vu; another memory of being chased down by a different vehicle. Pictures of the horrifying scene flashed in surreal fireworks bursts before her mind's eye, and she even heard the beginnings of a scream; a scream that was drowned out by the sickening sounds of crunching metal, splintering glass, and cracking bones.

Her head had begun to pound by the time she fell against the front door of the house. She fumbled with the latch for several seconds with trembling fingers before managing to throw the door open with enough force to send it crashing against the wall.

Her bare feet slipping on the slick foyer floor, Lacy was forced to slow her flight. The appearance of her mother-in-law in the living room doorway quickened it again.

"Why, Lacy, whatever—"

"Don't!" Lacy shouted, though it came out a hoarse whisper on her ragged breath.

Don't what? she wondered as she fled past the older woman. *Don't try to stop me? Don't talk to me? Don't send your hired killer after me?*

A bubble of hysterical laughter escaped her throat as she grabbed the balustrade and started up the stairs. *I've lost it,* she thought. *All of it. Control. Reason. Sanity.* But no sooner were the thoughts formed than she felt Jesse enter the house. She *heard* him, too. The sharp click of his booted heels against marble, but it was the feel of energy and rage that caused her knees to nearly buckle beneath her.

Unlike his mother, Jesse didn't try to stop her with words. He was coming after her. The staircase trembled beneath the weight of his hurried pursuit and Lacy heard her fear whistle through her clenched teeth as she reached the landing.

Oh, God, had he brought her home just to kill her?

And then everything was happening at once.

He grabbed her shoulder, spinning her around though only partway as she refused to give up her grip on the railing. And then she struck him, hard on the side of his head with the heel of one of her sandals. She heard his grunt of pain and realized that his hand slipped from her shoulder in the same instant.

Turning fully now, Lacy met her husband's shocked gaze. Splayed fingers of blood were already spreading across his face, and he was struggling for a hold on the banister as he pitched backward in a certain fall.

Horrified by the injury she'd inflicted, yet still terrified by the memory of Clay Waters and his role in her life, Lacy turned away and raced up the last few steps.

As she dashed for her room, Jesse cursed and then something hit the wall. His body as he toppled down the stairs? She didn't look. Couldn't. But she knew she was right in the next instant when she heard Rose scream and the sequence of heavy thuds.

Lacy slammed her bedroom door shut behind her, twisting the lock. Her heart pounded in her chest as she dropped the shoes, and slid along the door to the floor beside them and hugged her knees. Rocking back and forth, she squeezed her eyes shut, willing the picture of Jesse's bloody face and the rude soundtrack of his fall from her mind.

Oh, God, she'd probably killed him!

Before he killed me?

She pressed her knuckles against her mouth, stifling the shriek that begged release.

What now? She couldn't just sit there. She had to get away, and she had to hurry. This time she wouldn't be merely fleeing a would-be murderer as she suspected she had the last time she'd left. This time she might well be running from a murder charge.

Jesse hurt like a son of a bitch. And that was every-where *except* the wound to his head. *That* felt like it'd been opened up with a fire-hot branding iron.

"You need stitches," Rose said as she pressed another swatch of gauze to the gaping cut.

Jesse sat on his mother's vanity. Gently pulled her hand away, he assessed the damage. "No. It looks worse than it is. Just put some of that ointment on it and tape the gauze in place so I can get outta here."

"What you mean is, so you can get upstairs to that witch you married," Rose said, angrily grabbing a tube of medicated salve from the dressing table and twisting off the cap.

In spite of his discomfort, Jesse grinned at his moth-er's reflection. "Easy. That top is not Lacy's neck, much as you wish it were."

"Don't be flip," Rose said sharply, though a grin tugged at the corners of her mouth. It disappeared with the memory of her son tumbling head over heels down the stairs. He'd finally stopped himself only a couple of stairs from the bottom by catching hold of the wrought iron. A shudder born of keen imagination rocked her as she perceived him lying on the hard marble flooring in the foyer, blood spilling and his neck broken.

Tracking the route her mind was following, Jesse reached behind him and patted her arm. "It's all right. *I'm* all right."

"No thanks to her. Thanks to God for intervening and saving your life."

Jesse let loose a long whistling breath of aggravation. The warring between mother and wife had been a con-stant in his life since the day he'd first brought Lacy home as a bride. Not that he hadn't done his part in redoubling the situation today. He frowned, then winced with the ensuing sharp pain. "Ow!"

That started another litany from his mother, but Jesse wasn't listening. He was running a fast movie reel in his mind over the events leading to his fall down the staircase.

She'd been hurt when he talked with her in the bathroom.

Defiant when she'd come downstairs.

She'd seemed assured in the first few seconds as they'd stood on the side of the road talking to Randy and Clay.

So, where the hell had the fear come from? Nothing he could recall explained the sudden change in her. Nor was it a figment of his imagination. His body could attest to that.

He glanced at his mother's grim face as she taped the gauze square to his brow. Rose believed Lacy had struck out in a fit of anger. He knew better. Terror had motivated her. But why?

Brushing his mother's hands from his head, he checked the bandage in the mirror. "Good enough," he told her as he slid off the stool and headed for the door.

"Jesse!" Rose called.

"Not now, Mother. I've got to go talk to Lacy."

He didn't look back when she called out again. Not even when she masterfully altered her tone to a cajoling whine. He was used to her ploys. Besides, though she had learned how to beg with her voice, she should have practiced in front of a mirror, for she'd never realized the importance of softening her gaze as well. Her black eyes never changed. They remained as cold and hard as obsidian.

Unlike his wife's blue eyes, which could be as dark as midnight skies when she was angry, as bright and shimmering as sapphires when she laughed, or as murky as storm-churned seas when she was frightened.

He clenched his jaws as he realized that was the one color of blue he'd never seen in her gaze before today. He would never have believed it if he hadn't witnessed it himself. Lacy was many things, but frightened was not one of them. So what the hell had happened? Why was she suddenly so afraid of him that she'd run from him outside, then turned and fought like a cornered terrier when he finally caught up with her on the stairs?

There was only one possible answer.

The aches and pains in his battered body and injured head ebbed with the knife-sharp sting to his heart. His wife was afraid of him! But why? What had she remembered?

Chapter Ten

Lacy's emotions had run the gamut. From fear to anger to depression. Now she was exhausted and resolution had taken a firm hold. She was going to leave the Southern Star. She had no choice. Not if she wanted to live. She did. She'd already proven that by fighting her way out of a coma after the near fatal accident.

Accident. Now even the certainty that she'd been the unlucky victim of a driver out of control had been snatched away by the hazy visions that had tumbled from the recesses of her mind, one after another, helter-skelter.

Having mustered enough strength to pick herself up from the floor, Lacy had made it as far as the bed, before falling back onto the welcome softness of the mattress. She lay sprawled across it now, pressing her hands to the sides of her head. She groaned. What was real? Any of it? All of it?

Clay Waters. She'd remembered him. As soon as Jesse uttered the young man's first name, her mind had supplied the last. But was it really possible that he'd been hired to kill her? Was that what had prompted her abrupt flight weeks earlier?

It seemed too farfetched to be believed. Though why when it was so glaringly obvious that Rose Pryde, the family matriarch, *hated* her? Lacy didn't doubt the woman would do whatever she deemed necessary to be rid of her son's wife once and for all.

But Jesse?

Pulling herself up to a sitting position, her legs dangled over the side of the bed. Her gaze was focused on her restlessly moving feet though her thoughts remained concentrated on Jesse. A sharp dagger of remorse pierced her heart as she recalled the shocked expression

on his face when she'd struck him. Oh, God, she'd been
crazy with fear, but she hadn't intended to hurt him.
Thank the stars she hadn't injured him too seriously.
Rose would have called an ambulance had his condition
been grievous or, at the very least, driven him to the
hospital herself. She'd done neither. Lacy knew that
much.

The French doors leading to the balcony had been
open when she entered the room. Even in her misery,
she'd noticed at once, as the mid-morning breeze dried
the tears that had slipped from the corner of her eye
and run along the bridge of her nose. She'd sat there,
face raised, drinking in deep gulps of stabilizing air. Regaining her equilibrium. Slowing her galloping heart.
Long enough to overhear the housekeeper on the patio
below cluck her tongue as she called up to Cybil who'd
apparently been on the veranda only a few yards away.
"Senor Jesse is bleeding badly from the *puta's* attack, *si.*
You are not to worry though. *Mamacita* Rose is tending
him with God at her side."

If fear hadn't had such a firm hold on her emotions,
Lacy would have laughed at that. God at Rose's side!
Ha! She'd wager the only time God was at that woman's
side was when his presence was necessary to protect
someone else from her evil.

The thin smile that was born with the observation died
with the startling memory that had triggered the terrible
chain of events. If she wasn't hallucinating, someone had
hired Clay Waters to kill her. She wasn't positive that
her disabled mind wasn't conjuring the murder conspiracy from a book once read, or a movie she'd seen, and
attributing them to the hapless cowboy. But she was certain she believed in "better safe than sorry."

That decided her. She headed for the closet to retrieve
a few pieces of luggage she'd discovered on a shelf and
an economy of selected outfits. She'd returned to
Rooster Corner, Texas, and the Southern Star with the
hope of regaining her memory. Leaving might well jeopardize that goal. But dying would remove the possibility permanently.

Time to get out of Dodge, she mused. The decidedly
country saying made her think of Jesse and inspired a
real smile. She wondered if he would appreciate the

irony of such a Texified adage crossing such a citified mind. Somehow, she thought he would.

She laughed.

"Something funny?" Jesse asked from the bathroom doorway that linked their rooms.

Lacy jumped, then froze in place. The unexpected intrusion had startled her. But worse than that, his timing embarrassed her to the core. She'd been laughing. Laughing! Only an hour or so after tearing across the lawns like a woman chased by demons and then attacking him with the sharp, lethal heal of her shoe. Good Lord, he must think her not only without a memory but without a conscience as well.

Setting down the two suitcases she'd just retrieved, yet careful to keep her back to him, she asked, "Are you all right?"

"Well, I'm standing here, so I guess you didn't kill me if that's what you were hopin' you'd done."

Guilt and remorse flying right out the French doors she'd left partially ajar, she spun around to face him. Anger at his remark heated her cheeks as she met his insolent gaze. But that, too, quickly dissolved as she noticed the square of bandage on his brow. She shook her head. "No, that wasn't what I was hoping. I didn't mean to hurt you. I'm sorry."

Ignoring her apology, his gaze left her face, settling on the twin pieces of luggage. "Where are you going?"

Lacy shrugged. "I'm leaving. I don't know exactly where I'm going. Back to California, I suppose. I'll probably call Peach or that girl from the patient advocacy group. Either one of them will help me find a place until . . ." She shrugged again, raking her hair back with all ten fingers at the same time. "I'll figure it out while I'm packing."

"How're you going to get there? You suddenly remember where you put the money you took when you left the last time?"

Lacy felt her blood drain from her head. She was suddenly dizzy and had to grab on to one of the bed's tall posters to keep from falling. "I stole money from you?" she asked in a hoarse whisper.

One corner of Jesse's mouth actually tilted up with the question and something flickered in his dark eyes.

Relief? Hope? Scorn? Lacy was too confused to understand anything at this point.

"Well?" she pressed.

"No, Lace, that's one thing I can't accuse you of doin'. You didn't take anything that didn't belong to you. The money you withdrew from the bank was your own."

"Oh," she said, unconsciously letting her stiffened shoulders sag.

"Why?" he asked, all humor absent from his tone again.

Abandoning the safety of the bedpost she'd clung to, Lacy crossed the room to her dresser, keeping her back to him as she opened a drawer and began extracting articles of lingerie for packing. She could have pretended not to understand that he was asking her why she was leaving. Stall for time while she searched for an answer that didn't reveal too much. But what difference did it make? She was afraid and whether a hired killer was a figment of her imagination or a very real threat, it didn't matter. It was real to her. And she wasn't staying.

Facing him again, she met his eyes steadily. "It's simple, Jesse. I don't like it here. I'm afraid of you. Not just you. Your mother, your brother, Cybil. All of you. So, I'm getting out while I can."

"Afraid of us? Why? What's happened? You didn't look too afraid when you came sauntering down the stairs asking for the keys to one of the cars to go into town. So why all of a sudden? Have you remembered something that frightens you?"

Lacy didn't answer at once. Instead, she searched her husband's handsome face. Looking for fear. Fear that she'd remembered something she shouldn't have. Evidence of guilt or even remorse in the dark eyes that smoldered with some unreadable emotion. In his sharply chiseled jaws where a muscle ticked. Even in the impatient set of his full lips.

Frustration at her own inability to recapture the truth of what had happened to her marriage and why she had fled her husband's home caused her to cry out, "Damn it, Jesse!" She shook her head fiercely, sending her pale hair whipping in front of her eyes. "You all hate me! You can't deny it. Your mother took great delight in telling me just how much last night.

"That's a good enough reason for me to want to leave right there. But there's so much more. Think about it, Jesse. You want to keep me a prisoner out here on your ranch. Not allow me any contact with the outside world. Why is that? Is there some terrible secret I might uncover about my life here before I ran away the last time?"

He arched a brow, mocking her with both his expression and his tone when he answered. "You suspect me of keeping you from Rooster Corner so you won't find out I'm some kind of monster with a hideous secret I'm guarding?" He laughed derisively. "Oh, that's rich, Lace. I'll tell you something, sweetheart. Apparently you not only lost your memory when that car ran you down, you lost your mind."

Sobering, he added, "Ever occur to you I might be trying to protect you from yourself?"

Lacy ignored that. Her voice tinged with sadness, she said, "You can try to turn the tables but you can't deny that you hate me." She sighed heavily and turned her back to him again, this time to grip the edges of the dresser as she posed one last question. "I guess what I really need to know is if you hated me enough to kill me."

She waited for his answer, her eyes squeezed tightly shut, and her breath held. Silence was her only reply. It seemed an eternity passed before she finally made herself look at him again, though this time she was seeing his reflection in the mirror that hung above the dresser.

He stood as still and rigid as a granite statue, his gaze directed at the floor.

"Jesse?"

Eyes as dark as night met midsummer blue as he raised his gaze to hers. "I don't know, Lace. About hating you, I mean. Maybe I did." An abject, weary grin played across his lips. "Or maybe it was that I just loved you too much; loved you enough to want to kill you."

Chapter Eleven

Jesse lay across his bed, an arm slung over his eyes as his confession to his wife played itself over and over in his mind. Was it true? When he'd learned what she'd done and that she was leaving him, had he been so shattered he'd actually considered killing her? No, there had never been an overt, conscious threat. But maybe, just maybe, he thought now, he'd unconsciously longed for revenge. Longed to destroy her as swiftly and shamelessly as she had murdered their love.

He'd been shocked and repulsed by the admission that slipped from his lips as he answered her question. But it was the expression on Lacy's face that had stunned him most. There was no surprise. No amazement. No apparent change in her countenance at all. Only the slightest of nods as if he'd merely confirmed what she'd already known.

But he wasn't a violent man! Not even when the harsher elements of running a ranch necessitated severe and often seemingly callous action.

When a bobcat gone berserk stalked his herd, Jesse suffered pangs of remorse when he was forced to bring the animal down.

Guilt rode his back for weeks when he had to fire a ranch hand for flagrant violations of Southern Star rules.

And though he'd been goaded into fights in honky-tonks brimming with drunks, he'd almost always managed to settle the matter with a single well-delivered punch.

Rage simply wasn't an emotion Jesse let get the better of him. Until Lacy.

His arm still lying across his eyes, he inadvertently brushed the bandage covering the wound on his brow with his sleeve. He groaned, but he knew the hurt he was feeling emanated from his heart.

Where had Lacy's fear come from? Had his need to punish her—a need he hadn't even recognized—telegraphed itself to her?

He shook his head. No, he wasn't after revenge. *Maybe* once, when he'd learned what she'd gone and done. Not now. Not anymore. Now, all he wanted was closure. He wanted the return of her memory so he could confront her, find out why.

He sat up, swinging his long, powerful legs over the side of the bed. He had to convince her to stay and in order to do that, he had to go to her under the aegis of making peace. A grin that was born of irony rather than humor crooked the corners of his mouth.

He needed an offering and it didn't take a rocket scientist to figure out what it should be. Crossing the room in a brevity of long strides, he snatched a set of keys from a dish on his dresser.

A moment later he entered Lacy's room once again, tossing the keys onto her bed. "There," he said in answer to her raised brow. "There's your freedom."

Lacy shook his heard. "I don't get it. What are they?"

"Keys," he said with a teasing grin.

She rolled her eyes impatiently, then reconsidered and, playing along, folded her arms. "Okay. Keys to what?"

"You bought me what you called a six-month anniversary present a couple of weeks before you left. A black Jag. I'm giving it back to you. Now you have a way out of Dodge."

Lacy's voice erupted in laughter.

Jesse frowned. "What's so funny? You said you want to leave. I'm giving you a way to do just that. I'll write you a check you can cash in town, too. For fifty thousand dollars. That ought to last you until you get settled and regain your memory."

Lacy almost stopped laughing at that. Almost, but the giggles that she was beginning to suspect were being nurtured by hysteria refused to stop completely. They slowed, came in fits. Tears leaked over her lashes, and she swiped them away with a halting apology. "I'm . . . I'm sorry, Jess . . . Jesse. This isn't funny, I know. It was just that remark about getting out of Dodge." She laughed again as she waved the explanation away. But this time, thankfully, she won control after only a few seconds. In fact, her emotions suddenly executed a flip-flop, and she sank to a chair, drained and depressed. "Never mind, it's too hard to explain."

Jesse shrugged. "Doesn't matter." He smiled then, and she was touched by the gentleness that accompanied it in his eyes. She noticed that the sharp angles of his arrogant features appeared to soften as well, and for the first time, she *believed* that she'd once fallen completely and utterly in love with this handsome stranger . . . until something had happened to destroy it.

"What's the matter?" he asked as he watched sadness cloud her eyes.

"I was just wondering what could have gone so terribly wrong between us to make me leave so soon after giving you a gift to celebrate our first six months together."

"I don't know," he admitted honestly in that resonant voice that caressed her like kid-gloved fingers. "I wish I did. I wish you'd stay so we could find out together."

"But why?" she asked, her tone as soft as his, though only because she'd spoken around the knot of mingling fear and hope. "Aren't you afraid the truth will hurt you more than you have been already?"

Jesse turned his gaze out the window. He couldn't let her look into his eyes as he answered; couldn't allow her to see that she'd already picked his soul as clean as a vulture on carrion. At last he said, "No, Lace, I'm not afraid. Not of that. I'm only scared that once you leave, I'll never know."

She considered his answer for a long moment. When she finally answered it was accompanied by a deep sigh. "I can't help feeling that I'm damned if I do and damned if I don't." She stood up and crossed the room to stand only inches from him. Tilting her head back so that she stared directly into his dark eyes, she offered a tremulous smile. "Something frightens me about staying here. I'm not certain if I'm remembering danger or merely conjuring it up because I need an excuse for my unhappiness."

"I would never hurt you, Lacy. I swear to God. And Mother—"

Lacy cut him off with a shake of her head and a hand laid against his chest. "You don't have to defend her. Whatever she does, it's out of loyalty to you. I understand that. I don't have the faith in her integrity that you do, but that's neither here nor there. I don't know that I can get over this premonition or whatever it is of certain disaster if I stay, but I owe you." She flinched as her gaze inadvertently erred a couple of inches higher to the swatch of gauze, then ventured an abashed smile. "Not only because I nearly killed you today but because you came for me in L.A. after the accident. You obviously weren't obligated since I'm the one who ran out on our marriage vows." She shrugged, suddenly embarrassed about the rapid fire of her words that betrayed her nervousness. "Anyway, promise me just one thing and I'll stay till I can look you in the eyes and tell you the truth—no matter how hideous it may be—about what happened."

Jesse raised a suspicious brow before nodding his agreement. Maybe it was time for concessions. "Name it. If you stay, I'll do whatever you ask. I give you my word."

Lacy granted a halfhearted smile, but when she spoke, her expression was sober and her tone tainted with fear. "Help me remember . . . and keep me safe."

Moments later, his promise given, Jesse and Lacy stood there in the middle of her room not knowing what else to say. They'd agreed. She was staying, and he was going to help nudge her memory while protecting her from the demons that threatened—bona fide or otherwise. What now?

Lacy posed the question aloud. "Okay, we're agreed on that much. So, kemo sabe, where do we start?"

His easy, sexy grin slid into place. "The Lone Ranger? Not me. I wouldn't hide behind a mask. Besides, I'm a quarter Indian, remember? Strong, stealthy, silent."

Deciding she liked this teasing, playful Jesse too much to let him go right away, Lacy kept up the game. "Tonto? Un-uh. Sorry. No way. I definitely would argue typing you as a sidekick. You're a leader. No doubt about it."

"Geronimo?" he asked, his dark eyes dancing with mirth.

"Nope," she said firmly. "He was a wild card, don't you think? Maybe Cochise."

He pretended to consider the alternative before shrugging his agreement. "Okay. And what about you? Who would you be typed as?"

She held out her hands, palms up. "How would I know? I don't know enough about myself to find a likeness." She lowered her gaze to the floor, the joy gleaned in the past few minutes of lighthearted banter momentarily dulled with the reminder of her lost self.

Jesse felt his smile wilt with hers at the unintentional reminder of her amnesia, but his recovery was quicker. "Okay, so I guess now we start over with my original proposal to show you the ranch." Grinning with all the devilry and charm of a mischievous schoolboy, he covered his head with his arms as if warding off a blow as he added, "Provided, that is, you don't decide to slug me again."

"Stop!" she said, swatting his arms away from his head. "I wasn't trying to hurt you, and you know it."

"Does that mean you'll take the tour with me?"

Lacy glanced at her watch. "Do we still have time for you to show me the entire ranch?"

"Not all of it, no. We couldn't see everything in two days, but there are a couple of places that were favorites of yours that I think might jog some memories."

This time when her smile faded, she turned away so he wouldn't notice. His comments had reminded her of Clay Waters, and the memory she *thought* she'd found. She remembered the man, his face and name. That much was real. *That* much she knew. But what about his part in a conspiracy to kill her? Wasn't it possible that the realities of her past had mingled with fantasy? After all, Jesse had told her she was an aspiring novelist. Wouldn't that mean a creative imagination, and plots that could include intrigue and murder? No, she wasn't ready to share what might well be a crazy mix of fact and fiction.

Glancing over her shoulder at Jesse, she smiled tentatively.

"What's the matter, Lace?" he asked, his sun-darkened brow furrowed with concern.

"Nothing," she said. Then with more conviction, "Re-

ally. I was just thinking about the two men who stopped
out on the road. Let me change clothes so we can go. Then
maybe you can start our trip down memory lane by telling
me about them. What did you say their names are?"

Chapter Twelve

Ranch business and errands completed, Randy Hawkins and Clay Waters were now relaxing in Cookie Conchita's, a tavern and Tex-Mex diner combo. They sat with three other locals—hands employed by the Sunny J, a smaller though formidable spread. Elbows resting on a Formica tabletop, their callused hands curled around long-necked beer bottles. Booted heels that rested on jean-clad knees clicked against chrome table legs in time to requisite country music blaring from a jukebox.

Randy was downing boilermakers—Kentucky bourbon chased with Texas beer. He'd just polished off his third when one of the guys from the Sunny J brought up the subject of Lacy Pryde's return to the Southern Star.

"Heard how your boss had to go fetch his old lady back from California. Heard how she's lost her mind, doesn't know shit from shinola."

"Yeah?" Randy asked, alcohol adding a measure of belligerence to his tone. "Heard from who?"

Tommy Lee Pritchett scratched his neck and shrugged, seeking support from his friends with a glance as he answered. "Shit, I don't know. Folks. Everybody's talking. Hell, word's all over town."

The other two Sunny J cowhands nodded.

Randy looked at Clay, who sat hunched forward, his body folded around a plate of fajitas and chin actually resting on the lip of the bottle he was nursing as his fingers smoothed a long handlebar mustache. "Well, Waters and me, we just seen her," Randy boasted. "She didn't look anything 'cept hot as a pearly handled pistol to me. Hey, bud, she look nuts to you?"

Reticent by nature, Clay considered the question for a long moment before shrugging. "Like you said, she looked good enough to eat, but I don't guess that's any kinda proof her mind's not fucked up. Got to admit, I thought it was strange her standing on the road hookin' a ride and all, no matter what the boss claimed they was doing."

"Jesus H. Christ, Clay. They was playing games is all," Randy said before quickly turning his attention away from the topic of the beautiful Mrs. Pryde to signal the restaurant owner for another round of drinks by holding up a bottle and drawing a circle in the air over the table with his finger. At Cookie's nod, he returned to the topic at hand. "I say people just got to have something to flap their jaws about."

"Shitfire, Hawkins, you ain't got the brains God gave a gnat. Everyone in Rooster Corner knows he kicked her pretty ass out."

His ruddy complexion darkening by the second, Randy pushed his Stetson back on his head with a frustrated jab and muttered another expletive under his breath. "Then just tell me this, asshole. If he kicked her out, why'd he take off for California last week and show up again with her in tow yesterday?"

"Didn't have much choice," Cookie answered as she arrived at the table and began passing out drinks. Everyone's order in place and brimming ashtrays, empty bottles, and smudged glasses all gathered, she cocked an ample hip, resting the tray on the ledge it provided. "Jesse got a phone call from the cops in Los Angeles. Said his wife had been hurt in an accident. Mama Rose argued something fierce against him going to see about her, but Jesse Pryde's one honorable man." She stopped talking long enough to let her gaze sidle over the faces of her audience, make sure she had their full attention. With a satisfied grin dimpling her full cheeks, she continued. "Mama Rose was on the warpath until Jesse explained that it was duty rather than desire driving him. Only thing neither of them know was that Lacy's pretty face and body weren't the only parts that got all broken up when the car hit her. She lost her memory, too. Jesse had no choice but to bring her home to the Southern Star. But the way I hear it, nobody's very damned happy out there these days."

Silence hung over the table as heavy as Cookie's perfume until Randy shattered it by shoving his chair away

from the table with a teeth-jarring screech. Tottering
drunkenly for a second or two, he eventually steadied
himself with a hand on Clay's shoulder and glared bellig-
erently at the tavern proprietress. "*Shiiit,*" he drawled,
turning away before reconsidering and facing her again.
"I've gotta take a leak, but jest so ya know, I think that's
one hundred percent, pure-D bullshit, Cookie. Clay and
me seen 'em today with our own eyes, and I'm here to
tell ya, if those two was any happier, they woulda been
doing the poke 'n' ride right there on Highway D."

Laughter erupted from the men seated around the table
as well as from a few other patrons scattered nearby.
Only Cookie and Clay seemed unable to find the humor
in Randy's crude analogy.

With an exasperated shake of his head, Clay got to
his feet and rounded his chair to slip an arm around his
wobbling buddy's shoulders. "Come on, Ran. Let's go
find the john."

"Yuck it up, fellas. I heard it myself from the man's
brother, and you tell me why Dillon Pryde'd have reason
to lie." It was a rhetorical question, and Cookie turned
her attention to the late afternoon sky, which was bright
and clear. Her thick, three-hundred-pound frame jiggled
with a sudden shudder. "There's big trouble brewing out
there at the Star ranch. I can feel it in my bones as
surely as I can feel a thunderstorm heading our way."

Clay guided his drunken companion toward the men's
room and pushed the door open. He stepped back and
allowed the other man to enter the bathroom. "You handle it from here? I've got to make a telephone call."

"Oh, yeah?" Randy said, grinning sloppily as he held
on to the sink for balance. "You been holding out on
me, bud? You got some new little filly you haven't told
ol' Randy 'bout?"

Clay forced a laugh as his annoyance mounted. Right
now there was no one else in the vicinity of the pay
phone across the hall, and the call he had to make required privacy. "Strictly business, pal. Gotta talk to a
man about a job." He rubbed his first two fingers together with his thumb. "Earn myself some extra moola."

Randy's carrot-orange brows raised at that. "You
need money, bud, you jes' wait right here. Ol' Randy'll
show ya how to do that at the pool table."

"You got it. Let me make my call, then we'll kick ass with some eight ball."

As Clay started to pull the door closed behind him, Randy called out, "Hey, you any good?"

"Yeah, baby," Waters said over his shoulder. "The best."

"*Shiiit,*" Clay heard Randy say as he extracted a calling card from the billfold in his back pocket and crossed the hall. Lifting the telephone receiver from its hook, he chuckled under his breath and defended his claim to the drone of the telephone line. "Depends on the game, amigo," he said. "*And* what're the stakes."

Chapter Thirteen

Lacy changed clothes, discarding her sexy dress and shoes for a more practical outfit of tomato-red sleeveless shirt, blue jeans, and black boots, all the while struggling to maintain a trail of positive thought by concentrating on Jesse and his proposed tour. It was proving a hopeless quest. Maybe because each mental step was taken in blindness and the path littered with half-culled memories her mind kept tripping over.

Like Clay Waters.

Was he really a gun for hire and if so, then who hated her enough to have ordered her killed?

No! She wasn't going to do this. Dropping the brush she'd just run through her pale blond hair, she turned her back to the mirror, leaning against the dresser and folding her arms in punctuation to the resolution.

Her memory was returning. Slowly. At a snail's crawl. A frustrating iota at a time, in snatches, flashes, and dreams. But okay, she'd strive for patience. If only the memories had clarity. This was real. That was not.

Her gaze fell on the doll positioned in the center of the chair. Lacy's brow puckered. The likeness was uncanny. It would have been impossible to forget her and yet the dress should have been blue. She was sure of that. So, wasn't that proof that her mind was playing tricks, giving her memories that were only partially accurate?

Her mind segued right back to the enigma of Clay Waters.

It might well be that once she recaptured all of it, had all her ducks lined up in a row, she'd realize that she simply hadn't liked Clay Waters. Wouldn't that explain her mind's ability to attribute villainous intentions where there were none?

Maybe. Maybe not. But she wasn't going to allow herself to panic again. Not without proof. In the meantime, she was going to place her trust in Jesse. He might well have brought her home to the Southern Star merely as a matter of duty, but she knew in her heart he would never allow anyone to harm her. He'd loved her once. Deeply. Else how could she have hurt him as deeply as he claimed she had?

And it didn't take cognizant memory for her to know that she had loved him, too, with every measure of her being. They'd been together again only a few days since his arrival at the hospital in L.A. During that time he'd been cool, even hostile, and on occasion downright mean. More often, he'd been kind and caring. It was true, she couldn't revive a single second of the most intimate moments they'd shared—their lovemaking, their laughter, their talks. Even so, her heart hadn't forgotten. That was evident in the way she felt every time their eyes met, desire communicating itself as provocatively as a lingering kiss. Oh, yes, she could admit it now. She wanted this man and nothing—not her amnesia, the mysterious wrong she'd done him, or his tenacious grip on his hurt and anger—was going to stop her from getting to know him again. By the time her memory was fully recovered, she vowed, their marriage would be intact as well.

She'd been standing in the middle of the room, confronting her heart's desire. Resolve firmly in place, she returned to the closet one last time to snatch her Stetson from a shelf. She started from the room on her way to the date with her cowboy when she remembered the open doors to the balcony. Turning back, she hurriedly crossed the room to shut and latch them. She was stopped by her sister-in-law's voice.

"Y'all are just too good, Lacy, honey," Cybil said, her speech as slow as maple syrup and exaggerated by an alcohol-induced slur. "I mean it, sugar. It's a thrill to witness you in action."

Lacy hesitated for a moment, then on a defeated sigh opened the doors wide and stepped out on the balcony. "Okay, Cybil, I'll bite. What are you talking about? What am I so good at that you love to watch?"

"Why, the way you *do* it, honey. The way you drive

that man crazy. One minute, being so hateful and all, and the next, as sweet and temptin' as honey on a blueberry dumplin', and him just eatin' it all up. I've just never seen anything like it."

"You're drunk," Lacy said with an exasperated shake of her head.

Sprawled on a lounge chair, a glass in hand, an ice bucket and an uncorked decanter of clear liquid that wreaked suspiciously of gin on the table beside her, Cybil laughed, the sound coarse and gurgling; a testimony to her tobacco and alcohol abuse. She didn't argue the charge. "Whenever I'm able, honey . . . which is almost always."

She wore the same purple satin housecoat she'd appeared in earlier on the landing above the foyer. Now, the bodice gaped and one shoulder had slipped revealing razor-sharp bones beneath sallow flesh, small, sagging breasts resembling a bitch's teats sucked dry, and a stomach bloated by alcohol. Makeup she hadn't bothered to remove from her eyes the night before blackened the pronounced hollows under her eyes, and her dark auburn hair—normally artfully tousled—was a snarled mess of tangles and spikes.

Pity nipped at the edges of Lacy's heart, though memory or instinct whispered a warning of caution. "Are you angry with me, Cybil?" she asked gently, hoping her tone disguised her horror at the revelation of her sister-in-law's self-destruction.

"Angry?" Cybil asked, her surprise at the question seemingly genuine. "Of course not, silly. I think you're wonderful." She stretched a thin arm toward Lacy, wiggling her fingers like a spider's legs creeping up an invisible surface.

Lacy frowned, not understanding the gesture until Cybil supplied an explanation.

"I've been sittin' out here thinking about it ever since Jesse left your room. I don't know how you do it. There's not a man in the state of Texas who wouldn't kill you for what you did to him. But you, you just tossed it in his face like it didn't matter more'n a fingernail you'd chipped. Then, off you go for parts unknown leaving Jesse as torn up as a willow caught in a twister, and now here you are right back home, crawling right back inside him same as you did before." She raised her glass. "To you, Lacy James-Pryde. If I was wearin' a hat, I'd surely take it off to you, 'cause you're definitely the best."

Lacy sank to the twin lounger beside her sister-in-law. She'd overheard the argument between Dillon and Cybil in their bedroom, so she shouldn't be surprised by this attack. Yet, she was. She was stunned. Maybe because in spite of her sister-in-law's cruel depiction of her as trash, Lacy'd felt an empathy; a bond that tied them as sisters if only by marriages that had apparently both gone terribly wrong.

"Yesterday when Jesse brought me here to the Southern Star, I knew I'd hurt him. He'd already told me that much. What I didn't know was how, what I'd done. I still don't know because everyone insists that's one of the things I have to remember on my own. I pretty much took it for granted that I was totally at fault, until I went for that walk with his mother.

"Now there's a lady who plays by her own rules. Oh, she makes a good show of acting the southern gentle-woman, but as soon as no one's looking, *wham,* she's sucker-punching her opponent. I'm sure you know how she despises me. Because I hurt Jesse? I thought so until now, but here I am again, and why? Not because of Jesse, surely. Or is family loyalty really enough to make all of you hate me?"

Cybil's laughter when it came this time was sharp and full. Her entire body trembled with the force of it. "*Hate* you?" she managed at last as her hilarity ebbed. "Why, I don't hate you, Lacy. I swear to God, I don't. I'm just jealous, you silly." She took a long sip of her drink as if that said all there was to be said, end of discussion. But as Lacy stood up, deciding against trying to reason with a drunk, Cybil set her glass aside with a loud clank and continued her rationale. "Besides, you just don't belong. Why, it's as plain as this zit right here on my chin. You're not a Texan—not exactly a sin but not a point in your favor either. More importantly, you don't hail from money. Oh, you've got style, panache as they say, but I've never had trouble discernin' between sterling and polished-up tin.

"If that's not bad enough, you're a writer, for good-ness' sake! A *romance* writer. Leastwise that's what you claimed even though none of us has ever seen evidence to back that up." She stared out at the beautiful vista of rolling hills and powder-blue skies and seemed to forget Lacy's presence entirely.

"Not that it matters. Could be the queen of England, and it wouldn't matter to Mother Rose. No one's fine enough for her precious boys."

Some minutes later Lacy exited her room and started down the hall. The possibility that Jesse might have tired of waiting and given up on her came and went in a skittering thought she barely noticed as she ambled slowly toward the stairs. She was still thinking about Cybil, and deep lines pinched her brow as she went over and over her sister-in-law's pathetic little drama.

Lacy had been hurt by some of the accusations. A couple of times angered. More often, though, it had been pity that had stirred in her chest. Pity and sadness. She'd wanted to turn her back on Cybil, close and lock the doors behind her, and forget what she'd seen and heard.

Sadness coiled around Lacy's heart as she approached the landing. She stopped, brought up short by the realization that the weight of her grief was every bit as heavy as it was the day she'd finally awakened from the coma in the hospital and faced a world of strangers that included herself. A thin smile of irony parted her lips. She hadn't thought it possible to sink to that level of depression again. Of course, she hadn't known then what she did today. Hadn't understood that sometimes ignorance was preferable to knowledge.

Not for the first time, she thought how much happier everyone would have been if she'd never learned her identity. She had no doubt that Rose and Cybil would shout an amen to that. What about Jesse? Wouldn't his future have loomed brighter if she had managed to stick to the original plan of a disappearance that was forever?

A fiery iron pressed against her heart with the certain answer to that question. This time the pain didn't just sear. It burned all the way to the center of her soul. But why when she had to admit that she, too, would probably have been happier as well? She asked herself this as she started down the staircase, her fingers absently trailing the cool surface of wrought-iron railing. At least lost in the netherworld of the unconscious, there had been the peace of presumed innocence.

She hadn't had a conscience that niggled with guilt.

Neither hate nor jealousy had existed.

Grudges and vendettas hadn't even been a consideration.

A noise—the tapping of heels against marble—caught her attention. Raising her face, her gaze cut to Jesse standing below in one of the arched doorways. A grin that went all the way to the dark centers of his eyes only intensified her heartache though she managed to hide it behind a smile of her own.

He took her hand as she stepped from the last stair. "Damn, woman, you're gonna have to learn to get ready faster," he teased as he led the way through the back of the house, his big, strong hand encasing hers.

Allowing him to tug her along, Lacy finished her list: She hadn't been in love.

Moments later, seated in a different vehicle than the shiny Cherokee that had been parked waiting for them at the airstrip the day before, Lacy strapped on her seat belt. She looked around, noting the roll bar above their heads where a roof normally was. "I feel like I'm going on safari," she said.

As he locked the wheels in place, readying it for their excursion across rough prairie lands and up steep hillsides, he chuckled. "Guess it's about the same thing, except I don't expect to run across any elephants or giraffes." Following her gaze to the rifle that rested beside his leg, he shrugged. "We do see an occasional mountain lion or rattler. Sometimes coyotes even venture in close enough for us to have to scare them off with a round fired over their heads. Mostly, though, the gun's just a precaution. Don't worry about it."

Shifting into reverse, he moved his right foot from brake to accelerator. A roared *"whoof"* that seemed to emanate only inches from the vehicle caused him to stomp on the brake once again.

Both Jesse and Lacy turned their heads just in time to witness a gigantic, living breathing ball of fur hurdling through the air in their direction. As instinctively as dodging a launched missile, they ducked, Jesse with an angry invective, Lacy with a startled squeal. The entire vehicle shook as the enormous animal, miraculously avoiding the overhead bar, landed squarely in the back seat.

Jesse's anger was immediate. "You crazy mutt. *Out!*" he shouted. The command was followed with a thrust of his arm in the direction of the patio.

Instead of obeying, Thorn pled his case with a low-pitched grumble. It was more argument than threat until Jesse repeated the mandate. Then the wolfhound disputed his position with a curled lip, sharp teeth bared, and the rumble of his growl more ominous.

"I think he wants to go along," Lacy said, alarm replaced by amusement.

"Well, he's not," Jesse said, his angry tone almost a match for Thorn's snarl. Yanking open the door, Jesse started to climb out.

"Oh, *please,* Jesse. What's he hurting? Let him come along," Lacy begged, a hand placed persuasively on her husband's arm. Instinctively, she understood that it was the dog's disregard of authority more than the surprise air raid that had fired Jesse's dander.

He hesitated. "I don't know what's gotten into the damned mutt. I've never seen him act like this. He's always been so obedient."

Lacy glanced at the big dog who had turned doleful, golden brown eyes to her now, actually seeming to anticipate her rebuttal. "He's hardly more than a pup, isn't he? What—two? Three?"

"Yeah, somewhere around there," Jesse admitted, a brow lifted suspiciously. "How'd you know that? Lucky guess?"

Weary of the walls of mistrust she was ever running into since her return to Rooster Corner, she sighed. "No, Jesse, it wasn't a guess, and neither was it a slip of the tongue, damn it. This isn't some elaborate game of pretense that I occasionally mess up. Any idiot could tell he's young, for God's sake. His coat's thick and shiny. His teeth certainly look healthy ... sharp. And he's definitely spry. An old dog could never have made that leap." She chuckled, for just an instant letting go of the tension and frustration of the past two days as she reached over the seat to ruffle the dense crown of fur between the hound's ears. "You're just like any other adolescent, aren't you, boy? Entitled to an occasional rebellion."

Thorn didn't disagree, and Jesse gave it up. "Okay, he can ride along, but you get to deal with Mother when we come back."

Looking past the dog now, Lacy followed Jesse's gaze to the patio where Rose stood staring at them. Arms folded, head held high, and her posture ramrod-straight, she looked like a statue, Lacy thought. A totem pole.

Suddenly the image made Lacy laugh as she recalled what Cybil had told her about Rose's heritage.

"I doubt you'll think it so funny later," Jesse said as he backed the Jeep away from the garage. As he shifted into first, once again changing direction to circle the garage, Lacy replayed the last few minutes on the terrace with Cybil.

Mildly annoyed by Cybil's unsubpoenaed sentiment that Lacy didn't belong because of her lack of pedigree and nonstatus as a native Texan, she'd maintained her cool. But she asked, "What about Rose? You certainly can't claim she looks the grand Texas lady, not the way she wears her hair braided down her back."

Cybil chuckled at that even as she slopped gin from her glass with a dismissing wave of her hand. She rolled her eyes and even managed a cluck of her thickened tongue. "Shit, Lacy, even without a memory I think you'd've figured that one out. It's all about the Native American thing. She's not only a real, honest-to-goodness Pryde, she's half Indian. Sacagawea or Pocahontas or maybe brave little Tiger Lily of Peter Pan fame. Trust me, honey, this Indian thing is a big deal with her. Add the prestige of her Anglo-Texan heritage to that ... well, suffice it to say, it doesn't get worse than that. A real fuckin' Texas Indian princess with an ego as big as the state itself."

As the Jeep Wrangler jogged over ruts and gullies in a crudely cut trail around snaking curves and up steep slopes, Lacy laughed appreciatively. It was true. Cybil had hit the nail square on the head regardless of her blurred vision. Rose Pryde was the creation of two characters she'd blended to perfection. She'd acted the parts, played both roles—proud blood relative of the long-suffering, much maligned Indian race as well as an arrogant Texas empire heiress and matriarch—for so long and with such alacrity, pretense had become reality and the personalities inseparable.

Jesse grinned, though it was evident he didn't know what she was laughing about. "This is better. When you were so late coming down, I'd begun to think you'd changed your mind. Then when you showed up, you looked upset again. I thought maybe I'd only imagined the truce we'd come to. But you're okay now."

There was a note of question in his words that Lacy answered. "You know, I'm beginning to think I'm just swell. I might not remember enough about my past to put together a paragraph, but I'm starting to believe that's a whole lot better than being crazy."

Surprised by the enigmatic explanation for her sudden good mood, Jesse said, "Okay, I'll bite. Who are we talking about?"

"You mean who's crazy? Well—now don't take offense—but I think I'm talking about all of you. You, your mother, Cybil. Probably Dillon, too, though to be fair, I haven't spent enough time with him to know for sure if he should be included."

Jesse frowned. He wasn't annoyed. In fact, he almost thought it was as funny as she apparently did. He didn't know exactly what had inspired this unexpected sentiment. Maybe the conversation Lacy mentioned she'd had with Cybil. After all, his opinion of his sister-in-law wasn't a whole lot more charitable. But it had to be more than just Cybil. Lacy had included both his mother and him in the category. His frown deepened when he caught her watching him, then heard her laugh again.

"You Prydes are probably the most supercilious bunch of snobs I've ever run across. In fact, I think I can offer that with a pretty fair amount of certainty even though I don't remember ever meeting a single one of you before the accident. In fact, except for the hospital staff and the police officers, I don't remember another person on God's green earth, and I still stand by that claim. I doubt the queen of England is any more full of herself than you Prydes."

Jesse had been on the verge of laughing. About to tease back, counter some of her charges with a few of his own. But all at once, he realized she'd pricked his ego and drawn a bead of blood. "*Supercilious?*" he repeated, incredulous.

Lacy heard the mix of injury and irritation in his voice. She wasn't bullied. In fact, if anything, he'd just proven her point and that started a whole new fit of hilarity. She drew her knees up to her chest and buried her face as she let the giggles spill out.

Abruptly jerking the wheel to the right and shifting gears down as he prepared to climb an ominously steep hill, he muttered to himself under his breath. "Not only crazy and arrogant. Apparently funny as hell, too."

Her amusement died as she conjured images of the Jeep tumbling front over rear in its failed attempt to conquer the sharp incline. Lacy ignored his sarcasm, held her breath, and squeezed her eyes shut.

Even the engine that had been designed for such abuse abandoned its steady purr in favor of a strained whine. Thorn growled nervously and hunkered down on the floor between the seats for better purchase.

Seconds later, with a final jarring thud, all four wheels came down on level ground. Lacy let loose a long sigh of relief. She was surprised at the whimper that accompanied it. Pain that radiated from her head to her knees had replaced fear. The jolting, bone-bruising climb up the rocky terrain had aggravated her slow-healing injuries from the accident. Involuntary tears filled her eyes, as a groan slipped from her lips.

Jesse slammed on the brakes, bringing them to an instant stop. The seat belt that crossed her breasts and shoulder became a weapon of torture as Lacy was thrown forward. She grimaced, but this time it wasn't accompanied by a feeble whimper or puny groan. This time she yelled. "Why don't I just get out and lie down in front of this tank and let you drive over me!" The angry outburst didn't ease her body's aches, but it sure revived her spirit. Unfastening the seat belt with an angry snap, she yanked open her door and started out of the Jeep. She'd intended a forceful, angry exit but was obliged to move gingerly, sacrificing dignity. She settled for a glare fixed on Jesse that she hoped would cripple if not kill.

"Oh, God, Lace, I'm sorry! I wasn't thinking about

how tender you must still be," Jesse said, his tone so repentant and sincere her forgiveness was immediate.

"I'm all right," she said, though she hugged her rib cage, which still ached pretty fiercely. "Really," she added. It was true. Her body might be sore, but physical bruises healed quickly. Much faster than wounds to the mind and soul. She was living proof of that.

No matter what she claimed, Jesse could see the pain in her eyes, and he cursed his stupidity as he slammed the steering wheel with the flat of his palms. "Damn it!"

Thorn, who'd remained watchful and alert in the back seat, responded to Jesse's show of temper with a low, guttural warning. Springing up in the same instant, the wolfhound's giant front paws rested on the back of the driver's seat, and lethal fangs bared only inches from Jesse's neck.

"Down!" Jesse ordered.

Thorn's intimidating growl deepened.

Lacy couldn't help it. She laughed.

Chapter Fourteen

Lacy's laughter ended as abruptly as it had begun. The second she turned her head to the view ahead of her, she was moved to utter silence. Even the aches her body had complained of were forgotten. Her gaze passed almost reverently over the awesome beauty of the scenery afforded by their vantage point high above a valley of verdant meadows. A breeze stirred the long grasses creating ripples of silver. Wild flowers grew in bright hues like streamers tossed carelessly from the sky, and trees in varying shades of green dotted the landscape like sprinkled confetti. It was a virtual festival of color and beauty, Lacy thought fancifully. And then, *Maybe I really was a writer.*

Jesse, meanwhile, was appreciating none of the magic Lacy had discovered. Conversely, his nerves were on one hell of a roller coaster ride, and getting more jangled by the moment. One second he castigated himself for the injuries his careless disregard had aggravated. In the next, her obvious appreciation of Thorn's posturing threat pissed him off royally. He was still muttering a few creative epithets for the big dog. But her sudden, absolute silence renewed his concern.

Thorn, already out of the vehicle and resting comfortably on his haunches at Lacy's side, cast Jesse a warning glance as he climbed from behind the wheel and circled the Jeep. "Are you—?"

Lacy cut him off. "Oh, Jesse, it's magnificent," she said as he stepped up beside her. Clutching the powerful biceps of his right arm with both hands, she pressed her cheek there as well. "You don't have to tell me. I know this was my favorite spot on all of Southern Star land."

Leaning away from him slightly, she turned her gaze up to his. The blue of her eyes rivaled the bright azure sky and her cheeks and lips colored with excitement and happiness. He couldn't recall a time when she'd ever looked lovelier. Not even on that first day, when he'd met her and thought her the most exquisite creature on this whole great planet Earth.

She was smiling, her full lips parted expectantly. He could taste her then in that second as he had so many times in their six months together. Could still feel the incredible torture of her kisses that had too often led to lovemaking even out here where they were as likely as not to be caught by a ranch hand at work mending a stretch of fence, out searching for a stray calf, or merely enjoying some idle time meandering by his lonesome.

He forced his gaze away from her face. Memories like that were off-limits. "It was one of them, one of your favorite places. You came here a lot." His voice sounded strained even to his ears. Changing the subject away from the bittersweet memories, he brought them back around to the question of her injuries. "I'm sorry about the rough ride up the canyon wall. We could've circled around. I wasn't thinking about you still being so tender. Just say the word, and I'll take you back to the house." He grinned then. "Using the long, smooth route, of course."

Ignoring both apology and suggestion as if she hadn't heard him, she asked if they'd ever talked of building a house up here. "It seems so ideal."

"We did once or twice in the first few weeks." There was accusation in his tone that he hadn't intended, but then maybe there were some things a man just couldn't get past. Like being blindsided and deceived. On the other hand, he wasn't angling for another argument. On a lighter note, he amended his statement. "Mostly, though, I think you liked it well enough at the house with the family. Besides, you kind of had your head set on doing some traveling, so there wouldn't have been much point in sinking a lot of money into another house."

She turned her gaze once again to the valley that had so enchanted her, though her train of thought stayed with Jesse and his comments about her hopes and dreams in the early days of their marriage. She was pleased by his willingness to talk about them and eager to hear more.

"The way you say that, it doesn't sound like I was only after sightseeing for a week here and a week there."

"No, as a matter of fact, you were planning on several months in Europe. You claimed the extended exposure to different countries and cultures would help your writing. No substitute for firsthand research, you argued persuasively."

"And you?"

"What about me?" he asked, staring past her. Of course, he knew what she was asking. But he couldn't answer her. How could he admit how big a fool he'd been? That he'd been willing to give it all up for her. The Southern Star. His family. His own dreams. How could he tell her he would have moved the earth to a different universe if she'd asked.

"Were you willing to leave the Southern Star just so I could research books nobody seems to have ever seen me working on?"

"Doesn't matter," he said tightly. "We never made it that far." After a strained pause he changed the subject and reached for her hand. "Come on," he said, "time's getting away from us. I want to show you a place I think might jog your memory."

Lacy hesitated. She wasn't ready to let go of the conversation about their marriage. Then again, like all the other revelations about her six-month tenure here, she'd begun to detect the familiar ring of accusation. She wanted desperately to know everything. To learn who she was and to learn it from Jesse. What she liked, what she hated. What made her laugh, could bring her to tears, evoke rage. And she wanted to know about *them*. She knew she'd hurt him, angered him, but had she ever made him happy? Even if only in the early days and weeks of their marriage? And then she remembered the condensed version of their elopement to Mexico that he'd related to her. Her cheeks burned at his implication that she'd fully satisfied at least one aspect of their relationship.

Suddenly even the innocence of their handholding was supplanted by a semblance of intimacy, charged with sexual innuendo. Desire so fierce it was surely born of memory rather than mere suggestion inspired a quiver that emanated from the pit of her belly to the tips of her fingers. She was embarrassed, horrified that he might somehow realize the errant course her thoughts had abruptly taken.

Pulling her hand from his, Lacy turned away, using the subterfuge of inviting Thorn along as an excuse. She patted her thigh in a coaxing gesture to the dog lagging a few feet behind. "Come on, Thorn. Jesse wants to show us someplace special. I bet you already know where it is. Did I love it there, fella? Do you think I'll recognize it?"

She laughed at the happy wag of his tail and the accompanying agreeable bark. She tilted her head slightly to meet her husband's gaze. "He's big and scary-looking, but he's really just an oversized, easygoing oaf, isn't he? I can't imagine that he and I didn't always like each other. I wonder why that was. Do you—"

"Judas Priest, you can get on a roll, Lace," Jesse complained, though he chuckled with his words.

Lacy felt her face heat with embarrassment. She knew she'd been talking too fast, machine-gun fast. Inane, stupid prattle about a dog, for God's sake! But better that than quiet with her thoughts about the two of them making love. Her face caught fire again, and she searched for a new, *safe* topic as she swiped her hat from her head and gave the flattened hair on her crown a quick toss and a hasty finger-combing.

"Do you hear it yet?" Jesse asked, mercifully distracting her as he grabbed her hand to lead her down a narrow, winding path cut between giant boulders.

She didn't. At least not consciously, but as they rounded the last bend, stopping midway between summit and valley floor, she saw and heard, both in the same instant. A waterfall, cascading over the lip of a canyon wall, dropping noisily some sixty feet or so below before settling to an easy-flowing river.

"Oh, wow," she said in a breathless whisper. "This has to be paradise."

Jesse didn't reply, though for several long moments Lacy hardly noticed his silence. Enraptured by the waterfall, the surrounding landscape, and the accompanying sense of serenity, there didn't seem reason for further conversation. Sighing with contentment, she leaned against him, the back of her head resting against his chest in a gesture so natural, she didn't register it. Not until his arms slipped around her waist, and she felt his body bow slightly so that his chin rested atop her head. Even then, she didn't pull away. It felt so right, her slender frame enfolded in the power of his.

"Damn you," he said and his sharp, sudden intake of breath, like that of a man just sucker punched, shattered the aura of normality so completely, Lacy was almost afraid to look down at her feet. She was as good as certain she'd find herself lying there in tiny broken shards.

Tears filled her eyes, but she resolutely held them back as she stepped forward out of his arms. She still held the brim of her Stetson in one hand, although now tightly crumpling it to still the tremor that had begun in the instant of his rejection. With an almost inaudible groan, she jammed the hat in place on her head and started off toward the bottom of the trail. "You guys coming?" she asked in a tone that was amazingly nonchalant. Damn, she was good. Maybe she'd been an actor in her previous life. She sure deserved an Oscar for this performance.

Daring a glance over her shoulder, she could tell that Jesse was as impressed as she. With his murderous glare, his eyes glinted like flint, and she read his mind as ably as if she were inside it.

Deceitful bitch. Fragile, my ass. Just another ploy to distract me while you try to work your way inside me again.

It wasn't true. She wanted to tell him so. But not now. Not when it was so obvious how close she'd come to actually achieving the goal he was silently accusing her of. Not when she saw the self-loathing that mingled with anger directed at her.

Suddenly weighted with regret, she let loose a soft, shuddering sigh. As fierce as his animus toward her, he was still hardly more than a stranger to her. No matter how well he knew the woman he'd married, nothing could change the fact that her mind couldn't recall a single facet of *them*. And yet her heart recognized what her mind could not. She was still deeply, profoundly in love with him. Or maybe she had fallen in love all over again. It didn't matter. His conspicuous revulsion at holding her in his arms hurt more than all the physical agony induced by the automobile accident.

Despite her resolve to appear undaunted, she was suddenly too weary for game playing. She stopped her descent, turning her face away from Jesse though this time staring at nothing; not even aware of Thorn as he pressed against her leg and offered a muted grunt of understanding and sympathy.

Chapter Fifteen

"You remembering any of this?" Jesse asked, his tone sounding to Lacy's ears as flat as her spirits. The three of them—man, woman, and dog—followed the stream, approaching a wooden footbridge. The question posed by Jesse was the first he'd spoken in more than thirty minutes. Lacy answered it on a long, defeated sigh. "No. You know I'm not. It's beautiful, a proverbial wonderland, but as far as I can recall, I've never stepped foot here before in my life." She'd lagged behind him for a time, but she quickened her pace now, catching up with him and passing him by to turn and face him. They both came to a standstill. Thorn stopped as well, juxtaposed between the couple, his massive body that of a warrior tensed for battle, and Jesse clearly the enemy.

"One day, Jesse," she said, holding up her index finger. "I've only been here a single day and already I can't stand this. You've got to talk to me, answer my questions, tell me about *us*!"

A muscle rippled in his jaw, the only indication he'd heard a word she'd said. His eyes, as cold and hard as the granite boulders they'd passed, stared at a point far beyond her. "You heard the doctors," he said after a time.

"To hell with the doctors! Peach, Dr. Ivers, all of the so-called experts—they're all wrong! I'm not playing by anyone else's rules. Not anymore. Either—"

"Either what?" he asked, the edge in his voice sharp enough to slice her to ribbons. "There are no either-ors, Lace. No options. No alternatives. Not for you, not this time. You have nowhere to go and no way to get there unless I help you." He shrugged his shoulders in a gesture rich with sarcasm. "It's as simple as that."

Lacy trembled with barely contained frustration, but

she refused to let him realize just how desperate she was. Folding her arms over her chest, she met his gaze squarely. "You know what I think, Jesse? I think you prefer that I not remember. I think you're a power monger. An arrogant bastard who has to keep the little woman in line. Couldn't do it last time, so she left. Isn't that how it really went down?

"And now—this time, with her memory gone—you have the advantage, and it's as easy as ropin' a blind calf. How's that for a good guess and an even better analogy? Why, shucks, honey, I think it's mighty damned clever of an empty-headed little ole gal like myself to come up with something a big macho cowboy like you can relate to."

Rage darkened Jesse's face as his hands gripped her shoulders. "You bitch—" he began in a choked whisper.

Lacy cried out. Even with adrenaline coursing through every vein she was no match for his strength. She began to crumple in the same instant Thorn bounded to his hind legs, his steely jaws closing around Jesse's wrist. The growl that accompanied his attack was a low warning as fierce as a snake's hiss.

Neither Lacy nor Jesse had noticed the approach of riders on horseback. Neither of them would ever be able to say when the newcomers joined the fray or what happened when. Utter pandemonium caused everything to whirl around them like pieces of colored glass in a kaleidoscope. Cries and shouts melded together, arms and legs became knotted and snarled, and then Jesse was rolling down a sharp bank toward the stream, Thorn leaping after him through the air.

The weight of the massive wolfhound checked his fall just inches from the final drop into the icy river water. Jesse yelled at Lacy, "Goddamn it, Lace, call him off before he rips my throat out!"

Before she could respond, one of the riders, a small Asian man, bellowed an order to the dog. "Thorn, here!"

His companion, a beautiful woman several inches taller than him, crouched down, clapping her hands and urging the animal to her with a friendly tone. "Good boy, Thorn. Come here, you big lug."

Lacy was on her backside, though whether she'd been

pushed or had sat down of her own volition to escape
the bite of Jesse's fingers, she didn't know. She was
shaken and confused, but otherwise unharmed as far as
she could tell. She pushed herself to her feet just as Jesse
climbed the bank, slapping at grass stains and clods of
mud that clung to his shirt and jeans.

The striking blond woman, the small Asian man with
hair tied back in a long ponytail, and the giant dog lined
up together, an incongruous trio with an unmistakable
shared opinion that the man voiced. "Jesus Christ, have
the two of you lost your minds?"

There was really nothing funny about his question.
Nothing even remotely amusing about a single moment
that Lacy could recollect. In fact, now that she'd recovered her wits, she rubbed at a tender spot on her elbow
and grimaced at a few new aches and pains around her
tailbone and left shoulder blade. Involuntary tears had
even spilled over her lashes at some point and still clung
wetly to her cheeks, but suddenly she was laughing.
Within seconds, she was hugging herself as giggles became gales that doubled her over. "B-b-bingo," she stut-
tered between fits of laughter. And then, damn her, she
was crying again, and crumpling—falling, really, into a
dark abyss—and Jesse, the s.o.b., was trying to catch her
in his arms.

Lacy sat on the edge of a blue and white plaid sofa,
every now and then shaking her head in disbelief.
Fainted! She had really, truly fainted right out there in
front of God and those strangers, and *in* Jesse's arms,
for Pete's sake.

Scared them all witless according to the Asian guy
with the lively, expressive eyes and the easy gliding
grin—*Like stockinged feet on a waxed floor,* Lacy
thought, her eyes widening at a sudden recaptured memory of laughing children—a boy and a girl dashing from
a carpeted hallway into a large country-size kitchen, then
sliding across the glossy linoleum with high-pitched
squeals of laughter. One of them she recognized intuitively as herself as a girl around eight or nine!

"What is it?" Jesse asked, concern tightening his
voice. "What's wrong? Your face is flushed. You're not
dizzy again, are you?"

Lacy shook her head. "No, I'm fine. Stop fussing over me." There was an acrid bite to her tone, which she regretted immediately. She tempered it as she spoke again. "I told you, I haven't eaten all day. That's all. I've probably never fainted before in my life, and I'm sure I never will again." She displayed a reassuring grin. "Okay?"

"No, not okay," Jesse said, his dark gaze still watchful and mistrustful of her ability to diagnose the reason for her fainting spell.

Deciding to keep the snippet of happy childhood memory to herself for a while—a lollipop to be saved and pulled from her pocket whenever she was in need of a sweet comforting treat—she changed the subject away from herself. "Where are we?"

She accepted a glass of water from the beautiful woman whose face seemed familiar all at once, though her identity still eluded Lacy.

"We brought you to our house," the man said. "Don't you remember? When you came to, Jesse carried you here. He was going to take you into Rooster to the hospital."

Lacy nodded, recollecting it all now. One minute, she and Jesse'd been fighting, the next she was laughing and crying, and then just as Jesse'd put his arms around her, she'd felt the world start to slip away. She'd awakened on the ground with four anxious faces all staring over her. One of them—the big adorable oaf, Thorn—had almost burst her eardrums with his joyous, piercing bark at the sight of her open eyes. Everyone was suddenly laughing and then Jesse was scooping her into his arms and off at a dead run.

She recalled offers to take her on horseback, and his stubborn refusal to hand her over. Then, as gently as if he were handling a frail bird, he'd set her on the sofa. "I'm going to go get the Jeep and get you to the hospital," he announced, breathing hard from exertion and strained nerves.

She argued that, eventually persuading him that she was all right, just a bit weak. The strangers added their two cents worth—chimed opinions that all she needed was some rest and nourishment.

The woman worked in the kitchen, her long legs moving gracefully between counter and refrigerator, her shoulder-length swing of gold-blond hair shimmering under the late afternoon rays of sun that shone through the oversized kitchen window.

From the corner of Lacy's eye, she caught the man's quizzical stare on her face and turned to meet his gaze, coming up with a friendly smile as she answered the query she read in his raisin-black eyes. "You're wondering why I keep looking at you both so curiously. Evidently, you don't know about my amnesia. I can tell from your expression that I should recognize you. I'm sorry. I don't."

The man shrugged, a gesture of apology that was reflected in his contrite expression. "Actually, we've heard . . . about the accident, how seriously you were hurt, and your claim of amnesia."

"My claim," she echoed. "I guess that's succinct enough. You don't believe me." She pushed herself off the sofa, anger motivating her, weakness the deterrent that forced her down again. So much for an indignant, self-righteous march out the front door.

"Joey didn't mean it the way it came out," her hostess said, proffering a tray laden with sandwich, chips, and a glass of ice water. "It's just his uncommonly effortless talent for putting his foot in his mouth."

The man named Joey sat on an ottoman some distance from the sofa, and the woman facetiously defending him sat down behind him, her long legs straddling his as she wound her arms around his neck and used his shoulder to prop her chin.

Lacy flinched inwardly at the intimate pose that was so keenly reminiscent of the way she and Jesse had stood by the waterfalls earlier.

Joey's lover went on. "Anyway, it's not a matter of what we do or do not believe. We flat out don't know. Tongues are wagging in Rooster Corner and opinions are divided." Her shoulders hunched in question. "My guess is a Nielsen poll would show that about thirty percent believe your memory loss, and seventy percent think your story is a bald-faced lie."

Lacy blinked at the candor as well as the disproportionate numbers against her credibility.

Jesse was quick to her defense and for half a beat

Lacy foolishly let her heart be encouraged. Then more pragmatically she accepted his aegis for what it was: His responsibility and honor as a noble knight, which, she was learning, her prideful Texan considered himself to be.

"Lacy has amnesia," he said flatly. "She was almost killed when a car smashed into her. Her physical injuries are healing rapidly. Unfortunately, research hasn't uncovered a cure for injuries that can't be seen in the mind." He stood up from the spot where he'd sat beside her on the sofa, turning his back on their hosts. "I'm going for the Jeep. Eat your sandwich and rest till I get back. When we get home, you can go to bed. Luz will bring your dinner up."

Not risking a reply, Lacy could only nod. He was angry again. Well, it didn't take a rocket scientist to figure out why. Defending her to his friends stuck in his craw like catchweed.

A long-haired kitten, sneaking from behind a chair to slink covertly along the wall toward the stairs, relieved her of the obligation for one more bite of humble pie. The smile she'd struggled against spread like fresh-made jelly across her face. "I guess the shy little fellow who just tore up those stairs explains Thorn's absence."

"Believe me, it's for *his* protection," Joey said. "For all her soft, delicate appearance, that baby can be a vicious she-devil. Got claws that could shred metal."

A heavy, embarrassed hush fell over the room, no doubt inspired by the seemingly innocuous comment. But why? And then it was as clear as the sparkling water on the tray before her. At one time or another, two, perhaps even all three of them, had shared a conversation about her that rang harshly familiar with Joey's description of the kitten. "Don't tell me you named her Lacy?" she asked.

"Of course not!" Joey's friend said, her tone reflecting utter amazement. "Why would you think that?"

Why indeed?

Jesse cleared his throat and raised his hand in farewell to their hosts, thanked them for being there to help and promised to return soon. *To take her off their hands.* That was the implication the others heard as well judging by the way their eyes suddenly darted for the floor followed by the statue stillness of their bodies. Afraid of betraying their discomfort.

Lacy rolled her eyes. She might have lost her own mind—at least that part of it that pertained to her past—but she was getting damned good at reading others'. Too damned good.

The moment the door closed after Jesse, she sighed though it sounded more like a blast of storm winds against the absolute quiet inside the house. She could have cheered when the refrigerator fans clicked in, creating a hum to fill a bit of the void.

She actually jumped when Joey finally spoke.

"Goddamn, how rude can we be? Sorry. I swear it wasn't intentional. I just can't get a handle on this thing. Keep thinking you know us as well as we do you."

"I *think* he was going to make introductions, but he feels silly since we've known you for several months," the woman suggested with a chuckle that was easy, comfortable.

Lacy responded with a smile.

"Anyway, this is my husband, Joey Wong, and I'm—"

"Liberty Ambrose," Lacy said just as the front door opened and Jesse stepped into the room again.

Three sets of eyes widened, then settled on her face, each directing a guilty charge.

Lacy gave her head a hasty shake, denying their hasty judgment. "It's not what you think. I don't *know* you. But I was watching you while you fixed my sandwich. I thought you looked familiar. Just now—I think it was the way your eyes lit up, maybe, when you introduced your husband—I got it, where I recognize you from." She could almost swear she felt the heat on her face from Jesse's burning gaze and turned to look at his accusing glare. "I saw her on the cover of a copy of *People* magazine on your mother's coffee table yesterday. There was a brief accompanying blurb: 'International cover model, Liberty Ambrose, trades in the fumes of her jet-setting lifestyle for country living, a wedding veil, and tight-fitting jeans.' Something like that."

"Almost verbatim," Joey confirmed.

"I just came back to tell you that Thorn refuses to budge from his guard post outside the door. He's pantin' pretty good though."

"I'll get him a bowl of water," Joey said, already on his feet and heading toward the kitchen.

"Thanks," Jesse muttered to him though his eyes were directed on Lacy with an offering of apology.

Lacy refused it, looking away and focusing on the model. "Your house is nice, Ms. Ambro— I'm sorry, I don't know what to call you. Is it Ms. Ambrose or Mrs. Wong?"

Again the full, melodious laugh. "Both. Neither. Professionally I'm Liberty Ambrose, I suppose. Privately— on the utility bills and junk mail—I'm Mrs. Joey Wong. Mostly, I'm just Libby."

Lacy'd been aware of Jesse standing there watching her before giving up and leaving again, but her attention was focused fully on her hostess now. Lacy smiled. She liked Libby, wondered if they'd been friends, and decided to ask.

Joey answered the query with a telling bark of incredulous laughter as he passed between the women with Thorn's water bowl. "In a word, no," he added for emphasis before stepping outside.

"Okay," Lacy said slowly, reaching for her sandwich for the first time. Picking up a hefty wedge of bread, ham, and cheese, she met Libby's eyes, which were as blue as her own. "Well," Lacy said, nibbling thoughtfully on a bite, "I guess that just about makes the dislike of me unanimous."

Chapter Sixteen

"Tell me about them—Joey and Libby," Lacy said a full hour later as Jesse steered the Jeep toward home.

He didn't answer at once, and Lacy knew he was weighing the cost of a lon-n-n-g ride in dignified silence against a concession of neutral conversation that could gobble up the miles.

She didn't press him. Instead, as she awaited his decision—to talk or not to talk—she reached between the front seats to pat Thorn's shoulder. Exhausted from his vigil as her guard, he didn't bother to lift his head, only sighed loudly, contentedly.

"Lib and Joey?" he finally said. "Well, Lib grew up right here in Rooster Corner. She was always a sad little kid. Her mama was a clerk in the county assessor's office. Never married though folks were pretty clear on who Lib's daddy was: Rooster's very own esteemed mayor, Evan Ray Paulson. Course, Lib's last name on the birth certificate was Ambs, same as her mother's people, and in the space provided for father's name, it read 'unknown.' Anyway, it was tough being an illegitimate kid in a town the size of Rooster. Hell, the population's only in the neighborhood of twenty-five hundred.

"But the real kicker was that Evan Ray's wife, Julia, gave birth to their first child—also a baby girl—the same day, same hospital. Named her Evana after her daddy, of course, and I suspect as her way of heapin' another shovelful of humiliation on poor Maybelle."

Jesse gave his head a quick shake—the kind of gesture that connotes amazement. "Had to hand it to Maybelle, Lib's mama, though. Held her head high through the worst of it. Even named her daughter Liberty as a declaration of sorts. My mother called it a kind of symbolic 'up yours.' Course those weren't the words she used. Folks snubbed Maybelle for a while, and it must have taken a toll on her, 'cause she moved away with her baby for a time. Took her out of state to live with Maybelle's mother for the next few years. But just when everyone was pretty well convinced they'd seen the last of them, here they came right back to town again just in time for Lib to be enrolled in kindergarten at Sam Houston Elementary.

"Julia Paulson pitched a fit everyone still snickers about. Called Maybelle every name in the book right out on the front steps of the Rooster Corner First Southern Baptist Church in front of God, Reverend Stinson, and his entire flock. Dillon and Cybil were there. Said Maybelle simply held Libby's hand, smiled and nodded to everyone they passed, and stopped only long enough to tell the minister what a fine sermon he'd preached. Most sided with the mayor's wife for a time, of course, but eventually their holier-than-thou attitudes changed to grudging respect and eventually even to admiration."

Lacy looked down at her hands that were clasped in her lap and smiled. In some odd way, she could relate to this woman named Maybelle. Lacy knew so little about herself, her life, but she knew what it felt like to be a pariah. She was somehow encouraged by the story, as if she, too, might eventually turn contempt to respect. And then she remembered his original comment about Libby, about the sad little child she'd been. Intuition told her what Jesse had not. "It wasn't as easy for Libby, was it? I mean, kids can be a hundred times as cruel as adults." Her eyes widened with another realization. "And she and Evana were probably in the same class in school. How terrible!"

"You got it. Evana was a little bitch even as far back as grade school. Always bringing some pretty new doll or showing off a new dress and always bragging to Lib about it being a gift from her daddy." He was quiet and pensive for the next few minutes until he added a last quiet commentary on Libby's excruciating years in Rooster Corner. "When she was seventeen, she got on a bus and headed for Dallas. She got work as a model the first week she was there. A year later she went to New York. They changed her last name from Ambs to

Ambrose and in no time at all she became a household name. Three years later she came back to town. On a self-elected hiatus from an exhausting schedule is the way she put it."

"And of course everyone fell all over themselves to make her welcome," Lacy said, vicariously experiencing the certain triumph.

"Most of the town, yes. Not Julia Paulson, of course, or Evana, who was unhappily married by then and as spiteful as ever. For the most part, though, Libby rode back into Rooster Corner to a queen's reception."

The last was said on a note tinged with sadness ... and guilt? Lacy's brow knitted as she tried to decide if that was what she'd heard in his tone. Tentatively prodding, she asked, "But?"

He drove slowly, considerately avoiding the deepest ruts and gullies in the dirt road. His eyes narrowed to slits of concentration, and Lacy wondered for a long moment if he would respond at all. Just when she decided on fast-forwarding the life story of Liberty Ambrose to her marriage to Joey Wong, Jesse spoke.

"She stayed in Rooster for three or four months. It was a good time for her. She was really happy for the first time in her life. She wasn't just accepted, she was idolized. I bet every girl between ten and twenty-five had Liberty Ambrose's poster on their bedroom wall. Hell, every guy from fifteen to eighty had one, too. Then Libby fell in love with the wrong guy." He hadn't once looked at Lacy in all the time they'd been talking, but he took his eyes from the road long enough to identify the man who'd broken Libby's heart. "I was that guy, Lace." He turned back to the business of driving as he told the rest—the worst of it. "We saw a lot of each other that summer. Went to Dallas for the annual Oil Barons' Ball. Jetted off to New York in the middle of the afternoon to hit a party one of her friends was having. Even flew to Cancun for a few days without a word to anyone about where we were headed. Just barely made it back in time to change into the tux I was wearing for Dillon and Cybil's wedding. At the reception she started talking about the kind of wedding we would have. I swear to God, I don't remember a word she said after that for the rest of the night. I was caught up short as if someone'd just stuck a knife in my gullet. Spent the rest of the night getting drunk as a brewery rat.

"I don't remember anything else about what we said or did. Found out the next day that one thing I did do was tell her how I didn't feel about her. I must have laid it out pretty straight 'cause she went home to her mother's house, crawled into a tub of hot water, and slashed her wrists."

Lacy regretted her shocked gasp the second it slipped from her lips. This was hard for him, and she'd just made it worse. The muscles in his jaw and neck quivered as if reacting to the fierce string of a bullwhip laid across his back, and there was nothing she could do.

She changed the subject.

"Tell me about her and Joey. How did they meet? And why are they living in a house on Southern Star land?"

He looked her way, only a fleeting glance, but she saw his appreciation and smiled even though she was already focused on the hill they were mounting.

"Joey Wong is one of the world's all-time greatest chefs, believe it or not. Born and raised in Boston, to humble parents, he worked in kitchens in Manhattan, washing dishes, chopping vegetables, basically doing the grunt work until he'd watched and learned enough, and saved enough money to go to Paris to be formally educated in culinary arts. To make a long story short, last year Libby went to dinner with friends at one of New York City's finest restaurants. She asked to meet the chef so she could give him her compliments. According to both it was mutually requited love at first sight. They dated a few weeks, announced their engagement, then got married six weeks after that. A real whirlwind affair that had everyone speculating about the reason for the 'chop-chop' wedding, to quote one tabloid.

"You and I went to New York for the wedding. When Libby asked how we'd met, you told her about leasing the old house and the fun you'd had redecorating it. A few minutes later Lib was asking if they could rent it for the two weeks they were squeezing out of their demanding schedules for a honeymoon.

"The next thing the world knew, Joey was giving notice that he was quitting his coveted position to try his hand as an entrepreneur. He's currently the most sought after caterer in the business. His clientele are the crème de la crème of international society. He coordinates elaborate sit-down dinners for ten to five hundred guests—weddings, yacht parties—any occasion the privileged wish to celebrate. And he operates from the Rabbit Patch while they look around for land to build their own place on. Libby flies to her shoots from here as well. They both work three weeks out of every month, reserving one week for time together."

Lacy's smile was wistful. "What a beautiful love story. It's obvious how perfect they are for each other. They're so in tune." She turned in her seat to look at him. "While we were waiting for you to drive the Jeep down from the bluff, Joey went out to take care of the horses. I was really ill at ease because I'd just opened a can of worms by asking if she and I had been friends."

Jesse's head snapped right and his narrow eyes widened in astonishment.

Lacy sighed, weary of always saying the wrong thing with this man. "Anyway," she said, firmly refusing to acknowledge his "how stupid can you be" look. "She was very generous. Said she was a staunch believer in letting sleeping dogs lie. I don't think she was being completely honest—especially with herself—about her ability to forget our differences as completely as I have. I'm pretty sure she's leary yet, but she was extending an olive branch so I grabbed ahold."

"That was big of you," he muttered under his breath, though obviously purposefully loud enough for her to hear.

Lacy wrinkled her nose at him, though tenaciously managing to hang on to her cool. "They're perfect together. She was telling me about their return to Rooster Corner as a couple. Laughing about how amazed everyone was when they realized she'd married an Asian chef, a full foot shorter that her height, and with hair a good ten inches longer than her own. Joey came back in at that point and joined in, telling me how he was sure folks in Rooster were calling him Hop Sing behind their backs. It took me a minute to track that, but I finally remembered watching reruns of *Bonanza,* and I cracked up. But the funniest part was when Libby told me how whenever they go into town, she calls him Little Joe. We all laughed at that one. Joey says no one knows if she's pulling their leg so they're afraid to laugh. They swear they're going to name their place The Ponderosa and name their firstborn Hoss whether it's a boy or a girl."

Lacy was laughing at the fun memory, and she saw the corner of Jesse's mouth twitch with his struggle not to laugh along with her. "Oh, Lord, Jesse, lighten up. I won't take a chuckle or a grin as a sign you're enjoying anything about being with me, I swear to God. But, damn it, life's too short." She reached over to jab him in the ribs just as he turned the last corner in the road and came up behind the garage. "Just think, you could wake up tomorrow just like me—as noisy and empty and irritating as a baby rattle."

"Not empty, Lacy," he said, selectively. "You may have lost your memory, but you're still clever."

She recognized the sarcasm, decided to match it. "Why, thank you, Jesse. And may I say, you might well be little more than a stranger, but you're awfully nice to put up with me."

That did it. He grinned. "My pleasure," he said as he pulled the Jeep to a stop.

Thorn sat up, stretching mightily and yawning hugely, his entire massive body riffling with his exertion to wakefulness, and then in a single bound reminiscent of the way he'd entered the Jeep hours before, he was out and running for home.

Obviously, even he had a barometer that measured when enough was enough, Lacy laughed to herself.

Turning off the ignition, Jesse leaned across her to open the glove compartment and pull out some kind of remote-control box. "Here. This opens the garage door over there. That's where we keep the Porsche."

The garage was designed to hold five vehicles. There were three doors—double wide, double wide, and single. The last was the one he'd indicated with a jut of his chin, and she couldn't help but wonder if the luxurious sports car was garaged there because of its value or as a matter of practicality—the out of the way portal that housed the symbolic reminder of the woman everyone hated.

Lacy accepted the control box with a thin smile and murmured thanks. Good humor was proving desperately hard to hold on to.

Jesse was already opening his door when Lacy stubbornly gave one last college try at keeping the channels of communication open if only with banal chatter and silly questions. "Jesse, wait, please. I want to ask you something."

His door open, and one leg already out, he paused. "I'm waiting," he said.

"Yes, but will you answer?" she teased. At his silence, she posed the question: "Is the reason Libby and I weren't friends because she was once in love with you?"

"Nope," he said, stepping the rest of the way from the dust-covered Jeep.

She hurried after him. "Nope you won't answer on the grounds it might incriminate me or nope you're not incriminated because you're not the reason?"

"Luz'll bring your dinner up after you've had a chance to shower and rest," he said, not even slowing as he strode toward the house.

The smile shriveled along with her promptly withering spirits. "Clever Lacy," she mimicked. "So damned clever you don't have a friend in the world . . . and wouldn't remember even if you did."

Chapter Seventeen

God, she loved this man.

Lying in implicit darkness, the light of a full moon occluded by scallop-edged, designer window shades, she closed her eyes and within seconds relived their lovemaking. She felt the delicious thrill of his bruising kisses, tasted his breath that was fiery and minty like a rich liqueur. Imperceptibly, she arched her back as she once again experienced his hands cup her breasts, fingers massaging as his teeth nipped the sensitive tip of a nipple. Slowly—almost as deliberately as their artful foreplay and the final carnal ride only moments before—she let her mind take her again through the profound journey of every exquisite phase of their lovemaking.

Liberty Ambrose was known for her striking beauty and photogenic inequality. But she knew as few others did that passion was truly her keenest attribute. From her earliest recollection, she'd possessed a special sensitivity that allowed her to re-create incidents engendered by intense emotion. Episodes of pleasure, joy, pain, or anger; it didn't matter which. She had only to close her eyes and relax. Within seconds, her breathing slow and shallow, the present disappeared, and she was once again virtually reliving the experience.

According to her therapist a few years back, it was a form of self-hypnosis that was a rare and potentially valuable tool. An innate talent. A gift, actually, he'd said, though he'd also warned—as if the persistent throbbing ache and thick gauze bandages around her stitched wrists weren't reminder enough—that she should recognize it as a possible curse as well.

But that was then, in the days of ecstasy-cum-agony when she'd pinned her future to an impossible dream; an emotional suicide attempt as real as the slashed veins.

Now, in the darkness, she smiled. Funny how the world changed with time ... . with the right man.

Turning on her side, she tucked one hand under her pillow, reaching with the other to run her fingers through Joey's long blue-black hair. "I love you," she whispered.

"Why does that sound so mournful?" he asked, surprising her, for she'd thought he was already asleep.

"It didn't, did it?" she asked.

She felt the brush of his shoulder against her arm as he lifted it in a shrug. "Maybe not. Could be I'm merely hearing what I've felt in your aura ever since Jesse and Lacy left."

She thought about it for a few seconds. Moving her arm so that it draped across his chest, she let her fingers play over the hard knot of sinew and muscle in his biceps. But the feelings that responded to her mental probe were too prickly. She changed the subject back to the two of them.

"You know for a guy who looks so thin and wiry under his clothes, you've got one *fine* bod, my love."

His chest moved beneath her arm with his almost silent laughter. "The credit goes to my ancestors. Trickery and deception have always been the credos by which we Chinese live. As Confucius say, 'Present a mask of frailty and humility, then conquer with might and pride.' "

Libby laughed, moving closer to lay her head on his shoulder and throw a leg over his. "Confucius, my ass. Original Joey Wong bull crap if I've ever heard it."

"Yeah, okay, but not bad, huh?"

She pressed herself closer to him, ignoring the question.

"Holy shit, Lib, you're not horny again already!" Joey teased.

"No. Just can't get close enough to you, I guess."

"Then we'd better talk about it."

"What?" she asked.

"This thing you're feeling. This mix of sadness and anger. It's there, and you can't get rid of it by crawling inside me."

She was silent for a long moment, probing her heart for the rationale behind the feelings he'd nailed. When she found it, she explained, "I really hate that woman, you know? I mean, really deep down in the pit of my gut, but today I actually felt sorry for her. Worse than that, I believed her! And you know what? I think I'm more angry with myself than with her, because I just know I'm being snookered. She's so goddamned good, Joey, she's going to tear him apart all over again, while everybody—us included—stands around like we're in some sort of fucking trance and lets it happen. I mean, instead of just sitting by with our thumbs up our asses while she brainwashes us all, why don't we get right to it? Fix up a brew of cyanide-laced Kool-Aid like that crazy prick in Jonestown did, give it to Jesse, and be done with it. At least spare Jesse further torture."

"Whew," her husband breathed. "We still here in our bedroom or on some wild amusement park ride?"

In spite of her anger, which had admittedly mounted with her speech, Libby laughed, punching him playfully at the same time. "I know, I'm straddling the teeter-totter—one minute sitting there talking with her like sisters, the next talking *about* her like she's some monster—but that's the whole point, isn't it? The way she makes everyone crazy when she's around?

"One minute, she's looking at me with those saucer-size baby blues of hers and baby-doll pouting lips—which, yes, damn it, I'm still jealous of—telling me how pretty and warm my house is. And what am I doing? I'm thanking her like *I'm* the one who decorated it instead of her!" She sat up suddenly, repositioning herself so that she faced him. Drawing her knees up against her chest, she folded her slender arms over them and rested her chin. "We might as well have been former coeds catching up on one another's lives. You should have seen the expression on her face when I told her about you and me—the way we met and fell in love. Smiling wistfully like she'd just been told that fairy tales sometimes do come true."

"Yeah, you two looked pretty cozy when I came back in from watering Thorn and stabling the horses. But you know what I think?" he asked, no longer even a hint of humor in his tone.

"Ooh, so serious. I'm almost afraid to hear."

He rolled onto his side, propping his head on a fist

before telling her, "I think you responded to her because you really did like *this* Lace. That sixth sense of yours is telling you she's not lying; that the amnesia's as real as she claims. At the same time you're pissed with yourself. It makes you nuts that she's forgotten her role as Queen Bitch. You don't want to trust her and even more you don't want to like her." He waited for her response and when none came, added the harshest accusation of all. " 'Cause deep down, Lib, you know if *you* do, there's a pretty good chance Jesse might like her, too."

"Horseshit," she said flatly.

"I don't think so. You might not want to admit it, but the truth is, as much as you hated the person we all knew, you were glad she was such a self-centered bitch. It proved how faulty Jesse's judgment in women is, how wrong he was not to have chosen you." He felt her stillness that he knew forewarned an explosion if he went too far, but shit, it needed saying and she needed to hear it.

"Bottom line, Lib? The reason you were so willing to talk about us and our life here on the ranch today is because you hoped to jog loose a memory or two. You *need* her to remember. Otherwise, Jesse might just forgive what she did to him and take her back. You can't have that 'cause that would mean the end of the contrast: you the deliriously happy ex-lover, him the hornswoggled fool."

Libby's eyes widened in the same instant her head snapped up, spine straightened to a rigid rod, and her fists came down on the bed in loud thudding protest. "Let me get this straight. All of a sudden you're Sigmund-fucking-Freud? Stick to your culinary talents, sweetie, 'cause as an analyst, you suck."

"The truth hurts," he said softly, gently.

"It's not the truth, damn you!" she cried out though it came out hardly more than a whisper around the knot of hurt in her throat. Tears burned behind her eyes. "It's mean and it's vile, Joey."

"Yeah, it is, babe, but just as lies can sometimes be kind, truth can be ugly. You know I'm not trying to hurt you, but the fact is, you hurt me when you pretend the way you respond to Lacy isn't tempered by your feelings for Jesse. Don't get me wrong, I know it's not overt. On the other hand, I also know a small part of you will always care for Jesse Pryde. It'll always matter if he's happy, but at the same time, there will always be that little part of you—that tiny germ of meanness that exists in all of us—that will root for his misery."

She opened her mouth to profess her innocence, but he checked her denial with a simple plea. "Wait, babe, please."

Smarting like hell, she turned her head away from him, laying her cheek atop her knees as she swiped at a tear.

"I know you love me," he said. "There's not a fiber of my being that doubts how completely committed you are to me . . . to us, our marriage. But ever since Lacy broke Jesse's heart and took off, you've been reveling in it. Oh, I know all about the outrage—the gnashing of teeth and the tearing of hair with Rose, and Cookie, and everyone else in Rooster Corner—at her deed. I know every last one of you has sincerely worried about poor, betrayed Jesse. But, baby, hiding behind the truth under the guise of loyalty and righteous indignation doesn't change the fact that every woman in this town—Rose Pryde included—has gotten off on the thrill of what she did, because you all hated her the minute she laid her hooks into the best-bred specimen Texas ever had to offer.

"I suppose I'm pretty safe in the assumption that the honeymoon's over, considering that along with the tears and the denial, you've got murder written all over your gorgeous face." He shrugged. "What the hell? I've already gone this far, may as well unload the rest of the round."

"You're a son of a bitch, Joey Wong," she whispered.

He flinched but fired the rest of his charges. "Like I said, you're mad as a whore on Sunday because all her johns are in church. By tomorrow you'll forgive me by excusing what I've said to jealousy, because I can't get over the fact that the two of you were once lovers. Don't do it, Lib. Stay mad. Don't forgive me. But don't excuse it to concern about the threat Jesse is to me, to us. That's not it. I've had my moments, don't get me wrong, but I talked it out with myself."

He stopped short as he saw a tear drip from her

cheek. Jesus Christ, while he was shooting off, he should have saved a bullet or two for himself.

She was the other half of him, and the agony he'd incited knifed through him with razor-sharpness. He'd gone too far. He could only hope now he understood her well enough to recognize the correct route back into her heart.

Holding his breath, he ruffled her hair, signaling the end of his lecture and offering a return to playtime.

She lifted her head to glare at him. "Leave me alone. You're as bad as Chink," she said, referring to the Himalayan kitten Joey had presented to her on her twenty-seventh birthday a few weeks earlier. "Her name's Chink," he'd told her, handing over the cream and mocha fur ball at the same time. "Named in honor of the one and only chink in my armor." She'd laughed at his witty inventiveness, but as she'd looked into this clever, sensitive man's dark, slanted eyes, she'd wondered if the moniker wasn't more a self-deprecating epitaph, a telling expression of insecurity.

"I can't believe it," he grumbled now. "Equated to a fucking cat!"

"What's not to believe? You're just alike. Always trying to make up after wreaking havoc. I'll tell you the same as I tell her: 'You can't rake me with your claws one minute, then tease me into forgiveness the next.' "

Joey's grin suggested it was worth the try. "Okay, where was I? Oh, yeah, talking to myself. Well, I said, 'Self, you've got to get a grip on this thing. Libby's merely savoring the sweet moment of vindication, her proof positive that Jesse Pryde was a bigger idiot than the dumb animal he rode into town on for not marrying her when he had the chance.' "

She wasn't entirely over the hurt. Mild anger lingered as well. Still, an irrepressible smile claimed a place on her beautiful face. "Oh, yeah, and what did 'Self' say to that?"

Instead of answering, Joey reached for her to pull her on top of him as he rolled onto his back again. She came willingly. She'd once been a victim, allowing others to take what was hers, be it her pride, her friends, whatever they demanded. She wasn't that person anymore. Today, she recognized the worth of life's treasures. Joey was her most prized, and nothing, not even his hurtful words, could make her loosen her grip on the importance of what they shared. He had hurt her with his honesty. But forgiveness was a price she'd always gladly pay to protect their love.

Despite her superior length of several inches, the two of them sprawled one on top of the other was a pose both were accustomed to, and Libby spontaneously braced her feet solidly against the baseboard. Their gazes locked even in the dusk, he held her face between splayed fingers for a long moment before kissing her over and over again, firmly, possessively. Then he held her away from him, his dark eyes boring into hers, unblinking until she smiled.

He sighed with the deep satisfaction of a contented man as she slid down several inches, bowing her legs and crossing her ankles to accommodate her length. He stroked her hair as she began to plant kisses against the intimately familiar planes of his chest that were as smooth and hard as polished stone.

Immediately aroused by her response, his breath quickened and stirred wisps of hair on the crown of her head. Yet, he knew this woman too well to dismiss the subject of her ex-lover's wife until it was settled between them. Mustering every measure of resolve within him to combat the primal urges she was rousing with her teasing tongue and soft, moist lips, he answered her with hard-found levity.

"Okay, so . . . Self did confirm what I'd been confident of all along: In a nutshell, the best man won . . . me being the best man, of course. Oh, and one more thing I thought he rather cleverly pointed out: I got the prize while poor Jesse got the spoils."

She smiled as new tears formed and fell, leaking into the corner of her mouth and pooling on his chest.

Merciful Mother, how good this man was for her.

Several minutes later, drowsy and half dozing, she forced sleep away once more to ask if he was still awake.

He mumbled something about suffocating beneath her weight and rubbing her back in the same instant to keep her where she lay.

She stayed where she was, stretched over him, appreciating his ability to provoke a grin even when she was at her most earnest. Her tone somber and hushed, she said, "God saved me from myself twice, Joey. You know what I'm talking about. When He didn't answer my prayers to make Jesse love me back and ... and after, when I tried to—"

"Shh, I know."

"Well, anyway—don't laugh—He was there for me both times, and I guess I sort of feel like I owe Him big time."

Joey didn't laugh, but he did grin. How could he not when nearly everything about this woman made him so deliriously happy? Even this crazy notion of hers that she was somehow responsible for protecting her former lover. "In other words, you're telling me you're going to keep an eye on the mysterious Mrs. Jesse Pryde. As long as she remains docile and guileless, she's safe. But the minute she steps out of line or shows an inkling of recovered killer instinct, you're going to be at God's side, His avenging angel or something."

"I don't think docile's a word I'd use even now to describe Lacy," Libby said on a huge yawn that wouldn't be repressed. And a moment later, "Have you forgotten how furious Jesse was when we rode up on them today? You know she must have said something to provoke him to that kind of rage. I've known him since I was eight years old and I've never seen him so mad. Jesus, Thorn was ready to tear his throat out in defense of her. You don't suppose she was taunting him about—? No, that's silly. She doesn't even remember doing it, so how could she bring it up ... unless she accidentally stumbled across—"

Smacking her bare bottom lightly with his palm, Joey tipped their bodies so that she rolled to his side. "No, I *don't* suppose, but I do assume it doesn't take much to get him riled these days. As neither of us will forget, she ripped out his heart before she took off last month. As for what was going on between them today, I seriously doubt we'll ever know what that was all about."

"I guess you're right. Besides, what difference does it make? He's still in love with her. We both saw that clearly enough when she fainted. He hates her, too, but right now both emotions are probably tripping all over themselves. He's going to have to get over both—the love as well as the hate. Until then, she's still going to be able to yank his chain even if she doesn't know she's got hold of it."

"Can't argue with that," Joey said. "But my advice is for the two of us to stay out of it. Lacy may be as harmless as a garter snake right now, but the second she realizes she's a rattler with venom in those fangs, watch out. Memory or no, I can't help believe once a bitch, always a bitch."

"I guess," she said, her tone lacking just enough conviction to worry him. But before he could add another warning, she was already switching tracks on him, bringing up another subject and catching him off guard.

"I think I'll go with you to California tomorrow," she announced. "You'll be home Saturday morning, right?"

"Sure, the anniversary party is Friday night, but I won't have a free minute while I'm in L.A. Not with all the exotic specialties Bruce and Demi have asked for— crystal rosebud party favors at each of the five hundred place settings, forty-two of their favorite photos together over the years re-created into nine-foot-tall stand-alone posters, marzipan lovebirds settled in nests of spun chocolate for dessert. And those are the easy ones I've already got covered. You wouldn't believe the anniversary cake."

"Poor baby," she said, stretching to peck his lips. "I won't get in your way, I promise. But I want to go, get away. And I can always stay busy in that city."

"I thought you wanted to be here to help Rose with the last-minute details for Jesse's birthday party Saturday night."

"I may not stay the whole time. I might come home Thursday or Friday. Anyway, with you having everything already arranged, how many last-minute things could there be ... even for Rose?"

"You're right, as usual," he said, rubbing at his eyes with curled fists. "Let's go to sleep. We've had a long, hard day. For the moment, I think the two of us have pretty well covered the most significant areas in the world tonight—in our little world that is."

She scrunched her pillow as she allowed herself to be

pulled against him, fitting into the curve of his body as it spooned around her.

"Jerk," she groused.

"Wonderwoman," he countered.

Joey, the victor, God at rest, and everything forgiven. They both laughed.

Chapter Eighteen

It was a breathtaking night. A cool breeze lifted fine strands of Lacy's pale blond hair, played through the trees, and stirred potted geraniums along the veranda into dance. The sky was as clear and lustrous and dark as wet ink, dusted with twinkling stars and centered with a perfect round opal-white moon. Yet even while she was awed by the night's perfection, her attention was focused inward. Had she ever witnessed a night like this before? Had she ever sat out here alone in the early, predawn hours just because in its own way, the peace she found was more restful than sleep? Had she ever sat here in Jesse's arms, sharing the wonder of it all?

No, she couldn't do this. Couldn't create more turmoil with questions that would yield no answers. She pressed her eyes closed, mentally shattering the queries in a figurative burst of embers.

She'd come out here in search of serenity that was elusive in the daylight hours when solitude was unattainable, and every moment a wearying crucible under the watchful eyes of Jesse's family and friends: *her* judges, jury, and jailers.

The image of Clay Waters flitted across her mind. She shivered. Was he the henchman hired to carry out her sentence? With almost physical exertion, she pushed the question away. She couldn't think about him. Didn't dare contemplate the possibility that someone—Jesse, please God no—could hate her enough to hire a killer. Surely, her poor, damaged mind was merely confounding fact with fiction. Taking snatches from a mystery novel and mixing them with the last unhappy memories she'd kept of her months here on the Southern Star.

Shattered, the title for a movie with . . . with Tom Berenger. She was suddenly certain she remembered seeing the film. Berenger had played a character who'd awakened in a hospital bed with amnesia just as she had. The plot was vague, but she recalled complex twists that involved a murder attempt.

Her fingers pressed to her brow, she strained for a clearer picture. It was no use, for just as quickly as it had come to her, the dim memory was lost, replaced by that of another movie. This one filmed in black and white. Old. Made, she would guess, sometime in the forties or early fifties.

And then she had it: *Spellbound* with Gregory Peck. He, too, portrayed a character suffering from amnesia. And if memory served accurately at all this time, Ingrid Bergman played a psychiatrist helping him to recall the details of a murder he was accused of committing.

She blew out a hard breath of frustration. Could her mind in its own twisted version of blindman's bluff have stumbled over the reason for her fear of Clay Waters's role in her personal life's script? Oh, please, Jesus, yes.

She sank deeper into the thick cushion on the lounge chair, more tired than ever, though slightly relieved and even hopeful.

Plainly, she hadn't attained tranquillity even in the soothing quiet of night and away from the scrutiny of mistrusting eyes. Perhaps her goal had been too lofty. Absolute peace of heart was only going to be possible when ... if? No, damn it. Not if. *When* she regained her memory.

But for now, she would take comfort in the morsel of hope her mind had just offered.

For the time being, she would appreciate even the slightest relief of tension. The quiet hours alone had given her that much. And it was enough for now. But she had to tutor her mind with more vigilance. Not allow it a free reign of terror that conjured hired hit men.

She was going to learn who she was, but this time she was going to do it right. She was going to start at the beginning, take baby steps that were tentative and unsure until she was certain she was steady with each single one.

And something else. Jesse wasn't going to make her crazy with his glares, innuendoes, and part-revelations. She would continue to probe, ask questions, and examine everything she saw for a glimpse of recovered past, at the same time learning patience and how to turn the other cheek.

Folding her hands in her lap, she actually smiled for the first time in hours. She might well enjoy this: serving him with a dish of his own medicine. It was a bitter brew she doubted he'd enjoy much.

In the darkness, she smiled again, this time widely and with an accompanying soft chuckle.

She had another satisfying thought as well: She might just spend all day sleeping, then pass her nights out here alone, gently nudging the return of her memory without the hindrance of a perpetually scowling husband, hostile mother-in-law, drunken sister-in-law, or anyone else.

She was feeling better already.

Jesse couldn't sleep. He'd tossed and turned for hours. Shoving the covers off, he left his bed to pace the room for a few minutes, before grabbing up a pair of jeans from the back of the chair where he'd left them several hours before. He didn't bother with a shirt or even underwear, for that matter, as he shoved first one foot into a worn denim pants leg, then the other. He didn't even bother with the buttons on the fly of his 501's. After all, he was only stepping outside for a breath of fresh air. He might even make it a walk around the second-story veranda. Just pass enough time to let the sounds and feel of the country nights that were as familiar as his own heartbeat mollify the gnawing monster that had returned to the pit of his stomach the moment he'd laid eyes on Lacy again in that UCLA hospital room.

Damn, shit, hell. Apparently not. What the fuck was she doing out here? he wondered the moment he stepped out the door and spotted her sitting not ten yards away.

She didn't hear him as he padded barefoot toward her across the terrace floor. He could tell that by the way she continued to sit so still. So blissfully relaxed. So goddamned comfortable and at ease.

"Why the Sam Hill aren't you in bed?" he asked when he stood within a couple of feet of her.

It wasn't exactly pleasure he felt when she jumped at

the sudden intrusion of his voice. Something close to it, though. Something sweet and satisfying.

"Oh, my God, you scared me nearly to death," she gasped, turning so that she looked up into his face and placing a hand over her hammering heart at the same time.

"Sorry," he muttered as flat and unrepentant as a frog's croak from a nearby pond. Repositioning himself against the wrought-iron railing so that he was almost directly in front of her, he said, "You didn't answer my question. It's after three o'clock. Why aren't you inside getting the rest your doctors told us you're going to need for the next several months?"

She considered a fib—something about not being able to sleep—as she stared past him into shadows and silhouettes of trees and hills. And then she remembered his penchant for anger and rudeness and even cruelty that was always directed at her. Why should she let him off the hook so easily?

Directing her gaze to the centers of his black eyes, she answered with the simple truth. "It's the only time the wolves are at bay." She looked away. "Least that's what I thought."

His grin spread with the easy interpretation of her double entendre. "Meaning me." He shrugged. "Well, don't worry, you're safe. I'm not out to eat you tonight."

"Pity," she countered. "I might have changed my mind about keeping you at bay if I thought that was a possibility."

"Always so clever," he said, the grin gone in a flash as quick as it'd appeared. "Even without memory, you still manage to twist and turn words for your own purpose. To seduce or pacify or cripple, whatever your whim." He stepped away from the railing. "Forget it. I'll leave you alone. Sorry I bothered you."

"Jesse, wait," she said, swinging her legs over the side of the chaise and coming to her feet. "Please, as long as you're already out here, sit with me for a few minutes and talk."

"About what?" he asked. "Most topics are off-limits, remember?"

"Fuck the limits," she snapped.

"Now that was vintage Lacy James-Pryde," he said

with an appreciative laugh as he dropped to a chair beside the lounger she'd rested on.

Lacy sat down again as well. "Never mind, Jesse."

Damn her, Jesse thought, seeing the light go out of her eyes and the defeated slump of her shoulders. Offering a compromise, he said, "Maybe you're right. Maybe the limits imposed by the experts have been too confining. What do you want to talk about?"

Us. About us. Which was the truth. Of course, she wouldn't tell him that. That plea would induce another remarkable Jesse Pryde scowl. "Anything. You, your family, your work. Just *tell* me something. I can't stand all this caution. This secrecy . . . and my God, the innuendo. I mean, how terrible could the consequence be if someone accidentally mentioned that you and I both liked old movies?"

He smiled and this time it was just that, a simple smile that wasn't sarcastic or condescending or rueful or even mocking.

Lacy returned it.

"Actually, you did. Like old movies, that is. A real buff. Had quite a collection and were real upset about the trend to update them with correlation techniques," he said, staring at the single dimple that appeared in one cheek with her smile. His eyes narrowed as he noticed for the first time a difference that he couldn't quite put his finger on.

Lacy's smile widened. "I knew it! I just remembered one. Really old. One of Gregory Peck's first movies I think."

"Yeah, you were into 'em," he said, though his attention was still focused on the deep crevice in her face that somehow, someway, was different than he remembered.

It took Lacy several seconds before she realized Jesse's concentration was on her face rather than the beginnings of their first real exchange. She knew what it was. This was the first time since he'd appeared in her hospital-room doorway that she was without the makeup she'd learned to apply with a careful hand to disguise the tiny scars that remained from the reconstructive surgery. She felt her face heat with sudden acute embarrassment and covered it with her hands.

Jesse understood at once what he'd done and grabbed her wrists, gently pulling them away from her face.

"Don't. Please," she said, turning away from him and trying to free her hands from his. "I know how ugly I look without ... without makeup. The scars are getting ... they're fading, but they're still red and angry and gruesome."

The moon bathed her face in profile now, and suddenly he had it—the reason the dimple he'd probed so intimately with his fingers, his lips, his tongue in the weeks and months of their relationship seemed in some way altered. He squeezed her hands, an offering of reassurance. "Don't turn away from me, Lace. Not because you're self-conscious about a few scars. My God, no matter what's happened to us, you will always be beautiful to me." He released one of her hands to cup her chin in his palm and turn her toward him once again.

"But you were staring, and you looked so ..."

"Confused," he finished for her. "That's what it was. I was looking at your dimple—that little button that shows up every time you flash that gorgeous smile of yours. It looked different tonight. And then I figured it out. It's that scar at the corner of your lip. So close to the dimple, it distorted it for me. It's hardly big enough to notice, the scar and the way it changes the effect of your smile. Really, it's only a tiny crescent, a little half-moon-shaped line I hope never goes away because in a way I can't quite explain, it's a flaw that makes the rest of your perfect beauty all the more startling."

Lacy didn't turn away, but she lowered her eyes so he wouldn't see the tears she was barely keeping from overflowing. No wonder she'd fallen in love with this man. He was rugged and macho, tough and sexy, sometimes cruel and petty. She would not have credited gentleness and charity to his list of personality traits. And then, in these few minutes, he'd touched her soul with his kindness. In a solitary gesture and only a few quiet words, he'd handed her back her dignity and rekindled her love for him. She thanked him for the first. She didn't dare acknowledge the last.

"For what? Being honest? It's the truth. Pure and simple. Trust me, Lacy, no tiny little scars are ever going to take anything away from you. You're one of a kind."

That produced a soft laugh of pleasure. "Not as pretty as Libby."

"Now you're going too far," he teased. "Begging for compliments." He sat back, folding his arms and placing an ankle on his knee. "Since you brought it up, though, I'll tell you this much. The two of you were confused for sisters whenever you were together in public. Myself, I couldn't see it. Okay, sure, you're both blond, blue-eyed ..." He grinned as his eyes drifted from her face to her legs that were bare except for a few inches of thigh that her oversized T-shirt covered. "Long-legged, for damned sure. But, hell, that description probably covers a few hundred thousand women. Besides, your bone structure is finer, more Thoroughbred than quarter horse."

She was thrilled by the generous comparison and his unrestrained confession of preference. She also had sense enough to know when not to press the issue. As long as they were on the subject of Liberty Ambrose, however, perhaps now was the time to ask about the rift between her and the famous model. She asked, "Speaking of Libby, will you tell me why we weren't friends?" Before he could agree or not, she buttressed her request with a justification. "I really like her, Jesse. You said you weren't the reason the two of us weren't friends. So, I think that only leaves one possible explanation for the animosity between us. I did or said something to hurt her. I'd really like the opportunity to undo the damage. Please give me that chance. Tell me what I did."

Rubbing his callused palms over the rough denim of his jean-clad thighs, he muttered something like "What the hell," then looked her in the eyes as he told her. "I can't say it was all one-sided, Lace. Not at first. Libby was wildly in love with Joey even then—the two of you met at her wedding, remember? But maybe it kinda ate at her a little that I married you in such a rush when I wouldn't commit to her. Anyway, who knows for sure, 'cause on the face of it all, the two of you seemed cautiously friendly until the night of the Oil Barons' Ball." He stopped there, and Lacy intuitively recognized the trouble he was having relating the rest of the story.

"Come on, Jesse. You're already in. Tell me the rest." He hesitated only a fraction of a second. "In a nutshell, I went with Joey for champagne. The two of you went to the ladies' room. When you returned, you were grinning like the canary-sated cat and Lib, well, Libby was acting plain weird. She was shaking and upset, and the next thing we knew, she and Joey had left.''

Disappointed, Lacy sagged back against the cushion, only in that moment realizing how tense she'd been. "Did you ever find out what I did to upset her so badly?"

"Oh, yeah. Cybil was in the powder room as well. I don't think it took her more than ten minutes to spread the gossip through the entire room of two thousand guests."

Lacy waited, breath held.

"According to her account—which, incidentally, you never denied—you and Libby were standing side by side in front of the mirror. Libby was putting on lipstick, and you leaned forward so that your faces were only inches apart. Cybil said Libby sort of stopped, lipstick tube poised in midair as you met her reflection and asked, 'Mirror, mirror, on the wall, who's the fairest of us all?' Then you stepped back, flipped your hair over your shoulder with a toss of your head, and said, 'Now, isn't that the silliest question? I am, of course. Just ask Jesse.' "

Lacy was speechless. Was it possible? Had she ever been such a cold, vicious bitch? My God, she'd accused Jesse of being mean. If there was even a modicum of truth to the story he'd just related, he was practically a saint compared to her. No wonder she was so hated. "I don't know what to say," she mumbled almost to herself, stunned and abashed. "Answer one more question, Jesse?"

"Depends, but go ahead and give it a try."

"Did *everyone* hate me?"

That provoked a laugh from him, which in turn produced a quiver of dread that coursed the length of Lacy's spine. "Never mind," she said. "I don't think I want you to answer after all."

Jesse stood up, reaching for her hands at the same time to pull her to her feet as well. Every muscle in his body, from his firm jaw and corded neck to his powerful biceps and the rock-hard pecs beneath his chest, rippled with some unidentifiable emotion. "On the contrary, sweetheart. I think you'll like the answer to that question a *lot*."

He circled her waist with an arm, drawing her tight against him so that she could feel the heat from his skin beneath her thin nightshirt all the way from his washboard-hard stomach to the bare vee created by his unbuttoned jeans. With his other hand, he held her face tipped up toward his. "Not the men, Lace," he said, his voice tight and low. "There wasn't a single man I knew who didn't want you from the minute he laid eyes on you." He laughed. "Jesus Christ, even my own brother had trouble staying away from you. It was the boys who work the spread, though, that you mostly kept stirred up. I had to threaten to fire every last one of them at one time or other. Whenever you went out to saddle up Black Billy—the prize gelding you'd begged me for as a wedding gift—every one of 'em quit working to watch you ride."

Lacy's breathing was quick, and her heart raced. He was angry again—this time with stirred memories of jealousy—but he was aroused as well. She could feel it in the heat of his breath against her face that was as fast and labored as her own, and in the sweat that beaded on the surface of his belly, then dampened her shirt. And she could feel it in the throbbing swell in the crotch of his jeans that was pressed against her stomach creating a delicious hunger and agony.

Anger may have started this latest confrontation. Burning desire was fueling it into a challenge that neither would be able to back away from if she didn't stop it now.

"Did I ride well?" she asked.

Chapter Nineteen

Jesse had a reputation for slow burn. He was as cool and reluctant to sting as a scorpion left to his lonesome. And he never took a dare for the sake of pride alone.

His character was as superior as his physical strength, his keen intelligence, and his head-turning good looks. He was a man's man, a woman's dream, but he was human . . . and flawed.

He hungered and he ached.

He could be riled if pushed too far.

And the day he'd met Lacy Pride, he'd discovered his weakness.

A languid smile slid across his handsome face. "Did you ride well?" he said, his tone laughing yet mean and threatening. "Oh, baby, you were born to it." Without another word, he scooped her into his arms in a move so fluid and quick, Lacy gasped with surprise.

"What are you doing?" she asked.

"Just what you've been begging me to do. I'm gonna help you remember exactly how good you are."

Lacy's emotions ran wild.

Thrill.

Panic.

Desire.

Fear that burgeoned to terror when he kicked open the French doors to her bedroom, splintering wood and shattering glass.

She struggled, twisting and bucking in a game attempt to free herself.

Jesse merely laughed and tightened his hold until he reached her bed. Then he tossed her down.

The breath slammed from her lungs with the force of the landing. Lacy hardly noticed, and she didn't hesitate.

Rolling onto her stomach, she scampered—half crawling, half clawing her way toward the headboard, toward escape—away from him.

Jesse took his time peeling his jeans off as he watched her. In any other instance, he might have felt shame for the fright he was provoking. Not now. Not this time.

Lust and hunger, fierce and raw, consumed him.

His breath coming in quick, hard rasps that rocked his chest, he kicked his pants away from his feet and reached for the only means to sate his need.

He caught her by the ankle, causing a startled squeak, then grabbed the thigh of her other leg as he crawled onto the bed after her. She darted a look over her shoulder just as he straddled her hips and gripped her arms, flipping her onto her back.

"Take it off," he said, his gaze, which had locked on hers, dipping to the T-shirt.

Lacy didn't move. She couldn't. She wasn't even touching her except where his knees pressed against her bare flesh below her bikini panties. Still, he held her in place with his piercing gaze like a butterfly captured and secured with a straight pin.

He grinned, a smile of pure satisfaction as he reached for the hem of her shirt and pushed it up above her breasts.

"No," she said, raising her hands in the direction of the shirt with every intention of pulling it down again. Too late.

Her eyes widened with shock as he caught both of her slender wrists in one hand while he ripped her panties in two with the other, jerking them from beneath her buttocks and tossing them to the floor.

"Damn you!" she exclaimed on a gush of air that made the protest sound almost more a plea.

He let go of her arms. As easy as that, he was giving up the insanity.

Lacy was stunned by the sharp sting of disappointment. Was she crazy? One minute fighting him like a woman on the verge of hysteria, the next so devastated she wanted to beg him to finish what he'd started.

What he'd started? What she'd invited!

Shame radiated from her belly to her cheeks. She'd taunted and teased, offering herself like a practiced

whore. She'd pushed him past reason, then backed off
the game like a frightened virgin. A prick tease. Isn't
that what they'd called girls like her back in school?
Only this time, she hadn't been teasing. This time, she
wanted him with every measure of her being and God
knew she didn't want him to stop now.

She needn't have worried. Jesse had no intention of
leaving her bed until he'd satisfied the raging hunger
he'd been suffering for far too long.

He'd only slowed the feast.

His eyes as black and opaque as slate, he held her
gaze for a long challenging moment while he lowered
his belly against hers. His eyes never moving from hers,
he began a deliberate, undulating dance. His penis, enormous and throbbing, slid across her silky flesh, driving
her mad.

Arching her back, she slipped an arm between them,
curling her fingers around him and lifting her hips in the
same instant to guide him inside.

He grinned, slowly, devilishly as he bucked away from
her, out of her grasp. Capturing both wrists with one of
his hands, he stretched her arms above her head. This
time he was the game master, and he couldn't allow
himself to forget that even for a second no matter how
she tempted him, no matter what trick she employed.

For Lacy James-Pryde was a seductress with skills and
powers that required no memory. When it came to lovemaking, her talent was innate.

"Un-uh," he said with a stern frown—schoolmaster to
pupil. "Not tonight. Tonight's your lucky night, 'cause
I'm going to do all the work. All you have to do is hang
on for the ride." Guiding her fingers around the brass
newels of the headboard, he said, "Keep them there, out
of my way."

Lacy shivered. There was a cold glitter that threatened
like sharp shards of broken glass in his dark eyes and
an even more ominous threat in his quiet tone. She was
both thrilled and scared—like a child about to experience her first roller coaster ride.

The comparison rocked her. Like a child. But she
wasn't a child. She was a woman ... a woman who
wanted the fever of excitement that could not be found
in any amusement park ride or any place else, for that

matter, other than in this, the most intimate context of loving.

And what's more, she understood Jesse, what he wanted, what he intended.

What he wanted was to make love to the woman who stirred his passion as no one else could do. She understood that because even without a single recovered thread of their intricately woven life together, she was certain there'd never been a man capable of arousing desire in her like Jesse.

What he intended was to reduce it, twist it, distort it, so that it bore no resemblance at all to the beauty of lovemaking but retained instead only the mangy image of sating base animal need.

She couldn't allow him that. Wouldn't allow it. Once, only a few weeks before, they'd been deeply, profoundly in love. No one had admitted that, of course. Not in so many words. Still, it was true, was evidenced by the tiny scraps of proof she'd gathered here and there. In their whirlwind courtship, their hasty elopement to Mexico, the expensive car she'd given him, and the prize gelding he'd presented her with ... and in the few, rare unguarded moments when she'd caught the glint of remaining splinters from that desecrated love in his eyes like slivers of a shattered stained-glass window.

Risking disobedience, she uncurled her fingers from the brass rods to capture his face between her hands with the barest touch. Her fingertips as provocative as feather strokes, she traced the telling features of his Native American heritage: the proud, high cheekbones to the hairline as black as ink, along the deep bronzed skin of his throat to the smooth rock-hardness of his chest.

He didn't resist nor even acknowledge the tentative exploration. He was preoccupied with his own reacquaintance with her body, though for the moment rather than his hands he used his gaze as his caliper.

His eyes moved deliberately over every inch of her, resurrecting their love for a moment. Long enough to compare it to the hate that had consumed him for the last four long weeks. Was it possible that love—any love—could even remotely approach the hatred that kept him restless in the day and without sleep at night? That made it impossible to focus on work? Or kept him from any meaningful discussions even with his mother for fear the topic might turn to the most intimate secrets in his heart? And worst of all made forgiveness a word without meaning?

No, love couldn't consume a man's being like this. And hatred couldn't sate lust. So maybe lust was the strongest emotion of all. Maybe by satisfying it, he could punish the blue-eyed witch who'd destroyed his life and at the same time exorcise the hate as well.

He grinned, remembering what it was his daddy, R. Davis, had always said. "Hell, anything's worth trying for if it's worth stewin' about. 'Sides, nothing ventured, nothing gained."

Jesse's expression made a slow turn from amusement to dark intensity. Time to drive out a devil.

He began at her throat, at the first appearance of a faint blue vein in her translucent, alabaster skin that he trailed with his lips and tongue until it disappeared somewhere deep between her full breasts. Then he flicked his tongue over a telltale, swollen nipple, teasing, tormenting before drawing it into his mouth with his lips, suckling, then nipping before backing away once again to feather its sensitive tip with the barest graze of his tongue.

Lacy pushed at him with the heels of her palms, resisting the exquisite torture he was only beginning. "Oh, God," she groaned. "No, Jesse."

"Yes, Jesse," he countered sarcastically in a hoarse whisper. Then louder, harsher, "Say it, Lacy! Two minutes ago you were grabbing me. You're not backing off now. So say it. Admit how badly you want it. Just one time, goddamn it, tell the truth." As he spoke, he slipped an arm beneath her, tipping her buttocks forward as he opened her legs with his knee and parted the lips of her sex with his fingers and traced her most intimate place.

He raised up on one elbow to stare into her eyes as he circled her navel with his finger, leaving a trail of damning wetness.

"Your body doesn't lie as well as your mouth, Lace."

She didn't flinch as he'd expected but smiled. "You're mistaken, Jesse. I wasn't telling you I don't want you. Only insisting you slow down a little." As she spoke, she raised up to trace his dark nipple poised just above her face with her tongue.

Goddamn her.

Jesse was almost crazy with need and frustration. He held her face, his fingers biting into her cheeks that were still tender with the remnants of reconstructive surgery.

He knew he hurt her. Damn it, he saw the pain spark in her eyes before she closed them in an obvious effort to hide it. A rivulet of guilt coursed his spine. But guilt he could live with. This need he could not. He had to exorcise it before it ate him alive.

Using his knees, he pushed her legs apart, catching her unaware when he plunged a finger inside her.

Her eyes flew open as she gasped with pleasure. She raked her hands through his hair, then sank her nails into the taut flesh on his straining shoulders as she raised up to meet his thrusting hand.

Though his gaze was locked with hers, Jesse was blinded to everything but his searing lust. "Tell me what you want, Lace," he said, his tone deceptively tempered. "Tell me how you want me to fuck you." His finger was plunging into her now with quick, deep thrusts.

She wanted him, this witch who had driven him crazy since the first moment he'd laid eyes on her. Goddamn it, he could see it in the dewy sheen on her brow and in those soul-devouring blue eyes. Hell, he could feel it in her heat.

He inserted another finger, driving harder, twisting both together, then parting them to open her wider and wider. "Don't tell me this is enough, baby. I know you too well, remember? Finger fucking was never enough for you. Grab my hand, Lace, like you used to. Try to take it all."

She was writhing, now, the fire he'd ignited with his hand fueled by his taunting words. She followed his instruction, grabbing his wrist and pulling it toward her, rearing up to meet him as she forced his fingers deeper.

She read the triumph in his eyes, in the undisguised arrogance of his wide grin, and in the almost animallike growl of satisfaction when he brought her to the exquisite instant of climax. She gave it to him, his moment of dominance and superiority ... then she turned the tables.

Capturing his face between both hands, she raised herself to him, covering his lips with hers and slipping her tongue inside his mouth. She heard his sharp intake of breath and circled his neck with one of her arms, checking his escape before he even tried to make it.

He pushed her down against the pillow, coming with her, meeting her greedy kisses with erotic, teasing nips of his teeth on her bottom lip.

He found her hands with his, entwining their fingers and pushing her arms above their heads. He laid full length on top of her and his pelvis ground into hers as he pried her legs wide with his powerful thighs. Then, in position, he rose above her, the weight of his upper body supported by the straining muscles in his forearms as elbows bent, he went back for one more lusty, ravenous kiss.

Lacy seized the moment. Slipping from beneath him, yet dragging him after her with taunting kisses that rendered him as helpless as a magnet trailing quicksilver, she won the moment.

Jesse flipped onto his back with only the slightest provocation of a hand pressed to his chest. He was suddenly reeling and as unbalanced as a drunk on a teeter-totter.

Lacy captured him in her hand at the same instant she straddled his hips. With the edge of her thumbnail, she grazed the head of his quivering cock, provoking a bead of moisture. Then she rose up on her knees and guided him to her sex.

He clasped a breast with one hand, his fingers alternately stroking and kneading, then closing on the swollen nipple. Her attention diverted for an instant, he slipped the other hand under her from behind her buttocks and inserted two fingers inside her burning, wet center and opening her with them spread wide. Then he reared up with his hips, catching her off guard and almost reclaiming the game.

Lacy's breath caught on a ragged gasp of mingling surprise and desire, but she wasn't prepared to concede just yet. Not until he was hers. He'd managed only the slightest entry before she raised herself away from him.

"Goddamn you," he said, his lips pulled back in a contorted snarl of agony. Grabbing both wrists, he forced them behind her, pinning them there with a single powerful hand. With the other, he guided himself under her, just missing his goal again and again as she teasingly evaded him.

Her voice hardly more than a husky whisper that reflected her own flagging control, she demanded of him what he'd not been able to force from her. "Tell me," she said. "Tell me what you want. Admit how badly you want me."

"The way I'm holding you, I could snap your spine with a single tug," he countered.

"Ah, how terrifying," she purred, stirring his passion with her body that never stopped moving. "But then you wouldn't be able to remind me how well I ride."

"Then let me inside before—"

"All right," she agreed easily, too easily, covering his hand with hers and drawing him to her. Slowly, deliberately, she lowered herself onto him until she'd taken every inch of him inside. Then the true torture began.

She didn't move.

Jess clamped her thighs with his strong hands and lifted his hips.

Her head bent and her blond hair flung forward around her face, she stared into his eyes, her expression enigmatic.

She'd snatched dominance and stripped him of his last measure of control. But it was her seemingly cool detachment that angered him, made him want to spear her so deeply, he could pierce her ice-cold heart.

As if sensing his mounting rebellion, her muscles closed around him in the same instant she tilted her hips forward ever so slightly. Shocked as if with an electrifying jolt by the subtly inflicted pleasure, Jesse cried out in a hoarse groan.

Lacy smiled, prying loose his fingers that gripped her thighs to lace them through her own.

But it was all an act, and she barely stifled the moan that begged release as she leaned forward creating such excruciating tension that for just a moment she was riveted in place. She bit down on her lip in her struggle for control against the sweet hurt of his huge cock so deep inside her even the slightest shift in position caused another fierce wave of ecstasy. Her senses reeled. She was on the verge of conceding defeat; admitting she didn't have the strength to resist the carnal tug-of-war.

"Lacy, for the love of—"

"Un-uh," she said, inspired by his plea to one last triumph. Meeting his gaze, she smiled slowly, seductively as she mimicked his earlier instruction with only a single important twist: "Not tonight. Tonight's your lucky night, 'cause I'm going to do all the work." Pushing his arms over his head as he had hers, her grin widened. "Just lie back, lover, 'cause I'm suddenly pretty sure riding—even riding a stud like you—is going to come real natural."

"Lacy—" he tried again, but her power was too much and his words were lost in a strangled cry of agony as she began a sinuous dance with her hips that increased in tempo until he was nearly mad with want.

True to her claim, she rode him hard and fast until her own need betrayed her, consumed her, forcing her to bow over him and cling to his shoulders as a climax exploded within her.

Jesse seized the opportunity to reclaim the game as he rolled them over in a motion so fluid and effortless, Lacy hardly registered the conquest until he was on top of her. And then he was driving into her with relentless force, his fingers altered to claws that gripped her buttocks as he plunged, harder, deeper, faster. His teeth bit into the tender juncture of her throat and shoulder. But she felt none of the pain he was inflicting as she wrapped her legs around his hips to meet every brutal thrust.

She held on to his arms and felt the straining muscles ripple and twitch. She witnessed the metamorphosis of the perfect chiseled features of his handsome face as they contorted into a pain-wracked grimace with the climax he was fast approaching. And she loved him more and more with every time he moved a little deeper inside her.

A tear spilled over her eyelashes; a tear inspired by the exquisite intensity of loving.

There had been nothing gentle or caring about their lovemaking from the first second when he'd tossed her onto her bed. Tomorrow her body, still mending from the catastrophic accident, would scream from the soreness induced by their need. Every inch of her would pay the price of admission she'd allowed Jesse tonight, but she would savor every ache.

On that thought, she smiled greedily and tightened her muscles around him, holding him, pulling him, wanting more, more . . . until the instant he penetrated her soul, allowing all of her love to spill from her in a dizzying orgasmic flood.

Her hands moving to his back, she dug her nails into his shoulder blades, tightening her legs around his hips and urging him to a stop just long enough to recover her equilibrium.

But Jesse was unmerciful, thrusting faster and faster, and bringing her to a third shattering orgasm just as he achieved his own climax and collapsed against her.

Lacy laid an arm over her brow as she placed the other around his neck. She was weak, almost numb, and physically sated but filled with desire that had nothing to do with sex. Only love.

Turning her face toward the veranda, she realized for the first time that a cool breeze fanned through the doors, which stood open and broken. She shivered as it stirred over their sweat-soaked bodies, and burrowed deeper beneath his fiery, heat-giving body.

"I love you," she whispered against his throat.

He didn't answer.

Lacy sighed. She hadn't expected him to. It was going to take him a long time to forgive the terrible wrong she'd done him. She understood that. Besides, maybe, just maybe, when she remembered what it was, she would be able to explain. For now, all that was important was the discovery she'd just made. He couldn't admit it even to himself. Might not even realize it. But it was true. She was sure. Jesse Pryde was still in love with her . . . no matter how hard he'd tried to prove otherwise.

She sighed as she ran her hand over his head, content to hold him.

Jesse reared up out of her arms and stood up from the bed. "Save it, babe. You wouldn't know the meaning of love if I looked it up for you, then hit you in the face with the dictionary."

She lay still, stunned at the sudden return of his anger.

"Let me think, what was it you said to me the day

you left? Oh, yeah, it went like this: 'Got myself a real cowboy. And not just any ol' cowboy. Jesse Pryde. Stinking rich, gorgeous mug, and a stallion's cock, to boot. But bottom line, still only a stupid hayseed who believes in horseshit like true love and happy ever after.'"
Snatching his jeans from the floor, he stood with his back to her as he jammed a foot into each faded denim leg. He was already walking away as he tugged them up over his hips. At the splintered French doors, he hesitated. "I'll have someone in here to fix these tomorrow."

"Jesse, wait—"

He stopped right there in the doorway, though this time he turned to face her. He stood there, a tall, darkly silhouetted figure with the moon at his back inspiring a frisson of fear that checked the protest she's been about to make.

But Jesse hadn't changed his mind about leaving because she'd asked him to. He'd stayed because, fool or not, there was still one last thing he had to do.

"I've never hurt a woman in my life, Lacy. At least not intentionally. I'm not proud. I'm ashamed and sorry." The timbre of his voice that was normally as soft and smooth as chambray was now as coarse and harsh as gunny sack.

"What I'm trying to say is I didn't forget how fragile you still are since that car ran you down. I meant to hurt you, Lace, and that makes me sick to my toes." He raked his fingers through his hair, shook his head, then added on a self-mocking laugh, "I swear to God, I never thought we'd end up ... well, in bed together, but I guess in a way I'm grateful we did 'cause I've thought about breaking your pretty neck these past couple of days since you've been home. Can't deny the consequences of that would have been worse for both of us."

"Wow, chivalry and contrition at its best," she said, sarcasm disguising injury and shock.

"The best you're gonna get from me tonight, beautiful," he said, turning away and exiting the room.

No, damn you! Lacy's mind screamed as she scampered from the bed, tugging the wrinkled T-shirt he'd never bothered to remove down to cover her nudity. She raced after him, catching up with him just outside the terrace doors to his own room. Grabbing his arm, she cut an arc around him until she blocked his path through the doors. "Don't you dare walk away from me! I've had enough of your damned games!"

"Shut up," he said, his voice low. "You'll wake up the entire house."

"You ass!" she said, raising her voice even louder. "You didn't much care who you woke up when you carried me crashing through my bedroom doors." She folded her arms and braced her legs in a stance she couldn't know was all too reminiscent of the way she'd stood the morning she told him their marriage was over.

"Get out of my way, Lacy," he said, a clear warning ringing in the words.

His tone startled her as he'd meant it to, but it was the murderous rage in his eyes that made her knees tremble. Still, she couldn't back down now. They'd crossed a threshold tonight. He wasn't going to put her back in that proverbial cage where he'd kept her imprisoned with silence and innuendo. "You've never hurt a woman before? Isn't that what you said? Then you're a damned liar. You've hurt me so many times just in the past few days since you showed up in my hospital room, I've lost track."

"That isn't what I meant and you know it," he argued.

"Tell me what the difference is. Let me get the rules straight. It's all right to harm as long as the wounds you inflict aren't physical, is that it?"

"Don't twist this, Lace. You pushed me into that bedroom as surely as if you'd held a gun to my head. And I let myself be provoked into hurting you. I'd undo every single second since I met you if I could. Since I can't, I can only apologize for tonight. That's all. There's not another damned thing I can do."

"Yes, there is," she countered, no longer angry. Desperate instead. "You can make me understand. You can tell me why I love you enough to forgive the brutality of our lovemaking and savor the passion we shared instead. You can stop glaring at me for sins I won't remember until you tell me what they are. And you can admit that even though you want to hate me, claim you were only trying to hurt me, what we shared back there in that bed proves how right we are together." She summoned courage, then added quietly, "If you didn't still love me, how could I get under your skin the way I do? For the love of God, you just admitted to wanting to kill me!"

He didn't answer. Instead, he took her arm, drawing her after him into his bedroom. When the doors were closed behind them, he reached for the shirt he'd worn earlier and left draped over the arm of a winged chair. "Sit down," he barked, motioning with a jut of his chin in the direction of the same chair.

Buttoning his fly, he pulled on the shirt though left it to hang open as he crossed the room and swiped his socks and boots from a corner of the floor.

He sank to the edge of his bed, dropping the boots again on the floor and laying the socks beside him on the spread. Then he clasped his hands between his knees and fixed his gaze on the full, bloated moon that shone directly into the room.

"Once, I loved you enough to give up the world for you, Lace. I've told you that, remember? Not anymore. What drives me now is shame, pure and simple." He heaved a sigh but still didn't look at her.

"Shame'll do funny things to a man. It'll incite him to drink or to go out looking for a good fight. Sometimes, not often, it'll make a man do the right thing. Like stand up and confess a sin or right a wrong. Mostly, though, shame just makes a man mean and causes him to take his anger out on someone else."

"I don't understand. From everything I've learned or figured out on my own, you don't have any reason to be ashamed. I'm the one—"

He silenced her with a glance that chilled her for its replication of his mother's icy glare.

When he spoke again, he'd lowered his gaze to his hands locked so tightly she could see the whiteness of his knuckles in the moonlight.

"Have I mentioned R. Davis since you've been back?" he asked but didn't wait for her answer. Whether he had or not, it didn't matter. He was going to tell her again. "Greatest man I ever knew." He raised his face only long enough to share a slight grin with her before looking down once more. "Course, I might be a tad prejudiced since he was my dad. Most folks would tell you the same thing, though. He was held in high regard by everyone who knew him, far as I know.

"He liked to talk . . . in similes, mostly. That's the way he always made his point with Dillon and me. By using examples. He didn't lecture, but we always knew he was giving us a lesson he expected us to learn and remember. He had high standards and measured others by them.

"I've always tried to be the man he was. I suppose, underneath it all, that's why I came to California when the police notified us about the hit-and run. No doubt that's why I brought you back home with me when I learned about the amnesia. It all boils down to what my dad would have done.

"He lived by a strict code of ethics, and he challenged Dillon and me to live by them as well. To be the kind who had courage enough to free a wolf from a steel trap even though he knew he might later have to shoot that same wolf for attacking his livestock. Charity. R. Davis— we never called him Dad or anything but his given name—always said that was the first mark of a man's worth. Bravery was second. Wisdom last. Most men possess one or two, he said, but that wasn't enough. Only a real man had all three, 'cause they were all three the components that comprised character. All the charity in the world isn't enough if a man isn't brave enough to offer it when it's the most difficult to give or wise enough to know when it just isn't possible."

Lacy didn't move. She hardly breathed. She wasn't sure what Jesse was telling her, but she sensed rightly that if she interrupted now, she might never have another chance to understand the man she'd married.

A tear fell from Jesse's eyes, splashing onto his hand. Jesus Christ, he thought, bowing his back and pressing the heels of his hands against his eyes. He hadn't cried since the day his horse, Piper, stumbled and broke his leg and R. Davis handed Jesse his rifle, directing him where to aim it to end the animal's suffering. It was the day before his tenth birthday, and Jesse had cried himself to sleep that night. He'd never cried again because the tears hadn't lessened the pain. They'd only prolonged it.

Rubbing his face briskly with his hands, he got to his feet. Keeping his back to Lacy, he jammed his hands into his rear pockets and walked to the doorway to lean against the jamb.

Tears filled his eyes again, and he pinched the bridge of his nose between his thumb and forefinger. Why now after all these years? He hadn't wept the day R. Davis died. Or at the burials of Dillon and Cybil's two stillborn infants. Not even when Lacy'd told him . . .

Oh, hell, he couldn't handle that one. The pain of even grazing the periphery of that memory was as sharp as a skimmed razor's edge.

Clearing his throat, he said, "Anyway, the point is, I thought I was finally man enough to walk in my old man's shoes. I'm not." Turning into the room once more, he went to his closet, disappearing inside for a moment. He came out again, shrugging into a suede jacket and buttoning his shirt. "I'll stay out of your way until you recover your memory and get back on your feet. All I ask is that you try and stay out of mine as well."

He snatched up his socks and boots, heading for the far door that led to the hallway instead of the veranda. Lacy dashed after him, and once again got between him and the exit to check his escape.

"No deal," she said.

"Goddamn it, woman, give it up. I'm tired. I've had enough, but I can still muster enough energy to lift you up over my shoulder, carry you back inside my bedroom, and lock you in the closet if you don't get out of my way."

"I'll scream," she promised.

"Okay," Jesse said with a weary, defeated shrug of his shoulders. "You win. Just tell me what you want."

They stood only inches apart now, and for the first time Lacy could see the wetness that still stood on his lashes and the telltale redness of his eyes.

This strong, quiet man whose pride meant more to him than all of his wealth had cried, and all because of her. In that moment she would have given anything to undo the hurt she had caused, to take away the pain. She desperately wished she could let him go. Just tell him how sorry she was and kiss him good-bye. But she couldn't. Not until she knew.

Hugging herself, she looked into his eyes. "I'm terrified."

"Of me?" he asked, his brows lifting with disbelief. "Why? I've told you I won't ever hurt—"

"No," she whispered. Then in a firmer voice. "No, Jesse, not of you. It's me. I'm terrified of suddenly remembering who I was. Of facing the heartless bitch everyone hates. But no matter how horrific that prospect is, I'm even more frightened of never finding a way out of this dark, bottomless abyss my mind has slipped into. I have to know what I did to you."

He slammed his head back, striking it against the doorjamb as if physically assaulted by her words.

She grabbed his arm. "Oh, please, don't do this. Listen to me. It's the only way out for both of us. Every time we even get close to it, I can see the suffering in your eyes, so I know how despicable it must be. My God, you have to realize how hard it will be for me to face that. But I have to. Otherwise, neither of us will ever be free." She paused, dragging in a long, ragged breath. Then on a simple word, she ended her argument. "Please."

Boots and socks falling to the thick carpeting almost soundlessly, Jesse bracketed her face between both hands. "Why not?" he asked. "What difference should it make to me how the truth affects your recovery?"

Though his hands held her like a vise, she managed to shake her head. "None."

"I could kill you anyway."

"I know," she said. "So tell me."

He stared into her eyes, his breathing quickening as his anger enveloped him. When he answered, the words were ground out like chips from his broken heart. "You murdered our baby, Lacy. Like so much unwanted garbage, you tossed it away." Tears rivered down his cheeks now unchecked, and his hands trembled with recalled agony and rage as they slipped from her face to circle her throat. "Then you laughed in my face while you described every detail of the procedure. I almost felt it die while I listened, Lacy. I almost felt myself die."

Lacy couldn't breathe. He was choking her, his hands tightening with every syllable he uttered, but she didn't defend herself. She didn't even raise her hands to stop him.

Her mind screamed denial, but what did it know? Nothing. Not one single shred of evidence that could defend the charge that was uglier than anything she could have imagined.

Chapter Twenty

Much later, under a fuchsia dawn, Lacy once again sat on the veranda enveloped in a cocoon of misery, confusion, and disbelief.

She didn't remember the moment when Jesse released her, stalking away as she crumbled in a heap to the floor. She had no idea how long she had lain there nor did she even recall how she'd finally mustered the strength to struggle to her knees. She didn't recollect the shuffling walk to the terrace or know why she'd passed through her bedroom without just lying down on her bed.

She remembered nothing but the horrible accusation and her cry of protest: "No! That's not true! I couldn't have done that. I couldn't have killed . . . not something I loved. Not a baby I created with the man I loved."

Maybe, she thought now, she hadn't protested aloud at all. Maybe her protest of innocence had stayed locked up in her mind just like her memory.

Not the tears. They'd come. She'd cried and cried. For the unborn baby whose life she'd ended before it had even drawn breath.

For Jesse, and the agony she'd witnessed him relive in that terrible moment.

And she'd wept for herself, for comprehension she couldn't grasp.

When the tears were all used up, she'd begun the frustrating process of putting together a puzzle of the woman named Lacy James-Pryde; a woman she was beginning to believe she would never remember.

There was no doubt that she'd been well liked by everyone on staff at the California hospital. Young interns and residents had come by the day before her departure with gifts, mementos, and souvenirs of her stay—some thoughtful and touching, others gag gifts to make her laugh and cover the awkward parting between new friends who would probably never meet again. A couple of nurses had even surreptitiously swiped at tears as she was wheeled away.

And little Johnny Decker. Lacy smiled as she thought of the ten-year-old leukemia patient she'd come to know while the two of them sat side by side in wheelchairs—she awaiting X rays, he on another dreaded, debilitating chemo treatment. She'd gone to visit him in Pediatrics almost every day until her dismissal. The last time she saw him, he'd come to her room long after visiting hours because he couldn't sleep until he told her good-bye. He gave her a picture—a crude depiction of the two of them sitting in their wheelchairs. Two things in the childish crayon drawing stood out in disproportionate exaggeration from the rest: the enormous smiles on their stick-figure faces and the gigantic, oversized wheels on their chairs. Lacy immediately understood the significance of both. Hugging him to her, she let him know. "I love you, too, Johnny, and I believe, one day, we're both going to be well and strong again." She scribbled quickly on a scrap of paper that she pressed into his hand and added, "This is my phone number and address in Texas. Your mom's given me yours. So when we're both well, we'll get together and have a party to celebrate."

Now, alone in the sad beginning of her third day at home, she squeezed her eyes shut with the bittersweet pain of that memory. How, she wondered, could she reconcile Johnny's heroine with the monster everyone here insisted she was?

She flinched as she recalled Jesse's revelation of her cruel taunt to Libby at the Oil Barons' Ball.

She could only wonder what she had said or done to Cybil and Dillon to make both of them so bitter and hostile.

And what about the charge she'd overheard Dillon make about her marrying Jesse for his money? No, that didn't make sense. Jesse himself had told her she'd bought the Porsche as a gift to him with her money; money he'd implied she'd brought into the marriage.

Rubbing her eyes that burned from crying and lack of sleep, she sighed. There was so much that didn't make sense. So many holes that needed filling.

Like Thorn's radical change of heart. From what everyone said, her staunch ally and defender had once appointed himself her archenemy. Ordinarily, weren't animals consistently predictable?

Or what about Jesse's claim that she was a writer? She'd seen no proof of that, although in all fairness, she really hadn't given it much thought. She'd been preoccupied with the unenviable task of getting her bearings—about as easy as tackling Mount Everest blindfolded—especially while constantly dodging bullets of innuendo and point-blank accusation.

Still, the feel of that—her being a writer—was wrong. Somehow, she fancied herself an artist, it was true. But not one who worked with words. She squeezed her eyes shut, reaching for the sense if not the actual memory. And then she surprised herself by actually pulling a recollection from the recesses of her mind.

She saw herself in a filmlike scenario, though the screen was dim and a little out of focus like a home movie watched in a room that was too well lit. Still, it was her, she was sure of it. Much younger, though. Maybe thirteen or fourteen, and the same dark-haired boy she'd remembered before was with her. He leaned over her shoulder, reaching around her to point at something in front of them. *Not bad, Rodin. I mean, it looks just like her, but who's going to know it's Mom? If you want to blow people's socks off and win those competitions, you need to sculpt someone famous like Michael Jackson or Cher. Now there's a fox everyone would recognize.*

The memory faded to black, but excitement tingled through Lacy's body as she pushed herself from the chaise and ran into her bedroom.

Picking up the doll, she stared into the face that was a likeness of herself. She had made this doll.

Sinking to the chair, she laid it in her lap and traced the porcelain face with her fingers. There was no lightning bolt of recollection. No electric shock of familiarity that emanated from her fingertips at the touch of smooth, flawless features. Nonetheless, Lacy knew without doubt that she was the creator of this miniature replica of the enigma who was Lacy James-Pryde.

So why the pretense about being a writer? Unless . . .

But that was crazy. Who else could she be if not Lacy James-Pryde?

How would the doll have gotten here if not by her?

How would she have remembered Clay Waters?

Most importantly, how would her heart recognize what her mind still refused to admit? That she was deeply, profoundly in love with her husband.

So in love, you aborted his baby? her mind demanded cruelly.

Lacy jumped to her feet, letting the doll fall unharmed and unnoticed to the plush, thick carpeting. Stepping over it without even a glance, she dashed around the room, snatching lingerie from a dresser drawer, slacks and a shirt and a pair of loafers from the closet. She tossed everything onto the bed, then hurried to the terrace doors, shutting them and dragging the bench from her vanity over to keep them in place until their broken lock was mended. She was already pulling off her T-shirt as she entered the bathroom and turned on the shower.

She was invigorated and excited by the discoveries—paltry and scarce as they might be—she'd made in the painstaking recovery of all she knew of herself.

Stepping beneath the hot spray of water, she leaned against the tiled wall. For the first time since crawling from the floor hours before, she noticed the aching in her body that seemed to permeate every pore. She felt dizzy and weak, and her head pounded from behind her eyes to the base of her skull. Some—most—were the residual symptoms of the almost violent urgency of their lovemaking that had been so physically taxing. The rest, merely testimony to her intense fatigue and lack of resiliency since the accident.

Glancing down at the tiled floor at her feet, she noticed a thin rivulet of red that swirled with the water toward the drain. Only then did she notice the faint sting of something embedded in the ball of her foot. Leaning forward, she raised her foot and immediately located the thin splinter of glass protruding from a small, inconsequential cut. It came out easily with her fingernails plied like tweezers. She flinched, though more with the recollection of the shattered French doors than with pain. Another war wound. Ironic that she should bleed from the least hurtful injury of all. Letting the tiny shard of glass slip down the drain, she dismissed it along with the blood that continued to run pink, and reached for the loofah and soap. Sighing, she repositioned herself under the steamy spray, closing her eyes and raising her face to it. Rest or sleep would have to wait. Too many questions begged answers that couldn't be put off any longer. She had too much to lose.

Her thoughts returned to Jesse. The darkly handsome face her mind offered was reproachful and angry, but Lacy refused to back away from it. If she was guilty of the crime he'd claimed, she was going to find out why, and somehow, someway, she was going to make it right if it killed her.

As if bidden by the innocuously intended expression, Clay Waters's image replaced Jesse's.

Lacy winced, immediately terrified and recoiling, but resolve returned at once. Not even Waters or the threat he posed—real or make-believe—was going to stop her from finding the key that would open all the locked doors in her mind and reveal the answer to the most important question of all: How could she be two such different people?

Matt Peacher was on the very edge of violating every ethical law in the book including his oath to his profession and his wedding vows to his wife, Janie. He was on the verge of making love to one of his patients when the telephone rang. Cursing both God and Alexander Graham Bell in a tone that was damn near a shout, he rolled onto his side and reached into the darkness in the direction of the rudely jangling phone. In his quest, he managed to knock the current issue of *Playboy* to the floor, tip over an uncapped bottle of aspirin, and upend a bud vase. Only then did he succeed in pulling the receiver to his ear to bark an irritated "Hello!" to his caller.

At the tentative "Peach? Is that you?" from the other end of the line, his face flamed as hot as the compromising dream he'd just awakened from, a very improper dream about this same caller.

He was sitting up even before he made his answer and casting a shamefaced glance over his shoulder at his wife's body, curled away from him in blissful slumbering ignorance. "Yes, Lacy, it's me. Can you hold on a minute?"

Good God, what time was it? he wondered, stepping from the bed and glancing at the illuminated digital clock on his way from the bedroom. Four a.m.! What the hell?

He spoke into the phone again as he pulled the door closed behind him. "Okay, I'm back. Sorry. Didn't want to wake my wife. She has to get up with the kids in— Oh, shit, what's the matter with me? Something's wrong or you wouldn't be calling, and here I am mumbling about disturbing Janie. Forgive me, Lacy. I'm just . . ." *fucked up because I was dreaming about fucking you,* he finished silently. Aloud, he changed the subject. "Never mind. Tell me. What's wrong?"

There was a long silence and for a few confused seconds, Matt was afraid she'd hung up. He was just about to call out to her when she finally spoke.

"Oh, Peach, everything. Me, this place, all of it," she said in that voice he'd remember all of his days for its rich musical clarity that nevertheless possessed an incongruously haunting breathlessness at the same time. He'd even mentioned it to Janie once, likening it to the ethereal sound of the winds in the moors on the Isle of Skye—their honeymoon retreat.

"Okay, Lacy, take your time. Tell me everything," he said.

"Umm, give me a minute, Peach. I didn't think this would be so hard, but it . . . damn."

Matt quickly reassured her. "Take all the time you need."

Only the faintest vestiges of his dream lingered. Still, he flinched as he thought of his long-time friend and associate, Jacob Ivers, who'd been part of Lacy's medical team during her convalescence. He didn't have to guess what the wily little shrink would say. Tonight wasn't the first time he'd dreamed about Lacy, and he'd actually confessed to his friend earlier.

"That one's so obviously Freudian, it's laughable, Matt. Put two and two together, man. You love your wife, but she's knocked up again and no doubt not too interested in playing who's on top. Now, add the most gorgeous patient either of us has ever treated, and I guarantee you, you'll arrive at four. In more technical psychiatric jargon? Your id is repressed by professional discipline and devotion to Janie. All well and good. That doesn't change the fact that you're a horny bastard whose *schlong* doesn't know repression from oranges." With a sound smack to the back, he'd added on a wicked laugh, "Quite simply, Matt, my friend, yours is a case of the dick wagging the doc.

"Nothing to be ashamed of. Quite normal, in fact. Believe it or not, even I—as close to perfect as God dared—indulged in a couple of wild daydreams before, alas and alack, I was forced along with you to sign the bewitching Mrs. Pryde's discharge papers."

Shaking off the craziness of lust and psychoanalytic mumbo jumbo, Matt shrugged back into his mantle of consummate professional. Padding barefoot along the thick Persian runner that ran the length of a spectacular curling marble staircase, he sat down on the bottom step and propped his elbows on his knees. Then he prodded gently.

"Unless this is something Dr. Ivers could better help you with. Is that it, Lacy? Is that why you're hesitant to talk? Do you want his home number? You know he wouldn't mind."

"No," she replied with quick decisiveness. "This doesn't have anything to do with him. It's just . . ."

He heard her groan and opened his mouth to offer reassurances, but she beat him to the punch, blurting the reason for the call at such an inappropriate hour.

"Is it possible that I ever had an abortion?"

For the first time in his twelve plus years as a physician, Dr. Matthew Peacher was totally dumbfounded. Not by the question. At least not precisely by the question. Maybe by all that it implied or merely what it didn't explain.

"Do you think you may have remembered having an abortion, Lacy?"

She didn't answer.

"Is that why you left your husband? Is it possible that you blamed him for forcing you to abort a fetus you very much wanted?" As soon as the last words were out of his mouth, he could hear her sobs—soft, hopeless.

"Lacy, don't do this. You called me with a question that is obviously very important to you. So, talk to me."

She sniffled a couple of times, apparently fighting for control, then said, "I think you already answered it, Peach."

More perplexed than ever, Matt rubbed his brow in a vain effort to clear his befuddlement. "I'm confused. I think we need to back up, Lacy. You asked if it's possible that you ever had an abortion, right?"

"Yes," she said, calmer. "And your assumption that I might have recalled the experience tells me everything I need to know. Despite the fact that you told me I'd never been pregnant, you weren't including pregnancies that were terminated."

The doctor scratched his scalp beneath a thinning patch of hair. "Okay, I'm totally lost, but let me explain a couple of things. Maybe that'll get us back on track. Whenever we receive a patient who doesn't have any ID or who—for whatever reason—can't help us learn who he or she is, we tag 'em as a J. Doe. John or Jane, depending on gender, of course. Then there are some routine, fundamental steps we take to ID the patient. We allow the police to take fingerprints and photographs to be compared to those of missing persons on file. In your case, a photo wasn't possible. Not immediately with all the facial damage sustained in the accident. And the prints turned up nada.

"From there, someone on our staff, usually a nurse, examines the patient for identifying marks such as tattoos or scars or distinctive birthmarks. We take measurements and assess age as nearly as we can. From there it gets a little more detailed.

"For example, X rays are taken of everything from teeth to toes. Sometimes our J. Does are runaways who have been abused and attended in hospitals in the past. We can often successfully match our findings against X rays of prior broken bones and come up with a name. Or we can get dental records for comparisons. In your case, we came up empty at every turn. You were pretty broken up, but there was no evidence of prior breaks and no matches to dental records."

He paused for a few seconds, allowing her to interject a question if she had any. When she remained silent except for a long exasperated sigh, he continued. "So, at this point, we reverse our tactics and start ruling out. We do a very cursory pelvic exam to determine virginity or lack of, prior pregnancies or not." He cleared his throat. "Sometimes, we can even detect sexual habits that will give us a pretty good idea of our J. Doe's personal proclivities."

Her tone reflecting her impatience, Lacy stopped him there. "I get it, Peach. Thanks. I'll let you go. I'm sorry for waking you. I just had to know." She laughed though it rang hollow and sad and was edged with a strange note of finality. "Remember how impatient you accused me of being? Guess the change of scenery hasn't helped me achieve that virtue."

"Lacy, wait. There's something I'm not getting here. You said I answered your question about whether or not you had ever had an abortion. That's not right. I didn't. I can't answer that, because I don't know."

He could have sworn he was shocked from the sudden jolt of electricity that sparked across the telephone lines all the way from Texas.

"How is that possible, Peach? How could you not know? If you were looking for evidence—"

"We might not have detected signs of a pregnancy that was terminated in the first four to six weeks. As I remember noting, it was evident that you were not a virgin, and that you had never carried a pregnancy to term. In other words, you might well have been someone's lover or wife, but you definitely were not someone's mother. I don't recall noting any cervical changes consistent with the termination of a very early pregnancy. I can pull your chart in the morning to determine whether or not I made any notes along that vein, but I'm relatively confident I wouldn't have. It wasn't evidence that would help us in our goal to identify you, and pelvic exams are an evasive procedure. You were a very sick girl, Lacy, and we couldn't take that risk. I wouldn't have wasted time, not with your condition as fragile as it was."

"But another physician looking for proof of an abortion performed in even the first weeks could detect changes in the cervix that would answer the question positively one way or the other, is that right?" Lacy asked.

He could hear the excitement in her voice and smiled remembering the hope he'd heard a little more than a week ago when she'd learned she had a name and a husband and a home. The smile wilted as he recalled her original statement about how terribly wrong everything seemed to have turned out. He could think of a dozen questions, but he pushed them back as he answered hers. "I'd say so. Yes. Definitely."

"All right," she said, her tone stronger, more confident. "Now I have to find me a doctor." Out of the blue, she laughed. Fully, happily, this time. "Too bad you're so far away, Peach. I'd be there in a heartbeat. You're the best."

"You're not so bad yourself, kiddo," he said on a smile. He didn't understand what had just happened. Or even what he'd given her that had made so much difference. Maybe if they just talked awhile, she'd offer some sort of explanation; tell him something of what she'd learned about herself, her life as Jesse Pryde's wife, and why she was so pathetically desperate and miserable.

And then he heard the quick, "Thanks, Peach. I really do love you," and the click signaling the end of the mysterious and confounding conversation.

"Yeah, you, too," he muttered as he depressed the OFF button on the cordless phone he held in his hand.

He hadn't heard Janie come down the stairs, but he felt her presence even before she reached the step he sat on and lowered herself to sit beside him.

"That had a mournful ring to it. Something serious with one of your patients?" she asked on a sleepy yawn as she laid her head in his lap.

"Former patient, yes. But I don't know how serious. Weird is a better word."

"How?"

He shrugged. "Who knows what I mean? I don't even know."

She reached up to tousle his hair. "If you don't want to discuss it for fear of violating physician/patient privilege, just tell me," she said. "I know how to mind my own business . . . as long as this former patient isn't the infamous other woman we housewives worry about."

He brushed her long sable-brown hair away from her face as he answered honestly. "It was Lacy Pryde. My Jane Doe until several days ago. Remember?"

He felt her grin against his leg. "Give me a break, Matthew. What woman in the world would forget another woman as beautiful as she? Remember when I met up with the two of you in the hallway at the hospital?"

"Of course. The day the bandages came off her face."

"She looked so pathetic," Janie said, "but even with all the swelling and redness, the beauty was still there underneath just waiting to emerge. I'm glad I'm not a jealous woman because I'd certainly be jealous of her. How's she doing down there in Texas? Must not be too good if she called you at home in the wee hours."

"No, I don't think so."

"Ah, I can see this conversation's not going to get us anywhere."

"Nope, but it's not because of confidentiality. Not this time. I really don't know what's going on." He popped her behind. "Come on, let's go back to bed and get that last ninety minutes until the damned alarm goes off."

As they walked back up the stairs again, arms around each other's waist, she asked, "You really don't have any idea?"

"About what prompted the phone call?" He shook his head and blew out a loud sigh. "No, babe, I really don't. I answered some questions about some tests and examinations I conducted, and just when I was getting ready to make a few inquiries of my own—find out if she was making any progress with the amnesia and how she was adjusting—she hung up."

"Not quite," Janie corrected as they reached their bedroom and separated, each of them going to their own side of the king-size bed. "First, she said something that made you smile all goofy like Little Matt when he talks about Cindy in his kindergarten class."

Plumping his pillow with a couple well-aimed jabs, Matthew laid back. "If you're going to try reading expressions for clues, you're going to have to do better than that. It was good to hear from her that's all. Besides, it wasn't really even a smile. I think it was more a grimace. Being disturbed in the middle of the night gives me gas."

Janie scooted over to his side of the bed, fitting herself into the crook of his arm. "Yeah, right," she said, contented and already sleepy again. "And that probably explains why you look like that when you're dreaming about her.

"But don't worry, I'm not threatened. Women constantly fall in love with their doctors. It's that transference thing Jacob is always talking about. And every man Lacy Pryde ever meets will love her because she's everything their little boy fantasies were all about."

Matt chuckled. "I'm glad Lacy called. Otherwise I might not have learned so much about you. I admit, I already knew I was married to a smart-ass but a psychic who interprets dreams even before she knows what they're about? Now, that's a new one." He rolled onto his side. "And just to allay any fears you're not having, I wasn't dreaming about Lacy Pryde." The little white lie told, he circled her waist with his arm, drawing her against him. "Satisfied?"

"Of course. As long as you never get any better at lying, I'll always be satisfied."

"What makes you think I'm lying?" he asked, raising up on an elbow with indignation.

"Because you were saying her name in your sleep and—"

"And that proves I was dreaming about making love to her?"

"And making all those goofy noises you make when we're doing it," she said. "So, don't bother denying it. I know you too well. Besides, she might be all the things every little boy dreams of, but I'm the stuff you got and are stuck with."

He couldn't help the chuckle. "So, you're not the least bit jealous."

"Not the tiniest bit. But I am sleepy, so hush, sweetheart."

He didn't say another word. Not for a good couple of minutes. Then he couldn't help it. "Why not?"

"Geez, Matthew. Why not what?"

"Why aren't you jealous? Am I so safe and dull no other woman would ever even look twice?"

This time, Janie laughed. "Of course not, silly. It's just that I know without a doubt how much you love me.

And, too, no matter how much I prefer the country house to this monstrosity your folks left you, you would donate your left testicle before you'd risk losing it."

"Is that a threat?"

"Certainly. I'm four months pregnant with your fourth child, remember?"

"God, I love it when the bitch in you comes out."

"Mmhmm. I know. So, go to sleep and dream about Lacy."

"I could think of something better than dreaming about another woman."

"Un-uh. It's God's unwritten law of time off for good behavior. I've done my stuff. Now, I get to just sleep and get fat." She raised up to look at the clock, falling back against him with a loud groan. "And get up in an hour to feed the three guys we already have."

"Okay, you win. I'll dream. You sleep."

She did her part, but he didn't dream. Instead, he lay awake and worried. The phone call from Lacy had disturbed him more than he realized. Maybe he'd find time to call Detective Dailey. Just see if anything new had turned up in the mysterious hit-and-run accident. Probably foolish. But a chill suddenly dotted his skin with goose bumps, forcing him to acknowledge the bad feeling that had settled in the pit of his gut the moment he'd answered the phone and heard her voice. It was an instinct he'd learned as a doctor and had come to trust in every facet of his life. He was feeling it now, all the way to his toes. The most unforgettable Jane Doe of his experience was in trouble.

Chapter Twenty-one

Lacy had made up her mind. She wasn't going looking for trouble, but she wasn't backing away from it either. Her conversation with Peach had settled some things for her.

A pretty detailed search of closet, drawers, and boxes had settled more.

For one thing, she was now certain she'd never been even remotely close to writing a novel. She'd arrived at that conclusion after turning up a box of publishing biz how-to's that appeared suspiciously pristine and unread. Otherwise, there wasn't a single shred of evidence linking her to her claim of career aspirations as an author. Besides, there was the absolute confidence she now had that she was a sculptress of sorts; the creator of lifelike dolls ... portraits in porcelain.

So why the lie about writing?

She shook her head. It simply didn't make any sense.

And what about the abortion Jesse claimed she'd had? Every fiber of her being was in denial of that one! Especially after talking with Peach. Not that he'd given her concrete proof. He had suggested reason for doubt. That was enough for her. Now, she was going to find the doctor who'd attended her and get irrefutable evidence of the lie for Jesse.

She shook her head. But there it was again. Another lie. If she hadn't had an abortion, why on earth would she have claimed she had? Why tell a lie that was so ugly and destructive? It didn't make sense unless ...

What if she'd needed an excuse to leave? Wouldn't that have been the one act that would have damned her forever in Jesse's eyes? Wasn't that the perfect way to assure he would never come after her?

Clay Waters's face hovered before her for a second

before she banished the image. Her fingers trembled as she leaned forward before her vanity mirror, applying eyebrow pencil. She was forced to wait a moment until her hand steadied again.

She wasn't going to think about that man. Nor about the fear he inspired every time he came to mind. But she couldn't entirely rid herself of the notion that he might have been the reason she'd run.

Her heart began a drumroll in her chest, and she gripped the edge of the table. So many questions, and every one conjuring up another . . . like who would have hired an assassin to kill her?

One thing at a time, she reminded herself. Right now, she needed nourishment. She'd not only passed an entire night without sleep, she'd been run through rigors to rival a Marine recruit obstacle course. She needed sustenance to get her through the day she faced.

She applied the last of her makeup to her eyes . . . eyes that felt like they'd been doused with sand, then rinsed with the brine of ocean water. She reached into a drawer for a rubber band she'd found earlier while inspecting every nook and cranny for papers linking her to a past life. She hadn't really been surprised at the little she'd turned up. Apparently she hadn't planned on coming back to the Southern Star. She might have had plans to have her wardrobe shipped out to her once she was settled. Nevertheless, she wouldn't have left behind important documents such as her birth certificate, passport, diplomas, or degrees. Obviously she had even taken photo albums of her life before marriage to Jesse, for other than the picture he'd shown her of the two of them on their wedding day, Lacy hadn't uncovered another single item linking her to him or this house.

A frown marred her brow as she tied her short hair back in a sad little nub only a couple of inches long. Hardly worthy of being called a ponytail. And definitely not the most becoming style she'd managed in the past several days.

Never mind. It was enough for today. She was too tired and sore to work for more. Maybe a scarf knotted around it—just not red, she was already sick and tired of red. Add a pair of simple gold loop earrings . . . and just a touch of lipstick—there.

She stepped away from the mirror to give her image a final once over. Not bad for a too-skinny chick with sleep-deprived red eyes and aches and pains she could discuss with one of Mike Tyson's opponents after a bout.

A framed photograph of Jesse stared at her from the top of the armoire on the far side of the room. She wrinkled her nose at him, but a smile was already tugging at her lips as she left the room. She had pushed him too far in bed. This morning, she was paying the price. Yet, she couldn't honestly say she regretted a single moment.

Okay, so maybe Jesse wouldn't call what they'd done lovemaking, but she doubted he could look her in the eye and deny that it had been deliciously gratifying.

She flinched as she glanced at his bedroom door, remembering what had happened afterward. Sweet Jesus, he'd cried!

She was almost doubled over by the time she reached the top of the stairs. Stopping, she clung to the balustrade. A couple of deep breaths and another healthy dose of resolve, and she was steady again.

No, whatever had happened—the hurt, the tears, the revelation—it had all been necessary. Now, she had a place to start from. And no matter what, she'd always have the memory of lying in Jesse's arms, of making love, and the absolute certainty that there wasn't another woman on earth who could have sated the need she'd sensed in him last night. He might well hate her, but it wasn't too late for them. Not yet. Because Jesse Pryde was no longer her husband in name only. He was her lover again.

Rose and Dillon sat alone at the kitchen table. Neither of them seemed to notice Lacy's arrival in the doorway. At least, Lacy believed, that was the impression Rose intended when she set her coffee mug on the table, her expression pensive, her brow mildly furrowed, and said, "Jesse's gone to Dallas. He phoned to say he wasn't certain when he'd be home. By Saturday, of course. Anyway, I meant to ask him if he heard a panther during the night." Picking up the mug once again, she wrapped her long fingers around it as if drawing comfort from its warmth. "Such an eerie sound. Like a woman's scream.

I hardly slept a wink after I heard it. Did it awaken you and Cybil? I know that's what kept poor Jesse up; drove him off so early, he's already arrived in the city."

Dillon's face was in profile to Lacy, but she saw the heat of his embarrassed flush as it stained his face. He, too, knew she was standing there now, just as he realized like she did that Rose's comments were impeccably timed to her arrival.

Her own face had warmed with humiliation as she'd quickly caught on to what was happening. There was no panther. Rose had no doubt heard some of what had gone on between her and Jesse, then come up with the comparison during the night. Lacy didn't dare dwell on the question of exactly how much the snooping woman had overheard. She'd probably been standing with her ear pressed to the wall from the first moment of door-splintering thrill to the mind-shattering climax.

Walking into the room, she pulled out a chair, smiling serenely. "I'm sorry, I didn't mean to eavesdrop, but I couldn't help hearing you say something about a pan ther. I would never have believed they live so close to civilization." She smiled again, this time to Luz, who'd arrived at her side, a carafe of hot coffee in hand. As soon as her mug was filled and her order for eggs, bacon, hash browns, and grits placed, she turned her attention to her breakfast companions again. "You're wrong about Jesse, though, Mother Rose. He was with me most of the night, and I don't think either one of us heard any cats." *And I don't scream like one either,* she added with her unblinking gaze.

Rose ignored the implication, turning to Dillon once again. "Anyway, alert the men to be on the lookout for a wild cat. I don't want to have to worry that someone might be hurt while I'm away."

Lacy didn't have to feign interest in this latest revelation. It quickly turned to mistrust as she thought of Jesse's whereabouts. "Don't tell me, Jesse asked you to join him in Dallas. That's why he called?"

Rose's answering smile was patronizing, her tone amused and condescending. "Silly girl. From the first day we met, you always were so threatened by me; so worried that I'd somehow get between you and Jesse. And here you are even without a memory, and still as insecure and jealous as ever. Interesting, isn't it? The human psyche, I mean. Apparently, these are innate rather than acquired character flaws."

"Mother's going to California, Lacy," Dillon said with a friendly smile that was like a white flag signaling truce. "Her sister-in-law, is very ill. Mother spoke with her husband last night, and he recommended that she come as soon as possible."

"I'm sorry," Lacy said, lowering her eyes to the napkin she'd spread across her lap and was working with agitated fingers. "Did I know her?"

"Emma?" Rose asked with an incredulous laugh. "Hardly. You know, I don't think you understand how temporary you were to our family. How do I explain it so you can fully understand?"

"Mother—" Dillon began, the warning in his tone even though he was cut off before he could continue.

Rose silenced him with a glance, then turned her attention back to Lacy, her gaze as cold and dangerous as black ice. "Ah, I have it. Think of yourself as a straight-line wind that blows through these parts from time to time. Not something we ranchers take lightly—potentially destructive, certainly dreaded—but never more than a brief moment of temporary insanity." She smiled and actually reached out to pat Lacy's hand. "And now, bless your heart, without your memory, you hardly even possess enough gust to ruffle feathers."

Lacy laughed. Genuinely, fully. Had she ever known anyone with such unmitigated gall? She didn't need a memory to answer that one! Her brief bout of shame cured by the woman's outrageous rudeness, she suddenly realized she'd been given reason to celebrate.

As Luz set her breakfast in front of her, Lacy raised her glass of orange juice. "I'd like to propose a toast to your sister-in-law. May her illness not take her before her family is ready to give her up." She took a sip, then set down her glass. "You know what, I just bet that's the case. Why, if she has even half your spunk, Mother Rose, you could still be sitting by her side long after we've welcomed in the next decade. Wouldn't that be wonderful?"

Rose's face had turned as gray as the morning that was cloud-covered and forbidding.

Dillon was suddenly choking on something he'd apparently swallowed the wrong way.

Lacy ignored them both and dug into the golden scrambled eggs, munched a slice of buttered toast, then dabbed at her mouth quickly as a new thought dawned, causing her eyes to widen. She swallowed hurriedly to explain. "Oh, about me and the straight-line wind, was it? That was good, but I think you might have underestimated me. From what I've been finding out about myself over the past couple of days, I may well prove more of a threat than that. More like a twister roaring smack down the middle of things and wreaking such havoc no one can recognize what's left in my path. Oh, and incidentally, something else you were mistaken about. I have had a memory or two." She sipped her juice for a long, irritating moment, then smiled at her breakfast companions. "Anyway, the thing is I've realized I've told you all some lies."

Rose's dark eyebrows arched with interest, and even Dillon, usually as wary as a cornered coyote, was leaning forward, caution forgotten.

"For one thing, I'm not a writer. I'm a doll maker." She shrugged apologetically. "Well, actually, all modesty aside, that's understating it. I'm a very gifted artist. The dolls I make aren't just dolls at all. They're perfect replicas of living people."

Rose had sat back and folded her arms across her chest. Now, she smiled with a parent's tolerance of an overimaginative child. "As anyone will tell you, I never for a moment accepted your claim to be a writer. But this new lie—a doll maker, did you say? This one is so clever. So original. How on earth did you come up with it?"

"I suddenly remembered my brother. He called me Rodin, and the next thing I knew, I was looking at the doll I left behind here at the Southern Star. Do you know, I could actually feel my hands molding the face and later painting the features while I looked into a mirror."

"Hmm, how interesting. Only I seem to remember you telling us about your loneliness as an only child without siblings. Do you recall that, Dillon?" Rose asked pointedly.

Lacy felt sorry for her brother-in-law, who was trying so desperately to straddle the fence in neutral territory. She was quick to admit her guilt and keep him safely out of the quagmire. "Okay! So, there you are! Didn't I just tell you I was a liar? I am. No doubt about it. In fact, I'm finding out there are a lot of things I lied about."

"Well," Rose said, pushing herself to her feet. "I'm not embarrassed to admit you've caught me off guard with this new tactic of yours. I freely concede I don't have an inkling as to what you're up to, but I have to finish packing. Randy Hawkins is bringing the car to the front in thirty minutes." She turned her back on her daughter-in-law to issue a few last-minute instructions to her eldest son.

Lacy was dismissed like a circus freak that had initially both repelled and intrigued Rose, yet now only bored her. At least that was the impression Rose had tried for. Lacy wasn't fooled. She had won this battle with her surprise surrender and had caught Rose off balance. Pleased with the outcome of a match she'd never wanted any part of, Lacy noshed leisurely and sipped her cup of richly brewed coffee, barely heeding the conversation taking place just outside the room between her in-laws until she heard Jesse's name mentioned. Rose had said something about being home in time for his party on Saturday. Something else about Dillon checking with Mattie to see if the beading on her dress was completed.

Saturday was apparently Jesse's birthday and by custom, there would be a birthday party in his honor. Lacy made a mental note to check her closet for an appropriate gown. Shouldn't be a problem unless every one of the dresses turned out to be red.

Right now she had more serious things to worry about and, she thought as she entered the foyer and stopped a few feet behind her mother-in-law's arrow-straight back, a few last barbs to deliver on her way out.

"If you'll both excuse me, I'm on my way, too. I've got to brush my teeth and freshen my makeup so I can get an early start for town. Got another lie to track down, find out why I told it so I can set things straight with my husband."

That won their attention. They both stared at her.

"Could I ask a favor?" She posed this to Dillon, ignoring Rose entirely. "Could I borrow a few dollars? Jesse tells me I have money of my own somewhere. As soon as I recover the rest of my memory, I'll know where I left it and pay you back." She smiled, surprising even herself with the fun she was having. "Of course, considering what a liar I've turned out to be, I don't suppose there's any reason you should believe me."

Laughing, Dillon shook his head as he pulled his billfold from his back pocket. "Nope, I don't imagine I'll hold my breath waiting for you to pay me back." He held out three twenty-dollar bills. "This should hold you today."

"Thanks," Lacy said, accepting the money without hesitation. "Have a good trip, Mother Rose," she said over her shoulder as she brushed past the woman. At the bottom of the stairs, she paused to look back. "I just had another flash of recall. Funniest thing. I just remembered my mother's favorite saying: 'Every time you forget what you're about to say, you're saved from telling a lie.' Little did she know what a storyteller I'd turn out to be, eh?"

"Odd that you never mentioned your mother either," Rose said.

"No kidding? Surely I didn't claim I was hatched from a seashell."

Her mother-in-law ignored the question, choosing to ask one of her own instead. "Speaking of your many fabrications, Lacy, which one is it you hope to disprove by going into Rooster Corner? After all, the lies you were so fond of telling relate to who you were before Texas and Jesse," Rose said.

"That's what I thought, but surely Jesse told you about the horrible one I told him the day I left here last month." She waited, though she knew there wouldn't be a reply. She carefully watched their faces, thinking she was getting good at gauging their reactions. For one skipped heartbeat, she was afraid she'd been wrong, that the unblinking stares they returned signaled their absolute confidence in her guilt. "I'm talking about the abortion I *didn't* have," she clarified.

Dillon surprised her with his anger. "I don't know

what the hell is going on here, Lacy. I don't know anything about you being a writer or a doll maker. Or having a mother and brother after telling us how you were brought up by your grandmother. But I know what you done to Jesse when you killed his baby. That wasn't no lie. No one with an ounce of decency would've lied about something as important as that. And what's more, I don't believe you would've done it to Cybil. Not knowin' what it did to her every time she had to bury one of the babies she'd carried for almost nine months." His voice trembled and cracked with slipping control. "I'm not saying you didn't have a lot of spit and fire in you that galled us all, but you hurt for Cybil. I saw it when you didn't know I was lookin'. So, say what you want—hell, do what you want—but don't be telling me you'd lie about something that you knew would tear us all up worse than anything else you could've done."

Lacy looked down at the floor as he strode angrily from the room, bumping into her yet not even slowing. She'd seen the tears flood his eyes, and she felt shame resurge. She was getting pretty damned good. She'd made two men cry in the last few hours alone.

She raised her eyes, on the verge of wishing her mother-in-law a hasty good-bye, but the words stuck in her throat, caught by what she saw in the other woman's eyes. Fear.

Determination reclaiming dominance over her emotion, she folded her arms. "That's right, I'm not giving up. I don't have enough pieces to put this puzzle together yet, and the few I've found aren't fitting. But I'm going to put it all together because no matter what my motives were or who I was before, I'm nobody today except the woman who loves Jesse Pryde, and more importantly the woman *he* still loves." She nodded at her mother-in-law's wide-eyed denial. "Believe it. It's true. Oh, yeah, you're right, he hates me. But think about it. Love and hate run so close sometimes it's hard to tell one from the other. I know you understand what I'm saying. You're not exactly pure and saintly. So, I'd bet this sixty dollars R. Davis must have gotten so mad at you, you worried that he hated you even though deep down you were confident of his love."

Rose gasped, though what the reaction meant, Lacy didn't have a clue. She ignored the uneasiness that tingled in her fingertips as she pressed her point home. "If I'm right, and there's even a spark of love left in Jesse's heart for me, there must be something worthwhile in me to love. So, I'm going for it, Rose." She rolled away from the balustrade, stopping only a couple of steps above her mother-in-law. She didn't turn around. "Maybe when you get home for Jesse's birthday, we can start over."

"I hope so, too," Rose said. At least that's what Lacy *thought* she heard. But probably not. Probably merely wishful thinking.

As she started up the stairs once again, she was suddenly so drained, she wondered for a moment if she could make the climb. By the time she entered her room, she knew her visit to Rooster Corner was going to be postponed again. For now. For at least a couple of hours while she rested, regained her strength, and recouped her equilibrium.

She was asleep almost as soon as she stretched across the bed, but just before she dropped into a deep dream she thought she heard someone move on the far side of the room. The impression was just as swiftly gone, however, replaced by a panther with eyes as dark as its coat. The cat was joined by another, one so thin its ribs stood out against its coat that was not black but red as flame. And then more cats joined the first two. One by one they came, forming a circle until she was surrounded by six restless, pacing animals. She recognized each of them: Rose, Cybil, Dillon, Libby, Joey, and finally Jesse. They didn't growl or snarl as she would have expected. Rather, they purred softly, rhythmically, hypnotically. She knew it was a trick to win her confidence, for she understood as well that it was only a matter of time before they closed in for the kill. Yet, oddly, she wasn't frightened by the certainty of death; or the excruciating pain she would suffer when she was torn to shreds by their claws, her blood dripping from their jowls. She was awed by their courage and relentless pursuit. It was only right that she pay for her lies. And then she saw him standing above all the others on the granite boulders beside the waterfall. Clay Waters. She wanted to scream. No! *This* wasn't fair! She was accountable to *them,* not their hired assassin!

And then she was screaming, and it sounded exactly like the cry of the cats that circled her.

PART II

Along came a spider
And sat down beside her.
—*Little Miss Muffett*

Chief Anderson was indulging himself in a five-minute break. His feet crossed atop his desk, he stared at the far wall, his gaze somewhere between the twin framed portraits of the President of the United States and the Director of the Federal Bureau of Investigation. A smile worked on his face like an accordion, expanding and deflating as he thought of his six grandchildren. They were the source of his greatest joy. They were also the prime reason he worried about a world rampant with crime. In three years he would be retiring. Then he could spend all his free time doing what he enjoyed most: spoiling every one of them until they were rotten to the core. He only hoped a halfway sane society remained for them. With a sigh, he raked his fingers through his graying hair. Sometimes he just wasn't sure.

Dropping his feet to the floor, he straightened in his chair and pulled it closer to his desk. His gaze went immediately to the family picture taken only a few weeks before. Maybe the battle against crime was uphill. Maybe the good guys were even losing it, but these people—his wife, Judy, his kids, and those beautiful babies—were definitely enough reason to keep fighting.

He riffled through the stack of file folders on his desk—all current cases, all unresolved—selecting one and pulling it from the middle just as a knock sounded on the door. A glance at the wall clock to his right explained why the interruption hadn't come via his secretary and the intercom system. Twelve twenty-five. Becca was still at lunch.

He called out an invitation to enter, setting the file folder aside once again as Agents Gary Maltz and Frank Mandell entered his office single file.

Chief Anderson turned his attention to Gary, the junior agent of the two, yet the first through the door and also the man carrying the telltale yellow sheets of fax paper.

"What have you got?" he asked.

"Word just in from our man in Rooster Corner about our—"

The chief waved the rest of his sentence away. "Our witness, Lacy James-Pryde. Yeah, I got that much." He tapped the folder he'd been about to go through. "I was just about to reacquaint myself with the trouble our girl got herself into a few weeks back. So tell me, how is the unforgettable Lacy James-Pryde doing?"

"Well, according to this, *she's* doing hunky-dory. From what the agent's been able to pick up, she hasn't regained her memory yet, but maybe that explains the fact that whoever Sammy Wyatt hired for the hit hasn't tried again. Could be, however," Gary said, thumping the paper with the back of his hand, "Wyatt's man just hasn't been given the opportunity. She's been pretty well holed up at the hacienda or with her old man the whole time since she's been back."

"So, what you're telling me is that we're looking at a catch-22 here," the chief observed. "On one hand, we can be grateful she's safe for the moment. On the other, we can't forget that until she regains her memory we don't get what we want."

Both agents had taken seats in chairs directly in front of the bureau chief's desk. Agent Mandell shook his head as he sat back, maintaining his easy, relaxed posture, which was as much a reflection of his laid-back personality as of his seasoned maturity in law enforcement. Only his odd pale eyes that looked a century older than the rest of his youthful face gave away his excitement with their unusual luster. "No, sir, that's not exactly accurate. As a matter of fact, it looks like things could be ready to pop."

Agent Maltz reclaimed the ball; though unlike his partner, he sat on the edge of his seat. "Frank's right, Chief. Early this morning—now, I'm talking before the sun was even thinking about rising over the Lone Star state—Jesse Pryde left the ranch, headed for Dallas. Later," he paused to check the times given in the fax, then continued, "at eight-thirty, Jesse's mother, Rose Pryde, departed by chauffeured limousine for Dallas. Some twenty minutes after that, Liberty Ambrose and her husband, Joey Wong, headed for Dallas as well."

"Something big going on there?" Warren asked.

"No, sir," Gary answered with a shake of his head. "Far as we can tell, simple matter of coincidence.

"However, Jesse called the ranch from Dallas at six a.m. to tell his mother he was taking care of business at the offices of Southern Star Enterprises. She, in turn, announced that she was leaving for California to visit her terminally ill sister-in-law in Santa Barbara. Said she'd just gotten off the phone with her brother-in-law, who'd begged her to come."

The chief heard the "but" in the last sentence and raised his brows. "Go on."

"There was no incoming call from her brother-in-law or anyone else before Jesse's call. There *was* an outgoing call made by the senior Mrs. Pryde to American Airlines making reservations for a flight to Los Angeles."

"Which, incidentally, turned out to be the same flight that Mr. Wong and Ms. Ambrose departed on," Frank put in. "Their plane should be landing in about an hour."

Chief Anderson looked from one agent to the other as he rubbed his jaw. "Okay, so I guess we know where Rose Pryde is headed. We have to be careful there. Wyatt would love an excuse to scream violation of his civil rights guaranteed under the Constitution. Bottom line, there's probably not a darn thing we can do except advise everyone to be on the alert just in case Mr. Cool loses it and blurts something loud enough for us to pick up." His frown deepened. "But what about the others? Why were they on that flight?"

"Wong's catering a big do for Bruce Willis and his babe, Demi Moore. A milestone anniversary celebration or something," Maltz said. Then with a click of his tongue and shrug of his massive shoulders, he went on. "Liberty Ambrose. We don't know from nothing. Wong's thing has been scheduled for weeks. As far as we knew, Ambrose was enjoying a sort of extended hiatus except for one gig in Paris a couple of weeks back and another one a week or so earlier in the Big Apple.

Then this morning she purchased a first-class round-trip fare over the phone. Probably just decided she couldn't stand to be away from her new hubby. She's booked on a return flight home Friday night, though, instead of with lover boy's return flight Saturday."

"You got surveillance on them?" the chief asked.

Both agents looked at each other, then back at their boss. Maltz responded. "No, sir. Far as I knew, our orders were to do nothing except register arrivals and departures of all Southern Star residents. You want someone on them, we'll have to hustle."

Warren shook his head and waved away the suggestion. "No, forget it. Let's keep our attention focused on the clever Mrs. Lacy Pride. Is she still hanging tight at the ranch?"

"As a matter of fact, she was sleeping most of the morning. One of the reasons Jesse called from Dallas was to tell his mother that his wife's bedroom door—the one leading to the veranda, not the one inside—was busted. He wanted her to get someone up there to fix it right away." He grinned. "Guess who was one of the men she sent up to inspect the damage?"

The chief flashed a quick grin. "Waters. Yeah, I got that. So, what did he tell you? How did the door get broken?"

"Who the hell knows?" Maltz said.

Warren stared down at his hands that were laced except for the thumbs, which were frantically revolving one another. It was the only telltale sign of agitation anyone would ever detect. When he spoke, he was perfectly calm, even reflective. "But she was there asleep in her own bed, so it doesn't look like anyone tried to break in. Otherwise, one would think she'd either be too upset to sleep or at least hidden in another room."

Gary Maltz laughed. "If I was guessing, I'd bet she broke it in one of her famous temper tantrums. I don't suppose her short fuse is connected to her faulty memory bank."

"Anything else?" the bureau chief asked.

"As a matter of fact, there is." Frank pulled a folded sheet of paper from the inside pocket of his jacket, opened it and smoothed it out, then handed it over the desk. "Not much good to us as it turns out, but something interesting and proof positive that we're finally getting some cooperation from LAPD."

Anderson's eyes widened as he read the first line. "They found her car," he said, rare surprise ringing in his tone.

"Yep. Out off some dirt road in the Mojave, but gutted and burned."

The chief put down the paper, directing his gaze to the young agent. Why read what the man could tell him in half the time? "Any prints?"

"Yes, sir. Two sets. They've run 'em both. One belongs to our gal. No surprise there. The other one doesn't match anyone we have on record."

"Where were they lifted from?" Anderson asked. "Driver's side? Passenger?"

"Both. Passenger *and* driver side. Hers, too. Both sets, both sides."

"What does LAPD get from that?" Chief Anderson asked.

"Same as Frank and me," Maltz answered after a brief glance at his partner. "What about you?"

Warren drummed his fingers on the thick stack of manila folders for several thoughtful seconds, all the while staring at the six little faces of his grandchildren in the photo on his desk. "Hmm," he said, finally. "Along came a spider, who sat down beside her. That's what I get. What about you guys? That what we all getting?"

Both agents laughed.

Maltz said, "Well, we weren't exactly thinking nursery rhymes, Chief."

"Mother Goose, Gary. You ought to read her work sometime. She had a way of cutting straight to the heart of it."

Both men came out of their chairs, their bureau chief's message ringing as clear as crystal tapped with a spoon. Frank spoke for both of them. "We're on it, sir. I just wish we had something more to go on. 'Cause quite honestly, if Wyatt's hired a hit with someone we can't even tag, you know it ain't no rank amateur. He's paying some bucks and that means import."

"Maybe, maybe not. We've checked out anyone and everybody who's come to Rooster Corner in the past six months. We have histories on every last one of them."

"But she wasn't hit in Rooster Corner," Frank said. "She was hit right here under our noses. So, maybe our perp knew he couldn't get close to her there and drew her out to California somehow."

"Yeah," the chief agreed, nodding his head tentatively at the veteran's well-made points. "Or maybe he was right there all along, and we just didn't ID him ... *she* did. That would explain why she took off, leaving us all sitting around with our thumbs crammed up our butts. Remember how it didn't make sense to any of us? She wanted out of her past and inside that lifestyle bad enough to risk everything for it. Why would she just up and give it all away one day like someone swearing off chocolate?"

Neither man answered. What could they say? If they had the sixty-four-thousand-dollar answer to that one, they'd have it solved.

They were almost to the door when the chief stopped them. "If she so much as leaves the house to take a stroll with that dog, Godzilla or whatever the heck his name is, I want her watched."

"Right," Maltz said, turning the handle and opening the door.

"Hold it!" the chief said. "Mandell, go home and pack some things. I want you out there on that ranch tomorrow morning. I'll get it set up."

"Me?" Frank asked, the timbre of his voice rising an octave with his surprise. "Okay, sure, but may I ask why?"

"You escorted her to the airport when she went into the program, didn't you? And you stayed there until she got on the plane that took her to Texas, right?"

"Well, yes, sir, but—"

"So, maybe seeing you will strike a responsive chord in her memory." He snapped his fingers. "I've got it. They're having a party for her husband Saturday night. I'll get you inside the house. You'll work for that Wong fellow. While the old lady's away, you can make like a mouse and play. We've got to break this thing in the next few days or we'll lose her and everything else. The everything else I can live with if I have to, but I've never lost a single witness I've put into the program. I'm not going to start now when I'm only three years away from turning in my badge."

"Yes, sir," both men said in unison, their expressions as somber as his.

As soon as they stepped out of the office and pulled the door closed behind them, they exchanged silent queries with their eyes. Becca, the bureau chief's assistant, was at her desk once again, so neither man spoke until they'd wended their way through the building via a restroom stop, a check for messages at their desks, and a long ride in a lethargic elevator.

Then it was Gary who broke the fast.

"Jesus Christ, nursery rhymes! Is the guy just losing it, or so fucking sharp, he sent that one sailing over my head?"

"Which do you think?" Frank asked, pulling a pack of Camels from his shirt pocket. He lit one and took a couple of long pulls before going on. "The man's so right on, he's scary. Think about that spider thing for a minute. Somehow, someway, some*one* not only slipped in beside her in *her* car, he also managed to get behind the wheel, then tricked her into standing there while he drove it into her. Now, you tell me, just a verse from a bleepin' kiddie rhyme or did the chief pop that nail square on the head?"

"Yeah," Gary agreed grudgingly. "But you know what freaked me? His mention of the dog. Now, how the hell did he remember that? Shit, did anyone even ever mention that there *was* a monster mutt on that ranch?"

"I'm telling you," the younger man said. "He's The Man 'cause he never misses a beat. Gives me the heebie-jeebies. I've always admitted that."

"Okay, so it's not senility creeping in. I don't think it's just that he's The Man either. He's different about this one, about this witness. It's like he's committed the most minute detail of her file to memory. And you know what? I think it's about something more than keeping her alive or sticking with her on the hunt till she leads us to the treasure. *I* think our fearless leader's got himself a hard-on he can't get off."

"Give me a friggin' break, Maltz. The man's so committed to his wife, he makes Jimmy Carter look like the worst kind of lecher for lusting in his heart. There's his religion, too. Hell, he's some high muckamuck in the Mormon church. And geez, even Becca ducks out when she sees him heading her way with a new photo of the grandkids." He took another drag, blew the smoke out his nose again, and added his final evidence. "Anyways, you heard him. He's less than three years from retirement."

"Exactly. And what happens when a man starts feeling the bite of old age on his ass? He gets to looking around for a way to prove he's still got the stuff. Next thing you know, he's hungry for a hot young thing like our Lacy Pryde."

"Or," Frank countered, "if he's as smart as Chief Anderson, he simply accepts the inevitable. You know, that ultimately the *cojones* are gonna go the same way as the hair. Frisky suddenly takes on a whole new definition, and playing horsy for the kiddies is as good as it gets."

"Naw, now it's you who's not giving credit where credit's due. Babes have been after him long as I've known him. He may have a little iron at the temples, but that doesn't mean there's any less lead in his pencil. Fuck no! Besides, our witness wasn't just your everyday, garden-variety sweetmeat. She was such a hothouse specialty, a eunuch could get a hard-on looking at her." He paused long enough for Frank to start with an interjection, then cut him off. "*And* she's a ball buster, to boot. The kind of challenge dear old granddaddy might just start obsessing over."

"Ah, you're full of shit," Frank said, tossing his cigarette down on the pavement and smashing it under the toe of his plain brown standard-issue shoe.

"Hey, I'm not too stupid to know that those things'll kill you."

Frank laughed, not in the least upset about the latest cigarette lecture. He heard it every time he lit up, which was every time he was anywhere it wasn't prohibited. He didn't buy into the government scare tactics. Hell, he worked for the government. He knew firsthand how it operated. He was fond of telling his wife that Big Brother would be so far up the ass of every American citizen one day, he'd give the shit alert before the bowels got the word. That is unless the smog, terrorists, or Armageddon got 'em first. Cigarettes were definitely on the bottom of his worry list.

Gary slapped him on the back. "Go ahead. Yuck it up, pal. I'll send you a funny get well card when you're in the oncology ward dealing with the lung cancer that's gonna get you."

"Shiiit," Frank said, going on to share the nightmare he'd lived with for the past five years since becoming a federal agent. "I'm destined for my name on the wall. Frank Mandell, KIA. You can count on it. Some crazy's gonna take me out in the line of duty."

Killed in action. Not a joking matter. Not to the men and women who woke up at the start of every day with the potential of death staring them in the face. Gary wasn't laughing. In fact, he was suddenly as sober as the priest Frank had confessed his fear to just the past Sunday.

Frank chuckled and pulled another cigarette from his pocket. "Chill out, man. I'm just blowing smoke." He laughed again. "Hey! Blowing smoke! Is that good? Am I too clever, or what? Anyway, it was just a stupid defense against fanatical antismoking rhetoric."

"All right," Maltz said, his tone quietly accepting. "But if it becomes more than that, go in and see Dr. Ancolli." A smile spread. "Maybe it wouldn't be such a bad idea to go on back upstairs right now and talk to him before you head out for Texas."

"What? And let him pull the scabs off all my phobias so they really get going? No way, man. Besides, I'm masochistic. I like living with fear, on the edge. It's like sex. A real high and it hurts so good."

Moments later, their farewells said, Frank watched Gary get into his four-door powder-blue sedan. He climbed into another one, almost identical, and headed for home in the valley. Maybe he shouldn't have said anything to Maltz about the thing inside that awakened him in the middle of the night and caused sweat to bead on his upper lip the minute he was given a field assignment.

On the other hand, he had a particularly bad feeling about this one, and he sure couldn't tell Denise, his wife. Not with her seven and a half months pregnant with their first ... and second as it had turned out. Twins.

Geez, he could understand how proud the chief was. But for Frank, it was more than just about becoming a dad. It was about getting lucky enough to find a sweetheart like Denise who loved him when no one had ever thought of him as more than a homely Howdy-Doody. Then suddenly there he was thirty-eight and resolved to his destiny as a bachelor, and wham! In walks Denise. Comes into work one day, the new secretary on the job. Next thing he knows, they're datin', and last year, bing bang, they're doing the ol' stroll down the aisle. And now this. Almost forty years old and pregnant ... well, sort of. How lucky could a guy get? Just the thought of becoming a daddy made his heart do a real cool flap-jack imitation.

So, just in case his luck didn't hold out ... he had to tell it. Just in case things went down the wrong way, someone knew and could vouch for his instincts.

He lit another Camel, turned on the radio to his favorite station—easy listening—and rolled down his window.

Catching his reflection in the rearview mirror, he rubbed the top of his head briskly. Had luck with him now, that was for damned sure. He'd forgotten the surest rule of all: Rubbing a redhead was a guarantee of good luck.

All right! He was unwinding now! And glad he'd told Maltz, too. Insurance just in case. Now he could start focusing on the assignment: getting close to the witness who called herself Lacy because she was beautiful enough to wear it, and because it covered up everything that was marred and ugly underneath.

Chapter Twenty-two

Lacy awakened to the sound of muted voices and a dull, insistent banging. Blinking away the last vestiges of sleep, she pushed herself to a sitting position and struggled to focus.

The first thing she noticed was the time on the bedside table. Twelve-forty! Damn it. She'd slept the morning away.

"I'm sorry, Miz Pryde," a voice said from the direction of the veranda. "We didn't mean to wake you."

Alarm was slow coming as Lacy, still sluggish, sought to identify the voice. Heavy storm clouds and a hard rain had turned the world to blurred lines and fuzzy silhouettes of variegated gray. One by one Lacy separated them until she made out the forms of two men.

The first, crouched low in profile, appeared to hold one of the French doors in place, while the second one stood above him, working with a screwdriver at the jamb.

Though it was clear they were repairing the broken doors, Lacy's heart began an irrational race as she recognized the man standing. Clay Waters. Why him? Was it only coincidence that he'd been sent to her room or something more sinister?

A test to see if she recognized him?

A reminder of how easily he moved around the spread, even into her room, her private space?

Maybe more specific than that, a message: *I can get you anytime I want, anywhere I choose, easy as one, two, three.*

But not in her bed like a sitting duck, and not cowering like a cornered mouse!

She scrambled to her feet, forcing a smile onto her face and confidence into her walk. She looked from Waters to the other man, someone she didn't recognize. "Clay, isn't it?"

He seemed surprised. "Why, yes, ma'am. And this here's Johnny Golight." He chuckled, scratched the heavy stubble of a two-or three-day-old beard on his cheek, then smoothed his long mustache with his fingers. "But he's worked here longer than me, so you probably know him better'n I do."

Lacy shook her head. "Actually, no, I'm sorry. I . . . There's a lot I don't remember, people I don't recognize."

"Hey, that's okay," the man named Johnny said with a wide snaggle-toothed grin. "Probably don't help none that you're seeing me up here in yer room for the first time again neither. I'm hardly anywheres 'cepten the barn. Mostly, I jest sorta tend the livestock. Randy was helping Clay, here, fix these broke doors till Miz Rose asked him to drive her to the city."

Lacy suddenly remembered the strange dream she'd had, and on its heels, the impression she'd had as she drifted off that she'd heard someone moving around her room. "Were you in here when I came up from breakfast?"

Clay looked down at the toes of his scruffy boots, and she thought his face darkened with discomfort, though it was hard to tell in the heavy shadows.

"Um, yes, ma'am. Sorry about that. I was takin' the door off the hinges when you surprised me by coming in. I slipped out as quiet as a mouse the minute you laid down."

"But you came back before I was awake. Why?"

Johnny was standing now as well and exchanged a quick embarrassed look with Clay before answering for him. "I'm afraid that's my fault, Miz Pryde. I got the call for the doors to be fixed before Jesse gets home from the city tonight. So, when Clay told me you was sleepin', I said we should try to get the doors off and take 'em out to be fixed. We done that without disturbing you and was just putting 'em back again."

Lacy nodded, no longer caring if the whole damn bunch of ranch hands was standing in her bedroom. Jesse was coming home tonight! For some reason, she'd gotten the impression from his mother that he intended to stay in the city at least until his party on Saturday.

"Miz Pryde?" Johnny asked, his leathery face wrinkled into a thousand creases with his concern.

She smiled. "Oh, that's okay. Go ahead and get it done. I've got to leave, anyway."

"Are you all right?" Clay asked. "You, uh, if you don't mind me saying, you seem kinda funny, like maybe you're not quite awake yet."

Lacy shook her head, already walking away as she answered. "I'm fine. Just distracted. I shouldn't have slept so long. I've got things to take care of before Jess— my husband gets home."

Dismissing them, she went to the mirror to apply a touch of makeup and smooth the front of her hair once again. Her eyes still had that swollen, sleepy look. Otherwise, for the business she had in Rooster Corner, her appearance was good enough. She snatched the keys from the dresser and turned toward the door. She stopped short with a startled squeak as Clay put a hand on her shoulder.

"Sorry," he said, the rueful smile that accompanied his apology lending him a boy-next-door harmlessness. "Either you're a tad jumpy or I've picked up a knack for scaring you without intendin' it."

Lacy studied his face for a long moment before giving it up. His expression was as guileless as an infant's. So, what did she expect? The overt sinister mien of Snidely Whiplash? A cold-blooded killer would have mastered the art of disguising his true nature behind an appropriately deceptive mask. "I'm sure it's just me, Clay," she said, a bit too hastily, her tone clipped. She managed a thin smile. "I'm in a hurry is all. What did you want?"

"Well, that's just it. You being in such a rush 'n' all and it raining cats and dogs out there, I thought you might want me to drive you into town. I could just hang around and wait till you've taken care of your business."

No way! Lacy thought, though she was proud of the nonchalance in her tone when she replied aloud, "Oh, gee, thanks. That's really nice of you, but I need to get out by myself. Besides, I know Jesse wants these doors finished, and I've got a lot of errands." She raised her hand, waving to both men as she paused long enough to grab the purse she'd packed with her driver's license, a tube of lipstick, and the electronic garage-door opener Jesse had given her. From the corner of her eye, she saw the three crumpled twenty-dollar bills she'd borrowed from Dillon. They were lying on the bed next to where she'd fallen asleep. Snatching them up and putting them in the purse, she backed from the room. "Thanks again, Clay. You, too, Johnny. See you later."

She didn't stop again until she reached the hall closet. Damn it! There must have been more than a dozen coats and jackets hanging there. More than likely one of the windbreakers or full-length raincoats belonged to her, only she didn't know which ones. Stomping her foot in an abbreviated tantrum, she yanked a three-quarter, lightweight khaki parka from its padded hanger. Too small for Rose, she reasoned as she shrugged into it. It could belong to Cybil, but if so, she'd apologize later. She flinched as the thought of her sister-in-law called to mind Dillon's angry eruption about her claimed abortion and its effect on his wife.

Not now, she told herself firmly. She'd deal with that later. Right now she had to stay focused: She had to prove the lie she'd told when she claimed to have had an abortion. No matter what the implications or the consequences of that lie, she'd deal with them later, *after* she'd convinced Jesse of the truth.

Resolve firmly planted once again, she made one last stop at the telephone table in the kitchen. Flipping impatiently through the yellow pages of the phone book, she found the one she was looking for, ripped it out, and shoved it into her pocket. Then she hurried through the house and out the back door, pulling her hood up over her hair and ducking her head against the hard-driving rain as she ran toward the garage. She fumbled in her purse for a few seconds before pulling out the compact remote-control box and aiming it at the garage where Jesse indicated the Porsche was parked. By the time she reached her destination, the door was rising and already high enough for her to dip beneath.

A moment later she buckled her seat belt and turned the key in the ignition. Then she gripped the steering wheel and took a good deep breath. "Here goes everything," she said.

*   *   *

She turned south on the highway, heading in the direction Randy and Clay were going two days before when she'd first met up with them again. They'd said they were going into town. She only hoped that the way was a straight shot or at least well directed with road signs. The windshield wipers on the smooth-running little car were dueling valiantly with the rain. Still, for the first several minutes, Lacy drove slowly, carefully studying signs and watching the road for unexpected bends and twists. Soon, however, she relaxed enough to study the names on the crumpled sheet of yellow telephone book paper she'd taken from her pocket and smoothed against the steering wheel. Only three doctors practicing in Rooster Corner; one of them in family medicine, another in pediatrics, the third in veterinary medicine. Her gaze flashed quickly to the street, then back to the name of the obvious choice: Dr. Raul Trajillo.

She registered the address, then dropped the paper to the seat beside her. Her hands tightening their grip on the steering wheel, she glanced into the rearview mirror. Resolve. That's what she read in her eyes and found in the flatness of her lips.

Headlights flashed off the mirror as a vehicle came up on her at a hair-raising clip from behind. Seconds after, its horn blaring, a whir of red streaked past with alarming closeness before swerving into the single southbound lane once again and forcing Lacy to slam on her brakes as a blinding tidal wave of water was thrown up onto her windshield.

Lacy watched it disappear into the storm-blackened distance as she recovered her equilibrium and let loose a long-held breath. Only then did she realize that it was a pickup truck similar to the one Jesse drove that had very nearly scared the crap out of her.

In the next couple of miles, two more trucks flew past her at stupendous speeds, dousing the windshield of the compact car and jangling Lacy's nerves. Did everyone in Texas drive like they were hightailing it from a posse?

Headlights came out of nowhere from the opposite direction. The car was on her in seconds, then flying past her in a whir of blue, and as Lacy looked in the rearview mirror, the red taillights disappeared in seconds. Well, that answered that one. Apparently fast and loose was another thing Texans did bigger and better than everyone else.

At last she saw the sign announcing Rooster Corner, population 6,290, and a half mile farther the vague watery outlines of buildings and streetside mercury lights that glowed prematurely in the darkness of the summer squall.

Slowing from the crawl of twenty-five miles per hour to fifteen, Lacy squinted at storefronts and street signs searching for the address she'd memorized.

It only took her a few seconds to realize that though the lights burned outside on the street, on the inside most of the buildings were dark. Had there been a power outage?

Then she heard them. Sirens blared and whirred nearby and above the roofline to the west, black gusts billowed and churned in a sky already darkened and roiling by storm clouds. Smoke!

Lacy pulled into a parking place along the deserted street, turned off the ignition, and jumped from the car. Her heart was slamming in her chest as she dashed along the sidewalk, fighting the wind for control of the hood on her jacket. Rain slashed against her face and soon her jeans clung to her as heavy as canvas sailing brought down by a storm. Lacy ducked her face and ran.

A fire blazed nearby despite the heavy downpour. She could hear it as she rounded the street corner and by the time she reached the next intersection, she could see flames licking the sky as if it rained fuel instead of water.

The sirens had stopped now, but hundreds of raised voices kept up the din.

A stitch in her side slowed her to an awkward, gimpy pace just as she arrived at the corner of Second and San Crista. Recognition brought her up short. San Crista. This was the street she'd been looking for, the street that Dr. Trajillo's office was on.

A crowd of dozens stood watching—some in clusters, hugging and weeping, others alone and awestruck—as dozens more fought the fire that blazed from the windows and roof of what moments before had surely been a grand two-story white house. Even from a distance of several hundred feet away, Lacy could feel the heat of the blaze on her face and taste its acrid fumes on her tongue. Smoke stung her eyes and burned in her lungs. She swiped away tears and coughed up soot and felt fear curl along her spine.

Someone wailed pitifully as twin pillars toppled with the collapse of the front porch. Seconds later, three men ran, half carrying, half dragging the same woman across the street to hand her over to a small crowd of people standing only a few feet from where Lacy watched.

"Hold her here, goddamn it! There's nothing she can do for him and getting herself killed ain't gonna help nothing!"

"You shore he's still inside?" one of the men keeping the hysterical woman from dashing back across the street asked.

"Don't know! Only going by what she claims!"

Her face and hair transformed into a helmet of black by smoke and soot, the woman writhed and bucked for freedom, and Lacy turned away, sickened by her inability to help.

"Hold on, now, Lenora," an elderly man who stood only inches from Lacy was saying. "If he's inside that inferno, he's gone, but he's past sufferin' and on to a better place. So you hang to that, gal, just like he'd want you to."

The others, men and women alike, turned to each other, seeking and offering comfort at the same time in their embraces, sobbing and babbling as they all sought to assuage the rawness of their fresh hurt.

Lacy felt like a voyeur standing there baldly witnessing their pain. She could sympathize, but she was apart from them and their tragedy.

Turning her gaze to the flaming house once again, she tried to focus her thoughts there as well. This was sad, tragic, but none of her business.

"I don't understand," a voice said from a place just to her left.

Lacy looked at the young man who had just spoken. Dressed in a grimy flannel shirt that hung open and dripped rain, and mud-splattered overalls that were tattered and ripped clean through in both knees, his lank, shoulder-length dark hair was uncovered and plastered to his forehead. He couldn't have been more than sixteen or seventeen though he dragged on a filterless cigarette that he cupped in his hand with the air of a seasoned smoker, and his pale gray eyes, though reflecting disbelief and sadness, nevertheless had an odd flatness about them.

Lacy turned back to the fire, but not before thinking that he was looking on this tragedy as just another of life's cruel hoaxes to be added to a list that was way too long and one he was way too familiar with.

He spoke again, his voice so quiet and emotionless, it took Lacy a moment to register the punch he delivered with his words. "Folks is talking about how he was murdered. But why'd anybody want to kill a guy like Dr. Trajillo, who was always there to help, then burn his house to the ground? Just answer me why."

Lacy's head whipped around, and she grabbed the boy's arm. "Did you say Dr. Trajillo?" she asked.

"Yeah," he said, pulling his arm from her grip and tossing the spent cigarette butt into a puddle. "Who the hell'd you think it was?"

Lacy watched him as he stalked off, while she stood rooted in place as she struggled against overwhelming horror. Then, her hand pressed to her mouth, she held back a scream as she staggered to one of the buildings behind her and leaned against its stuccoed wall. Tears that had nothing to do with the smoke and fire spilled over her lashes and a new wound opened in her heart.

Sweet Jesus! Dr. Raul Trajillo, dead. Murdered. And that poor woman who'd been led away from the burning house, his wife? Of course, his wife. Oh, God. And why, dear God, why?

But that was a question Lacy didn't dare probe. Not too closely and not now.

She focused on the less significant consequences of the dreadful tragedy; the effect it would have on her. She'd suffered a major blow, no doubt about it. She'd come looking for vindication that might now be lost to her forever.

Oh, God, how could she be thinking about herself? A man was dead, his wife a widow and homeless. What kind of selfish bitch was she to worry about disproving the lie to Jesse when so much more had been lost?

She covered her eyes with her arms crossed in front

of her face, though the moment she removed her hand from her mouth a low-pitched moan slipped from between her lips. She rocked from side to side in anguish, and shame, and disbelief.

Men were suddenly shouting, and she felt the ground beneath her tremble as they raced toward the crowd.

"Run!"

"Get out of here!"

"Fire ... propane!"

"—Gonna blow!"

"Run, damn it!"

Lacy joined the hysterical crowd running for their lives. She ran past the street where she'd parked the car, past a church where many of the group broke off to huddle and weep. She ran until she was the only one left, not stopping until she reached a school yard that was abandoned by both rain and summer recess. Gulping in air with all the gusto of a sprint runner, she sank to a railroad tie that banked a sandbox on the playground. Hugging her waist, she squeezed her eyes shut and listened to the blood pound in her ears. Seconds later the explosion rocked the earth and startled a weak squeal from her lips.

A second, milder explosion followed, then a third. Lacy sat tensed for a long time waiting for more aftershocks. Eventually, her shoulders drooping, she let go of worry about what was happening at the site of the terrible disaster.

Hugging her ankles and burying her face against her knees, she wept.

She wept for the slain doctor, and for herself, and for the whole world that was so ugly and mean and topsy-turvy it could never be righted again.

Chapter Twenty-three

"Well, damn it, missy, this is sure the last place I ever expected to find you." The voice came out of nowhere and was as startling as the earlier propane explosions.

Lacy jumped at the intrusion, raising her head at the same time.

A woman resembling a sumo wrestler for her grandiose proportions and high gloss jet-black hair that was pulled up in a severe top knot was crouched in front of her. A grin spread across the stranger's face as easy as warm donut glaze. At once, instead of jiggling rolls of malleable putty, her features were transformed. Her rouged cheeks became plump cherry gumballs. Raisin-black eyes sparkled and snapped. Her mouth that had been almost lost in folds of excess flesh metamorphosed to an uncommonly pretty smile of full, candy-apple red lips and toothpaste-commercial white teeth. A myriad of friendly lines that bracketed her mouth and jutted from her eyes testified to her penchant for laughter.

Forgetting her misery for a few seconds, Lacy found herself responding to the stranger. "You know me?" she asked, though she immediately realized how silly the question was. Obviously, the woman did, else why the comment about finding her in the last place she would have expected? Besides, even though everyone was a stranger to her, most of the townfolk probably were acquainted with her at least by sight. "Never mind. That was stupid. Of course, you know me. You as much as said so from the start. It's just that—"

"*You* don't know *me* from Adam," the woman finished for her. "That's all right, missy. I know all about that amnesia thing. Leastwise, I heard the *claim* same as everybody else." Again the smile that could warm the toes of a polar bear napping on an iceberg. "Only now I see for myself, this isn't just a mean trick you've come up with to get back inside that comfy life you had going for yourself before you screwed it all up."

Lacy flinched at the harsh candor, though she was almost instantly mollified by the matter-of-factness she'd detected in tone. Obviously, the words hadn't been intended as an attack.

The woman reached for her hand. "Here, help me up. I'm not as spry as I once was. Going down's still a favorite exercise, if you get my gist, but the getting up's a whole different thing."

Lacy didn't get the risqué implication for a moment. When she did, she laughed spontaneously.

"I'm Cookie Conchita," the woman said when both of them were standing. "Got a little Tex-Mex bar 'n' grill about three blocks from here. My sister, Nola, opens up, and I do the closing. Today, I'm going in a couple of hours early to inspect the damage." She glanced at her companion. "You know about the fire and poor Doc Trajillo?" At Lacy's nod, she went on. "Anyway, Nola called me. Says there were only a few broken glasses and a cracked coffee carafe from the explosion. But I've never been good at taking anyone's word for anything. Always gotta see it firsthand—like you and this memory loss thing, for example—so I'm going in early. Good damn thing, too. The storm may have passed over, but looks to me like you trapped most of the rain in your clothes. We gotta get you toweled off and into something dry."

"Thanks," Lacy said, though a note of doubt rang in the word.

Cookie picked it up and spewed laughter from her belly like lava from a volcano. "Hey, I'm lovin' this. I keep forgettin' that you don't remember the difference between shit and shinola. You don't remember Nola either, and you're thinking she's big as me. Ha! That's a good one. Don't worry, she takes after my dad who was a skinny little Irish runt. Me, I got lucky. Inherited from my ma's gene pool—a Greek goddess of regal proportions. Had the kind of softness a man could lose himself in. Most often what must've happened 'cause after one night we never saw 'em again." She laughed again.

"That's me, too. A regular amazon. But Nola's no bigger than a gnat, same as you. Point is, her clothes'll fit, and she keeps a fresh change in the broom closet."

Lacy was looking up at the sky, wondering when it had stopped raining. She wondered, too, how a woman who was half Greek, half Irish had ended up with a name like Cookie Conchita. Most of all, she was wondering if there was any connection between the doctor's death and her search for proof to absolve her of a bogus abortion. Oh, God, she hoped not. How many sins could one soul bear?

"Here we are," Cookie said as they arrived at the curb and a two-toned white and turquoise Chevy Impala that looked as if it had just been driven off the showroom floor though its winged rear fenders and extraordinary length dated it by more than three decades. She pointed to the front passenger door. "It's unlocked. Climb on in. This princess is a collector's dream. Seats are covered in plastic, though, and I've got disposable paper floor mats no top of the real ones, so don't worry about getting anything wet."

Five minutes later the princess parked safely in a one-car parking zone in a private lot behind the restaurant, and her reintroduction made to Cookie's reedy, red-headed sibling, Nola Applebee, Lacy sat on a bar stool sipping cider through a straw. She was dressed in a borrowed sleeveless plaid shirt and a studded denim miniskirt that she was having a lot of trouble picturing the sixty-something Nola wearing. Cookie was behind the counter running an inventory of the surviving glassware.

"Did you know me?" Lacy asked.

"Huh?" Cookie muttered with a half glance over her shoulder. Then, her full attention caught by the question, she turned to face her lone customer. "I thought we'd gotten past that point. Course I knew you."

"No, I mean did you *know* me? Did we talk? Did I tell you about me?"

"Yeah, as a matter of fact, I knew you about as good anyone. Better even than Jesse, maybe, 'cause you confided in me."

Yes! At last someone she could talk to. Someone she could trust. Lacy pressed her eyes closed as she gulped back grateful tears. Somehow, her heart had instantly recognized the only friend she'd had in Rooster Corner. Her bottom lip trembled as she braved a smile. "I knew it."

Cookie laid her clipboard and pen aside and leaned forward, distributing a portion of her weight to her forearms. "You remembered anything at all?"

Lacy shook her head, still struggling with her emotions that had been banged around pretty good with the day's events. "No, I mean, yeah, a few things. A doll, um"— she paused, swiping at tears that rebelliously poured over her lashes—"a couple of scattered memories from my childhood . . ."

Cookie patted her hand, "Hey, calm down. I flipped the CLOSED sign. It isn't gettin' turned around until I take a notion, which isn't going to happen till I'm good and ready. Nola's grilling beef fajitas. We'll talk while we eat. Start with the easy stuff. Work up to what's got you so down in the mouth. How does that sound?"

That did it. The dam broke and the floodwaters spilled out. Lacy was mortified to be weeping like a tearful three-year-old in front of a virtual stranger. She expected and dreaded the obvious—a suffocating hug between the pillows that were Cookie's breasts—and got the opposite: nothing.

Cookie left her alone until the tears had dried up, and she was beginning to wonder if both sisters had forgotten her and gone home. She was on the verge of going into the kitchen to investigate when the swinging aluminum doors suddenly burst open with Cookie carrying a tray filled with covered dishes. A jerk of her head and a "come and get it" were invitation enough for Lacy, who slipped from the stool and joined the proprietress at the table.

Minutes later Lacy rolled her eyes and swallowed a sumptuous bite of the concoction she'd put together under Cookie's direction—tortilla, a slice of tenderloin, onion, tomato, guacamole, and sour cream. "Mm, this is wonderful."

"Try the beans," Cookie directed.

"I did. They're great. Everything is."

They ate in companionable silence for a while. Music played from a jukebox and every now and then Cookie got up to fetch more chips and salsa. Nola had gone home, so except for the occasional ringing of the telephone that Cookie said the answering machine would catch, their peaceful respite was uninterrupted.

At last, feeling sure she was going to pop, Lacy leaned back against her chair. Legs outstretched, she slid down in her seat and groaned. "That was so good I don't want to quit, but I don't have room for even another sip of water."

Cookie had just polished off the last of several tacos and reached for a plate of enchiladas. "So, let it settle, then you can eat some more."

Lacy laughed. "I came here a lot, didn't I?"

Her mouth full, Cookie could only nod.

"Tell me about your name. How did you become Cookie Conchita?" When the other woman pointed at her mouth, Lacy giggled again. "Okay, when you've finished."

Cookie answered as she went to the bar for a beer that Lacy turned down with a shake of her head.

"Damn, I've told this so many times, I think I'll change it just to keep from boring myself to death. Okay, let me see. When I was fifteen, I went to work in a small little diner in St. Charles, Missouri. Fred Delinski owned the place. My real name's Courtney—but puleese, do I look like a Courtney? So Fred called me Cookie. Eighteen months after I started working for him, we got married. Nola was older, already married with a couple of kids. Fred hired her when her husband got laid off from the Ford plant there. Anyway, pretty soon, I was Cookie to everyone.

"Four years later Fred had a heart attack and died. Nola and Barry—that was her old man—moved to Houston, and a few months later I sold the place and went tagging after my big sis to Texas. I got a job as a waitress, of course. What else would I do, that being the only work I knew. This time my boss was a sexy little guy named Julio Hernandes. He nicknamed me Conchita. We married the next year and had us the best little business and the hottest love affair in the history of south Texas. When he came down with prostate cancer ten years later, we joked about how all the experts claimed sexual inactivity was the leading cause of that type of cancer. But it wasn't a laughing matter. Julio was gone six months later and I hightailed it outta there so fast, I hardly remember leaving. Just couldn't stand being where he wasn't. I was headed back to Missouri when my car conked out on me two miles outside of Rooster Corner. I called Nola from a motel room to tell her what had happened. That's when she told me they'd already found a buyer for our place. Next thing I knew, I saw this empty building, thought about settling, and here we are sitting in Cookie Conchita's twenty-two years later."

"You never remarried?"

"Hell, yes, I remarried. Four more times, now. Lookin' for number seven even as we breathe. As I always tell 'em, 'I ain't the luckiest person to tie yourself to, but I'm damned sure gonna make sure your years with me are the sweetest.' So far, no one's disagreed with me yet."

Lacy smiled for a few seconds before it faltered and failed. Then she said, "Guess my style's more love 'em and leave 'em."

"We gettin' down to what you been wanting to talk about now?" Cookie asked.

Lacy drew a circle in the tablecloth with a single tine of her fork while she considered whether or not she was ready. Then she nodded. "Yes. I'm ready."

Cookie sat back and folded her arms, though she hung on to the neck of her beer bottle. "So, shoot. Tell me what you know. Ask what you're not sure of."

Lacy hesitated only long enough to choose a place to start. She decided to dive right in. "Was the doctor who died in the fire today the same man I claimed to have gone to for an abortion?"

"Ha! So you've figured it out, have you?"

Lacy was confused. Then it hit her. "That I was never really pregnant, you mean?"

When Cookie nodded over her beer bottle, Lacy almost collapsed with relief. "But I don't know *why,*" she said. "Was I that cruel? That desperate? That . . . that crazy? *What?*"

"All of the above, I think."

"Damn it!" Lacy said, frustrated by more word play. "Just tell me."

"I don't know everything. Hell, I can't even prove it

was a lie—about there being a baby, that is. All I know is one day you came in here, pulled me in the back, and told me you were leaving. You were all wild-eyed, shaking. You said you'd just come from Raul's office. Told me you'd paid him twenty thousand dollars to get rid of the kid you didn't want.''

"But you just said I wasn't—"

"Wait!" Cookie said, her tone sharp and impatient for the first time. "I'm telling you like it happened, and it's my way or the highway, got it?"

"Sorry, go on," Lacy said, her legs crossed and a booted foot swinging in rapid, agitated strokes like an oar in a racing scull.

"I cracked up. Not 'cause it was funny, 'cause it was ridiculous! Told you flat out that no one was stupid enough to pay twenty grand for a first trimester abortion that wouldn't cost anyone else more than a few hundred bucks. You shot back that she would if it made the difference between staying alive and dying.

"That's when I got it. I said, 'He's found you and hired a hit' or maybe it was 'He knows where you are and he's sent someone to kill you.' Something to that effect. I don't remember my exact words.''

"Who?" Lacy cried. "Who were you talking about? Clay Waters?"

Cookie blinked. "Clay? Hell, no, not Clay. Least that's not the man *I* was talking about. Could be the fellow your boyfriend sent, I guess." She stared thoughtfully at the label on the bottle in her hand, then looked up. "It's possible he's the guy hired for the hit. Showed up a month or so before you took off. But ... naw, Clay's one of the good guys. I'd almost bet on it."

"I think you might lose," Lacy said, her voice as flat as her hopes that Cookie had deflated with talk of a boyfriend. Her fingers trembled as she pressed them to her temples and tried to steady her thoughts. "Oh, God. Tell me who you meant and what I said that gave you the impression I was lying about the abortion.''

"Whoa, missy. You want me to tell you everything, you got to sit there and listen, okay?''

So Lacy listened. Sickened. Disgusted. Shocked. Eventually numbed by the chilling, lurid truths about the *real* Lacy James-Pryde.

Cookie told Lacy an astonishing story about her decade-long relationship with mobster Sammy Wyatt; about how she'd testified against him, then fled southern California under the protective umbrella of the FBI following her lover's conviction in federal court for murder.

Her tone harder than ever, she repeated Lacy's boast about already having Jesse picked out before the key had even been turned in her ex's cell and shackled almost as soon as she stepped off the private plane on Texas soil. "I remember you said, 'Poor baby didn't have a chance. He was mine for the taking before he knew he was even on the auction block.'"

In the first few minutes as she listened, Lucy rocked back and forth, comforting her weeping soul as a mother soothes a wailing infant. Soon, though, devastation draining her, she simply sat, accepting the blows and bleeding inside.

There was an icy glint in Cookie's eyes, and a razor-sharp edge in her tone as she spoke. But it was a facade that failed to entirely conceal her innate softness as wisps of compassion and caring slipped through the cracks of her steely veneer.

Lacy's gaze darted for her hands that were clasped in her lap as understanding dawned. This woman had loved her! But why? How?

As if reading her thoughts, Cookie answered the question she hadn't posed aloud.

She explained that Lacy was always looking over her shoulder, afraid that Sammy would find her somehow. She said Lacy had finally told her because Cookie knew everything that went on within a hundred-mile radius of Rooster Corner five minutes before it happened. If a stranger showed up looking for her, Cookie would be the first to find out.

Lacy had told her she was returning to the Southern Star only long enough to pack a few things. Then she was out of there. Gone forever, and that's when Cookie had put it all together about the faked abortion. She asked why Lacy was bothering with it right then, that day, if she was so sure she'd been found when she could end an unwanted pregnancy anywhere after she was away and safe.

"And what did I say?" Lacy asked, interrupting for the first time in several long minutes.

"You said, 'Because Jesse will hate me. It's the only way to keep him from coming after me.'"

Lacy was startled by the tears that suddenly filled the older woman's eyes. "Cookie?"

"I'm sorry," she said, dabbing at them with a corner of her linen napkin. "It's just now, seeing what that scumbag Wyatt did to you—the scars. That's how the accident happened, isn't it? He found you and ran you down. I knew it!"

Lacy's eyes widened. It had never occurred to her that the car that had smashed into her could have been driven with deliberate intent to kill. Oh, God! But she couldn't think about that now. She had to be sure that the story of her abortion was just that, a fabrication offered to guarantee Jesse's hatred. "Forget about that, Cookie. Go back to the abortion. You still haven't told me why you were so sure it was a lie."

Cookie hunched her thick shoulders. "That's easy. You admitted it. Right after the part about Jesse. I'd said, 'So, now the truth will out. There hasn't been any abortion. It's a lie to keep Jesse at bay, and now you've come here to buy insurance by confiding in me because Jesse knows you trust me. Raul'll argue patient/physician confidentiality, but Jesse'll convince him to admit he performed the procedure just as you said. He'll come straight here after that 'cause he knows you wouldn't leave town without telling me good-bye, and I wouldn't let you go without telling me why you were leaving.'"

"And just like that"—Lacy snapped her fingers—"wham bam, thank you, ma'am, I caved in," Lacy said, derision sharp in her tone.

"Caved in? You? Ha! Not hardly. We were in the kitchen, like I said. You picked up a butcher knife and backed me against the freezer with it. Said if I told anyone the truth I'd better be saying my rosary and praying at the same time that Sammy's man got the job done, 'cause otherwise you'd be back to cut my tongue out."

Lacy pressed her fingers to her temples, shaking her head from side to side at the same time. "I don't believe this! None of it makes any sense. I don't understand why Dr. Trajillo would agree to something so unethical. And you, my God, if I was your friend, why would I threaten you, and why would you help me hurt a man like Jesse?"

"Think about it. Nothing complicated about it," Cookie said as she leaned on the table to hoist herself from her chair. "Gonna get me another beer. Want anything?"

Lacy ignored the question. "Explain it to me because I don't get it."

Cookie cracked the lid off the frosty beer bottle with a sharp snap, then tipped it up to her lips. A moment later she plopped heavily into her seat once again. "Raul was a good man—God rest his poor soul—but he was human and not any different from the rest of us here in Rooster. One way or the other, we all owe the Prydes. Raul was as indebted as any of us. More so than most."

Lacy leaned forward to point a finger at her hostess. "He owed Jesse. He was a good man. But I show up in his office, offer him twenty thousand dollars to fake a reported abortion, and he immediately forgets his allegiance to the Prydes, his oath as a doctor, and takes my money. Yeah, certainly sounds like a real prince to me."

"That's precisely what he was. A gentle, loving prince. But he has a daughter who's locked away in a very costly ivory tower called Brookhaven Sanitarium. Her name's Marissa. She's mentally ill and Raul pays through the ass to keep her in the posh private facility instead of moving her to the state institution. He put his practice up for sale several years ago when the money began to dry up, but your mother-in-law convinced him to stay. She pays most of Marissa's hospital bills in exchange for medical favors such as biannual physicals for the men who work at the Southern Star."

"That still doesn't explain why he'd risk incurring their wrath. I mean, could twenty thousand dollars come close to what she must have paid him?"

"What if she encouraged his cooperation in your scheme?" Cookie asked.

Lacy's eyes widened. Oh, God, it did make perfect sense. He must have called Rose right after she approached him about the claim to abort a nonexistent pregnancy! And of course Rose would have been only too happy to go along with the surefire means of ridding her home once and for all of her hated daughter-in-law.

"I asked if you were as sure of Raul's silence and that's when you shocked the shit out of me. Grabbed the shoulder bag from the counter where you'd dropped it and pulled out two thick stacks of bills—one in each hand.

" 'Twenty thousand dollars, Cookie,' you said. 'Same as I paid Dr. Trajillo. You're right. It wasn't payment for getting rid of a kid. I'm too careful to mess up like that. It was the price of insurance to make sure the medical records *confirmed* an abortion if Jesse insisted on checking. Now, I'm buying a second policy insuring me that the whole damned town'll find out what a cold-hearted bitch he married.' "

"So, you took the money and kept my secret," Lacy said, more to herself than to her hostess.

The tears long gone, Cookie's body jiggled from head to toe with her laughter. "Hel-l-l no!" She wiggled her fingers creating a kaleidoscope of color as the brilliant gems in her rings danced and flashed. "First of all, do I look hard up enough to you to take a bribe dirty as that?" Then in a quieter, almost reproachful tone, "Something even more important you probably don't remember. In the few months that you were here, I loved you, girl."

Lacy didn't want to hear this. Not any of it. "But why? How?" she cried, covering her face with her hands as utter horror and disbelief rocked her. Suddenly weighted with sadness, she let her hands fall into her lap once again. "Nobody liked me. And I went after you with a knife, Cookie!"

Cookie didn't answer right off. Instead she let her gaze move over the features of Lacy's face. Then she fixed her stare on a spot of wall past Lacy's shoulder, and her dark eyes, instantly as glassy as midnight pond water, told it all even before she replied with typical candor. "You were so fucking beautiful. Smart, too, and exciting." She laughed. "The excitement! That was what was so refreshing. You breathed new life into this predictable little town that I swear to God was dying from boredom. The Prydes are our celebrities, you know? And you even made all of them—except for Jesse, of course—seem ordinary. When you walked into a room every woman wanted to be you and every man wanted to fuck you. Jesus, it was like you were Sharon Stone or something. Everyone kissed ass—I don't know, hoping you'd flash 'em a smile or something else more interesting, if you get my drift—and I was the one you chose. *Me!* The joke of Rooster Corner."

"Don't," Lacy said. "Don't put yourself down like that."

"You think it's me? Honey, there's an unofficial Cookie Conchita joke-of-the-month club." At Lacy's skeptical look, she slapped the tabletop irritably. "Swear to God. Way it works, the person who comes up with the best one gets dinner here in my place. The losers pick up the tab. I've heard three this month. Wanna hear my personal favorite?" she asked as she raised the hem of her tablecloth-wide apron to wipe away tears that had begun to spill over her lashes.

"No," Lacy said, reaching over to lay a hand on the woman's arm.

But Cookie shook off her hand and told her anyway. " 'Know what a Cookie Conchita six-pack is? Dead soldiers.' Get it? Six dead husbands? Six dead soldiers."

"That's awful!" Lacy said, tears of pity filling her eyes.

"Oh, there's more. Worse. Sometimes they hurt. Mostly, though, I just pretend they're funny and laugh along with everyone else. Anyway, that's why I loved you. You were selfish and vain, oven mean, but you were so freaking beautiful you intimidated the hell out of everyone. And when they saw how you came in here to talk to me, they started looking at me different." The tears dried now, she met Lacy's gaze again. "Don't get me wrong. I wasn't fooled, not for a second. I knew you were using me, first to get to Jesse, then to keep tabs on what was happening around town. I just didn't care, because I needed you.

"I think it was that way for Jesse, too. Probably still is, same as for me."

Lacy shook her head. "I don't understand. What do you mean?"

Cookie laughed. "Who would have ever thunk it? Clever, scheming Lacy James-Pryde, denser than a hedge."

Lacy ignored the barb though it scratched. "Explain what you mean by it was that way for Jesse, too?"

"You remember anything about mythology?" she asked, though evidently it was a rhetorical question, for she went on without pause. "Not so sure I've got it right myself. But I always thought you were like one of those Sirens who trapped sailors with their unearthly songs. You do that, except your power's in your exquisite face. You use it to draw people to you and then you possess their souls. You abuse them—hell, you torture them— but they don't complain 'cause no matter how bad you hurt them, it hurts too damned good. So you came after me with a knife and I would have let you slit my throat just as Jesse let you cut out his heart with your claim about destroying his unborn baby."

Lacy retched. Covering her hand with her mouth, she jumped from her chair and raced for the bathroom where she'd changed clothes earlier.

Moments later, her stomach empty and her nausea past, she was still too weak and soul-sick to move. She lay on the bathroom floor, her cheek pressed to the cool tile, her head reeling with all she'd learned about herself. She'd opened the forbidden door with her questions and now she had to live with the consequences.

Pulling herself from the floor, she stumbled to the sink to rinse her mouth and wash her face. She glanced at her disheveled reflection in the mirror. How would she ever again stand the sight of the woman she now knew she was?

Unless . . .

She returned to the dining room slipping into the chair beside her friend rather than into the one she'd sat in before across the table.

Only a little while before, shame had hung between them like a soiled sheet, making it impossible for Lacy to face the other woman. But suddenly everything was changed. She reached for Cookie's hand, holding it between both of her own. "Thank you, Cookie. I'm disgusted by everything you've told me. No, disgust doesn't even come close to describing what I feel, but I can't change any of that. I'm just glad the abortion never happened. I truly couldn't have lived with that." She stood up, bending forward to peck the other woman's cheek. "I've got to go. I've got a lot of damage to undo and I've got to hurry before it's too late."

Cookie pushed herself to her feet, her eyes never leaving Lacy's face. "You never fooled me the first time, missy—"

Lacy shook her head. "And I'm not trying to fool you now. You'll just have to wait and see."

Cookie detoured to the counter to retrieve the plastic bag that contained Lacy's wet clothes, then caught up with the younger woman at the door.

"Thanks," Lacy said, accepting the bag. "For everything. Especially your honesty. It smarted—now that's the understatement of the century—but at least I know what I'm up against with Jesse."

Cookie arched a skeptical brow. "I don't know if this amnesia thing has changed you for real or if I'm being conned, but either way I don't want anything happening to you. So, you just get home and stay by Jesse's side. I think you're wrong about Clay Waters being the man Sammy Wyatt hired, but whoever it is will try again soon as he has the chance or he gets desperate enough." She glanced up and down the street, then leaned forward and added in a rushed whisper, "Like he must have been today when he killed Raul and burned the house to keep you from getting to the truth."

Chapter Twenty-four

A frown puckered Lacy's brow for most of the drive home. Cookie's parting words haunted her. Was it really conceivable that the doctor had been killed to keep him from talking to her? She couldn't deny the disturbing coincidence of the timing, but otherwise it didn't make sense. Why would it matter to anyone if she learned that, in fact, she had faked the abortion?

Nothing difficult about that one, stupid. No one wants you here, and if Jesse forgave you, he just might not let you leave.

Fear tingled all the way to her fingertips. She gripped the steering wheel tighter. No! People didn't commit murder just because they didn't like someone, and she wasn't going to think about it anymore.

She considered all she'd learned that afternoon. So much. Too much! And too horrible to take in. Already her head was spinning with all the lurid details; churning like a whirlpool littered with debris.

Easing up on the accelerator, she loosened her grip on the steering wheel and sat back in the soft leather seat, forcing herself to a mental slowdown as well.

Soon her thoughts began to sort themselves, and she was able to winnow through all the facts she'd gleaned about herself.

Most of it was pretty appalling; confirmation of what a first-class bitch she had been.

Like the way she'd deliberately lied to Jesse about aborting his baby. What kind of monster would do something so cruel, knowing how it would devastate?

And what about the way she had threatened Cookie with a knife? Good Lord, as far as she knew, the woman had been the only friend she had on earth. Nice payback!

Oh, God, then there was Sammy Wyatt. A gangster and convicted murderer. Her lover! How did she reconcile the woman who'd involved herself with a scumbag mobster to the woman a decent, honorable man like Jesse would fall in love with? She didn't. It was ludicrous and impossible, and she refused to think about it anymore. She didn't have to. Now that she knew absolutely that there had never been an abortion, all the rest— every dirty detail of her life before Jesse—could be kept locked away in the past where it belonged. If she tried hard enough, she could even tunnel her vision to the future and the happy-ever-after life she was going to share with the man she loved. Besides, no matter what Cookie had told her, the only reality was what *she* remembered and for now, her sins purged by amnesia, she was innocent. She could believe anything she wanted. She could even *do* whatever she wanted . . . maybe even face herself in the mirror.

As the garage door crawled to a close behind her, Lacy stood rock-still. The Southern Star had an abandoned feel to it. There was an unnatural hush and stillness she hadn't sensed in the three days since her return.

Absent was the laughter or cursing, whooping and hollering in the pastures and scattered outbuildings as cowboys went through their daily rigors of backbreaking, muscle-rending work.

A fenced parcel of land to the south of the hacienda was empty of the mares and foals normally pastured there.

The enormous prized Charolais bull always penned in the barnyard nearby, quietly chewing his cud or snorting and bellowing to the grazing cows and heifers some acres away, was missing.

Even Thorn, shirking his conflicting duties as guard dog and receptionist, failed to come bounding around the corner of the house, coat flying and feet slipping with the speed and sharp angle of his turn.

It was a few minutes past six, so perhaps everyone had retired to their respecte corners of the world for rest and repast.

That made sense. It just didn't convince her or make

the eerie quiet seem any less threatening. Quickening her pace a beat or two, she hardly resisted the crazy urge to dash running and screaming for the house.

Still, her hands trembled as she slipped inside and closed the door firmly after her. She was sighing with relief as she realized that the unnatural hush had followed her indoors.

A low-wattage light burned from a single lamp in the kitchen though no one was there and even the usual delicious redolence of food cooking on the stove was lacking.

Lacy moved about the main floor, calling out a tentative "hello" as she went. Every room was washed in shadows, and as vacant and unwelcoming as the pristine kitchen where she'd begun her search for Luz, Cybil, Dillon . . . anyone.

Giving up, she returned to the foyer and started up the stairs. She'd change from Nola's tacky getup into something comfortable from her own closet. Then, if no one had shown up, she'd make herself a salad or sandwich and take it back upstairs. Maybe, she'd even watch some TV, forget—

"Off to market to buy a fat pig, then home again, home again, jiggedy jig."

Lacy recognized her sister-in-law's slurred voice, though not before jumping with fright.

Spinning around on the step, she found her. Feet crossed at the ankles, Cybil leaned casually against a wall beside one of the several arched entryways that emptied into the grand, oversized foyer. "Damn it, Cybil, you scared ten years off my life! I've been all over the house calling out to anyone who might be home. Why didn't you answer me instead of sneaking up behind me like that!"

In place of the response she expected, a single chime rang out from the enormous clock positioned between twin porticos as its hands came together to celebrate their arrival at six-thirty. The house went immediately quiet again except for the clock's return to its more civil tick-tock. Lacy gripped the railing and held on to the last of her composure.

Ice clinked against a crystal tumbler as Cybil raised it to her lips. Clear liquid dribbled like drool down her chin, and she swiped it off with the back of her hand, never blinking as she returned Lacy's stare.

"Never mind," Lacy said, turning away to resume her climb up the stairs.

"*Now* you're dressed like the woman all of Rooster Corner knows and loathes."

Lacy rolled her eyes before dropping both the plastic bag and her purse to the step and sinking down beside them. "Okay, Cybil, get it all out. Say whatever it is you have to say."

Cybil swilled her drink with the pensive frown of a philosopher striving for the words to explain the complexities of human nature rather than merely a drunk struggling to form cohesive thought. "I was just wondering," she began, finally, "who you really are. Trailer trash? Gold digger? Whore? Actress? Or all of the above." She raised her glass with the thick, gargled laugh only the very inebriated can manage. "Will the real Lacy James Pryde please stand up!"

The front door opened at the same time, diverting Lacy's attention from the cruel taunt to her husband's entrance.

He'd changed clothes since abandoning her outside his bedroom door. Dressed in a cream-colored Western dress suit—split pockets, mocha-brown stitched arrows—pearl-buttoned, pale blue shirt, sterling silver bolo tie and all, he looked every bit the wealthy scion of a Texas dynasty, and so handsome Lacy's stomach flip-flopped. Brown Stetson in his hand, he raked his fingers through his thick black hair, then absently fingered the Native American pattern of the band as his gaze passed from his sister-in-law to his wife and back again.

Lacy's excitement at his homecoming dissolved quickly to disappointment as he directed his first words to Cybil. "Where's Dillon?"

Cybil shrugged, then mumbled her reply. "Don' know. Town, I s'ppose, helpin' clean up after the fire." Her eyes widened suddenly as she remembered news she had that Jesse probably didn't. "You hear, 'bout Dr. Trajillo? Someone—"

"I heard," Jesse said, cutting her short. "It's been on the radio all afternoon."

The gleam, which had hardly sparked, went out of

Cybil's eyes. "Oh. Well, that's where your brother is, I guess." She raised her glass in his direction as if offering a toast with her next words. "Hell, that's where everybody is; all hands answerin' the call just like the proud volunteer firefighters we love and admire." She rolled away from the wall, adding a byline as she disappeared into the shadows. "For all the fucking good it did our esteemed doctor. Dead as . . ." Her words faded as she ambled down the hall.

The two of them left alone, Lacy was suddenly nervous. Her hands clasped in her lap, she stared at his snakeskin boots. Her gaze trailing the variegated hues of bark, sienna, and almond, she longed to rush down the stairs and relate everything she'd learned from Cookie, but without proof . . . no, it wouldn't work. He wouldn't believe her. She'd wait. Tomorrow she'd find another doctor. A specialist. She'd call Peach tonight and get the name of the best Ob/Gyn in Texas. For now, she would keep quiet and just be thankful Jesse was home.

Raising her gaze to his, she welcomed him with an uncertain smile. "I'm glad you're back."

Tossing his Stetson as he passed the hat rack, he didn't question his aim or notice his precision as it landed squarely and spun on a peg before coming to rest. He was already leaning against the balustrade, one foot propped on a step as he dug in his pocket for an envelope. He dropped it into Lacy's lap.

Her eyes flitting uncertainly back and forth between his enigmatic grin and the mysterious manila envelope, she clasped the latter between trembling hands.

"Go on, open it," he said. Then while she complied, he added, "Incidentally, it's one thing to know all the tricks of the trade—how to drive a man out of his fucking mind when you're in his bed. But so long as it's my bed, I don't want you looking like a hooker. Don't let me find you dressed like that again."

A cry of outrage rang out as Lacy jumped to her feet, letting the contents of the envelope—a miniature blue book and a green plastic card—slip from her fingers to the floor.

He ignored her reaction but scooped the bank book

and credit card from the floor and offered them to her again.

She looked at the gifts he held out to her, trying to focus and register what he was saying.

"Go ahead, take them," he said. "They're yours. This one's a passbook. Lone Star Savings & Loan. I transferred a hundred grand to an account in your name. The other one, well, you can see for yourself. American Express. Took some doin' to get that one set up and delivered in just a few hours. Anyway, there's a credit limit of twenty thousand, but if that's not enough, you just let me know."

"Why?" she whispered; the best she could do with her throat scalded by the tears she was barely containing.

The front door opened again though neither Lacy nor Jesse noticed.

"Why?" Jesse repeated with such derision and sarcasm, she flinched with his obvious implication. Still, he spelled it out for her. "Because, darlin', you earned it. I'd almost forgotten how good you are; got it down to an art form. And, honey, I don't know how many others you've treated to your exceptional talents, but this is one cowboy who's only too happy to pay for service like that."

Lacy didn't hesitate. She slapped his face and spun away, racing up the stairs as fast as she could run. She slammed her bedroom door hard enough to make the perfume bottles on her dresser dance and the original Georgia O'Keefe painting that hung over her bed slip to a tilt on its wire hanger. Finally, she fell back against the door, regaining her equilibrium though refusing to let her rage wane. Her arm throbbed from her wrist to her shoulder and her hand burned and itched as if frostbitten ... which it might well have been considering the cold bastard she'd hit!

Eventually, the sting that went from her fingertips to her neck began to ebb, but there was nothing—no gesture, no balm, not even enough will—to pacify her raging temper.

All day—all day, hell—all *week* since he'd walked back into her life again, she'd castigated herself for the bitch he and everyone else had delighted in telling her she was. So, okay, she accepted their verdict, and now, she'd arrived at a few judgments of her own.

She folded her arms and tapped her fingers in agitation.

The bastard had practically called her a whore. Well, what did that make him? What did that say about their marriage? Couldn't be a classic case of two birds of a feather, could it?

What about dogs lying down with dogs?

Or water seeking its own level!

Damned straight she deserved the money, and everything else the jerk wanted to give her!

Pushing away from the door, she yanked it open just as Dillon raised his hand to knock, almost ending up punched in the nose.

Both of them stepped back in surprise, then apologized in unison.

"Okay, we're both sorry," Lacy said, flashing a tight, insincere smile. "Now if you'll excuse me, I've left some unfinished business downstairs."

Dillon grabbed hold of her wrist, letting go at once when she raised her other arm to show him her doubled fist. "Hey, whoa! You do what you gotta do. I just wanted to give you these." He held out the passbook and credit card.

Lacy snatched them from his hand, then brushed immediately past him. She only got a few feet before coming to a dead stop. He'd deflated her so effectively she hadn't even heard the pop as her angry bubble burst. Reversing direction, she retraced her steps though at a more moderate pace.

No matter how she felt about the Prydes as a whole, she really didn't have a quarrel with Dillon. "Look, I'm sorry. I'm not angry with you. Thanks for bringing these up."

"You're welcome," he said. "But, Lacy, just one thing?"

"Nope," she said, alerted by his cautious tone. "Not about Jesse. He's your brother and you love him so I understand why you'd defend him. But you have to understand why I won't listen."

Dillon held up his hands in surrender. "Okay."

Lacy turned away, making it all the way to the stairs

before curiosity got the best of her. She stopped, trailing the cool iron railing with a fingertip as she invited his comment, her back still turned to him. "Go ahead. Say what you came to say."

She heard him approach from behind so she wasn't surprised when he laid his hands on her shoulders. "I freed a wolf from a trap once. He would've died if I hadn't come along. He knew it same as I did and didn't even snarl while I worked to get his paw out. But that didn't change the fact that he blamed me for the trap and resented me for helping him. Soon as I had him free, the bugger bit the shit out of me."

Lacy turned and lifted her face to his. She smiled and laid a hand on his arm. "I get it, okay?"

"Do you?" Dillon asked, the angle of his head a better indication of his doubt than his tone.

"Sure. Jesse didn't mean to hurt me. It's just payback time and paybacks are hell. See what a quick study I am . . . and with half my mind blank as a new canvas. Pretty amazing, huh?"

Dillon grinned. "Yes, ma'am, as a matter of fact, I've always thought so, but the fact is you only got some of it. Not all. You missed the most important part. Little brother is hurting, and he is blaming you for the trap he firmly believes you set for him last night—you got that straight. But the part you're missing—and this goes right to the heart of it, so pay attention—he bit you downstairs just like that wolf done me, not 'cause he's paying you back. *Because* he's still in love with you, Lacy, and he can't stand that, so he found a way to make sure you'd keep your distance."

"Gee, thanks. Just what I needed. One more person reminding me that I deserve every kick I get," she said, sinking to the floor and drawing her knees up against her chest.

Dillon hunkered down in front of her and attempted a sympathetic smile. "Hey, you've got it all wrong or maybe I'm just not smart enough to explain it right. Thing is, I hate what you did to Jesse—the way you ran out on him—but I'm glad you're back and I'm hoping the two of you can work it out."

"Why?" she asked.

Dillon hunched his shoulders. "I don't know. Because

I love my brother, and he loves you, so that's enough reason to hope you love him, too. Or because it got all screwed up for Mother and R. Davis and they couldn't straighten it out. And now it's too late for Cybil and me, so it'd be nice to see at least one Pryde ride off into the sunset with some happiness."

Lacy shook her head. "Don't, please. Don't say things like that just to make me feel better. I don't know who I am, but I've got a pretty good picture of the woman you all knew, and I know how little chance Jesse and I have. You're trying to be nice, and I appreciate it, but it just makes me fell worse."

He hooked her chin with his forefinger, forcing her to look at him. "Hey, all of us deserve a little nice. Even we real unsaintly types. I'm not denying you did a real hatchet job on my baby brother when you—well, I guess the two of you've discussed all that. You don't need me rehashing it all.

"What I've been trying to get around to here is this. Jesse doesn't let many people inside. We're brothers, and he's never even opened up to me. Same with our mother. He loves us both, I guess. Respects her, for sure, and has a sense of the blood-thicker-than-water bond that ties us all. Except for you, though, the only other person Jesse ever loved enough to hurt over was R. Davis—our dad, you know?"

At her nod, he went on. "The day you left, it was just like doing the night R. Davis died all over again. Except for those two times—I've never seen Jesse fall apart like he did then. Went into his office downstairs with a fifth of scotch both times. Sent for Luz to bring him more when the first was gone. Smashed every picture he had of R. Davis, then went through yours when you left him. Both times, he drank until he passed out, then woke up to drink some more. None of us knew he was capable of that kind of anger until the night R. Davis—well, anyway, none of us knew how to handle it. We all tried talking to him, but no matter what Mother or Cyl or I said, we couldn't talk him outta there. Finally came out after three days the first time, 'cause he had to attend R. Davis's funeral. To this day, I'd bet he's still so pissed, he'd spit in his eye, given the chance.

"Anyway, when you left, Jesus, it was ten times worse.

He got a drunk going that he kept up for more'n a week. Then he just pulled it all together and no one mentioned your name again until the police called from California about you being in the hospital. None of us knew what to expect, but I can tell you the last thing was for him to bring you home after the way you'd deserted him out of the clear blue."

"Wait, back up," Lacy said, her brow knotted with her confusion. "I don't get something here. Your father *died,* he didn't abandon him."

Dillon shrugged. "Jesse thinks he did. Nobody talks about it 'cause we don't have concrete proof, but it looked pretty much like R. Davis killed himself. Mother convinced the medical examiner to rule the cause of death as an accident. But the fact of the matter is, R. Davis left the house in the middle of the night. Jesse found him the next morning after he hadn't returned, washed up on the bank a few yards below the waterfall. R. Davis was drunk when he left, but everyone knew no amount of liquor could make him go near those falls on a moonless night 'less he was plannin' on jumpin'.'"

Lacy clasped a hand over her mouth as pity rose inside her. *Greatest man I never knew.* That's the way Jesse had described his father the night before. How terrible that he'd been the one to find him, and how devastating to believe the man he'd loved so profoundly had been so despondent he might have committed suicide. "Isn't it possible something could have drawn him near the falls and he simply slipped or lost his balance?"

"Sure," Dillon said with a weak shrug. "Anything's possible. But there's other stuff. For one thing, he changed his will that morning, reapportioning his wealth."

"But that still doesn't prove—"

"There was a note, too, Lacy. He left it for Jesse in his study. Jesse found it there the next morning. That's when he went out looking for him."

"I still don't understand. If he left a note—"

Dillon stood up and busied himself brushing the creases from his jeans. "It didn't exactly spell it out; didn't come right out and say he was going to kill himself. It was more cryptic than that; innuendo more than straight talk."

Lacy pulled herself up as well using the wrought iron with one hand and accepting Dillon's help with the other. "Don't tell me. I don't think I could stand it."

Dillon narrowed his eyes as he studied her. "This is for real, isn't it?"

"What? The amnesia?"

"No, I know that's genuine. I'm talking about this side of you that aches for Jesse, that can't stand to hear about him suffering."

"I love him, Dillon," she admitted softly before slipping past him and heading back to her room.

"Lacy!"

She stopped, looked over her shoulder, waiting.

"I know you don't want to hear what R. Davis wrote to Jesse, and the truth be told, I really don't want to get into it. But one thing you should know. The reason he wrote to Jesse? He wanted to warn him." He stopped then to pinch the bridge of his nose between his finger and thumb as he struggled for control.

Lacy didn't understand, of course, but then there was so little she did. What was one more mystery left unsolved? "Never mind, Dillon."

"No, this is important. I'm a little emotional is all, just coming from finding Doc Trajillo's body and talking about my dad and all."

"Okay," Lacy agreed. "Tell me."

"I, uh," he began, stopping to clear his throat before going on. "I just want you to know it's not all your fault—the way things turned out for you and Jesse, I mean. It's this penchant we Pryde men have for falling in love with the wrong women."

"Was that what your father warned Jesse about? Marrying the wrong woman?" Lacy asked.

Dillon was staring at the pattern of roses in the carpet beneath his feet. He looked up. "Huh? Oh, the note. No. That's just what I came up with after you ran off. Took a good look at what life with me has done to Cyl; put that up beside the way you took off outta here and figured out that R. Davis was wrong."

"What did he say?"

"He warned Jesse about our mother. Said everything Rose touched turned to rot. Told him it was too late for Cyl and me. He wanted Jesse to get away before she destroyed him, too, but after I saw what happened to the two of you, I knew he was way off base. The thing that's wrong had to be in R. Davis, and now in his progeny. Mother's strong and stubborn, and even cruel at times, but she's not vicious and bad like he said."

Lacy shivered, suddenly chilled, for though there were still more questions than answers, she knew just how *right* R. Davis was about his wife. Rose Pryde was evil.

Chapter Twenty-five

Sammy Wyatt didn't exactly like prison life, but he didn't hate it either. Course for some it was hell. For some, there was no one on the outside seeing to the bribes that made life on the inside easier. And for most, there was the constant fear of getting shived or butt-fucked. Getting it in the ass was the worst 'cause it was never just a one-night-stand. At least when a man got cut, he usually didn't live to be hit again. But there was little chance Sammy would ever be stuck with a blade; no chance at all he'd ever be stuck by another guy's dick. He had what was known within prison walls as "the thousand-yard stare." Viet Nam vets—those survivors of the cunning, mind-torturing Cong—had it. So did Sammy Wyatt. He'd never been to Nam. Wouldn't know a gook from a chimpanzee. But he knew all about life inside the foster care system and far as he was concerned, there wasn't no one better at fucking with a guy's mind than the bastards who'd raised him. One look in his eyes, it was understood: Nobody messed with Sammy Wyatt.

There were some things Sammy would have changed about the penal system, of course. The food, for instance. Not that he bitched about it. After all, Lompoc being a federal penitentiary, the food was better than what inmates in the state facilities were served.

On the other hand, he thrived on the strict order. Wyatt was a Virgo. Neat, meticulous, obsessively clean; character traits that ironically suited him for prison life.

Facing his reflection in the mirror, he combed his hair, taking his time, enjoying even the orderliness in this simple routine. Rake it with the comb straight back, then follow it with the flat of his other hand, smoothing any ruffles. Comb. Hand. Comb. Hand ... until ... there, perfect! Every strand precisely in place.

Next, he unzipped his trousers, spreading his legs to keep them from sliding below his narrow hips as he straightened the hem of his shirt, tucking it in once again. He might be wearing khaki—the prison garb of Lompoc inmates—instead of his former attire of twelve-hundred-dollar silk suits. It didn't matter. Sammy took pride in the way he looked.

Donnell Johnson, the soft-spoken prison guard who waited outside Sammy's cell to escort him downstairs, was losing patience. "Come on, Wyatt. Visiting hours are over at three."

Sammy laughed. It was only a little after nine. "You shoulda been a comedian, Johnson. Too bad we never hooked up on the outside. You coulda done stand-up in one of my clubs in Vegas."

Donnell, a young black man with a deceptively slight build—Sammy had witnessed him take down a 260-pound inmate without even breaking a sweat—grinned amicably. "And wind up in khaki like you? No, sir. Not this homey. Got too many brothers wearing it and one thing I noticed? It don't do our skin tone justice. You get where I'm coming from?" He looked down at his own uniform of white shirt, navy blazer, and gray slacks. "Un-uh. I ain't got no doubt I'm looking mighty fine just like I am. Man, soon as I step out in this here uniform, babes start trippin' all over themselves just to get close to me."

With a final glance in the mirror, Sammy exited his cell, falling in step beside the guard. "I think you're right on, Johnson. It's gotta be the uniform, 'cause you certainly ain't no Denzel Washington."

"Uh-huh, and who you think you are? Michael-Fucking-Douglas? Guess that's why the only chick ever visits you's that old stone-faced Indian bitch."

Rose sat in the visiting room of the Lompoc Federal Penitentiary, back stiff, hands toying restlessly with the soft leather handles of her Aigne handbag.

She was exhausted, though jittery and anxious to get on with the business that had necessitated the lies about her sister's failing health and the subsequent unplanned rush trip to California.

She'd arrived at LAX in the late morning hours the day before, rented a car, and made the three hundred miles plus drive to Santa Barbara. Twenty minutes after her arrival in the beautiful coastal city, she was checking into a modest, yet respectable motel overlooking the Pacific, and moments after that, her single bag unpacked, treating herself to a few minutes on the lanai. As it had on her last trip here just two months earlier, the panoramic scene of glass-smooth aquamarine ocean dotted with yachts and sailboats began at once to work its magic on her, calming her jangled nerves and reviving her weary spirit.

She'd almost wished as she had then that she could stay here forever, anonymous and unreachable. A rare, wistful smile played across her face before fading with her sigh. With a last longing glance at the peaceful view, she turned back into the room to call home.

The phone rang a half-dozen times before Luz finally answered. Fear clutched at Rose's heart as soon as she heard the excitement and tears in her housekeeper's voice. She knew something terrible had happened. Just please, God, not to Jesse!

Luz was practically incoherent, sobbing and rattling in a mishmash of Spanish and broken English until Rose broke in, her tone firm.

"Stop this, Luz! Tell me what's happened, and speak so that I can understand you. I don't have time for your histrionics. You may indulge yourself after we've ended our conversation."

"The doctor, senora! Raul Trajillo! *Muerto.* Dead! Someone has keeled him. Someone shoot him in the head, then burn his house!"

Rose's emotions ricocheted from one extreme to the next.

Shock at the unbelievable news that Raul was dead. Murdered!

Relief that Luz's hysteria had nothing to do with Jesse.

Another rush, this time of gratitude that he'd died before Lacy learned the truth about his part in the conspiracy to convince Jesse of a phony abortion. She'd been so close!

Rose clamped a hand over her mouth, ashamed of the giddiness and laughter that welled. Raul Trajillo, her friend and confidant, was dead, for God's sake! Murdered!

She was sobered by the next thought, sickened and scared as well.

What if Lacy had confronted the doctor and learned the truth, then killed him in the heat of passion? God, that would mean ... *No!* She couldn't even consider such a possibility. But she had. All night.

So she was drained and bone-weary this morning. Well, at least reason had returned with daylight. The odds of Lacy being Raul's killer were so farfetched, she didn't know why she'd even considered the possibility. Not that she didn't believe her daughter-in-law capable of murder. Quite the opposite, in fact. Wasn't her former lover, the very man Rose was here at the prison to see, a convicted murderer? Still, it wasn't logical. For one thing, even if Lacy had met with Raul and learned the truth, so what? All he would have told her was that she had paid him to back up her story about the abortion. Hardly reason to kill the man. For another, she'd called the house just before boarding the plane in Dallas the day before and learned from Dillon that Lacy was upstairs sleeping. Luz said the doctor had been shot around the time her flight was departing.

Convinced now that there was no connection between the doctor's tragic murder and her family, Rose rubbed her aching shoulders. Now all she had to do was remind Mr. Wyatt of their agreement. She'd held up her end of the bargain, and okay, so maybe he'd made a valid attempt to hold up his. Nevertheless, he hadn't succeeded. It was time for her to stress the consequences if he didn't get it done right and get it done now.

She sighed. She was getting too old for all this responsibility. Still, she couldn't turn over the reins just yet.

She closed her eyes for a long moment remembering how she'd once questioned the lengths she'd go to to protect what was important to her. Such a stupid query, for she'd soon learned there was nothing she wouldn't do to safeguard her loved ones or secure the future of her dynasty. If the end was warranted, the means were always justified. Even if it necessitated allying herself with the devil—him being Sammy Wyatt, in this case.

But, oh, Holy Mary, Mother of Jesus, how she detested this. *Her*—Rose Delores Cahille-Pryde—sitting inside a federal penitentiary. Subjected to the crude search of her person and possessions. Surrounded by razor-wire fencing. Spied on with security cameras. Restrained behind locked doors the same as the imprisoned child molesters, rapists, butchers ... and the lowlife who waited in the visiting room with her.

She'd left the motel room in Santa Barbara early, timing her arrival long before the start of visiting hours in hopes of avoiding them. She wasn't like these people. She was the matriarch of a kingdom. They were the peasantry. *She* knew that, but she resented the fact that *they* didn't realize the disparity. She wouldn't let them link her to the dirty underbelly of society. Not even Joe Wolf, her scum of a father, had been able to do that. In fact, just the opposite. She'd learned a valuable lesson from her mother's mistake. She firmly espoused the need for eugenic mating. A smile curled her thin lips as she thought of Jesse; proof of that pudding! It wilted with the appearance of Dillon's image before her mind's eye. He, on the other hand, was testimony that nothing in life was guaranteed. Ah, well, she'd taken care to insure that history didn't repeat itself.

She turned her attention to the other early morning visitors in the room. Just look at them. Only a few minutes past nine, and here they were, representatives of the world's losers, all present and accounted for. The living breathing worthless. How they disgusted her.

The parents—polyester outfits as loud and cheap as their laughter—bound to their incarcerated offspring by nothing more consequential than ill-timed copulation.

The requisite young wife indentured by wedding vows too hastily made—in this case, a pathetically thin young woman struggling with two runny-nosed, hyperactive toddlers dressed in unmatched, stained short sets.

The friend—a euphemism for every groupie, weirdo, masochist, or sadist—who frequented the prison for some strange vicarious thrill.

And the ultimate dud—the thirty-something, chain-smoking impoverished appellate attorney; champion of lost causes. The law-school graduate originally shackled by idealism of low grades or both. Hanging on years later only because the hard-gotten lesson that no one escaped the leper colony always came too late.

Rose watched the reunion between inmate and parents, then the first minutes between convict and lawyer. She was relieved when Sammy Wyatt was shown into the room. She rose to meet him, a smile on her face, her hand extended. Oddly, she wasn't repulsed by him as she was the others. In fact, she'd actually thought a lot about him since her last visit, and realized she was attracted to him in a purely intellectual sense, of course. He was, after all, quite a brilliant man. Crude, roughly cut, surely, yet charming and provocative. She could well understand her daughter-in-law's association with the man. More than that, she admired Lacy's survival instincts; even applauded the way she'd jumped ship and allied herself with the opposition at the precise right moment. Of course, that still didn't mean she would allow her to stay in Jesse's life.

"How are you?" she asked as they sat down at a table across from one another.

"Can't complain," Sammy said with an easy grin that took ten years off his face. "How 'bout yourself?"

Rose returned his congenial smile, though there was no friendliness in her tone as she answered, "Actually, that's precisely why I'm here, Sam. I do have a complaint."

"Let me see," he said, tipping his chair back so that it rested precariously on two legs. "I get three guesses and the first two don't count."

Rose chuckled in spite of herself. "Yes, I guess so."

"You're not happy 'cause our little problem continues to exist." The last words hardly out of his mouth, all humor disappeared from his expression as the front two chair legs came down on the concrete floor with an explosive bang. "And what if I told you I'd decided to cancel our—what would you call it?—our pact? What if I told you how I've come to decide I forgive her her trespasses and am even gonna give her a second chance?"

Unruffled, Rose shrugged. "I suppose I'd have to

admit to rare poor judgment, but I don't see that as the case here. I recognized your astuteness and intellect the moment we met." She shrugged. "Besides, why would you send someone to run her down with a car, leave her for dead, then suddenly change your mind? You wouldn't."

"You're wrong. I might. I'm like that. Given to unexpected bursts of charity and love and forgiveness," he said with a smirk. "But fact is, Rosie, my man didn't run her over with no car. My man was still in Texas when she was hit. Word I got was he was as shocked as any of us when he heard about it."

Rose's temper flared briefly before she quelled it with years of self-practiced discipline. "Let me understand what you're telling me. I held up my end of our agreement by depositing a hundred thousand dollars in the bank account as you directed me to do. You, on the other hand, have made no attempt to see that your end was accomplished."

"Naw, now you've gone too far. I ain't no welsher. I gave you my word I'd get someone on our problem and I did. I already told you he was in Texas. Working on your spread as a matter of fact when she got run down in L.A."

Impatient now, Rose leaned forward, placing both hands on the table and locking her dark gaze on his. "Enough. I know about the man you hired. Now I want you to tell me what you mean when you say you might decide to forgive her, give her another chance. I've paid you for a service. If you don't intend to deliver, tell me now, so I can make other arrangements."

Sammy grinned again. "And no hard feelings? Why do I find that too tough to swallow?"

"I suppose for the same reason I don't buy this line you're trying to lay on me. You are serving a life sentence for racketeering, conspiracy to commit murder, and embezzlement and all because this woman gave the authorities proof and testified against you. Why would you forgive her?"

"Because she and I are two of a kind. We're survivors. She didn't do nothin' I wouldn't've done to cover my own ass. Sure, I was hot, plenty hot. Especially when I heard she was married to some rich son of a bitch oil

baron. Pissed me off royally. That's why I agreed to—"
He paused, looking around to make sure they weren't
being overheard, saw that nobody was paying any attention, then leaned forward anyway and lowered his voice.
"You know, the deal you proposed. Figured what the
hell, ya know? Why should she just step out of shit and
into some fancy glass slippers when I'm in here rottin'
away.

"Then when I heard how she up and took off, leaving
your high and mighty son with his thumb up his ten-
carat ass, I knew it was 'cause she'd never stopped loving
me just like I haven't gotten her out of my system." He
ran his tongue over his lips as if just thinking about her
created a hunger within him. "Hey, she still calling herself Lacy? It suits her, don't it? I mean, I know you've
got a knot in your undies 'cause she's back home and
you can't stand the thought of her with your pretty boy,
but you gotta admit she's about the sweetest babe you
ever seen. *Looks* like lace, ya know?"

"You idiot," Rose snapped. "She didn't leave Jesse
because she still loves you. My God, she was like a bitch
in heat the entire six months that she was there, and
Jesse serviced her like a bull." She saw his face darken
as her taunts hit their mark and smiled with satisfaction.
"She ran away because she found out you knew where
she was. She was terrified. You should have seen her at
breakfast the morning she took off. Her face was white
as chalk dust and her hands were shaking so badly she
could barely hold a cup of coffee."

"Fuck that. No way she coulda known I'd found her
unless you told her," he said, his brows drawn and his
eyes narrowed suspiciously.

"Don't be ridiculous," Rose scoffed, looking around
for a guard or visitor close enough to overhear. Satisfied
that the only one paying them any attention at all was
the uniformed black man standing a good twenty yards
away, she rested her elbows on the table and steepled
her fingers. Her head bowed slightly, she might have
been praying instead of covering her mouth to prevent
anyone from lipreading. "I paid you a hundred thousand
dollars in your account to get rid of her. Why would I
then go and warn her? It's obvious she recognized the
man you hired and panicked."

"Un-uh," Sammy said with a shake of his head. "No way."

"Why not? *I* knew who he was the day he hired on, and I've never met any of your, ah, associates before. I'll admit I was impressed. Somehow I think I expected someone more—oh, I don't know—more obvious. But I have to tell you he's very good. Subtle. He fit right in. Every man on the Southern Star took to him. Jesse even commented on how well the new hand was working out at supper the night before Lacy left. As a matter of fact, I remember now how she almost choked when Dillon joined in the conversation and mentioned the man's name."

Sammy didn't speak. Just sat looking at her like she had her head on backward or had sprouted horns.

"What's the matter?" she asked. "Get a little sloppy, did we, sending someone she'd recognize by name? I'll grant I was surprised by that myself. But I did relish the momentary rush I derived from watching the blood drain from her face the moment she heard the name Clay Waters."

Sammy didn't move a single muscle. Not for several seconds. Then his fists came down on the tabletop with a nerve-jangling *bang*! Even Rose Pryde, who'd never so much as squeaked at the sight of a field mouse, was provoked to a sharp exclamation of surprise.

Donnell Johnson was immediately at Wyatt's side. "What the hell's the matter with you, man? Am I gonna have to take you outta here?"

Sammy held up his hands in surrender. "Sorry, Johnson. Just got some bad news about a friend of mine. Seems she's come down with a serious illness; serious enough to prove fatal, Mrs. Pryde was telling me. Just got me upset's all. Won't happen again."

Johnson stood at the inmate's side for a long moment, his gaze passing slowly back and forth between the handsome elderly woman and the normally tractable con. Finally, he returned to his post beside the door.

Wyatt gripped the sides of the table with knuckle-bleaching intensity though his expression remained carefully neutral. "Waters. You did say his name is Clay Waters? Tell me what he looks like." He didn't wait for an answer, providing the description himself instead.

"Five ten or eleven, lean, sandy hair, deepset eyes, scar that runs an inch or so from the corner of his lips down his chin?"

"I don't know about the scar. He wears a heavy handlebar mustache. But the rest is accurate," Rose said, her voice as tight as her coiled nerves. "Am I reading this right?"

"I don't know what the fuck you're reading, sweetheart," Wyatt bit out between clenched teeth. "But I didn't hire Clay Waters."

"Then who did?"

Sammy's slow smile was as chilling as the blue of his eyes that were glazed with ice. Rose shivered as she realized how many murder victims must have felt their blood freeze under that arctic expression long before their life drained away. Thank God for the armed guards.

Wyatt frightened her, though of course he'd never know this. "Damn it, Sam, tell me who he is. A hundred thousand dollars of my money is in a Cayman bank account in your name. To date, I have received nothing in exchange."

"Clay Waters is an agent employed by the Federal Bureau of Investigation, Mrs. P. A fucking Feebie. Now are you clear where we are? You paid me to hire a player for our private game of tag. Only Waters has decided to get in on the action and he ain't supposed to be 'it.' "

"Stop this!" Rose exclaimed more loudly than she'd intended. Then in a hissed whisper. "We're not playing a game. This is my son's life! So tell me what an FBI agent is doing on my ranch disguised as a common cowpoke."

His hand snaked across the table until it covered hers. He never took his eyes off her face as his fingers closed around hers. Not when she winced. Not even when involuntary tears filled her eyes. "Actually, Mrs. P., I was counting on you explaining that to me."

"How would I know?" she cried, freeing her hand and dropping it to her lap out of his reach. "It's ludicrous. Absolutely without rhyme or reason. According to the papers I found hidden in the dormer of the Rabbit Patch—the cottage she rented from us when she first arrived—the FBI put her into the secret witness program. Isn't it logical to assume they wouldn't jeopardize that by following her . . . unless—"

"Unless what?" he demanded.

She shook her head. "No, that's stupid. I was going to suggest that they might have learned, somehow, about my prior meeting with you and the arrangement we subsequently arrived at."

"Fuck that," Sammy said with a quick, dismissive shake of his head. "If they'd learned about our meeting, I'd know. No, damn it! Once they put her in the program—you can trust me on this one—it was adios and good riddance. Besides, Waters isn't some cardboard cereal pop-up or your Saturday matinee cartoon variety G-man. He's one of the best. 'Jell-O Man.' That's his handle 'cause he can mold himself into anything they want him to be."

Rubbing his face with his hands, Sammy continued to think out loud. "No, it just fucking doesn't add up. Once a witness goes into the program, they don't send *postcards* much less agents no matter how temptin' and sweet the poon tang. Bottom line, they was done with her the minute she gave them everything they was after."

And then it hit him.

Unless there was one tiny little detail she neglected to mention . . . like the fact that *she* had the fifteen million dollars the government had been looking for; the money that had disappeared from his secret accounts two days before the Feebies had closed in on him.

Agitated, he raked his fingers through his carefully arranged hair and for several seconds forgot where he was, who he was with. "Danny Lampoca, my right arm," he muttered, "vanished without a trace the same day my accounts were cleaned out. All this time, I assumed he and my dough were tucked away in some swank South American crib. I was dead sure I'd been had by a double-crossing dick. And here I find out I was had by a two-timing cunt."

"Wait a minute. You're making this . . . this quantum leap from Danny Whomever to my daughter-in-law all because the FBI planted this man, Waters, at the Southern Star?"

Sammy ignored the question. "The last time you was here, you said you learned about me through some newspaper clippings you came across in a box of her things. What else did you find?"

Rose rubbed her temples with her long, slender fingers. "I don't know. An address book. Some photos of the two of you together. A few letters from someone named Letti, Lotty—I can't remember exactly. Not much else."

"No bank book? Ledger? Notebook? Nothing like that with a series of numbers?"

Rose thought a moment, then shook her head. "No, I—wait a minute." Excited, she sat forward on the end of her chair. "I just remembered. There was no ledger, nothing like that, but the address book was all wrong. I don't know, fake or made-up like the rest of her life. It was brand-new. Still had that rich scent of unused leather, and there were only a few names. I recall wondering why she'd gone to the trouble of creating an address book, then hid it with the rest of the evidence of her secret past. It didn't make sense, but I forgot about that when I leafed through the pages. I was struck by how alike and fake the names all sounded. Too easy, you know, like Tom Jones and Jane Smith. Let me see. Oh, yes, Bob Brown. Sue White, I think, and Joe Adams. See what I'm saying? Names you might find in a first-grade primer. The addresses and phone numbers were weird, too, as I remember now. I can't say exactly what it was. It seems to me that they were run together. Area code, number, address, all on one line. Oh, and the other amazing coincidence? Everyone from the same town—Scarsdale or Scottsdale ... I'm not sure which. Maybe neither, but no one from Portland, Oregon, where she claimed she was from. How's that for being as believable as our first lady's homemade cookies?"

Sammy had been listening, tapping his mouth with his finger, and nodding every now and then, a smile spreading until he burst into laughter.

"What?" Rose demanded, offended and certain he was laughing at her yet not comprehending why.

Instead of answering, he stretched across the table to grab her face between his hands and plant an exuberant kiss on her lips. He was grinning once again from ear to ear when he let her go. "Mrs. P., I think I've fallen in love with you."

"Be still my heart," Rose said acidly. "Will you please explain what I said that got our courtship off the ground?"

Sammy tipped his chair back on its two hind legs, chuckling again. "Guess I'm just a sucker for a clever woman."

Rose waited, no longer amused or patient, and clearly making her point with her fixed stare.

"Okay," Sammy said, relenting and letting the chair drop back to the floor at the same time. "You were right about the address book. It's not only phony, it's set up on a system I created. Only, I made sure mine was authentic-looking. You know—addresses scribbled in on the wrong page; business cards, envelopes, and scraps of papers with a first name and a phone number stuck in the pages. But on seven different pages there are the fake names all in Scottsdale, which is Wyatt-speak for Switzerland—Swiss bank accounts. Get it?"

"I get it very well," Rose said, pleased with herself for finding the key to the mysterious reason why Clay Waters was hanging around the Southern Star.

Sammy brought her back to the business at hand.

"She really had me going, Mrs. P. I was all prepared to forgive her for testifying against me. When I heard about how some maniac had run her down and left her for dead, I coulda cried. And when I found out she was so torn up, she had to have her face put back together, I wanted to kill the son of a bitch. Most of all, I wanted to get in touch with her. Tell her all that, you know? I was even going to arrange to give you the hundred gees back."

"And now?" Rose asked, holding her breath.

Sammy ignored the question for the moment as he scratched the back of his neck and said, "Always said I'd never get reamed in the ass, but who'd have thought I'd have gotten it from a chick?"

"A crude analogy," Rose said. "Yet entirely appropriate, I do believe."

He nodded as he turned his head to stare out the window, his gaze raised to the guard tower. "Tell you what, you give me that address book, and we're back in business, Mrs. P." He looked at her winking. "And to prove how bad I feel about almost reneging on our deal, I'm gonna give you back your money. This one's on the house. Pro bono."

It was Rose's turn to laugh. "As much as I appreciate your offer, Sam, I can't accept. I always pay for services rendered. It's the only way to insure a job well done.

"However, I'm afraid I don't have the actual address book." She held up a hand at his sudden scowl. "*But,* fear not. It so happens that I did make a copy of all her papers, the pages from that book included. I'll arrange for them to be delivered to you by Monday. How will that be?"

"That, Mrs. P., will be fan-fucking-tastic. You've got my attorney's address. Fax them to him. He'll take care of the rest."

"Consider it done."

"Then you'd better get back home or you'll miss the fireworks."

Rose inhaled deeply, savoring the satisfaction of another family crisis resolved. She extended her hand. "Thank you, Sam. I'm very grateful."

He accepted her hand, even drawing it to his lips. He'd been called a lot of things, but nobody had ever denied that Sammy Wyatt had style. "Anytime, Mrs. P. It's been a pleasure doing business with you."

Rose stood and started to turn away before remembering Jesse's birthday the next day. She looked back at the man she'd just sealed a murder contract with, her smile so pleasant they might well have been discussing nothing more significant than an arrangement for him to come to the Southern Star to paint her house once he was released . . . in twenty some odd years. "There's just one more thing, Sam. Could you . . . *would* you wait until Sunday to take care of matters? We're having a party for my son tomorrow. Our community's already suffered a tragedy—Raul Trajillo, Rooster Corner's only family doctor, was killed yesterday. There's bound to be a pall on the festivities as it is, but we couldn't very well have a birthday celebration if his wife is found dead, now could we?"

Sammy rolled his eyes. "Jesus, you're something else, Mrs. P." His thumbs hooked in the front trouser pockets, he leaned into her to add, "For a minute there I felt just like we was discussin' a box social instead of a contract to off my ex–old lady. But you want it Sunday, you got it Sunday. Any preference of time of day? Jesse like to sleep in late, I can arrange to have her hit after noon so he's not disturbed."

Rose laughed. "What a charmer you are, Sam. Too bad I won't have good reason to come this way again for another visit. My sister-in-law, Emma? Poor dear died last month, and I'm afraid I'm going to have to tell the rest of the family." She laughed. "After the party tomorrow, of course. Wouldn't want to ruin Jesse's birthday."

They'd reached the locked door that opened to two different worlds: freedom in one direction; a four-by-eight cell in the other.

Sammy laughed appreciably. "Your kid know how you look out for his happiness?"

"Do men ever appreciate what their women do for them?"

"Suppose not," Sammy said before nodding at the guard. "Visit's over, Johnson. You can take me back to my suite."

"Looked like you and Pocahontas was having a nice chat," Johnson said as the two men retraced their earlier steps.

"Let's just say it was educational."

"Yeah? And what's a smart guy like yourself gonna learn from a dried up ol' bitty like that, Wyatt?"

"Two things."

"Okay, so I could use some learnin'. Tell me."

"She reminded me that there's only two kinds of people in this world—cunts and dicks."

"Wow!" Johnson said sarcastically, adding a whistle for emphasis. "Woulda never figured out nothing profound as that on my own. Thanks for sharing it with me."

"Hey, not so quick. Think about it for a minute. You're straight, right?"

"As a friggin' arrow," Johnson confirmed.

"Okay, so you usually do the porkin'. Point is, my friend, there's times when a dude gets reamed in the ass by a cunt. Difference is, he ain't gettin' fucked, he's gettin' shafted."

The guard scratched his head. "Now that shit's heavy, man."

They'd reached Wyatt's cell, but the inmate paused to lean against the iron bars a minute before entering. "So? Ain't you going to ask what the other thing I learned was?"

Johnson's laugh was a low-belly rumble. "Why waste my breath when you gonna tell me anyway."

"You're going to love this one, Johnson. That Mrs. Pryde? Her saggy ole pussy starts twitching every time she says her son's name. Jesse Pryde, fruit of her loins, and *she's* got the hots for him. Sick, ain't it?" He stepped inside the cell, flopping down on his cot and tucking his arms beneath his head. "Just goes to prove there ain't no justice. Not with me in here and a pervert like her out there."

Donnell Johnson didn't answer. Just shook his head and started away. Sammy stopped him, calling him back.

"What is it now, Aristotle?" he asked. "More philosophical crap on the imperfections of our planet Earth?"

"I need to see my lawyer," Sammy said, all humor suddenly absent from his tone.

Johnson saluted smartly. "I'll get him the word," he said before walking away and disappearing down the hall.

Sammy sat up the minute the guard's footsteps faded away. Snatching a pencil and sheet of paper from the narrow tabletop that served as a desk, he lowered himself onto his cot once again, this time to sit hunched over the paper on his lap.

He wrote out a short "To Do" list for his attorney:

1. Make arrangements for a Sunday service at the Southern Star. And see to it that Lacy Pryde didn't neglect to make her confession about a) his money and b) the missing Danny Lampoca.

Sammy laughed, pleased with his brilliance. That was too funny! Sunday services and confession. Ha ha. Appropriate, too, seeing's how the bitch would be meeting her maker directly thereafter.

His smile disappeared and his blue eyes turned to ice again. He added the second item:

2. Hire investigator to track down the driver of the car that ran her down.

Whoever the son of a bitch was, he was going to pay for hurting what was his. Nobody had the right to do that 'cept him.

3. Tidy up with Mrs. P.

The woman thought she was the fucking queen of hearts right out of Alice in Wonderland— Off with their heads! *Off with your head, Mrs. P., you fucking sicko.*

Chapter Twenty-six

Lacy stood in front of the gilt-framed mirror in the foyer. Excitement mingled with the residue of yesterday's emotionally explosive events to cause a tremor in her hands. She was having a hell of a time putting her earrings on.

"Not even nine o'clock and all gussied up. Must have something special in mind for the day." Jesse's voice cut into her thoughts, as unexpected as his image suddenly slipping unwanted into the reflection. Lacy jumped, dropping the back to the diamond stud earring she'd almost had fixed in place. The tiny gold piece would be hard to find against the veined marble floor. "Damn!"

"Sorry," he muttered as their gazes locked in the beveled mirror.

Pinioned by the striking picture they posed—him so tall and dark and strong; her so small and fair and fragile by comparison—neither of them moved for several seconds.

Jesse broke the spell with a derisive remark. "I think this is what they call a Kodak moment. Too bad we don't have a camera handy. You could keep it as a souvenir to be laughed over in the years to come."

His sarcasm—like the sharp bite of a whip laid without warning against her back—smarted, provoking a sharp wince.

But she surprised him as well with her quick recovery. Turning from the mirror, she reached up to lay a hand on the back of his neck and draw his face to hers. She kissed him, letting her lips linger just long enough to feel his response; the intake of a breath drawn too quickly, and the slightest pressure as his mouth sought more. Then she stepped away. "Mmm, much better than a photograph. Pictures are only one-dimensional. They couldn't possibly tell the whole story."

A camera couldn't capture what the heart knew, for instance. Couldn't interpret what she'd captured with that kiss. Who would know from a simple snapshot that those two people framed in that mirror were really two halves of a perfect whole? Lacy was still thinking about the kiss several hours later as she crossed the Dallas shopping center mezzanine where she'd come to purchase Jesse's birthday gift. The present he would open publicly at the party his mother was hosting for him.

Her hand closing over her purse flap, she smiled. Inside, on a single white sheet of paper, folded and tucked into an envelope, was the *real* gift; the present she'd hoped against hope she would be able to bring home to him.

Her happiness brimming over, she laughed aloud. This was the special gift they'd share. This was the present they'd celebrate in private tonight.

After that, we'll find the answers to the rest of the questions. Why I was desperate enough to tell you such a vile lie about my life with the man named Sammy Wyatt. Why I hid that from you, then ran instead of trusting you to help me when I learned that he'd sent Clay Waters to kill me. We'll talk about everything, lay it all out in front of us. No more secrets. No more lies. I'll do anything I have to to prove my love and save our marriage. And then I swear to God, Jesse, I'll give you that baby we never really made together before.

She smiled at a passing couple, holding hands and walking close enough so that their hips collided with almost every step. Young love, lust, hunger.

She and Jesse would recapture that, she vowed, balling her hands determinedly. There were so many unanswered questions. Questions she would ask Jesse to help her resolve. And if he couldn't? It didn't matter. They'd wait until her memory returned. But even if that never happened, if her mind never recaptured the past before the moment Jesse walked into her hospital room, so what? She'd settle for the love she knew she and Jesse would find again once all the lies were behind them.

She'd savor every moment anew and let Jesse re-create it all for her ... their love, their life.

Tossing her head back, she laughed again. Lord, she was happy!

Readjusting the black and white plastic bag bearing the Saks Fifth Avenue logo she carried over her shoulder, she bit down on her bottom lip, hardly resisting the urge to twirl right there in the middle of the mall in front of God and everyone.

Tonight, she would sleep in Jesse's arms ... after they made sweet, sweet love. In the morning ...

"Shelby!"

She turned, her arm already coming up in greeting and a smile finding its way in place by the time she faced the man who'd called out to her. It was in the racing, ensuing seconds of tumbling emotions that she recognized him, the man who hurried, shoes clicking sharply against the tiled flooring. His features—dark hair, green eyes, toothpaste-commercial grin, and shadowed full jaw—were pleasant, though just a tad shy of good-looking. He had matured many years past the images of the boy she'd remembered. Still, she recognized him. This man ... this stranger was her brother. Only her name wasn't Shelby. Please God, tell her it wasn't!

Then before she could protest, she was in his arms; in a fierce bear hug, her feet at least six inches off the floor as he spun her in a circle. "Damn, Shel," he said as he finally set her down on the world that was all at once topsy-turvy. "You can't know how glad I am to see you! I can't believe it! Hell, I'm blown away! But, oh, little sister, so gosh darn happy I'm probably going to make an ass out of myself and start bawling like a baby!"

Tears scalded her eyes, tears of gladness, sure, for she *knew* him, this big oaf who was her brother. Alex Sands. The name had come back the second he'd wrapped her in his bear-sized arms. But the tears were inspired by hurt, too. Her memory was returning, but at what cost?

"Oh, hell, don't start crying," Alex said, rolling his eyes. "I can't stand that!"

She laughed though it came out more a hiccuping sob. "You never could. I'll bet Kiki can still turn you to marshmallow whenever she wants something just by screwing up her face and *pretending* she's about to start crying."

Kiki. Alex's wife for three years now. Lacy could see her face as clearly as if her beautiful sister-in-law were standing in front of her. And there were the twins, her niece and nephew. Little Mike and Missy, adorable toddlers blessed with their mother's red-gold hair and their father's easygoing disposition. She was crazy about them.

She'd been about to ask what Alex was doing there, in a Dallas mall, but then she remembered. He lived here. Well, in Arlington, actually, but same thing ... or close enough. He was a professional football player; a tight end for the Dallas Cowboys.

And her parents, Joni and Ed Sands. They'd moved here from La Jolla right after the twins were born.

It was all coming back to her—her childhood, her brother's wedding to his high school sweetheart, Kristen Kelly Kilty, then his successful move from college football at USC as a first round draft pick to the professional level. She even remembered her father's disappointment and weekend-long sulk because Alex hadn't signed with the San Francisco 49ers.

Lacy was connecting all the dots, creating a very real picture of her family ... so where was she? Where were the memories of her life over the past several months?

Alex's thick brows drew together with the suddenness of his frown as he peered into her face. With one of his plate-sized hands, he caught her chin, raising her face up to his. His eyes narrowed, he studied her features, and she knew he'd found the thread-thin scars on her face where the tears must have washed away the camouflage of her makeup.

"Okay, Shel, tell me what's going on? What the hell's happened to you?"

She looked away, not because she didn't want to answer; because she didn't know what to tell him.

"Hey, it's me, kid, your brother, remember? Talk to me," Alex encouraged. His brows lifted and he rolled his green eyes again. "Geez, I'm an asshole, aren't I? Of course, you don't want to tell me what's gone down ... not out here in front of all these jokers. Come on, let's go home. No, better than that, we'll go to Mom and Dad's. They're going to be so damned glad to see you."

The temptation was there, but the fear, too. It just seemed too much too soon, and she was terrified. And then there was Jesse. Most important of all, there was Jesse. She couldn't lose him, yet she knew, if she stepped back into that other world, that safe place of family, she'd never find her way back to him again. So she shook her head as she placed a hand against her brother's troubled face. "I can't, Alex. I can't see them. Not yet."

"Look, damn it, you're coming home with me. If you don't want to go to their place, you can come to my house. Kiki's probably out finishing up the shopping for the kids' birthday tomorrow, so we'll have the place to ourselves . . ."

Birthday. Tomorrow. Theirs was the same day as Jesse's!

Alex was talking, but she wasn't listening. She was praying, *begging* God not to make the trade she was so desperately afraid He was offering. She wanted Alex, her parents, the babies, and her sister-in-law. She wanted the memory of her own life back, but not in exchange for Jesse.

"Shelby, what's wrong with you? You aren't listening to a thing I'm saying."

"Oh, God," she said, covering her mouth with her hand. "Alex, I'm sorry. I know how weird this all is for you. And you're right. A lot has happened. But I can't go with you. I can't talk about it. Not yet. I'll call you. I promise. Just give me until Sunday. Then I'll call you, and Mom and Dad. We'll all get together and I'll explain everything I can, I promise."

She'd stood up, shoving the strap of her handbag on her shoulder and grabbing the plastic garment bag from the fountain ledge. Alex bounded to his feet at the same time, seizing one of her arms, though with gentle pressure.

"Damn it, Shel, I can't let you go like this. We've been worried sick, all of us for—"

"You don't have any choice," she said, her tone harsh. She stretched up on her toes to kiss his cheek and wrap an arm around his thick neck for a long moment. "I'm sorry. Forgive me. I love you, Alex. I love you all. Tell them, and trust me, please. I'll call you Sunday, I promise."

Alex didn't argue further. He gave her his phone number, then just stood there, this football giant, who'd once been her hero.

She hurried away, stopping to glance back only when she was sure he'd be gone. He was still there, and even from the distance as great as the field he played on, she recognized his expression. She'd seen it once before, in the desolate little boy standing on the curb holding his sister's hand so tight she almost forgot the hurt in her heart as their father put the remains of their Dobie pup into a plastic garbage bag minutes after he'd been struck by a car.

It was a two-hour drive back to the ranch. It took her nearly four. Partly because she'd sat crying for so long in the parking lot. Mostly because she drove so slowly. She was in no hurry to give up what she'd just almost, almost had in the grasp of her hand.

Jesse was pumping iron in the state-of-the-art workout room. Not that he hadn't put in a hard enough day. Hell, he'd gone into Rooster early that morning, leaving only minutes after Lacy headed north for Dallas. As his family had done since the town was founded, he was doing his duty by the Widow Trajillo; paying his respects, offering a place to stay since the house had been burned to the ground, and seeing to funeral arrangements per her instructions. Then he'd gone to see the sheriff to check out any leads on suspects or theories as to why the murder had been committed. Frustrated by the negative response, he'd returned home to change clothes and join his men in the arduous work of cutting out calves for branding. They hadn't stopped until the last one scampered away bawling and bearing the brand of a double S over a star. The sun was setting by the time he reentered the house.

The spicy aroma of barbecue beef wafted from the kitchen, and he spied Dillon and Cybil seated at the table in the dining room as he walked past. He had no appetite either for food or conversation. Besides, he'd learned a valuable lesson in the past two days. He didn't dare stop longer than a few minutes. His thoughts proved too traitorous, making a beeline for Lacy, his beautiful, treacherous wife, who, God help him, he loved and hated with equal vengeance.

So he was using a last means to exorcise her from his system: a workout guaranteed to exhaust him past cognizance of anything other than need for sleep. And, goddamn it, if that didn't work, there was always Crown Royal. It had more than once proven itself a man's best friend.

Dillon turned at the familiar sound of drunken shuffling coming from the library to his right. "Come on out, Cyl. I'll carry you upstairs to bed."

She slithered along the wall until she appeared in the slanting light that slashed across her face to create a chinless profile of red frizz and jaundiced yellow cheeks and eyeball on one side, a featureless mask of melted gray wax on the other.

"I was jus' wonnerin', honey," she began. "When I hear you braggin' 'bout how you're going to get some, why don't you just say it like it is? Just say it right out. 'I'm going into Rooster to fuck that cute little whore, Dina, I got waitin' for me'?"

Dillon tucked his thumbs into the pockets of his jeans, his weight distributed mostly on one leg as he stared with considerable emotion at his wife. He'd once loved her. More than she'd ever suspected. And truth was, she'd been pretty crazy about him no matter how she denied it today. It was the baby thing that had turned it all bad for the two of them. If he'd known, coulda seen into the future . . . well, wasn't no sense gettin' into that again. And besides, the truth of it was, he was headed just where she suspected. Gonna find a little comfort in the arms of someone who didn't want nothin' in return except a hundred-dollar bill left on her nightstand. But first he had to get Cyl to bed.

"Come on, baby. Daddy'll carry you upstairs and get you all tucked—"

The front door opened just then, slamming hard into his shoulder.

"Son of a —" His complaint ended on a half note as he caught sight of his sister-in-law's face. Jesus Christ, Cybil looked almost healthy compared to Lacy's pallor.

And her eyes ... looked like some joker had popped her a couple of good ones. Either that or she'd cried herself half sick. "Hey, sweetcakes, you don't look so good," he said, taking a step in her direction only to be stopped by Jesse as he entered the foyer from the hallway behind the staircase.

"Looks like you got enough to handle with your own wife, Dillon," Jesse said, his tone ominously low.

Cybil licked her lips as she took in her brother-in-law's damp, tousled jet hair, his powerful bare chest that gleamed bronze as sweat still trickled along his washboard abdomen into his navel revealed by the vee of his half-buttoned jeans. He was barefoot and sexy as the devil himself must've been when he went out tempting saints. Ooh wee, if only she was the saint this devil was piercing with his black onyx eyes tonight. Only thing was, maybe someone ought to point out that Lacy was anything but that.

"Come on, Cyl, honey," Dillon said, pushing his Stetson back on his head and catching his wife up in his arms. "Time we get you to bed."

Cybil grinned, clutching her bottle in one arm, her other one hooked around her husband's neck. "Hey, Dill?" she asked as they started up the stairs. "You ever notice how your mama built this house like a billiards table? No matter where we all are, we keep emptying out into that pocket. You think she planned it that way so she could keep an eye on all the balls at one time?"

"I think you're drunk," Dillon said, though now that he thought about it, she did have a point. Nobody in the house could escape crossing through that room and Rose could watch the comings and goings from wherever she sat.

Cybil was laughing. "You men are so silly. Of course I'm drunk. I *stay* drunk, Dill, honey. It's how I cope."

They'd reached their bedroom and he laid her gently on the bed, then sat down beside her. With his forefinger, he brushed a thick strand of red hair from the center of her forehead. "I'm sorry," he said, meaning it for the first time in a very long time.

"Oh, you don't have to be sorry, sweetie. It's not your fault. Used to blame you." She stopped, yawning widely, then sliding down onto her pillow and curling up around her bottle that she still clutched between her breasts.

Dillon sat there another moment until he believed she was asleep, but just as he got to his feet, she spoke again.

"Do you know how clear it all is at the bottom of a bottle, Dillon? I mean everything. You should try it with me sometime. You'd be amazed how different everything looks. Be amazed what you hear, too. You can hear the truth in the bottom of a bottle, honey. I'll tell you about it later, 'kay?"

Dillon was surprised at the tears that stung his eyes as he worked the comforter down beneath her hips and legs, then pulled it up once again to cover her. He kissed her cheek. "Love you," he said, surprised that a part of him still meant it.

Lacy knew how she looked, her eyes swollen from hours of crying that she couldn't seem to hold back . . . even now. Her face as pale as the white terry towel that was draped around her hus—Jesse's neck. She was as low as she'd ever been in her life. She'd remembered a lot about her family . . . her pre-Jesse family, and even recaptured a few memories about the pre-Jesse woman she had been. Shelby Sands. Single, ambitious, successful. An artist who lived above her shop in a cozy little apartment in the artsy community of Laguna Beach, California. She'd been a doll maker. No, that didn't say it all. She'd created portraits in porcelain. Dolls molded to almost perfect replicas of famous people. She'd made a name for herself, was reknowned in her own humble right. Doll maker to the stars, monarchs, the rich and famous, and the just plain egotistical.

And she didn't care a fig about any of that. She'd trade it all for a single thread of hope to cling to, a tiny scrap of evidence that would link her to Jesse *before* the accident that had taken her memory and was giving it back to her in useless little pieces.

So, she'd cried.

She had a right. She was miserable.

All the way home, she'd struggled with what she knew. A lot more now, though not much that added up either. Hardly anything that made much sense.

Jesse had married a woman who claimed she was from

Oregon. Who had told Rose and the others she had no family except for a grandmother who had recently died. Who maintained she'd moved to Texas because she was inspired by cowboys and the whole Western thing—music, attire, ambience—important to a romance writer such as herself. That lie had rung false from the first note.

This same woman had confided to Cookie Conchita that she was, in reality, a former showgirl from Vegas who'd been involved in a ten-year relationship with a mobster who was now out to get her for testifying against him.

Was it possible all three women were one and the same?

The doll maker part was right. That much she was sure of; she'd remembered that on her own even before the run-in with Alex. And there was no question, she was a dead ringer for the girl Jesse'd married. Besides, she'd been carrying the purse with the Texas driver's license issued to Lacy James-Pryde. Now, how could that be if she wasn't that woman?

But the last part, the part about Sammy Wyatt and a hired hit man, that was as real as all the rest, too. She'd actually recognized Clay Waters, knew his name before Jesse had spoken it, and recognized him as the guy who'd been hired to kill her.

Then why all the discrepancies?

Okay, so she understood the name change. If she'd been put into the federal witness program, of course they'd give her a new name. But how did she fit the pieces of a well-respected doll maker with the puzzle parts she had of the conniving woman Cookie had described?

It didn't add up, and yet when she'd had the perfect opportunity to get answers, she'd run. Why? Why hadn't she gone with Alex and spoken with their parents? Damn it, who was she kidding? She knew why. She couldn't risk an explanation that might prove she wasn't Jesse's wife at all; merely an accident victim who had somehow gotten tangled up in someone else's mess and ended up falling for a man who wasn't hers to love.

"Are you okay?" Jesse asked, surprising her with his gentle tone.

She didn't look at him.

She had only glanced his way once when she'd entered the house. That was enough. More than enough. God, he was handsome, standing there breathing hard and gleaming with perspiration just like when they'd made love. A groan she refused release had lodged in her throat almost choking her. She swallowed it now and forced herself to answer. "No, Jesse, I'm not all right. I'm tired and upset and . . . and could you just please leave me alone?"

He didn't answer, though she waited hoping against hope he'd say something, *do* something that would help her find her way back to certainty about who she was. Who *they* were to each other. She sighed. "I'm going to bed. Tomorrow—no, I almost forgot, tomorrow's your birthday. Sunday, then. We have to talk. Yes, we'll talk then . . . Sunday."

"Damn it, Lacy, just one time, could you step off that world that revolves around you long enough to think about someone else."

That hurt. Caught her like a knife square between the shoulder blades. She gasped, hesitating a second before starting up the stairs.

"Stop, damn it!" he shouted, reaching for her before she got more than a couple of steps past him. He missed her arm, catching her purse instead. The strap broke and the purse dropped, spilling the contents down the stairs. Lacy let them fall. She was suddenly too tired to pick them up. Besides, in an odd way, it felt appropriate leaving the trail strewn behind her. There wasn't much. Like the smidgens of her life, all of it together didn't add up to a hill of beans.

Chapter Twenty-seven

She pulled the car to a stop at the curb, then simply sat there staring at the roof peaks—all she could see of the house she'd always hated so damned much.

Moments later she keyed in the code to open the electronic gate. Stupid bitch hadn't even thought to change it. Not smart, Grandma, dear.

She had a key to the door as well. Could have unlocked it herself same as the gate. Well, not this time. This time she wanted to be announced like someone who mattered instead of just the prodigal granddaughter returned ... unwanted. She depressed the button, then grimaced at the melodious tinkling of chimes. Anything to impress. That was good old pretentious Lotte.

At the sound of chimes announcing a visitor to the Brentwood estate, Maria Fuentas approached the front door. An uncommonly pretty Latino woman whether dressed in sequins for a night out with Juan, her fiancé, or clad in her uniform of jeans and T-shirt as she was now, a ready smile was as much a part of her beauty as her flawless olive skin or brush-thick eyelashes. But as she peered through the door at her employer's visitor, hatred and anger radically warped her beauty.

"Who is it, Maria?" The question, called out in a voice ground to gravel by years of cigarettes, came from the living room where the girl's employer passed most of her waking hours since the mild stroke she'd suffered a month before.

Her dark eyes fixed on the familiar face distorted by the door's thick lead glass window, she answered the query under her breath. "The *puta*."

"Maria!" the old woman admonished.

Maria opened the door, announcing the visitor in the same instant. "It's your granddaughter, ma'am!"

The sound of the wheelchair's motor whirred to life as Maria stepped aside to allow the visitor entrance.

Then without a word, Maria turned on her heel and marched off toward the back of the house.

"What are you doing here?" Charlotte Daniels asked as soon as she rounded the corner from the living room to the foyer.

"What a silly question, Gran. I've come to see how you are, of course."

The old woman spun the chair around, heading it back in the direction from which she'd come. "Well, you've seen. Now you can show yourself out."

"Ooh, so hostile," her granddaughter said, tagging after her, then dropping to the sofa a few feet from where the wheelchair had stopped. "And me your loving, sweet—"

"Loving! Sweet! Ha! The only thing sweet about you is that cloying perfume you wear. As for loving, maybe when you're in rare form and acting out for a man. But don't try and lay that crap on me. *I* know you, remember?"

"Do you? Really? Hmm, I wonder. Let's find out. If you know me so well, what am I doing here today? Why after all these months have I deigned to treat you to a few minutes of my valuable time?"

The old woman pulled a cigarette from a crumpled foil wrapper, sticking it between dry lips with trembling fingers.

"Do you have to do that while I'm here? You know how I hate cigarette smoke."

The woman in the wheelchair cackled. "Just like you know how much I hate you coming here. Didn't stop you, did it?" She put lighter to cigarette, pulling only a little smoke into her lungs before being stopped by a wet-sounding cough that wracked her frail body.

Her granddaughter swung her long slender leg impatiently and tucked a strand of pale blond hair behind her ear. When her grandmother's fit of coughing began to wane, she laughed. "I don't know why I discourage you. Every time I hear you cough like that, I'm reminded that all this—the old, old money, this dreary mausoleum that you keep dark as a tomb, even all your wonderfully gaudy jewelry—will be mine sooner than

later. Come to think of it, the only time I don't hate
you is when I remember all I stand to gain when you
accommodate this world by kicking the proverbial
bucket. I've even decided what to have inscribed on your
tombstone. 'Here she lies, no more rotten than she was
in life, only more appreciated for being dead.' "

"Charming. I'm touched that you've given me so much
thought. Now you may go."

"Oh, I think not. At least not until I've found out
what you've heard."

"Found out? About what?"

"Don't play games with me, you old bitch. Has there
been anything on the news?"

"Oh, you must be talking about the poor girl who was
run down by an unidentified assailant on the pier last
month." She took another puff on her cigarette, this
time only sputtering a couple of times like a tired
muffler.

"Tell me," her granddaughter said, scooting forward
so that she sat on the very edge of the sofa.

"They identified the victim, of course. Lacy James-
Pryde. But you know that. Said she's back home convalescing in her billionaire husband's Texas hacienda."

"Where she has no right to be."

"But where she is," Charlotte pointed out, her voice
suddenly strong and mean.

"Only because she didn't die like she was supposed
to."

Charlotte aimed the fiery tip of her cigarette toward
her granddaughter's face. "Then it *was* you who hit her.
I had my suspicions. Was almost certain when they announced that the police had found the shell of a burned-
out import registered to the victim. Knew it had to be
you who tricked her into trusting you. Only thing I
couldn't figure was how you convinced her to just stand
there while you ran her down."

"Like you said, she trusted me."

Charlotte watched, puffing and hacking, as her granddaughter stood, smoothing her expensive cashmere skirt
and tossing her pale hair as she'd seen her do a thousand
times in front of a mirror or just before her picture was
snapped by a camera lens, even on stage. It was a character trait as inherent as her cruelty and selfishness.

"Where are you going now?"

"Why, home of course. Only this time, I'm going to take what's rightfully mine. Jesse was never hers. He belongs to me. I fly to Dallas tonight." Another toss of her silky mane. "Tomorrow's his birthday, and I have no intention of missing the party."

Charlotte followed after her into the foyer. "You didn't ask about the wheelchair."

"What's to ask? You've had a stroke. That's obvious, isn't it? My God, you're drooling all over yourself from the corner of your mouth and who could help noticing that withered, useless claw just lying there in your lap. Pathetic. Hardly the picture of the indomitable bitch I've always held near and dear to remind me how much I despise you. Funny. You'd think I'd forget all that seeing you this way—reduced to a wasted old crone—but I still hate you every bit as much as I ever did. Only now you repulse me, too."

Her grandmother pulled a gold locket from beneath her housecoat, gripping it with the hand that still had strength. "God help me, I created a monster."

Her granddaughter's laughter floated like the tinkling sound of bells around them. Exquisite; as beautiful as her perfectly sculpted face. But the ugliness inside seeped out with her words. "God can't help you, poor sweetheart. You sold your soul to the devil nearly twenty-five years ago just thirty miles from here. You do remember Topanga Canyon, don't you? So near, yet so far. A cliché to be sure, but so apropos, don't you think?"

The air that was warm and balmy on this summer California afternoon nevertheless chilled the old woman as her granddaughter stepped out the door. She shivered as her hand tightened momentarily around the locket, then fell away as the last of her vigor ebbed.

Her head lolled against her chest. Still, she knew the moment Maria stepped out of the shadows. "You're a good girl," she said, her speech so slurred the words were hardly understood.

"Shh, *Madre mia*," Maria whispered against the woman's ear. There were no blood ties between them, of course. But the endearment was sincerely uttered, for the young Hispanic girl loved the old lady as much as her granddaughter hated her.

Pushing the chair instead of switching on the motor, she kept her back bent, her mouth close to the woman's ear. "Maria will put you to bed now for a rest. Later, after you've napped, I will read from one of the romance novels you love so much. Perhaps Tiffany White's latest one. She makes you smile."

Charlotte wasn't listening. She was thinking about her granddaughter and what she must do before she could rest. She had little time left and somehow she had to atone for her sins . . . right a twenty-five-year wrong.

"Ah, you're back," Joey said, bounding to his feet and racing for the door to help his wife with the packages she was carrying. "We have company, babe."

She followed his gaze to the redheaded man who'd been sitting, head bent over some papers, with her husband as she came into their hotel suite. He'd come out of his chair almost as quickly as Joey, and was staring at her with the self-conscious grin of a little boy who'd just been caught in the doctor's office stealing Band-Aids.

"I can see that," she said in a reply to her husband's unnecessary announcement. Going over to the sofa, she dropped her load of shopping bags and boxes, all from Rodeo Drive and each bearing the logo of a famous designer. "How do you do?" she asked, extending her hand and simultaneously tucking a strand of hair behind her ear with the other one. "I'm Liberty Ambrose."

The man's face flushed an incompatible scarlet to his carrot-orange hair. "I doubt you could find a half-dozen people who wouldn't recognize you, Ms. Ambrose. My name's Frank, by the way. Frank Mandell. I work for your husband."

"You're a caterer?" she asked, looking at her husband at the same time. Come to think of it, Joey seemed as flustered as his young associate.

"Uh, yes. Well, not actually, no. I'm sort of an intern, I guess you could say."

She smiled, nodding as if she understood, which she didn't. What was going on here? Why were both men so jittery?

"I'm afraid Frank's being far too modest. In fact, he's quite well trained in the culinary arts. I've even decided to send him ahead on the flight to Dallas this evening so he can begin overseeing the arrangements for Jesse's party tomorrow. I want to make certain everything runs smoothly."

She canted her head slightly, her eyes moving back and forth between the men. Joey, usually unflappable and poised, was rattling like a machine gun, his tongue tripping all over itself. And Frank . . . there was something odd about him, too.

At first glance he looked like a twenty-something-year-old nerd eager for a taste of life outside the pages of textbooks. But there was something about the eyes that belied the impression of youthful innocence. She worked a mental shrug, dismissing the bothersome conflict she couldn't quite nail. "Well, I'm glad to have the company on the flight home, Frank."

"Pleasure's mine, Mrs. Wong, er, Ms. Amb—"

"Libby, please. It's easier for everyone." She leaned to the right far enough to peck her husband's lips. "I'm going to leave the two of you to whatever it is you're cooking up—pun intended, fellas—while I change my clothes and get these things I've bought transferred into my luggage."

She was almost to the bedroom door when Joey startled her with an unexpected question.

"You been shopping all day, hon?"

One of her perfectly arched brows lifted. "Mostly," she said carefully. "Why?"

Her husband pulled a gold credit card out of his pocket. "You left this at Tallarico's this morning. They were kind enough to send someone over with it to the hotel."

Silently cursing her carelessness, she crossed the room again in a few quick strides and snatched the card from his hand. "I'll be sure to call and convey my gratitude."

"And perhaps, in the meantime, you should check your purse. I'd hate to have to cancel all your cards if you're missing others." He grinned. "That could take several days."

The last was said on a teasing note. Still, she had the decided impression she was being tested. Joey's prodding and probing, however lightly done, were out of character. But then so was her negligence. Could be that the strain of keeping the true reason for her visit to L.A. a secret was having its effect on her. Oh, well, it was just until tomorrow. She could stand it until then. In the meantime, she had to reassure Joey, keep him off the scent until the party and her announcement. "I give you my solemn promise I have not left any more credit cards lying around. In fact, Tallarico's was the last store I was in." Winking at the man named Frank, she kissed her husband soundly on the lips. "There. Not just my word. Also sealed with a kiss."

Frank laughed. Joey frowned.

"Then where were you this afternoon?"

Libby was beginning to get annoyed. "Joey, sweetheart," she said, still managing a sugary tone, "why all the questions? I've never been treated to an inquisition before and I'm sure Mr. Mandell is as uncomfortable as I am."

Frank laughed. "Hey, just pretend I'm not here. My wife and I go through this all the time."

"But we don't," Libby said, head tilted a bit as she studied her husband's face for a clue. It wasn't possible, was it, that he had somehow found out about her secret visit?

Joey's smile cut the tension. "Hey, sorry, babe. I didn't mean my questions as a cross-examination. I just worry about you sometimes. Turning into an overzealous, overprotective husband, I guess." He ran his fingers through his long blue-black hair. "Just all the horror I hear on the news. Makes me crazy."

Her relief so heady Libby felt giddy, she laughed. "Hey, you're forgetting the little .22 I carry at all times." She turned to Frank, expanding on the details. "I'm not exactly Annie Oakley, but I know how to shoot. In my line of work, we attract all sorts of wackos. They come out of the woodwork. Anyway, I'm even licensed to carry a concealed weapon because I'm what the"—she held up her hands, wiggling her fingers to form imaginary quote marks—"cops call 'high risk.' Anyway, I'm going in to change, so you, Frank, keep my sweetie here from listening to any more paranoia-inducing news broadcasts."

She was in the bedroom unzipping the back of her dress and doing an instant mental replay of the strange conversation when it hit her what it was about Frank Mandell's eyes that didn't gibe with the rest of his youthful features. They reminded her of Ho Chen Wong, Joey's great-grandfather whom she'd met when they'd traveled to China to celebrate the ancient Mandarin's one-hundred-fifth birthday. She remembered the impression she'd had of seeing a century of endurance and knowledge in his weary gaze. Frank had that same age-old look of life too personally experienced. It was weird and unnerving in a man so young.

As she pulled the dress over her head, however, she gave up wondering about the wannabe-caterer Joey had hired. In truth, she was too tired to give much thought as to why his eyes didn't match the rest of the picture. Shirley MacLaine would no doubt explain it as a man's old spirit who'd passed through life too many times. *Brother.* Right now, Libby just hoped she could get through the rest of this day.

Working her panty hose from her hips, she sat down on the edge of the bed while she peeled them off the rest of the way, a leg at a time.

That done, she fell back on the king-sized bed, covering her face with her hands. Damn, this wasn't just tired, this was bone-aching weary, and she still had that flight, then the drive back to Rooster Corner.

Her eyes closed, she stretched her arms over her head and grinned. Exhausted, yes, but worth it? Oh, yeah! She'd accomplished everything she'd come for. Now, all she had to do was get home . . . and get a good night's sleep.

Tomorrow she was going to celebrate. It wasn't going to be *just* a birthday party. It was going to be the day she rocked a certain guy's world.

Once and for all she was going to settle the question about the tortoise and the hare.

She'd made a helluva lot of mistakes in the past, gotten off to more than her share of false starts, but tomorrow she was going to bring home the blue ribbon.

Happy birthday, Jesse. Happy ever after, Libby!

*　　*　　*

American Airlines flight 1804 was scheduled to depart LAX at five-thirty p.m. Expected arrival time at Dallas/ Ft. Worth: ten twenty-six.

Friday evening flights were heavily reserved. There was rarely an exception to this rule. Especially in the summer months when conventions were closely booked. Tonight, however, the L1011 was filled only to half capacity in the coach section. Less than that in first class. In fact, only four passengers occupied the forward cabin.

Rose Pryde occupied an aisle seat, front row.

Behind her, one row back and across the aisle, Liberty Ambrose had finally taken her seat against the window after graciously signing autographs for the flight crew as well as several passengers.

Frank Mandell had boarded last minute, plopping into his seat beside the famous model.

Kathy Ramona, the senior flight attendant, fussed over him, offering pillow and blanket, magazines, a drink—as if she alone knew the undercover agent's true identity and the reason for his late boarding.

Rose Pryde ignored them completely.

The woman seated in the far back row kept her eyes closed, her face turned toward the window and resting against the pillow the attendant had arranged beneath her head. But she wasn't sleeping. She was listening. Taking it all in.

She'd been boarded early—long before the others— because of her condition and the wheelchair. And when they reached their destination, she'd be off-loaded last, long after everyone was gone . . . on their way to the Southern Star. Her destination as well. Though she wouldn't be arriving until tomorrow. She'd be spending the night in Dallas. After all, it would be rude to get there before the festivities began.

She sighed, deciding on a nap. She was weary after an especially arduous and emotional day. Still, she was contented. Everything had been put into motion. She was on her way to setting a few things straight, righting a very gross wrong.

Besides, she was amused, a rarity these days. She'd long ago learned to appreciate the Fates for their caprice and sense of the ridiculous. She'd merely forgotten how delightfully naughty they could be, how often devilish their tricks. Like the irony of this instance: a flight normally booked to capacity, yet pared down to only four passengers in first class, and all by chance? She thought not. Not when one considered the even greater coincidence.

All of them headed for the same ultimate destination. The Southern Star. Most magnificent spread in the entire Lone Star state. The woman chuckled under her breath. Magnificent by the standards of other ranchers, perhaps, but on the whole face of the world? Hardly even a zit.

Chapter Twenty-eight

Jesse watched Lacy disappear along the hall upstairs. The day before, he'd recovered his hatred, every stinking ounce of it. Then tonight, seeing her like that. Her pain touched him. Touched him, hell. It cut into him as incisively as a fuckin' razor. Dropping to his knees, he snatched her purse from the floor and began scooping up her spilled cache of possessions. What had she found out in Dallas that had so devastated her? One by one, he picked up her things, dropping them into the leather handbag—a tube of lipstick, a pair of sunglasses, her billfold, two pens, a map, some loose change, an envelope bearing a doctor's name and address in the upper left-hand corner ... a business card, someone named Alex Sands. Dallas Cowboys Football Organization? *The* Alex Sands as in number eighty-six?

Confused, he stuck the card into the purse as well, reached for the passbook he'd given her, then turned and sat down on the bottom step. Flipping the small blue book end over end in his hands, he dismissed the question about the football player's card, backtracking to the envelope. Was that it? Was it something the doctor had told her? Had he given her a negative prognosis for recovering her memory? And then it hit him. The printed return address in the upper left-hand corner. Dr. Lewis M. Carrool. But it was the tag that followed that widened Jesse's eyes and quickened his heartbeat. *Obstetrics & Gynecology.*

His hands shaking, he fumbled through the purse.

The passing of seconds were ticked off by the clock in one irritating click at a time as he stared at the envelope. Why had she consulted a gynecologist? What business was it of his? And why had she lied about what kind of specialist she was consulting unless ...

No more questions. He was sick to death of the questions, the innuendo, the walls that were erected every time he rounded a corner or asked even the simplest question. Even Raul, poor bastard, had refused to answer the whys about his wife's sudden abortion. So maybe, just maybe, he'd find an answer here, in the report a specialist in Dallas had given Lacy.

But, if she was devastated by the truth, could he stand it?

Letting the purse drop to the stair beside him, he pulled out the flap that was merely tucked instead of sealed and took out the typewritten report.

His eyes scanned the brief two paragraphs, once, twice, then slower until he couldn't see through the tears that filled his eyes.

He jumped to his feet, taking the stairs two at a time

He didn't bother to knock when he reached her room. Just barged in, then came to a dead stop in the darkness. "Lacy?" he asked, surprising himself by the moderate tone, considering that he wanted to shout ... dance, anything to release the incredible joy he felt.

"Go away, Jesse," she said quietly, her voice coming from a corner across the room. Between the closet and the chest of drawers? But that was crazy unless ... "Lace, are you sitting on the floor in the corner?"

"Damn it," she muttered and then he heard the dull, muffled thud of what must have been her fists as she slammed them ineffectively against the thick carpet. He grinned. She was pissed. That was good. Better than her sitting here crumpled up and feeling sorry for herself.

"Don't you laugh at me, Jesse Pryde! No, scratch that. Laugh your ass off, but go away and do it somewhere else, okay?"

He hadn't realized that with the light from the hall bathing him from the side, she could see him even though she remained only an indistinct silhouette.

Shit. He wasn't laughing at her. He was grinning from ear to ear like a jackass because she was so damned cute and ... oh, hell. He started across the room, his step quick until he bumped his shin painfully against the stool that sat before her vanity. With little more than an acknowledging grunt, he kept going until he saw her. Then he went down on his knees before her.

"Oh, God, Lacy, I love you. I don't understand. I'm so fucking confused I'm not sure what's up and what's down, what's real and what's not. Shit, I'm not even sure this isn't all a dream. But I know I love you, woman, and that's all I care about right now."

He tried to draw her to him, but she brought her arms up in front of her, warding him off. "You're crazy. Leave me alone."

"Maybe. Like I said, I'm not sure about anything. All I know is you didn't kill our baby. Don't get me wrong, a part of me would like to shake you till you explain why you'd tell such a stinkin' lie or your teeth rattle. But the truth is I don't give a rat's ass why. So long as you didn't get rid of the baby I tried like hell to give you, nothing else matters."

She had to tell him. But what? That she wasn't his wife? She didn't know that for sure. So, what else? That her name was Shelby Sands, not Lacy Pryde. But hadn't Cookie told her that her name had been changed by some legal mumbo jumbo for her protection? Yet how could that be? She wasn't some Las Vegas moll. She was just an ordinary girl from southern California who made beautiful dolls. Then why had someone hired Clay Waters to kill her?

Jesse saw the panic as it came into her eyes. "What is it, Lace? What are you afraid of?"

But she couldn't answer him. All at once, she was crying again, this time so hard she thought she might never stop.

Jesse pulled her into his arms. He rocked her there, cradling her like a baby, kissing her brow and making shushing noises until her weeping eased. Then he got to his feet and carried her across the room, placing her on the bed.

She reached for him when he turned away, catching hold of his wrist. "Don't leave me, Jesse."

"I'm just going to the bathroom to get you a cool washcloth."

She shook her head. "No, please, stay with me. I need you."

He didn't hesitate. He'd never deny her anything again. As long as she wanted him, he would be there for her. He stretched out on the bed beside her, pulling her against

him and holding her tight enough so that the sound of
their hearts beating became indistinguishable from one another. One heart as it always should have been.

She still cried, though quieter, softly. He kissed her
brow, then her eyes, tasting the salt on her tear-soaked
lashes. He murmured vows of love against her ear between more gentle kisses of affirmation.

She raised her arms to wrap them around his neck,
running her fingers through his hair, and kissed his
throat. "I love you, too, Jesse, with all my heart. But I
have to explain."

"No," he said, his voice husky with the need aroused by
the simple touch of her lips against his neck. "Not now.
Just kiss me again and . . ." The rest of his thought vanished as her lips, hot and moist, started a fire that coursed
from his throat to the pit of his stomach and beyond.

"Oh, God," he muttered as he rolled her over onto her
back. Rising above her, he bracketed her hips with his
knees and worked the peach knit dress she wore an inch
at a time above her hips, over her waist, up above her
breasts. He stopped there, forgetting the dress as his hands
cupped the perfect globes and a growl of fierce desire escaped his lips. Scooting his body lower, he parted her
thighs with one of his knees as he bowed his head and
captured one of her swollen nipples in his mouth.

Lacy was as hungry as he. She writhed and arched her
back. Working an arm between them, her hand closed
over the full swell of his crotch. She groaned, frustrated
by the coarse denim denying her access to his smooth,
pulsing hardness she wanted to hold and massage and
ultimately caress with her lips.

"Take them off," she said.

Jesse reared up, his powerful muscles rippling beneath
his glistening sun-bronzed skin. Lacy traced his bare skin
from his stomach to his shoulders as he unfastened the
last buttons on his jeans. "You're like a beautiful golden
stallion," she said in a husky whisper as her hand dipped
inside the opening he'd just created to free him. Her
hand circling him, she pushed him down on his back with
the other arm, then drew her legs beneath her as
she lowered herself and took him into her mouth.

She sucked, taking him into her throat, then releasing

him to the tip and closing her mouth over him again and teasing the tiny slit with her tongue.

"Oh, God, Lace." It came out a long, ragged complaint, but he thrust his hips in the same instant making it more a plea. Lacy didn't disappoint him. She had no intention of letting him go. Not just yet.

And then his hands found her breasts beneath her dress that had fallen down to cover her again. His strong fingers massaged them, grinding them against her chest, then closing around her nipples and pulling them roughly. She cried out. Yet it wasn't the exquisite pain but the surprisingly quick orgasm he'd brought her to.

She jerked to an upright position, keeping him in her hand, though for a long moment, she couldn't move; could only let the dizzying waves wash over her. Her fingernail grazed back and forth against the head of his quivering cock.

As soon as the last of the wave passed, she bent forward once again, intending to pleasure him some more, but he stopped her with knees drawn up to hold her pinned while he inserted his forefingers into the waistband on both sides of her frilly bikini panties. With a single pull, he slid them from under her and tossed them to the floor.

With his powerful arms, he lifted her up on her knees, then conveyed a silent order not to move with his piercing black eyes.

He shoved his jeans from his hips to his knees, not bothering to shrug them the rest of the way off, and though neither of them had spoken, she understood his desire for her to pull the dress off.

When she was naked, her legs parted still on either side of his thighs, he ran his thumb along her sex testing her wetness. Then he lifted her, hands on her waist, bringing her forward and lowering her above his shaft.

Using only intuition to guide her, she spread her knees wider and moved her hips in small, concise circles over the head of his erection until she felt the tip slip inside the opening she immediately closed around him, drawing him deeper and deeper until the immense length of him was buried entirely inside. Then she began to rock, slowly at first and only an inch or two back and forth. Then harder, faster, farther. His fingers bit into her buttocks, then slipped between them, joining his penis inside her so that not a single nerve ending in her most sensitive place escaped his touch. She cried out, then began to ride in earnest. He was a bull, crazed with passion, thrusting and turning and bucking, and she rode him, meeting every brutal thrust until the instant he captured her hips, pinning her against him as he exploded in climax and the beast she'd awakened inside him cried out.

So completely in tune, their instinct as profoundly joined as their bodies, he brought her crashing to orgasm just as his let go. She fell against his chest, her breasts heaving and the muscles that still surrounded him trembling uncontrollably like a storm-wracked ship dashed yet pierced and held by a shaft of granite.

When he could move, he kicked his jeans from his legs, then flipped the two of them over so that he was above her. He caught her face between his long fingers and gazed into her eyes that were still tear-stained and swollen and indescribably beautiful. "Don't you ever think of getting away from me again, Lace, 'cause I'm not ever letting you go."

She shook her head, a silent message of agreement never to try.

If only she was sure it was a promise she would be able to keep.

Tomorrow . . . tomorrow she'd tell him everything she'd learned. They'd work the puzzle together. But not tonight. Tonight was theirs. And she wasn't sharing a single second of it. Not with all the questions thrumming around in her head after answers. Not with Shelby Sands or Sammy Wyatt and his back-stabbing girlfriend. Not with Clay Waters, the hired killer working right here on the *Southern Star.* Not even with the terrifying possibility that once they discovered the truth, he might not want her anymore. *Especially* not with that.

"Hold me, Jesse."

"Until the twelfth of never."

She grinned against his chest. "Wow," she said.

It was his turn to smile, and together they agreed, "That's a long, long time."

Chapter Twenty-nine

It was approaching two a.m. when the car driven by Randy Hawkins stopped in the driveway just behind the hacienda.

Frank Mandell was out of the back seat and already opening the door for Rose Pryde by the time Randy started his slide from behind the wheel.

Weary, yet maintaining her regal demeanor, Rose accepted the affable caterer's hand, even granting a rare smile. "Why thank you, Mr. Mandell." Her gaze turned hard when it fell on the more laggard Hawkins. "Perhaps since you're so sluggish tonight, Mr. Mandell will help me with my bags while you drive our Liberty to the Rabbit Patch." She looked at Frank. "Would you mind?"

"Not at all," he said, looking to the driver and positioning his hands like a baseball catcher's. "Toss me the keys, Randy. I'll get her luggage out of the trunk. Let's see, yours was the blue tote and matching garment bag, right?"

Rose nodded, then faced Hawkins again. "You know, I never noticed how slow you really are. I suppose I've become so inured to the consequences of so many generations of inbreeding, I've forgotten that there exists a plethora of men out there with both agile minds and vigorous bodies. And here I was beginning to think Jesse the last of an extinct species. Incidentally, speaking of inbreeding, your wife, Suzette, is what? Your second or is it your third cousin?"

Randy felt his face catch fire as he threw the keys to the pansy caterer. First the fucking Chink coming in here and taking one of their women—everyone else might have forgotten that little Liberty was a local gal, not to mention his first love, something Randy Hawkins wasn't likely to admit, by damn. Now, here was another one. Looked like Opie-Fucking-Taylor, but he'd bet he was one of them perverts that liked beatin' off while he watched little boys. Guy certainly had the look. Happy-go-lucky smile and weird freakin' eyes, the way they never stopped movin' like they was scopin' out the place just like in them movies when they crazy fanatics took over the airplanes. Had the same crazy eyes. Always movin'. Nonstop. *Strange.*

Rose snapped her fingers in front of his face. "Stop glaring at Mr. Mandell and get going. Liberty's tired and would no doubt like to get home, preferably before dawn."

The palm of Randy's hand beginning to itch, he rubbed it over the ass of his worn jeans. Only itched like that when he got pissed and needed to hit something. Lucky for the old bitch he had more important things on his mind than worrying about her and some fancy-pants cook. Otherwise, he might just give her a sample of the meanness that comes outta *in*breeding. 'Sides everyone knew keepin' it in the family beat the hell outta crossbreedin' like her mama done when she let herself get fucked by that Wolf fella. 'Stead of poppin' *him*, shoulda drowned the kid just like ya do mongrel pups. Woulda done the world a service, gettin' rid of this old bitch.

Walking around to the back of the car, he slammed the trunk shut and snatched the keys from Mandell's hand. "I'll be around if ya need me tomorrow, Miz Pryde."

"As a matter of fact, I'm not done with you tonight, Randy. After you've seen Liberty inside and looked around the house for her, come back here. I want you to show Frank to the bunkhouse. He'll be sleeping there until he returns to California on Monday."

Randy ground his teeth as he formed something remotely akin to a smile. "Sure thing. Be back in a bit, fella. Get you squared away straight off."

Frank nodded. "I appreciate that. Thanks."

Randy had one foot in the car, his tush already settling on the rich leather seat when Rose called out to him again. *Okay, you old squaw, this is it. Just one more, and you're going to be looking for a new boy to yank around by the balls*. He grinned, waiting . . . like he didn't have a thing in the world better to be doing than kissin' her flat ass.

"One more thing. In the morning let Thorn out of his pen. I'm sure he's anxious to run a bit." She started for the house, stopped, and looked back. "He has been penned since I left, hasn't he?"

"Hey, you order it, it's done. You can count on that being fact."

Her answering smile was actually warm. "Why, thank you, Randy. I appreciate your attitude."

He tipped his hat, then climbed into the car. He met Liberty Ambrose's gaze in the rearview mirror for a brief second before shutting off the dome light as he pulled the door shut. "Nice night for a homecoming. Was raining like a sombitch while you was gone. Suppose to start up again tomorrow night."

"Well, maybe it'll hold off until after the party."

"Yeah, maybe," Randy said, leaning his head back and throwing an arm across the back of the seat. "Course, got a feeling most folks ain't gonna feel much like celebrating what with Doc Trajillo being put under tomorrow morning."

Libby slid up to the edge of the seat, making for easier conversation. "Oh, that was so tragic. I didn't know anything about it until I met Rose at the airport. What does the sheriff say. Do they have any suspects? Any motive?"

Hawkins shrugged. "Not that I've heard. Course, I wouldn't be the first to be told, now would I? I'm sure your high and mighty friend, Jesse Pryde, would hear before the rest of us."

Liberty laid a hand on his arm. "Don't be that way, Randy. Not with me. You and I were friends long before . . . well, before Jesse and I ever had anything going. Besides, this is Rooster Corner. Everyone's family here."

"Yeah, tell that to the bank who turned me down on the house I was trying to buy. Or better still, call up 'brother' Jesse and ask him about the raise I asked for last year. Maybe he'll be able to explain it to you."

Libby sat back. Bitterness was something she knew about, so she wasn't offended by Randy's anger. She was merely too tired to take on his troubles. Anyway, all the sympathy in the world wouldn't change the way a man felt until he was ready to change. She'd certainly taken some knocks before coming to terms with that reality. Yes, Randy was going to have to learn for himself. On a sigh, she changed the subject. "Has Clay been tending the horses and feeding my kitten?"

"Why, yes, indeedy. Like I always tell the Boss Lady, we aim to please. Or seeing how you and me's got a history, I'll explain it like it actually is. You all just keep your high and mighty asses stuck out there for us, and we boys'll keep our kissers puckered."

"Screw you," Libby said, curling away from him and closing her eyes.

"Hey, we done that before, remember? You never had no complaints that I can recollect. Guess I jes' wasn't tall enough to lift you out of that there gutter you was born in. Needed a highfalutin Pryde or someone connected high enough like that fancy Chink you married."

"Shut up, Randy, or I swear to God, I'll—"

Randy hit the brakes hard, then slammed the gearshift into park and turned in his seat to glare at her. "Or you'll what? Complain to the Boss Lady or maybe go straight to Mr. Jesse Pryde, the big man himself? And what're either one of them gonna do? Demote me? Deprive me of the pleasure of working harder than anyone else jes' so I can get my ass kicked twice as often, too? Or maybe they'll up and fire me? Whoa, now that scares me shitless." He could barely make out her features in the darkness of the back seat, but he could see that her eyes had widened. He'd frightened her. Ordinarily, the bully in him would have gleaned a measure of satisfaction from that. Somehow, though, tonight it only made him feel as low as she apparently considered him. With a muttered curse, he faced front again, eased the shift into drive, and started off toward the Rabbit Patch once more. "Thing you folks up there in your ivory towers don't understand, Lib. Once you got a man down, it don't do you no good to kick him again. Can't get him any lower than that, so what's the use?"

Ten minutes later Libby sat in the window of the bedroom she shared with Joey, stroking the kitten and nuzzling his soft fur with her cheek.

Neither she nor Randy had spoken much the rest of the way. Not at all, in fact, until he'd carried her bags inside and gone through the rooms as was the custom whenever she returned home from a trip without Joey.

She was beat. As tired as she could ever remember being, but depression had usurped weariness. Randy was right. The two of them had once been friends. More than that. They'd been lovers for a time, a few months. And as he'd said, things had changed. After them, there'd been her affair with Jesse. Her *love* affair that had almost killed her. Then she'd moved away and attained fame and fortune, married Joey. But *she* hadn't changed, not so much that Randy should hate her. Had she?

Given a slight nudge, Chink slipped between Libby's hands to the floor. She paused to meow and arch her back before disappearing into the hall. Libby smiled as she stood up, mimicking the kitten with a deliberate, slow stretch of her own.

Two-thirty! Ah, well, it was going to be a short night and long day. Joey should be home by noon. But she'd be gone long before that. She planned an early morning ride, then a long, leisurely hot soak before going into town to attend Dr. Trajillo's funeral.

She ruffled her thick blond hair with her fingertips and yawned widely. Definitely, a long day. And sad ... at least for a bit, but she wasn't going to let tragedy mar the magic. Not for Jesse. Not for herself. That's what her therapist had taught her. Her happiness had to come first. As long as it did, she'd be able to give it to others.

She slipped beneath the covers, savoring the thrill she felt as always at her homecoming. This was where she was meant to be, here in Texas, with the man she loved. A smile parted her lips as she drifted off to sleep.

Clay rarely slept with more than one eye closed. It was no different tonight. He was awakened by the first creak of the dry hinges on the bunkhouse door. Lying on his side, he didn't stir. Not at the sound of footsteps—two sets, both male, one heavier, clunking, the other light and tapping. He didn't even blink against the sudden harsh ache behind his eyelids induced by the unexpected probe of a flashlight passing over his face. Not even when he made out the words between the intruders, whispering and hushed, and recognized the name Mandell.

Waters was good at everything he did. His senses, like stone chiseled by time, had been honed by experience. He could count down minutes with the accuracy of a stopwatch and he watched them pass now in his head ... two ... four ... seven until the man whose steps he'd known anywhere as Randy Hawkins's exited the doorway.

He didn't move a muscle.

The springs on the bunk across the room squeaked and groused as Frank dropped down, obviously still fully dressed and two damned tired to care. The car engine—the Lincoln Town car Randy had driven to Dallas to chauffeur the missus home in—roared to life in the almost exact same moment.

Waters gave it a retarded count of thirty before slipping soundlessly from his own bed and sneaking to the other agent's side. "Meet me outside in five minutes," he said, his lips pressed against Frank's ear.

Less than three minutes passed before Frank wandered out the door, moseying like a man just too wired from travel to sleep and taking a look around. He ambled forty or fifty yards from the bunkhouse before he stopped and unzipped his trousers. He was already pissing into a clump of bushes when his old friend arrived at his side. "How's it going?" Frank asked, a grin sliding easily into place and his cautiously friendly expression the one he kept reserved for strangers.

"Going great considerin' it's the middle of the night."

"Hey, I wake you? Sorry, pal. Didn't mean to disturb anyone. That's why I came out here to take a leak."

Clay grinned. He and Frank went back, had a history and a long-time friendship. The man was good and he respected that, but more than that, he admired his style. Had the boy next door persona down pat. "Heard ya arrive, sure, but no big deal. I'm a light sleeper. Hear everything. When I realized you was coming out here, thought maybe I'd better follow along, warn ya about the snakes and varmints like to roam around at night. Ain't safe wandering out here on your lonesome in the dark."

Frank zipped his pants, then moved his long, lanky body in a way that made it appear boneless. "I hear what you're saying, buddy, but I'm wired, you know? Can't sleep. Been going all day and need to slow it down inside."

Waters shrugged, his thumbs locked inside his jean pockets. When he rounded an ancient oak, he stopped and leaned against its massive trunk. He faced the hacienda and nodded at the single light that burned in the third-story window when Frank stopped beside him to pull a pack of Camel cigarettes from his pocket.

"You come in with Mrs. Pryde?" Clay asked once his friend's cigarette was lighted.

"Yep, same flight. Hawkins picked us up in Dallas. Liberty Ambrose, too."

Clay nodded, then asked, "Why'd Anderson send you?"

Frank pulled on the cigarette, taking time to exhale before he answered. "I'm working inside the house tomorrow for Joey Wong. Actually, I'm supposed to be setting it all up before he returns from our slightly smog-defiled city of the angels. Had a crash course in catering etiquette and the gourmet hors d'oeuvres menu from Joey Wong himself just this afternoon.

"Didn't know I'd be flying with the dragon lady and the statuesque Liberty, of course. Our borrowed motto of 'Have Gun Will Travel' required some pretty fancy footwork. Had to ditch both of the aforementioned in order to board without displaying the hardware and flashing the metal."

Clay fingered his lush handlebar mustache as it spread with his smile. "So, the chief's hoping that by working within our fair Lacy's view all day, you'll jog loose a memory or two."

Neither man detected the silent steps approaching from behind. Clay thought he caught the alien whiff of cologne as it was carried on a mellow summer's night breeze. Frank heard the all-too-familiar click as the hammer was pulled back and a gun pressed to his temple.

"And what have I come across out here? Not one stinkin' little piggy like the man said I'd find. I've hit the buy-one-get-the-other-one-free, blue-light special. Whatcha know!"

The agents' eyes met, only for a fraction of a second, yet long enough to transmit what both men knew: In a heartbeat, it was over, had all gone sour. After years of mind-blowing training and ball-busting work, they were going down like two rookie recruits without a single hair on either ass. Motherfucker.

Chapter Thirty

Cybil climbed out of bed with amazing dexterity, successfully keeping her half-emptied bottle of Stoli from spilling so much as a drop and at the same time holding on to the small handgun she'd been fondling for the past couple of hours.

She'd been listening for her mother-in-law's homecoming with the same pent-up anticipation of a child awaiting Santa or Independence Day fireworks. And now the moment had arrived. The bitch was home, and it was time to kick off the celebration.

She padded barefoot to her bedroom door, leaning against it as she listened.

Some ten or fifteen minutes earlier, Jesse and Lacy had gone downstairs, giggling and pretty much doing a good imitation of adolescent teenagers. Cybil wasn't exactly sure how that had come about. She would have sworn theirs was a Romeo and Juliet love story, destined for tragedy. Then, there they were, making like honeymooners again. Not that she cared. In fact, it was pretty damned amazing how little anything mattered to her after the discovery she'd made on Thursday; anything, that was, except the confrontation she anticipated with her mother-in-law.

At last she heard the all-too-familiar footsteps of the Indian princess herself. One could always tell dear Mother Rose's step from all others. She did everything—including *walk*—with that same obsessive deliberation. The way she spoke, her hygiene and manner of dress, the means by which she ran her household, her dynasty, her *sons*. She was meticulous and thorough—nothing was left to chance. She had even found a way to manipulate the future of which she would have no part. Control was the life blood of Rose Cahille-Pryde, and Cybil was about to sever the artery and watch it all drain away.

Before she left her room, Cybil picked up an album she'd gone through the day before. She tucked it under her arm and carried it with her to her mother-in-law's room.

She didn't knock. She simply opened the door, stepped inside, and waited for Rose to notice her presence, which, of course, the grand dame did at once.

"Oh, for God's sake, Cybil, you could have given me a heart attack. Why didn't you ask to come in?" Rose paused, looked at the clock, then at the younger woman once again. "Do you see the time? What could you possibly want at this time of night?"

Cybil smiled as her gaze fell on the peach-colored sheet with the lace edge ruffle that her mother-in-law held out in front of her, examining it with an uncharacteristically perplexed frown. "Ah, Lacy must have lost that in her hurry to get up to her room once they heard you arrive."

"What are you talking about? Why would Lacy have her sheet downstairs and why would she run if—"

"Caught on, have you? Yep, I can see you have. Jesse and Lacy have been playing catch-up for most of the night. By now I'd say they're close to one orgasm for every night she was away. I've been lying in my room just listening to them carrying on. My own personal X-rated audio. Ain't love grand?"

"You're not only drunk, you're disgusting," Rose charged, dropping the sheet and turning her back on her daughter-in-law. "Now, go to bed and leave me alone. I'm tired and tomorrow's Jesse's birthday. I have to sleep a few hours so I can be refreshed for his party."

"Sorry, Mother, sweet, but I've been waiting for you to help celebrate with me," Cybil said.

Rose looked over her shoulder, alerted by the unusually authoritative tone in the normally malleable woman. "I beg your pardon?"

Cybil smiled. "Call me a spoiler, but I've made other plans for us, you and me, that is."

"Go to bed, Cybil," Rose said, her tone stern.

"You haven't been listening," her daughter-in-law said, biting out each word like a drill spitting out decay.

"You and I are going to have a little party. I'm afraid we're going to party so hearty you won't be in any shape to attend Jesse's birthday bash later on. But then, no one's likely to feel too festive after attending poor Dr. Trajillo's funeral, do you think?"

"I think you're a lunatic," Rose said, her patience gone. "Now, take your bottle of booze there and your—what is that? A photo album? Oh, Cybil. Just go to bed. You can do your memory lane thing until you pass out."

Cybil shifted the album so that the gun that had been hidden now showed, pointed at her mother-in-law. "And what would I do with my other little friend here. Let me introduce you. This is the only other guest I've invited to my party. She—her name's Lady Smith—is the guest of honor ... along with you, that is, and me of course." She raised the gun and scratched the side of her nose with the barrel. "Are you confused? I bet you are. I haven't been very clear. Let me see if I can explain it better. This is like one of those engagements they have over there in England. A command performance, I think they call it. I went once, to see the queen, that is. My father was governor of this great state. And my mama, why, folks thought of her like our very own queen. So beautiful." Cybil's laughter filled the room before ending abruptly, cut short by the unpredictability of intoxication. "Course that was then, this is now. Isn't that what you were thinking? That was before Daddy got caught defrauding the government and Mama was left without a dime to her name or a friend in the world?"

Rose was amazed at the woman's perception. She had, in fact, been thinking those very thoughts. Of course, she couldn't admit that so she lied. "You're wrong, dear. I was actually wondering why you dare suppose for a moment that I won't start screaming if you point that gun at me."

Cybil laughed heartily at that one. "Well, because that would mess everything up, Rose, and I know how you detest chaos."

"Which means what exactly?"

"Why, that I will shoot you, then kill whoever comes bursting through those doors in your defense. Since Dillon isn't home, I guess the first person through there would be your precious Jesse, and I just don't believe you'll risk that happening."

Rose held up her hands in surrender. "Then by all means, let's go celebrate this mysterious occasion of yours. May I ask where we're going?"

"Certainly, though I'm sure you'll be disappointed to learn I haven't planned anything elaborate. We're going to start the party, just the two of us, but we're going to do it in the dining room so we don't miss Dillon when he arrives. I want to include him no matter how late he gets here." She jerked the gun in the direction of the door, motioning for Rose to go ahead of her, then changed her mind. "Oh, sorry. One more thing. Pull one of those scarves from that hat tree over there. Whichever one, it doesn't matter. Choose the one you favor most, if you like. Perhaps the gold and black chiffon with the musical notes that Jesse gave you a couple of Christmases back."

Rose cast an amused look at her daughter-in-law over her shoulder as she slipped a shimmery aqua length of silk from its hook instead. "I prefer this one, I think. It's one you gave me, isn't it?"

Minutes later, the scarf secured between Rose's teeth and tied around her head, she sat in the chair nearest the portico to the foyer.

"There's something I have to get from the kitchen, Mother, dear. Sit there while I fetch it, okay? I was quite drunk earlier, though I do believe I've sobered up considerably while I was waitin' on y'all to get home. Not that my sobriety is either here or there. I'm quite an expert markswoman, you'll please remember, whether pickled or sober as I was the night Dillon brought me home to meet you and his daddy. Just stay put so I don't have to shoot you and wake up Jesse and his little bride."

She was back in a matter of seconds. She held up a long carving knife. "Don't expect Luz will mind me borrowing this, do you?"

Rose could only shake her head, then shrug her shoulders in an attempt to cooperate with some sort of answer.

Cybil laughed. "Of course, how silly of me. I should

explain what's going on. Why, I don't believe I've even told you what we're celebrating, now have I?"

Rose didn't answer. She was suddenly very afraid and the realization was creating a very tangible pain in the middle of her stomach. Panic. It was an alien emotion. No one had ever threatened her before. At least not like this. And yet, what had Cybil actually said? Nothing concrete about harming her unless she didn't cooperate. Still, the threat was in her eyes—in the madness that shone as bright and obvious as the four-carat diamond ring Dillon had put on her finger twelve years before. And it was there in the sing-songy tone of her voice as well. Rose hadn't quite figured out what had set her off, but she knew Cybil's fragile mind had finally cracked.

Cybil sat in the chair Rose usually occupied at the head of the table. The one from which she was able to keep her eyes on all three doorways leading to the room as well as the two main exitways from the house.

Cybil tipped the bottle, swigging the vodka as easily as if it were Perrier. "Mmm, I do appreciate expensive liquor."

She set the bottle on the table, then rested her elbow beside it and cupped her chin in her palm. "I know I'm taking the long way about here, but I'm making a point, so bear with me, 'kay?"

Rose hesitated a second, then nodded.

Cybil rewarded her cooperation with a smile. "Why, thank you. That's so nice.

"Anyway, the point is that Dillon warned me about you after we met and fell in love. I don't recall exactly the way he said it, but it wasn't bad or anything. Really, it was just like I said. He loved you and all, and he was proud as hell that you were his mama, but I guess he knew you can be a little hard if a person's not used to you, so he warned me not to be intimidated or afraid or like that. He promised that once we got to know each other—you and me, that is—we'd get along just fine. And silly me, I believed him.

"Course I didn't know then like I know now that some things a body just doesn't get used to. Besides, I was too busy feeling like a failure most of the time to care what you thought of me.

"It was that whole baby thing. Dillon wanted a baby

so damned much, he used to make love to me every night. And every time he emptied his seed inside me, he'd look me in the eyes and holler read loud, 'I put one there this time, honey! I guarantee ya, we made us a Pryde!' "

Cybil stopped then, pressing her fist to her heart with the hand holding the knife while she drank from the bottle again with the other one still clasping the long knife.

Tears stood in her eyes for a long moment before spilling over her lashes, at odds with the arrival of her smile. "Do you have any idea how bad it hurt me every month when I had to tell him I'd failed him again?

"Oh, oh, I almost forgot! I was going to show you." Picking up the knife, she shifted the gun to her left hand as she ran the blade over her arm inches above her wrist.

Blood oozed from the gash in a two-inch-long diagonal line, and with the telltale evidence of her daughter-in-law's self-mutilation, fear bubbled inside Rose. There was no longer any doubt, Cybil was a madwoman.

"Dr. Trajillo was so good to me. Running all those tests just as you asked and assuring me that the only problem we had was trying too hard. Do you remember that? Of course you do. You're the one who told him to pat our hands and give me his wonder shots. Those amazing vitamin injections guaranteed to keep me from getting pregnant. And to think, neither Dillon nor I ever suspected."

Rose was shaking her head and mumbling something unintelligible against the scarf that was biting painfully into the corners of her mouth.

Cybil chuckled as she picked up the bottle and guzzled greedily. She wiped her mouth with the back of her arm, uncaringly smearing her face with her own blood. "Oh, don't worry. The wicked old witch didn't win the day. At least not yet. Dejected, the princess left the horrible castle and went to visit her mother, in Europe visiting friends. But the prince was unhappy without his beautiful Cybil and came to fetch her home. And miracle of miracles, she got pregnant.

"It was the happiest day of their lives, the day when their fairy godfather disguised as a kindly Hispanic gynecologist told them that they were going to have a baby.

You can just imagine, can't you? The princess was in her thirties by then and quite convinced a miracle had happened.

"And then the doctor told Cybil that she was anemic and he recommended that she have a test to assure that the baby was all right. Amniocentesis. Very common. Very routine. But suddenly it wasn't all very normal. She was in labor and the baby was delivered stillborn."

As if forgetting she still held the knife, Cybil clasped her hands together. "Oh, God, did you see him? Our little Richmond Davis Pryde II? All that black hair, and those beautiful fat cheeks? Seven pounds twelve ounces and only two weeks early. No reason he should have died.

"But miracle upon miracles, the prince and the princess who had not even looked at each other in months found one another on a cold wintery night when the wicked old witch and her kindly husband for whom the baby had been named went to Dallas to meet the girl their youngest son was seeing. And you know what happened then? Well, how silly of me. Of course you do, you being the wicked old witch and all-powerful. They made love and without the doctor's *vitamins* to prevent her from ovulating, a second baby was conceived. And then history repeated itself . . . almost, except this time the perfect stillborn infant was a girl baby.

"Well," Cybil said, staring at nothing, though seeing her daughter's face just before the casket was closed on it for the last time, "you know the rest of the story. *I* didn't know. *Dillon* didn't know. How could we? We didn't ask questions. Why? Who would suspect that those beautiful, precious little babies' own grandmother would order the doctor to inject potassium chloride into their tiny hearts? No one, because it's too sinister to be believed. Oh, and not just sinister, clever, too. It brought on premature labor, so no one suspected anything amiss. Just one of those sad cases of a woman who couldn't quite make it to term and deliver a healthy breathing baby.

"So we just blamed God and turned away from each other so we didn't have to see the pain in the other's eyes. I turned to my old pal, Stoli, here, and Dillon, well, he just went into the arms of any woman he could find.

"Sad story isn't it? Something right out of one of those horrid fairy tales complete with the wicked witch and everything. Only, this one didn't have a happy-ever-after ending. At least not until I went to town to see Dr. Trajillo."

Rose began tearing at the scarf, alternately struggling to free it from her lips and untie the knot in the back.

"Do sit still, Mother, dear. I know it's uncomfortable having to hear how your sins have been found out." Cybil tipped her head to the side slightly, laughing softly, then said, "I was just thinkin' what a coincidence that is. Ever since I was a small child, I've been terrified of Judgment Day. I'd do some little something wrong—you know, like steal a cookie before dinner—and then I swear, I'd be so ashamed and afraid of what God was going to do when it came time to face Him on that terrible day when I had to answer for my sins, I'd make myself downright sick. But I've learned something since then. There are a lot worse things than having to fess up to your sins. There's the pain that comes with burying your newborn infant."

Without warning, she slashed her arm again with the razor-sharp knife. Then again. Blood welled, then ran in rivulets before pooling in the bend of her arm and spilling to the chair and carpet.

Rose's eyes widened with horror.

Cybil laughed. "No, no, no. Don't look like that. It didn't hurt. Not compared to giving birth." She slashed her arm again, twice more. "See, nothing like the pain of being told they were dead."

Blood poured now, and her arm dropped weak to her lap though she didn't let go of the gun.

"Is it warm in here to you?" she asked drowsily.

Rose didn't move.

"Must be me, then." Cybil shrugged as she laid the knife in her lap and reached for the vodka. "Goes down like water these days," she said. "But you're not interested in my prowess as a boozer, are you? No, I'm positive you're much more anxious to hear how I found out about everything."

Rose mumbled something unintelligible.

"Ah, have you figured it out already? Well, let's pretend not, so I can brag a bit, okay? I've had so little to be proud of these past few years. Surely, you can give me my moment."

Rose nodded.

"Why, thank you," Cybil said. "Now, let's see. Well, it's pretty simple. Thursday morning I was coming down to join you and Dillon for breakfast. I know, hard to believe, but something prompted me, telling me, 'Cyl, honey, you get on out of that bed,' and I did. That's when I overheard the conversation between you and Dillon and Lacy. I was real curious about that abortion, and I even went back up to Lacy's room. I was going to offer to drive her in to town and take her to Dr. Trajillo's house. But she was lying down, so I went on back to my own room.

"I just couldn't stop thinking about it, though, so I decided to go on my own. I got there about noon and the funniest thing happened. The minute I parked the car and looked up at that house, I got mad. I can't really explain it. I just remember thinking he better tell me the truth. If he and Lacy had lied about that abortion, he better damn well tell me why, 'cause it had hurt Jesse something terrible and I knew how that kind of pain felt.

"Anyway, I took the gun Dillon bought me several years back out of the glove compartment where I keep it when I'm in the car and put it in my purse. I went on up to the house but they were just leaving—Raul and Lenora, I mean. He was real nice. Asked if it was an emergency and when I told him no, that I just needed to talk to him, he patted me on the back and told me to have a seat. He was just taking Lenora over to the beauty shop to get her hair all done up for Jesse's birthday party. Said he was going to grab a sandwich and be right back." She laughed. "Even asked if I'd like him to bring me something. Can you imagine that? Offering to buy me lunch and knowing the whole time how he'd killed my babies!

"Anyway, you can pretty much put two and two together, can't you? I looked at the files. The abortion was there in Lacy's file all documented, but there was something else. Some kind of coded notes ending with 'per R.C.P.' Course, I didn't figure that one out right away."

Tucking the knife under her armpit, she stood up, and

shifted the gun to her right hand, while her left arm hung weak at her side, blood still dripping from her fingertips. She circled the table, never taking her eyes off her mother-in-law.

"I don't know what provoked me to look at the other files. Maybe for no reason except there they all were—us Prydes clumped together in that file cabinet just like we are in this house. So, anyway, I went through them all. Started at the back with yours. *Rose Cahille-Pryde.* Nothing interesting about that except six or seven pages with the heading 'Contributions/Services.' And the amounts were incredible! Ten thousand dollars. Five thousand. Fifteen thousand. Eight. Even twenty thousand a couple of times. And beside every amount some more coded notes.

"Anyway, I was going to skip R. Davis's file. After all, the man was dead. But then I remembered the whispers about his death being a suicide although after a time everyone seemed to accept the verdict that it was death by drowning due to an accidental fall. And I wondered if that was the way it was worded in the file. And guess what? It was, verbatim, just like you always said it. Except there was another of those funny notes and the initials R.C.P. And this time I think I figured it out. There was another file drawer that read autopsies. So I looked in there and found it all spelled out. Seems R. Davis had a fractured skull sustained from a blow to the back of his head inconsistent with the other scrapes and bruises he got from the fall. The doctor noted his findings regarding the skull fracture as inconclusive, however. And then there were those same initials and the note 'cross-reference page eight, 9/14/90.' And I had it."

Rose's olive skin darkened as a spark of hate flashed in her eyes and her nostrils flared with her quickened breathing.

Cybil stopped to lean against the table, chuckling softly. "I see you believe me. Yes, I knew then. The initials, of course, were yours. Don't know why it took me so long to connect that. And those ridiculous contributions were payoffs. I checked out every one of them while I sat there. The one you paid him for lying about the abortion. The ten thousand back sometime in the early seventies when he sterilized you because of a nonexistent reoccurring precancerous condition and kept it from R. Davis.

"And, of course, for not going to the sheriff when he put two and two together and realized you'd hit R. Davis, then pushed his unconscious body over the falls."

Her face contorted with anger, Rose jumped to her feet and started across the room toward her daughter-in-law. Cybil brought up the gun. "Sit down."

Rose backed up, but continued to stand until the younger woman pulled the hammer back.

"You're thinking I'm getting too weak from the loss of blood to end this the way I've been thinking about for two days now. Ordinarily you might be right. That is to say, if I were *ordinary*. But you see, I am crazy. Quite mad with grief and hate and a need for vengeance, and if you knew anything about mental illness, you'd realize that we are stronger than your average sane person. I think medical science credits it to a greater flow of adrenaline. Personally, I credit it to sheer will. I am going to die. I *want* to die, to be with my babies, but not just yet. First, I'm going to get my affairs in order." She laughed again. "And you, dear heart, are the last affair to be attended to. So, since you're already standing, let's go attend to you." She motioned with the gun for her mother-in-law to walk toward the kitchen. "Grab the keys—all of them. We'll decide which vehicle to take when we get to the garage. But in the meantime, should our honeymooners upstairs come down and be alerted by all the blood, they'll at least be slowed up by the absence of the keys hanging here by the back door."

As they neared the garage, Cybil stopped short at the sight of her husband's truck. Her brows knitting with her confusion, she tried to figure out the meaning for this surprising development. If he hadn't taken his truck, then how had he gone into town? Maybe he'd ridden in with one of the men. Yes, that was surely—

Rose, sensing Cybil's hesitation, then glancing over her shoulder and seeing the woman's confusion, decided to take advantage of the only opportunity she might have to save herself

She lunged forward, but Cybil reacted with amazing swiftness and strength, striking her on the face with the gun.

Rose dropped to her knees, groaning and then gagging on blood that quickly soaked the scarf still tied around her head.

"Get up!" Cybil snapped. "We're taking Dillon's truck. You'll drive." She opened the door for her mother-in-law, then keeping the gun trained on Rose's face, she circled the front of the truck and slid in beside her. She selected the right set of keys, handed one to her mother-in-law, and dropped the rest to the floor.

"Wait!" she ordered when Rose was about to start the engine. Rose's eyes were wild with fear and pain now and when she saw her daughter-in-law's hands coming toward her with the knife, she cried out, spraying blood and choking.

Cybil slit the scarf in two, pulling it from between the terrified woman's lips. "Now, we can talk if you like while we drive. We're going to the falls, incidentally." She had intended to say something else, but Rose's hand slipping near the center of the steering wheel and the horn stopped her. "Don't be a fool, Rose. Don't risk the last minutes you have left. You know I'll kill you. I wanted to wait a bit. Keep you alive until Dillon or Jesse found us so I could listen while you admitted everything to them, but it doesn't seem so important now. I've written it all down in my diary anyway. So touch the horn and I'll just shoot you now and then kill myself."

Rose spat a mouthful of blood to the floorboard, then shook her head slowly from side to side. "I . . . I won't do anything."

"Good girl." Then that mad laugh again: high-pitched and unnatural. "Good girl? What am I saying? I don't think you were ever anything but bad. Some people, like me, are driven to evil. Others like you are born that way." She laid her head against the window. She was getting weak, was having trouble focusing on her hatred. But she had to hang on. She couldn't let it go. Not yet. Not until she had avenged her poor innocent babies.

PART III

Eeny, Meeny, Miney, Moe.
  —A children's verse

LAPD Detectives Arnie Dailey and Terrance Larosa sat grim-faced and silent along with their captain, Micky Danalucci, and the chief of police, Paul Howard. They were gathered in the latter man's office. All four men were bleary-eyed, sober, and strung tight. It was seven a.m.

The detectives had been on the scene of a grisly double homicide not four miles from the site of a similar murder a couple of years back. No one was making comparisons. No one had to. There wasn't a man employed by the city of Los Angeles who didn't remember the heat the department had taken for the way that one was mishandled. The accused—a man quicker recognized than the Pope—had not only walked but also quadrupled his fortune. Hell, everyone involved—a coke-snorting bimbo friend of one of the deceased, the ex-wife of the chief defense counsel, even members of the losing prosecution team—had profited big time from the publicity. Two people butchered, and no one but the LAPD had paid a price—taken it on the chin, in the gut, and up the ass.

Well, not this time. This time, brothers and sisters, they were doing it according to the LAPD bible and their very own god—which was to say, they weren't stepping left or right without consulting the procedural manual, then double-checking it twice with Chief Howard.

Not that such vigilance was critical this time around. Hell, they had the perp ID'd on videotape by one of the victims. All neat and nice. Of course, wouldn't you know? This one could've gone a long way toward changing public opinion, and they weren't even going to get the credit.

The door to the police chief's office had been closed.

It opened now, a uniformed officer stepping aside to allow Gary Maltz to pass by as he entered the room.

Paul Howard came out of his seat to greet the FBI agent, reaching across his desk and shaking the man's hand.

The chief was surprised. He'd requested the bureau chief's presence in his predawn phone call to the federal agency. Such a request meant only one thing: top priority. Never in his personal history could he remember a time when such a call had been responded to with anyone other than the head man himself. If Anderson was unavailable, he would have expected his deputy. Ah, well, speculation would get him another Pepcid AC tablet, little else. "I was expecting Chief Anderson," he said to the agent he'd met only once before.

The young man, grim-faced and red-eyed, cleared his throat as his gaze darted for the floor. "Yes, sir. We've had, uh ... that is, two of his men went down in the field earlier this morning. Right now, uh, the chief is ..." He didn't finish the statement. It was obvious to all the men in the room that emotion was winning its war with professionalism. All four LAPD officers lowered their gazes. It was empathy not embarrassment that tugged at them. They all knew what it meant to lose a "brother" in the line of duty. No one spoke for the next several seconds.

Then it was Chief Howard who broke through the heavy silence. He introduced Agent Maltz to the other men in the room.

Greetings—quiet, somber, respectful of the victims— were exchanged around the room, followed by condolences. Then Gary sat in the chair vacated by Captain Danalucci. His smile of gratitude was thin, polite.

He turned his attention to the police chief. "What have you got, sir?"

"Two victims. Both female. One Caucasian, the other Hispanic." He ran his hands over his cap of thick white hair, leaning back in his chair and directing his attention to Detective Dailey. "Go on, Arnie. This one's yours. You can spoon-feed the details before we watch the tape again."

Every eye in the room turned toward the thirty-year-old homicide detective. "Bodies were discovered at approximately zero one hundred hours by Juan Lopez, the fiancé of the female Hispanic victim, and his brother Carlos.

"According to Juan, Maria was supposed to get off work at six. Traveled by bus, so should have been home by seven, easy. They had plans to attend a birthday party in honor of the dead girl's aunt. He waited until eight-thirty, then tried calling her at her employer's." The detective had been consulting his notes. He stopped, looking up at the bureau chief. "She worked as a housekeeper for the old, ah, Charlotte Daniels."

Gary recognized the name at once. Let his foot that had rested on his knee fall to the floor as he sat forward. "Go on," he said.

"Well, in a nutshell, the boyfriend, Lopez, called the house several times between eight-thirty and midnight. Made some calls to various family members as well. Even put in a call to us—dispatcher has it on record as coming in at eleven-oh-three—then went to his brother's house. That's Carlos Lopez, incidentally. Lives in the East L.A. barrio, as does the whole bunch of them. Anyway, according to Juan, Carlos offered to go with him to the Brentwood house. Says they arrived—let's see—a little after midnight. Rang the bell. No answer. Went to a pay phone—three, four blocks away—and put another call into us again at twelve thirty-eight. Got the routine promise of a driveby, and returned to wait in front of the house. Sat in their car another twenty minutes. No patrol cars showed, so bingo-bango, the Lopez brothers went over the fence.

"Front door was closed. Everything looked okay from outside, but when no one answered the doorbell, Carlos tried the knob. Door was unlocked, which Juan insists it never is. Anyway, the brothers went in. Found the young one first. On the second-floor landing at the top of the stairs. She was cut to ribbons." He stopped, pinched the bridge of his nose for a brief stabilizing second. "Sorry."

Agent Maltz shook his head slightly. He understood. A man could get used to a lot, but the best never got inured to savagery and carnage. "Not necessary. I know where you're coming from." He thought of Mandell and Waters, shot to death on the Southern Star, and felt tears burn behind his eyes again. He blinked a couple of times, turned his head away as the other man continued.

Arnie tugged uncomfortably at his earlobe. "Yeah well, it's just—anyway, there was blood everywhere. Neither man made it past the girl. Patrol officers discovered Charlotte Daniels's body in her bedroom. Her throat had been cut. Other than that, she sustained only a few superficial cuts on the right hand. Got off easy."

His partner, Terrance Larosa, jumped in. "He's got that right. The Fuentes woman, shit, she put up some kind of fight."

"Poor girl," Gary said, softly under his breath, then turning his attention to Paul, once again he asked, "What else? You mentioned a videocassette addressed to Chief Anderson?"

The police chief nodded in the direction of the VCR and television set to their left. "We just got done watching it. Want us to play it for you or you want to take it back to the federal building?"

Maltz held up his hands. "I'm here. If you don't mind, let's see it."

Paul nodded to his captain who was seated closest to the video apparatus. "Would you do the honors, Micky?" He turned back to the guest of honor. "This is gonna blow your mind, my boy, as well as explain a whole lot of something about an investigation we've been working on in cooperation with you boys."

"You're talking about the unsolved hit-and-run of Lacy James-Pryde."

Paul Howard was hunched forward, arms folded on his desk. He untucked one of them to point a finger at the Federal agent. "You got it." Then to Mickey. "Anytime you're ready."

His face expressionless, Gary watched the homemade tape that showed a recording date and time less than fifteen hours earlier.

He recognized the face of the woman in the wheelchair as that of Charlotte Daniels. Though just barely. He'd seen a picture of her. Had it in a file folder in his office. But that photograph was of a vital, handsome woman. This one, this frail, sick woman with the drooping left eyelid and slurred speech, facing the camera and talking specifically to his superior—even calling him by name—was a pathetic remnant of the woman he'd never met, yet remembered for her cold, hard eyes.

He listened in silence, the practiced delphic expression he'd learned from his more seasoned comrades never once slipping. She amazed him, though. People like her always did. Obviously ill and enfeebled, she had nonetheless rallied long enough to make her confession—her deathbed confession as it turned out. Yet, even before she began to point a finger, he knew what to expect. Understood that her ultimate goal of vengeance had been the true motivator.

The phone rang, getting off only a half jingle before the police chief snatched the receiver from its hook. "Howard," he barked.

He felt the sweat bead on his forehead and soak his upper lip as he listened briefly before holding the receiver out to the federal agent. "Maltz," he said, his tone curiously soft. "Call's for you." Then as he handed off the phone, he snapped an order to the police captain to shut off the g.d. TV.

"No, leave it," Gary countered, perching a hip on the corner of the desk and watching the continuing tape as he brought the phone to his ear. "Agent Maltz here."

Paul Howard pulled a wad of tissues from the Kleenex box on his desk and dried his face, his eyes never leaving the other man's profile. He watched his normal healthy complexion blanch as white as the man's snowy shirt. Saw the almost imperceptible tightening of his jaws, then the flash of emotion—mingling rage, impotence, and devastation—in his eyes. Paul knew exactly what the younger man was experiencing. He'd been there, done that, more than he wanted to think about. There was nothing worse.

He flagged his hand at his captain, catching his attention, and motioning again for him to turn off the VCR.

But Gary hung up the phone in that same instant and once again overrode the instruction. "Wait . . ."

Too late. That was it. He'd heard what she said. He just couldn't believe it. Or maybe it was that combined with the news he'd just received. He wasn't a man given to rage. But if two of the Bureau's best men had fallen because they'd missed this . . something so damned obvious, they were all idiots . . .

Paul was around the desk now, his hand on the agent's shoulder. "I'm so fuckin' sorry, son, I don't know what to—"

"Thanks," Gary said. He looked around the room at the other men as he offered an explanation. "Chief Anderson's en route to Texas. As soon as our dispatcher reached me about this homicide, I put in a call to him, another to the local authorities where two of our men had gone in undercover. Left word where I could be reached. Unfortunately, they haven't been able to get to the chief, but that was the sheriff in Rooster Corner. He'll relay the urgency if we don't reach him first. In the meantime, I'll take the tape. I've got to get going. Got to go break some bad news." He hadn't lost control, hadn't raised his voice a single note. But as he started past the television set that was shut off and quiet now, he slammed his hand against the dark screen, rocking the entire wall shelf and provoking a surprised start from every man in the room. "So help me God, I'm going to get that bitch!" And in a final croak before he exited the room, he added, "Then I'm going to pray for a way to forgive myself for letting this happen."

"Two of his fellow officers," Chief Howard began. He stopped, shaking his head. "Well, I don't suppose I have to spell it out for you."

Captain Danalucci sighed heavily. "But what's the connection to this?"

"Remember the call we got from airport security in Dallas just before the agent arrived?"

"The old lady's wheelchair. Yeah, the serial number proves it was registered to Charlotte Daniels, so what? We already knew our perp was aboard the American Airlines flight disguised as the old dame." Micky's thick black eyebrows shot upward. "Holy Mary, you telling me those two agents—"

"Yeah, Danalucci, that's exactly what I'm telling you." He circled his desk, dropped into his chair. Then in a sudden fit of anger every bit as potent as Gary's, he sent his most prized souvenir—the baseball autographed to him by the legendary Sandy Kovaks—crashing into the far wall. "And we shoulda been on this."

"How were we supposed to know?" Detective Dailey asked.

"We're cops. It's what we're paid to find out," the chief answered.

"Yeah, well if the Feebies didn't figure it ..." Terrance began.

The chief placed both hands on his desk and came halfway out of his chair to glare at the detective. "Then what, Larosa? Those two men deserved to get blown away? That poor girl, Maria Fuentes, she deserved to get cut up like a side of beef? Even the old woman? You saying it's okay we didn't know and she died because the FBI didn't know either? Son of a bitch! Will one of you please explain to me how one tiny pissant planet in an entire fucking universe could get so screwed up!"

Chapter Thirty-one

Lacy was awakened with a kiss. Her immediate reaction was a smile and languorous catlike stretch. Sudden wakefulness dawned, snapping her out of her languor. They'd shared an incredible night of passion, and she had no doubt how she must look in the brightness of day—eyes puffy, hair more than likely standing out in spikes on one side of her head, mashed flat on the other. And then there was always morning breath. Yuck!

Crawling from the bed, she made a successful escape only seconds before he caught on and started after her. She slammed the bathroom door behind her, giggling as she pushed in the lock and heard his playful growl of frustration.

"I'll get you, woman. You won't get away from me so easily."

Still laughing, she stepped away from the door, turned on the water in the sink, then faced her reflection. "Ugh. Now there's a face not even a husband could love," she complained, bending forward and splashing icy water over her swollen features.

She applied gel to her toothbrush and began cleaning her teeth and freshening her breath as she dabbed away the wetness from her face with a hand towel.

Jesse yanked open the door leading to his bedroom, startling her. She half squealed, half choked on the rich lather she'd created with her vigorous brushing.

"Now you're going to pay! Making me dash through the hall naked as a jaybird! The gall of you, woman!"

Lacy giggled and sputtered as he circled her with his arms from behind and kissed her neck. She twisted and writhed, succeeding only in splattering the mirror with toothpaste. He was relentless, and judging from his smiling reflection, enjoying himself immensely. His hands closed over her breasts as he stepped closer, pressing the length of his nude body against hers. His swollen penis jabbed insistently at her back until she surrendered. Spitting foamy blue toothpaste into the sink, she cupped water in her hands and ladled it quickly into her mouth a couple of times before turning in his arms and covering his lips with her own.

They'd made love three times during the night. In between, they'd snatched an hour or so of sleep and once padded barefoot to the kitchen, wearing only togas fashioned from the sheets pulled off her bed. They'd been deeply involved in a contest of creating the most imaginative though edible sandwich when headlights, boomeranging from the garage, bathed them in a bright glow. Instinctively, they ducked behind the protective covering of the cabinets. With amazing dexterity, they managed to slide plates and milk glasses from the counter—Jesse even snagging a bag of potato chips that he carried between his teeth—and scamper unseen back to her bedroom. They almost succeeded in doing it all in stealth and quiet until the instant only a step or two from the upstairs landing when Jesse stepped on Lacy's sheet, eliciting a relatively noisy squeal as it fell away from her.

They dashed into her room, she following his lead as he disappeared inside the closet. Laying plates and glasses aside, Jesse dropped the chips to the floor as well and pulled her into his arms.

They huddled together, laughing like juveniles only narrowly escaping being caught sneaking out after curfew instead of grown-ups doing what happily married lovers do best—sharing a night of love and passion and play.

They heard the squeak of the kitchen door being opened, followed by Rose's footsteps on the stairs, and finally the sound of the car leaving once again.

Lacy sat between his long, muscled legs, which curled around her in the darkness.

They waited for Rose to pass their room. Perhaps she had and they'd simply not heard. After all, the carpeting was thick and lush, a good muffler. On the other hand ...

"I think we may be in deep *caca*," Jesse whispered against her ear.

Lacy giggled. *Caca?* She sobered quickly with her next

thought. "You don't think she'd come in here? Oh, please, say no."

"No," he replied dutifully, then like an ornery boy added, "Unless she can't wait till breakfast to wish me happy birthday."

"Oh, she wouldn't . . . would she?"

"Umm, I don't know," he said slowly. "If she hears us, wonders what's going on . . . well, Mother's always been nosy."

"How could she hear us all the way from the hall to the closet?" she scoffed, though still keeping her voice to a whisper.

Jesse's fingers found a nipple, teasing it and making it swell as his other hand parted her sex and he slipped a finger inside her hot, welcoming warmth. "Her senses are very acute," he said, his voice hoarse with desire against her ear. "And you're pretty noisy when you get turned on."

Lacy gasped with pleasure, then smiled with utter joy. "Let her come, then. I'll never know she's here."

But in the next moment Rose was forgotten, and their early morning nosh abandoned, as they sated a deeper, sweeter hunger, then fell asleep still joined in a carnal embrace.

Sometime very early, in the dawning of first morning pink light, Jesse'd awakened and gathered her into his arms to carry her to the bed. She had only the vaguest memory of that now as he lifted her onto the marble counter in the bathroom, then guided his erection inside her.

Jesse watched their coupling in the mirror. It wasn't the act itself that was driving him, creating a craving in him that wouldn't be satisfied.

His gaze fastened on her back, he marveled at the sheer beauty of her. The creamy luster of her skin, the sculpted perfection of her body.

His hands gripping her thighs, he held her anchored against the counter, as he drove into her and watched the way she hugged him with her legs, thrusting her slender hips forward as she took him deeper and deeper inside.

He couldn't get enough of her. His hands moving away from her legs, his fingers probed every inch of her body from her slightly flared buttocks resting against the very edge of the marble countertop to her face as he cupped her chin and kissed her with a passion that intensified every time he looked at her. A fire burst of love and lust exploded inside each of them in that instant. Buying his face in her hair, he groaned and nuzzled her ear. "I love you, Lacy Pryde," he breathed. "I don't know how I lived without you those weeks you were gone." It was true. He couldn't fathom a day without her in it, and yet, it hadn't been like this before. Something was wonderfully different, new. He'd always wanted her, lusted for her body. Hell, he'd been consumed by her beauty, eaten up with desire. He'd thought he loved her, but it was only since her accident that he'd truly fallen completely, profoundly in love.

His arms circling her waist, he eased her from the counter until she stood on the floor before him. "Turn around," he said.

When she stood in front of him, her back against his chest, her head resting against his shoulder, he met her gaze in the mirror and made his confession. "I thought I loved you, Lace, before. The first time we made love, on the day we married, even when you left me and I thought . . . never mind that." He paused long enough to kiss her throat and watch them as his long, tapered fingers traced the planes of her exquisite face, eventually capturing her hair and pulling it back.

Her heart quickened at his declaration even as her mind recoiled with guilt. Throughout the night, she'd let him hold her, be her playmate, her lover, felt their souls meld and learned the wonder of giving everything she was to the man she adored.

"Jesse," she began, knowing the time had come to tell him everything. If their love was going to survive, it was going to be based on truth. There would be no more lies. And they would survive. All at once, she was certain of that. No matter what the complete truth turned out to be, they'd make it through it all, because they were really, truly, in love. Raising her chin, her eyes locked on his, a slight smile tugged at the corners of her lips. "Yesterday, when I left here, I was going to see a specialist Dr. Peacher, my neurologist at UCLA, recommended. I was confused about so much. Who I was. Why

I'd left the way I had. And so on, and on. But I knew two things for sure. One, I love you with all my heart, and two, I could never have aborted a baby we made together. I just couldn't have done it. No way, no how.

"Day before yesterday, I was on my way to see Dr. Trajillo—that's his name, isn't it?" At his nod, she continued. "Anyway, I didn't make it there. He'd been killed by the time I arrived. But I met Cookie or, I guess I should say, got reacquainted even though I don't remember, of course. What I'm getting to here is that she told me some things about myself, some pretty ugly stuff, I had a hard time accepting. Then yesterday while I was in Dallas I met someone else, another person with a different story to tell about the woman I am."

He opened his mouth to object. He didn't give a gnat's patootie about what anyone else thought, or who others thought she was or wasn't. He knew all he needed to know: He was deeply in love ... perhaps for the first time in his life. And as luck would have it, with his own wife! What more could a man ask?

"No, wait!" she said quickly. "Let me finish."

He was staring at her face, his gaze fixed all at once on her cheek and the slight smile that toyed there even though she was trying her level best to keep her expression as serious as the subject at hand. He almost had it, something he'd come near to pinpointing before. It was right there ... only a glimmer away until the screams began.

"What the hell?"

Lacy grabbed her robe from the peg on the back of the door as he darted for his bedroom, snatching a pair of jeans from the upholstered bench at the foot of his bed.

They stepped into the hallway together, hands locked, hearts hammering. Something was very, very wrong. That much they knew. They just didn't understand yet that while they'd played, their world had begun to crumble around them.

Chapter Thirty-two

The scent of blood was overwhelming. Immediately sickened by the sweet coppery odor, Lacy clamped a hand over her mouth.

Jesse gathered her against him though queasiness was making his own mouth watery. "It's Luz," he said. "She probably cut herself, then went running around the main floor hysterical and bleeding."

Neither of them believed that. Not for a second.

"We'd better go see," Lacy said.

"No. You stay up here. And lock the doors to your room. All of them. I'll come back and tell you what's going on as soon as I know."

Lacy shook her head, refusing to obey. She didn't want to go down those stairs, but she couldn't stay up there without him either. "I'm going with you."

He didn't argue. The housekeeper's cries were lessening, and he was almost sure he could detect the sound of men's voices. Two of them, maybe three. "Come on," he said, giving her hand a reassuring squeeze and signaling her to follow.

Luz was sitting at the old wooden table in the kitchen, rocking back and forth. Her wails dwindled to keening, she swabbed her eyes with the hem of her apron.

Two men clad in impressive brown and tan uniforms—complete with Stetsons, arm patches identifying them as members of the Rooster Corner Sheriff's Department, leather holsters, guns, and the prerequisite boots—were with her. The older one—round-faced yet surprisingly long and lean of body—stood over the housekeeper, patting her shoulder and murmuring reassurances in a heavy Texas drawl. The second man, decades younger with a swarthy, badly pocked complexion, sat in the chair opposite Luz, speaking in Spanish, then scribbling her answers in a pocket-sized spiral notebook.

With a piercing cry, Luz jumped from the chair, dashing across the room the instant she spied Jesse standing in the doorway. She grabbed him around the waist, tipping her tear-stained face back to meet his eyes as she rattled off something in Spanish.

"Is this true?" Jesse asked, looking to the older man for his answer.

"The first part, yes, son, I'm afraid so. As to the rest, well, we just don't know yet. I can tell you what we got for sure. Can tell you what's about to happen from the FBI's end. As to the other, I just don't have an answer yet." He stopped, the last words hardly out of his mouth when he remembered his manners. Tipping the bill of his hat, he nodded in Lacy's direction. "Miz Pryde. Sorry to have to make your acquaintance all over again under these tragic circumstances. Thought I'd be doin' that at your husband's birthday party this evening."

"This is Sheriff Doug Fenton, Lace," Jesse explained as he put an arm around the housekeeper's trembling shoulders and led her back to the table, gently urging her into the chair once again. "And Enricco, there, is one of his deputies. The newest recruit in the department. I don't think the two of you've met before."

"Pardon me, ma'am," the sheriff said. "I completely forgot about that, uh, amnesia thing you got since you was run down out there in California."

Lacy had been watching her husband and had seen the blood drain from his face. She waved away the sheriff's inane apologies. "Never mind that. Something terrible's happened. Just tell me what. I don't speak Spanish so I don't understand anything Luz has said. Has someone been hurt in there?"

The sheriff's eyes made a quick dart in the direction of the dining room, then snapped back to her face. "Look, we don't know nothing about what's happened inside this house. The fact is, we got a call from one of your husband's men and came out here to check that out. After we confirmed what Trey Grayson had told us on the phone, we came straight on over here. Afraid that's when we found the mess in the other room and well, as you probably guessed, Luz, here, came upstairs from her apartment downstairs about the same time we arrived and started screamin' and carryin' on. Didn't think for a minute she was going to let us in."

"Why didn't Trey call the house first?" Jesse asked.

The sheriff shrugged. "Claims he did, boy. Says no one answered the phone."

"But that's crazy. Lacy and I shut off the phone in our, uh, in our bedroom, but we heard Mother come in around two this morning. She was just getting back from a visit to my aunt in California. She always keeps the telephone on in her room in case of an emergency. And what about Dillon? I'm pretty sure he was plannin' a trip into Rooster last night, but he's home by now, I'd think. Have you checked upstairs?"

"No, Jesse, we haven't. Like I was tellin' you, we just three or four minutes ago got in the house ourselves. We went with Luz to the dining room, then brought her back in here and was just getting her settled down some when the two of you showed up."

"I'm going upstairs to check on Mother, and Dillon and Cybil," Jesse announced.

As soon as he left, Lacy turned back to the sheriff. "I still don't understand what brought you out here in the first place. Would you mind going over it for me in English?"

"Uh, yes, ma'am. Sorry about that. Two men were found shot to death in a gully out behind the bunkhouse. Ordinarily, the first thing I would have done is come on up here to the house and notify you all. However, when we arrived, we went through their things and found a badge tucked away in a suitcase belonging to one of the victims. Seems he was an agent employed by the Federal Bureau of Investigation. Well, course that changed things a whole lot, shifted priorities, and the first thing I did was put in a call to the federal office in Dallas. About twenty minutes later they got back to me, only the call came from Los Angeles. Turns out *both* men was working undercover, which caught me by surprise seeing's how we all knew one of 'em real well. Guess it just goes to show, a man never really knows—"

Jesse's rapid steps on the stairs, followed by his almost immediate arrival in the kitchen doorway, stopped the windy lawman midsentence. "Well?"

"They're not there," he said, running his hands through his hair with a frustrated curse. "Damn! What's going on?"

Lacy circled her husband's waist with her arms, resting her face against his chest and offering comfort. "Don't worry, sweetheart. I'm sure they're fine. Your mother's probably gone into town to spend the morning with Mrs. Trajillo. I'm sure she's aware that the doctor's funeral is today."

Encouraged by the sense in his wife's suggestion, Jesse nodded. "Yeah, of course, That's exactly what she'd do. And come to think of it, Dillon's still in town as well." He met the sheriff's gaze. "You might want to check and see if he's with Dina. He stays the night with her from time to time."

"I'll get right on both of those. Got any suggestions 'bout where we might find Cybil, while we're lookin'?"

Lacy and Jesse exchanged glances, then shook their heads.

"I don't think she's been out of the house in weeks," Jesse volunteered.

"Well, for once I'm glad to be able to contradict you, boy," Sheriff Fenton said with the first smile he'd pulled off since getting rousted from bed this morning with news of a double homicide on the Southern Star. "Could be she's gone into town along with your mother or maybe she's out looking for her old man, huh?"

Jesse folded his arms across his chest, his expression clearly doubting. "There's no use pretendin' here, Doug. We all know Cybil's drunk nine tenths of the time these days. I don't think it's too likely she'd be up this early with my mother, and it's even more unlikely she'd bother hunting for Dillon. She's gotten pretty used to his ways, I'm afraid."

"Well, the fact is, she's been in town a couple of times this week already. Seen her both times myself.

"First time, I was just coming out of my office when I saw her drive past. That was—well, hell, what's the matter with me? I'd just gotten the call 'bout Raul's place being on fire. Anyways, I seen her again yesterday. She was coming out of the hardware store. Rory Galbadon was even helping her out, holding her arm and showing her to her car, ya know? I was thinking just what you was saying a minute ago about her not being too steady the way he was holdin' on to her and seeing how she's been hittin' the bottle lately. I thought about pulling her over. You know, just offerin' her a ride so I didn't offend her. But she backed out of that parking space just pretty as you please, so I figured Rory was just being nice, and I even felt a little cheered, thinking how Cybil might be putting the bad times behind her and pullin' her life together."

No one spoke for a long moment until Lacy, suddenly chilled, hugged herself, rubbing her arms briskly, and looked in the direction of the dining room again. "Let's just hope she is with Rose and they're both in town comforting Mrs. Trajillo, but I think somebody better try finding them, Jesse. Dillon, too ... I don't have to go in there to know that someone was bleeding enough to have bled to death by now."

"You're right. Tell you what, Jesse, why don't you come with me to the bunkhouse? You can make the calls while I fill everyone in on what we've found in here. Then if we come up with any missing persons, we'll organize a search party. Even if everyone turns up accounted for, we'd better do some investigatin' because your wife's right, Jesse. Someone was stuck like a pig in that room and we better find out who."

"What about those poor men? Is it possible that's their blood in there? Could they have been shot in the house?" She saw all three men's brows knot with doubt and shrugged. "I know, that's crazy. I guess I was just trying to come up with some reasonable ˮ

Her words bit off in midsentence, she covered her mouth with her hand as she remembered the hit contracted on her. "Where's Clay Waters? Has anyone talked to him?"

The sheriff's gray eyes narrowed and darkened to slate. "Matter of fact, he's one of the victims we've been discussing here, Miz Pryde." He swiped the Stetson from his head, revealing a bald pate that he rubbed vigorously with his knuckles before settling it in place once again. "Now, why on earth would you have asked about that man in particular? Someone clue you in as to who he really was?"

"Yes. I mean no, no one *told* me who he was. I just

remembered on my own. At least, I thought I'd remembered. Now you tell me he was a federal agent, I'm so confused, I'm not sure about anything. None of this makes any sense."

"You ain't alone," the deputy said. "I'm more confused now than I was when we got here."

"Just tell us what you do know, Doug," Jesse said.

"Well, I know the one named Waters is dead. The other one was breathin' ... barely. Probably gone too by the time he reached the hospital." He went to the table, reaching over his deputy's shoulder to flip through the notebook. "His name, case you recognize it, too, Miz Pryde, is Mandell. Frank Mandell."

At the negative shake of her head, he continued. "That's okay, always worth a try. But who knows, maybe he'll fool us all and pull through. He still had a pulse, which is more than Clay, the poor bastard, had. Roger Troup—your neighbor just to the north—owns a chopper. When I seen how bad off the fella was, I got him on the radio. He was here in ten minutes. Took him to Longview. They got one of them trauma units there." He scratched the back of his neck, then remembering where he was in his telling, went back to it. "They was both shot right about here." He tapped the base of his skull with his forefinger. "Clean shot. Bang! Real professional. Execution style."

"Jesus, Doug. The ladies don't need all the gory details," Jesse snapped.

"Uh, yeah, sorry. Anyway, looked like they was shot right where they was found. Once Roger took off with Mandell, we loaded the other one into the back of my truck. Had another of my deputies take him into town and drop him at the mortuary."

The clock in the foyer behind them struck eight. "What time did you get out here, Sheriff?" Jesse asked.

"What was it, Rick? Seven-ten? Seven-fifteen? Somewhere in there. Your man Hawkins offered to call in all your crew on them walkie-talkies they carry. I left Chuck Harmon at the bunkhouse." He looked at Lacy, explaining that Harmon was another of his deputies, then continued. "I came straight to the house with Rick here and heard Luz here screamin' same as you did. We got her attention, and after a minute or so, she let us in and you know the rest."

"Okay, I'm going upstairs to finish dressing. I'll call around, see if I can find the rest of my family, then meet you in the bunkhouse," Jesse said.

Sheriff Fenton caught another whiff of the pungent scent of blood coming from the dining room and squeezed his eyes shut for a count of two. Might not be the smartest guy around, but he'd bet his next month's salary it was a Pryde whose blood had been splattered all over that room.

He rubbed the end of his nose. It was itching something fierce. Hated it when it did that. Always meant trouble. His wife said he was crazy, that it didn't mean nothin' except he should rub it. But he knew better. 'Sides, everyone knew trouble always came in threesies. so, count 'em off.

One, a professional hit on two agents caught working undercover.

Two, a whole lot of blood that could mean only one thing.

Three? Cripes, he could hardly wait for that shoe to drop! The way things were going, and with his luck, it'd wind up being something big like when President Kennedy was shot up there in Dallas. Yep, he had no doubt it'd be something real big like that ... as if the Prydes weren't big enough to have to worry about dealing with.

Shiiit! he thought on his way to the back door. If he could just keep the ones he did have in sight and away from the crossfire they might have a chance.

He stopped at the door, facing the others and assuming his most confident-looking pose: hand on his holster, weight resting on one leg, eyes shadowed by his hat brim. "Feds are on their way in from Dallas. Way I hear it, the Los Angeles bureau chief is flying in personally to oversee the investigation. Be here this afternoon. Those were his agents who went down. In other words, in the next few hours, this place is going to be teeming with fuzz.

"So do everyone a favor, Pryde. Make your calls, find your family members, and let us know, but after that, keep it tucked inside, if you catch my drift. You go running around half-cocked trying to save the day, you're just gonna end up putting you and that pretty little lady of yours in jeopardy. You hear what I'm saying?"

"Come on," Jesse said, circling his wife's shoulders with his arm and turning his back on the buffoon he'd helped elect. "You start getting dressed while I make those calls."

At her bedroom door she stepped away from his side, reaching for the knob. He stopped her, pulling her against him and catching her waist to spin her around. "You okay?" he asked, bracketing her face with his hands and staring hard into those crystal-clear blue eyes.

She raised her own hands to hold his wrists. "Truth?"

He nodded.

"I'm scared to death, Jesse. Something's terribly, terribly wrong. I'm not just talking about that blood. Something bad's happening, and it's got to do with me."

Jesse kissed her tenderly before backing off to meet her gaze again. "No, baby, that's where you're dead wrong. Something's not right here, I'll agree with that, but it's got nothing to do with you. I don't know what's going on, but I know one thing for sure. You're the only right thing that's happened here as long as I can remember."

"But—"

He shook his head. "No, I'm not going to listen to any arguments. I've got the same bad feeling in my gut that John Wayne down there was trying to convey, but it has nothing to do with you. Trust me on that one, Lace. I'm scared, too, I swear to God, but the only thing that doesn't frighten me this very second is you and me. You got that?"

Tears filled her eyes. She loved him so damned much! She only hoped it was true, that she wasn't a part of the hell that had been loosed on the Southern Star.

Chapter Thirty-three

Jesse rapped twice on Lacy's bedroom door, then opened it.

"Well?" she asked, turning from the vanity where she was brushing her hair.

"Nada," he replied with a shake of his head. "Nobody's seen Mother or Cybil, and Dina couldn't be reached. So we're right back to square one." He placed his hands on her shoulder and kissed the top of her head. "You look beautiful," he said, meeting her reflection in the mirror.

"Um, I think poets call it the bloom of love," she said, covering his hands with hers. He was trying to hide his worry and she wasn't going to let him down by revealing how anxious she was either. "You going out to the bunkhouse?"

"Yep, and you're going to stay put, right?"

"Yes, sir. I'm going to do everything I can to help make this situation as easy for you as possible."

"Good." He bent low to nuzzle her neck, then straightened and hurried to the door. "Oh, and turn the phone on again so I can call you as soon as we know anything."

Lacy turned on the stool to watch him leave. "And you stay safe," she countered.

He grinned, melting her heart and almost making her forget that two men were dead—murdered—and three people were missing. "I love you, Lacy James-Pryde."

The words caught her off guard, jabbing at her conscience as she remembered her run-in with Alex the day before. She had planned to tell Jesse about her family this morning and then everything had been changed by Luz's screams and the sheriff's news. But it might be more important than ever now.

Jesse had already closed the door behind him, but she hurried after him, fumbling with the lock that he'd also turned before managing to open it. "Jesse, wait!" she called, but he was already gone by the time she reached the banister.

The young deputy, Enricco, appeared in the foyer from the kitchen. "You okay, Mrs. Pryde?" he called up to her.

"Yeah," she said with an affirming nod.

Back in her room again, the door locked behind her, she slipped off the robe she'd pulled on over her jeans and T-shirt. She went to the closet and grabbed her boots and Stetson, gnawing on her bottom lip as she went.

Guilt was heavy, but she lightened the load with excuses and rationalizations.

She wasn't lying to hurt anyone. She was trying to help and mostly, she didn't want to worry Jesse. He had enough on his mind.

Besides, she couldn't just sit in the bedroom holed up like a frightened rabbit. She'd go nuts wondering what was happening outside.

And most important, she had an idea; an idea she thought might just work. But she had to hurry.

It was after nine a.m. already. Time was running out. The two federal agents had been found much earlier than he'd anticipated. Hell, the place was already crawling with badges. Just lucky for him they were all of the local, dumber-than-dumb variety. By noon the place would be run over by state boys who knew where they were coming from. Within an hour or two after that, the federal guys would be there. Then it would be all she wrote. He had to have his business completed long before any of that happened.

The man was on a bluff overlooking the valley that accounted for a good quadrant of acreage of Southern Star land. Mostly meadowlands except for the river and the falls just a half mile or so behind him to the north.

He'd been out there for ten minutes, give or take a minute or two. Thinking. Trying to figure a way around the sheriff and his men. He grinned. Jesse wouldn't be a problem. Hell, the man didn't want nothing to do with his old lady. If he knew him at all, and he damn sure did, good ol' Jesse would be out in the bunkhouse giving Fenton a lesson or two on tracking a killer. If that was indeed the case, it should be easy enough to get to her. Just slip up to her bedroom and do her quiet as a mouse. Then he could put in the call to that lawyer in California. Send a message the everything was all tidied up.

The man frowned. Word had come down that he was to take care of Waters, then wait till after the big to-do that night before offing the beautiful Mrs. Pryde. Well, no could do. Everything had changed. For one thing, the doc had been murdered. That had definitely put a pall on the party mood around town.

Then that Frank guy being found still breathing. Son of a bitch. Not that he had a chance in hell of surviving. A man didn't take a bullet in the head like that and live to talk about it.

And then there was the mystery about all that blood in the—

The man lost his train of thought as he caught movement in his periphery vision and the sound of horse hooves pounding the earth on the valley floor below in the same instant. He flattened himself out, his hand closed around his rifle as he worked his way to the edge of the bluff with his elbows.

Damn Sam, he was a lucky man. A slow grin took shape as he lined up the rider in the crosshairs of his rifle scope. Yessirree, it wasn't his mind playing tricks. He'd recognize that gal anywhere. And not just the pale blond hair blowing back beneath the brim of her hat. Hell, her signature red T-shirt was as telltale as a jockey's colors.

The horse was moving at an easy lope, and the man bided his time, giving rider and animal time to come out fully in the open. *Make it a clean shot*—he shut one eye and closed his finger around the trigger—*right through the heart*.

He hesitated, enjoying watching her. Damn, she could ride. Back erect, arms laid easily at her sides, only the toes of her boots resting in the stirrup, and just look at the way her hips flared. Umm, umm, only wished he could have her riding him like that just one time before . . .

But it wishes were dollars and yada, yada, yada, he wouldn't be out there lying in the wet grass earning money by shooting pretty ladies he really wanted to fuck, now would he?

Screwing up the left side of his face again, he drew her to him via the magic of the telescopic lens and worked his tongue around his lips. Damn shame, but then no one had ever said he was lucky. He was just smart.

He pulled the trigger, then slammed down the gun, cursing almost as loudly as the report from the gun.

Damn, shit, hellfire! That crazy horse had shied to the left in the exact second he'd fired. Oh, he'd gotten her, seen her go down. The question was where? Had he shot her clean enough to kill her or merely grazed her?

Peering over the ledge he saw her spread out on her back. The horse was running like crazy, but the man's attention was focused on the woman. He should probably get another bead on her and pop her again. This time in the head. He reached for his gun.

Someone yelled behind him. It wasn't close. Maybe up by the falls. Didn't matter. Whoever it was might have heard the shot, be calling to someone else. He had to get out of there, fast.

Half crouching, he ran for the wall of brush behind him where he'd left his horse tethered while he passed a few minutes getting his thoughts together.

Sliding his rifle into the scabbard on his saddle, he grinned. Who said he wasn't lucky. Hell, a minute or two either way and he would never have even seen her. She would have gotten clean away maybe preventing him from another chance at fulfilling his end of the contract.

As he swung himself up into his saddle, he continued to smile, even chuckling as he reined his mount north. He wasn't going to worry about the beautiful Mrs. Pryde anymore. His luck was too damned good today, which meant hers wasn't.

Joseph Wong was exhausted but glad to be home. The Willis/Moore bash had been a huge success, but at the first opportunity to escape, he'd headed for the airport, just making the two a.m. red-eye.

Shutting off the car, he stretched, yawned, then opened the door. He wasn't even going to take his luggage from the car. He was going straight upstairs to bed.

Do not pass go, do not take a ride on the Reading ... go directly to bed and kiss your wife. He laughed. Crazy man. No, make that crazy man in love ... and worried.

His thin brows came together over the bridge of his nose as he let himself inside the house. He was worried about Lib. Truth be told that was why he'd changed his plans and come home early.

She hadn't looked good yesterday when she returned to the hotel. She'd been pale and acting funny. Well not funny. Just strained, sort of. And that business about Frank Mandell. That worried Joey plenty. Mandell had told him all he could, which wasn't a hell of a lot. Only that he needed to work inside the house during the party. So, Joey'd gone along. What choice did he have?

Chink, the Himalayan kitten, came bounding down the stairs meowing and rubbing against his legs. He stopped, picking the tiny fur ball up and stroking its head between the ears. "Where's our lady, huh? She still sleeping? Good, then let's go wake her up."

Libby awakened with a groan as raindrops splattered against her face. She hurt. Damn it, she didn't just hurt, she *HURT*.

She started to raise her right arm, intending to throw it over her eyes, protection against the rain, but fire as hot as a branding iron spread from her shoulder up to the back of her head. She cried out.

What the hell—

And then she remembered. She'd been riding Black Billy. He'd been frisky, full of vinegar as Joey would say, but she'd managed to slow him down. They'd just settled into a comfortable collected canter when a black snake had wriggled in front of them, stirring the tall meadow grasses and spooking Billy.

Her eyes widened, then closed again at once as the raindrops began to fall heavier. She turned her head to the side, trying to lift her left arm instead. It hurt, but she was able to cover her face. At least she wouldn't drown in the rain like some stupid turkey.

Hell, no. She'd probably lie out there and bleed to

death. She'd been shot. She'd remembered the loud
bang, then the punch of something slamming into her
back, strong enough to unseat her. Didn't take a certificate from Mensa to put it together.

And then she remembered her surprise and started to
cry. She hadn't even had a chance to share her news
about the baby with Joey. *Oh, God, why?* she demanded
silently, anger replacing grief. And then she heard the
car.

Moving her arm, she tipped her head back as far as
she could. She saw the Land Rover stop, and Joey, her
Joey, running toward her.

"Libby, my God, what happened? Did that horse
throw you?"

She shook her head, then cried out when he raised
her up from the waist.

"My God, Lib, you're bleeding!"

"I've been shot," she whispered though the words
were hard to get out through her suddenly parched lips.
She licked them and tried again.

"Shh," he said. "Don't talk. I'm going to have to get
you to the Rover. I can lift you, but it's going to hurt
like hell."

"Hurry," she said. "We've got to save the baby."

She didn't speak again. Mercifully, she'd passed out
once more. She didn't feel him pick her up and hold her
against him as he balanced on his knees, then struggled
to his feet. She didn't feel the moisture falling against
her face, though this time it was her husband's tears
instead of the rain. And she didn't hear the threat he
made if God didn't help him save his woman and child.

It sounded like a child's whine. Dillon was sure he'd
heard it, but now as he listened, nothing. Only the loud
roar of the waterfalls. He'd reined his horse in at the
noise coming from above him somewhere in the rocky
cliffs that banked both sides of the river at the top of
the falls. But now he wasn't only hearing things, he was
seeing ghosts and mirages.

He squeezed his eyes shut and gave his head a brisk
shake. But when he opened them again, they were all
there. His truck parked out in the middle of nowhere,
and Topaz, his mother's Palamino mare, tied to the back

gate. And there, twenty or thirty yards away, Lacy climbing up the mountain of stone behind Thorn! What the hell was going on?

He watched them, Lacy following the dog and Thorn moving with deliberate caution and glancing back over his shoulder every now and then as if checking on her, making sure she was okay and still coming. Looked like something straight out of one of those Lassie shows he'd watched on TV as a kid.

Only this wasn't make-believe, he reminded himself as he heard the strange cry from the top of the falls just as he had before.

Lacy had heard it as well, he could tell. She was moving faster, scrambling with renewed vigor and not as much care. He thought he even heard Thorn growl, but that could have been merely the noise of the water.

It didn't matter. This whole situation was out of whack. But he didn't have time to figure it all out now.

He dismounted in one fluid motion, then slipped through the brush, taking a shortcut up to the top.

He arrived huffing and puffing in the narrow clearing at the same time as Lacy and the dog. But his attention wasn't focused on them. It was fastened on the grisly scene unfolding only a few feet from the edge of the waterfall.

His mother was standing against the rock, her waist-length hair, which he hadn't seen hanging loose since he was a small boy, plastered against her by the spray from the water as well as stained the same red-brown in places as her clothing, and the left side of her face swollen and bruised. His wife lay at the lip of the bank overlooking the top of the falls on a slab of granite, blood-soaked and as pale as death that was clearly not far off.

"She's crazy!" Rose shrieked in an alien high-pitched tone he'd never heard in her voice. He recognized it at once as the shrill, childlike shriek he'd heard above the crashing water from below.

Thorn was growling, a low, threatening rumble emphasized by the way his lip was pulled back to bare his fangs.

"She's going to kill me, Dillon!" Rose shrieked again.

Tears rose to the surface of Dillon's eyes as the wind stirred the blood-weighted fabric of his wife's nightgown enough to reveal her left arm. Washing clean of the blood he could see bone and tendons and wasted muscle beneath the pale flesh that had been slashed to ribbons.

"Oh, God," he groaned, dropping to his knees at her side. Slipping an arm under her back, he raised her gently, careful not to disturb the injured arm, and cradled her against him.

"Are you crying, Dill?" she asked in a tone so soft and weak, Lacy had to step nearer to hear her words. "Don't cry, sweetie. Mama's going to be with her babies now."

"What happened to you?" Lacy asked when it became clear that Dillon was too choked to pose the question himself.

Cybil twisted her head a few inches until she found her sister-in-law with her eyes. "It happened a long time ago, honey. Too long ago for you to worry about now. She ripped us to shreds when she killed our babies." She stopped again, coughing feebly, then moistening her lips with her tongue and focusing her gaze on Rose who had begun to sidle subtly along the wall of stone. Summoning strength no one would have credited the dying woman with, Cybil raised the gun. "Stay there and listen while I tell your son what you did to him."

"No, Cyl. Don't talk. I'm going to get you to the hospital. When, you're, um ... better, stronger, you can tell me."

But Cybil knew there wouldn't be time later. Her gaze fixed on the woman who had destroyed her and everything she loved, she made her charges. "She killed our babies, Dill. Had the doctor give them something. Can't remember now what it was. And your Daddy, too. Followed him the night he got drunk and came out here to be alone. He'd found out about everything. He was trying to decide what to do when she sneaked up on him and hit him with a baseball bat. He drowned just like the autopsy report said, but he didn't kill himself."

Horrified, Lacy faced her mother-in-law. "Why? How could you do such a thing?"

"Oh, for God's sake, look at them! They're pathetic. That's what's wrong with the world today. Nobody takes responsibility. Any idiot with hormones can reproduce. Well, not the Cahilles! I made a mistake with Richmond,

my husband. I thought we would make good babies together. Jesse was our success. You can see our failure
right here and, even worse, the poor excuse for a woman
he married. And you think I should have allowed them
to procreate? Don't be ridiculous."

Tears spilled over Dillon's lashes and still fire burned
in his eyes as he looked at his mother, but Cybil needed
him now, was speaking to him, diverting his attention
from the vile monster whom he had called mother.

The gun dangling from her fingers, Cybil laid her hand
against his leg and met his gaze. "I did it, Dill. Killed
Raul. I was waiting for him after reading the medical
records. I forced a confession out of him. Then I killed
him. I shot him and burned his house."

Voices, four or five or even more, were yelling from
below, calling out to them.

"Dillon!"

"Lacy!"

"Miz Rose!"

Over and over, the names of the people they searched
for echoed through the rocks before they were swallowed up by the clamor of the falls. Lacy turned toward
them, cupping her mouth and hollering down a reply.

Something, a sixth sense perhaps, alerted her to movement in her direction from behind. She swung around in
time to see Rose lunging for her and stepped back barely
avoiding being grabbed and flung into the water. Thorn
leaped, and the gun exploded from behind them in the
exact same instant. Lacy fell against the rock as dog
and mistress hurtled past her, crashing into the swirling
water below.

Lacy screamed as they disappeared over the top of
the falls.

And then Dillon was above her, reaching for her as
Rose had, and Lacy was fighting him, kicking and
screaming.

"Hey, whoa, girl," he said as the sheriff and a real
honest-to-goodness posse arrived to save the day ...
only a few seconds too late.

Chapter Thirty-four

Jesse sat alone in the living room, his head in his hands. Luz had persuaded the sheriff to allow Enricco to drive her to her son's house in town.

Shortly after that, Randy Hawkins had called in on his walkie-talkie, notifying Jesse and Sheriff Fenton that he'd spotted Dillon's truck parked at the foot of the site known as Granite Falls. He'd also told them, his tone grave, that the cab of the vehicle was covered in blood.

The sheriff had quickly selected a small knot of men to accompany him to the site. "How about you, Jesse? You coming with us?"

Jesse had declined the offer. Right now he had only one thing on his mind. Making sure his wife was safe inside her bedroom in the hacienda. "Randy didn't say anything about seeing Lacy, did he?"

"No, just what you heard. He found your brother's truck and a lot of blood. I've ordered him to look around, make sure there's no one hiding in the brush to ambush us, then ride this way and meet up with us. Sure you don't want to come along?"

"I want to, Sheriff, I just can't. I've been calling the house for the past forty-five minutes. I know Lacy is more than likely still locked inside the bedroom and has just forgotten to turn the phone on, but I'm going to find out for myself first. If she's safe, I'll ride out and join you."

But the house was empty. He'd gone through every room, then checked outside as well. He'd looked in the barn, gone to the dog runs, even returned to the bunkhouse on the chance that she'd gone there looking for him and somehow they'd missed one another. Now he was trying to decide where else to look, what his options were.

Well, one thing was certain, he wasn't going to find her sitting here. Bounding to his feet, he turned toward the door just as she appeared there.

She was soaking wet, trembling and pale as a pearl moon, but she was there. Safe.

"Jesus, Lace, I've been worried sick. Where have you been? What the hell happened to you? Do you know you scared me half—" He cut off the rapid fire of questions on a deep growl as he gathered her into his arms. "Son of a bitch, you scared me."

She hugged him, held him so tight her arms ached, and she cried. She'd never seen anything so horrible ... or if she had, she didn't remember and hoped to God she never did. "Cybil ... oh, Jesse, she's dead ... and your mother ..." She didn't finish the statement. How did she do this? Tell the man she loved more than life that his mother was dead, had been shot to death? How did she tell him why? Sweet Jesus, how could she stand even thinking about it? She began to sob, and held him tighter, her hands gripping the fabric of his shirt as memories of the horror she'd witnessed played themselves over and over in her mind.

Jesse's heart was hammering in his chest. Cyl dead? And what had Lacy been about to tell him about his mother? Lord God, had the whole world suddenly been pitched upside down?

He needed answers, but he didn't ask any questions. Not now, not yet. Not until Lacy was calmed down. Right now she was practically hysterical, and he couldn't forget how fragile her health had been since the incident in California.

His brow puckered with a new thought provoked by the last. Cybil was dead, she'd told him. He could only surmise that the blood in the dining room had been hers, which meant more likely than not that she'd been murdered—slaughtered—like those two FBI men. The LAPD had told him Lacy had been run down by someone intent on killing her.

Icy fear spread through his veins.

He remembered Lacy's words before he'd left for the bunkhouse earlier: *Something bad's happening, and it's got to do with me.*

He was suddenly sure she was right. He had no idea

how, and right now he didn't care, just so long as she didn't get hurt. Somehow, he had to make sure that didn't happen.

"Shh," he whispered against her temple as he rubbed her back and tried to soothe her.

Over her head, he saw the sheriff appear in the doorway and come to a stop. Dillon stood directly behind the lawman.

"She tell you?" Sheriff Fenton asked quietly.

Jesse shook his head. "Not much." He'd answered the sheriff, but his eyes were fixed on his brother. His face was tear-stained, paler than Lacy's had been when she'd come in. But it was his brother's eyes that held Jesse's gaze. They were red—further evidence of his grief—yet it was the way they flashed that warned of something running deeper than sadness. Hatred shone there. Hatred and murder. "Dil?"

A muscle worked in Dillon's jaw though he didn't answer. He let go a long jagged breath and turned his attention to the sheriff. "Why don't you get on back outside and tend to the business that brought you out here to the Southern Star, Doug? I'll fill Jesse in about . . ." His voice snagged on the sharp, ragged edge of pain that had lodged in his throat like a piece of broken glass. He swallowed, started again. "I'll get him told, take care of what needs tending to in here. You can let us know when the state and federal boys arrive."

Doug lowered his head, cleared his own throat that had suddenly filled with gravel, and nodded smartly before turning away and disappearing from the doorway.

"Cybil's dead, Jess," Dillon said without waiting until the last of Doug Fenton's heavy steps had faded from earshot. "Mom, too."

"Oh, God," Jesse groaned, tightening his hold on his wife. "How?"

Dillon's chin had dropped to his chest, but he looked up with the question, shook his head. "Un-uh, baby brother. This one I can't do right now. Can't talk about the kind of sickness and evil I learned about out there. Not just yet. Later, okay? After the bile settles."

Lacy's weeping had quieted, ebbed enough for her to step out of Jesse's embrace and speak for her brother-in-law. "He's lost everything, sweetheart."

"Of course. We'll talk later, Dil. Whenever you're ready."

Dillon cast a glance in the direction that the sheriff had gone. "Before that can happen, I'd guess the state boys and FBI will be after some answers. I expect I'll be the one to give them most of what they're after."

Jesse frowned, not so much bothered by what Dillon had just said as by the angry glint that had sparked in his eyes again. "There's something that goes beyond grief here, Dillon. Maybe you'd better tell me after all."

"And maybe you'd better shut up!" Dillon snapped.

Lacy took a step back, Jesse a step forward.

"Hey—" Jesse began.

Dillon held up a hand. "No! Shit, I'm sorry. Just at the end of my rope, I suppose. Forgive me, Jesse, Lacy. I need some time alone. A few minutes. I'll go upstairs. Clean up, get a grip, then meet you down here in a half hour or so. By then, I should have it pulled together again."

He turned on his heel, not waiting for a response from his brother or sister-in-law. Doing what he had to before he lost it good. Before he snapped once and for all. He had no doubt, in the end, once he allowed himself to think about all of Cybil's revelations, he'd go over the edge just as she had. Fine. He didn't care much one way or the other, but he had to keep it together just a bit longer. Until he tidied up the last of his business. Then, everyone and everything be damned right along with him and Cyl and his crazy fucking mother.

"You okay?" Jesse asked his wife once his brother was gone.

Her eyes downcast, she nodded, then shook her head no. "Yes, no. I don't know. It was so horrible, Jesse. Poor Cybil. She was butchered. Apparently, she'd done it to herself." She covered her eyes with her hands as if to blot out the image. "And then your mother and ... and Thorn—Oh, Jesse, they went over the falls. Cybil shot her, I think. Or maybe it was Dillon. I don't know. It all happened so fast." She was weeping again, and Jesse was more confused than ever, but he gathered her to him once again.

"Go upstairs, Lace. Lie down. We'll get this whole

nightmare sorted out when we can. For now, I'd better get outside with the sheriff."

He walked her to the foot of the stairs, kissed her brow, his hands slipping from her face to her shoulders as his lips followed as far as her mouth. "I love you, woman. Don't think about anything except that until I come back. Promise me."

It was a promise she would never be able to keep, but she nodded and even managed a wobbly smile. "Go on. I'll be all right."

He started for the kitchen and the back door, but got only a few steps. "Lacy, wait," he called, already bounding up the stairs. He grabbed her shoulders, turning her around to face him just as she was about to step onto the landing. "There is one thing you can answer for me before I leave."

She was taken aback by the gruffness of his tone, alarmed by the change in his expression from loving concern to something darker. Annoyance? Anger? "What's wrong?" she asked.

"I just remembered how frightened I was when I came back to the house earlier and found you missing. I've never known that kind of fear before. Never. Not even when you left me and headed out for California." He stopped, gulping down the panic he was reliving. He motioned behind them to the floor below. "When we were down there with Dillon I wondered at the anger I saw in his eyes. I didn't understand it until I recalled how helpless I felt when I found you gone. He's blaming himself for losing Cyl. For not being there when she needed him. He's got nobody to blame but himself and it's killing him. I couldn't live if anything happened to you. Don't leave the bedroom, Lacy. Please." The last was said on a choked whisper so desperate, tears filled her eyes.

She laid a hand on his cheek. "I'm sorry, Jesse. I didn't mean to scare you. I just wanted to help. I got Thorn from the pen, used him to track your mother." Pride flickered in her eyes. "I rode one of the mares, and we found them."

"I don't care," he said, gripping her arms tight enough to cause her to wince. He was immediately contrite.

"Oh, shit, Lace, I'm sorry. I didn't mean to hurt you. I just . . ."

"I know," she said, covering his hands with her own and offering a tremulous smile. "You don't have to worry. I won't leave my room. Go on. Take care of your ranch and finding out what happened to those poor men. I'll stay locked up until you come back, you have my word."

It was a promise she would have kept, too, if she hadn't passed Cybil and Dillon's room in the next moment and heard the man's heartrending sobs.

Chapter Thirty-five

Lacy didn't hesitate. She changed course, stopping in front of Dillon and Cybil's bedroom instead of going on to her own. She gripped the door handle, called out his name. There was no answer, though she hadn't expected there would be. He was suffering mightily and loudly, his sobs harsh and hiccuping. Lacy tested the handle, then carefully pushed the door open when it proved to be unlocked. Pity and compassion sluiced from her heart and she dashed across the room to where he sat on the side of his unmade bed, his face buried in the covers he held in his hands.

"Oh, Dillon, I'm so sorry," she said, crawling onto the bed beside him and wrapping him in her arms. "I'm so, so sorry."

He didn't answer.

Lacy rocked him like a baby, crooning to him, uttering words of comfort, empty platitudes about the healing power of time. She spoke of Cybil, of the peace she had finally found in death. Silently, she cursed Rose for the devastation she'd wreaked on her firstborn son. And eventually she gave up even that and simply waited for his anguish to bleed itself out in tears.

Tears began to fall from her own eyes. Silent tears that she hadn't even felt coming on. And rain pattered heavily on the veranda outside the room as if even the heavens wept for his loss.

Lacy's back ached, her shoulders burned, and her arms numbed while she continued to hold him. And just when she thought she would have to let him go, he pulled away from her, dashing the last of his grief from his face with the back of his arm. "I can smell her in the sheets. Lilacs and vodka. Her perfume and her booze . . . all I have left of her."

Lacy didn't answer. What was there to say? She scooted from the bed, standing and rubbing her shoulder and stretching the kinks from her back.

"I'll leave you alone—"

"No!"

The protest was made in a loud, unexpected bark that startled her. She reached out for his hand, squeezed it, and offered a smile though he wasn't looking at her. "It's okay. I'll stay. As long as you need me."

He looked at her then, his red, swollen lids half shielding his eyes and lending his countenance an aura of menace that inspired a shiver in Lacy.

But that was ridiculous. Hadn't she witnessed the gentleness in this man when he'd gathered his wife's body into his arms, carefully tucking her ruined arm in her lap in spite of the fact that she was past hurting? Hadn't she watched as tears rivered down his cheeks while he carried her down the hillside? And hadn't she heard him murmuring to Cybil, begging her forgiveness?

No, there was nothing about Dillon Pryde that should cause fear. Still, she stepped away from the bed, looked around her, and selected a chair on the far side of the room. "I'm here, Dillon. I won't leave. Why don't you lie down and try to rest. Jesse's outside with the sheriff. I'm sure he'll tell us what's happening as they find out. Until then, there's nothing for you to worry about except getting yourself together."

Ignoring her, he reached behind him and extracted a pistol from the back of his waistband. "I have to turn this over to Doug. It's the gun that killed Mother."

Lacy merely nodded because she didn't know what to say.

"Killed my own mother. What do they call that? Matricide?"

"Yes," Lacy agreed. "I didn't know. Who shot her, I mean. You'll probably have to give Sheriff Fenton a statement later."

Dillon rubbed the barrel of the gun thoughtfully, then said, "I loved her."

"She knew that," Lacy said.

Dillon shook his head. "Naw, not Cybil. I'm talking about my mother. I loved that bitch so much it was sick." He looked up from under his heavy brows, grinned. "You wouldn't believe the lengths I went to prove that to her. Got gored by a bull when I was ten just because she happened by the paddock and I wanted to show off. Know what she whispered in my ear just before the ambulance took me off to the hospital? Said she should have drowned me at birth like she would've an unwanted kitten. Said I was too stupid to live." He laughed. "Never forgot that, and soon as I was old enough, I left here. Went on the rodeo circuit. I was good, Lacy. Not just good, I was great! Think it impressed her?"

Lacy didn't know how to answer though she was pretty sure she knew what the answer was. He confirmed her suspicions.

"I showed her my bank book; all the prize money I'd saved up. And you know what she did? She threw her head back and laughed. Said even a trained ape could climb on a horse and hang on till he got bucked off. What did that prove except that I was either simian or moron."

Lacy's stomach knotted at the cruelty. She'd known Rose was cold, mean even. She just hadn't understood how vicious. "I'm sure she didn't mean it," she offered weakly.

"I finally quit trying to prove myself. I met Cyl, fell hard. Jesus Christ, maybe I was stupid." Another laugh slipped between his clenched teeth though this time it was heavy with bitterness and tinged with irony. "I thought I had the world by the tail. Hell, the only tail I had ahold of was my own."

"That's not true. You had a woman who loved you. If . . . if Rose hadn't . . ." She stopped, cleared her throat that was clogging with tears, and started again. "If she had just let you both alone, everything would have turned out the way you expected. You can't blame yourself for what she did. And maybe you can't even really blame her. Maybe she couldn't help it. Maybe she was sick."

"Oh, yeah, she was sick all right. Leastwise, she got sick every time she looked at me. You heard what Cyl said about why she had the doc murder our babies. Didn't hear any denials from Rose, did you?" He hung his head, shook it a couple of times, and looked up again. "But you still don't get it, do you?"

No, maybe she didn't, she thought. Not if he was going to blame himself for his mother's crazy need for total control. "I guess not," she admitted aloud.

"I—shot—my—mother!" He drew a deep breath, started to say something else, but Lacy interrupted.

"You didn't have a choice!"

"Fuck, I know that. You think I don't know that? I know that. But that's not the point. The point is, she was right all along. If I hadn't been so stupid, she wouldn't have hurt my Cyl or our babies, 'cause I would have killed her soon as I was old enough to heft a gun."

Lacy shook her head, her eyes fixed on the pistol he was fondling. "You didn't know then."

"Oh, yeah, I knew. She cut me out of her will. Left everything to Jesse. I knew that."

"Oh, surely—"

"I found out a couple of years back. Didn't tell anyone. Not even Cyl. But I started making plans. Went into business for myself. Became an entrepreneur, you might say. After the babies died, I made plans. I was going to take Cyl away from here. Arrange to adopt a kid or two. Buy one off the black market if need be. But I let too much get between us. That's why she's dead now."

"You're not to blame, Dillon," Lacy said firmly.

"Oh, yes, ma'am, I surely am. The buck definitely stops here, kiddo. I should have been home with her last night. Instead, I was in town, boffing the town whore. Even when I got back, I might have stopped—" His words were choked off by a sob. He shook his head, throwing off pain like a duck casting off water. "Even then I might have been in time to save her if I'd just come in the house instead of going to the bunkhouse to sleep." He'd been staring at the gun. He looked up at Lacy now. "Can you understand that kind of guilt, girl? The kind that won't allow a body to even face himself in the mirror much less crawl in bed beside his wife?"

Lacy nodded. "I still don't have my memory back. Not all of it, but I know about guilt, Dillon. I know how I hurt Jesse."

"Yep," he agreed. "You did do that, so maybe you do know what I'm talking about."

"But you can't blame yourself for everything that happened. Rose killed your babies. It was her fault that Cybil was so miserable. You didn't do that."

"Can't argue with you there. She was one cold-blooded bitch all right." He ran a hand over his face, then stood up and walked to the French doors. "Guess it's true what they say about the apple not falling too far from the tree."

Lacy frowned, not sure what he meant by that. Was he saying they both shared in the blame for Cybil's breakdown? She wasn't sure and then he changed the subject.

"Shit, girl, you should see all the cops out there. Place looks like a fucking anthill."

Lacy walked to the door, stopping beside her brother-in-law to peer out. "State troopers?"

"Yeah, that and the local boys and even the feds." he pointed to a knot of men, one of them dressed in civilian clothes, the other two, Jesse and Sheriff Fenton, standing below on the patio. "The suit's FBI," he said. "Come to see about those two men I popped."

Lacy felt her blood freeze. Jerking her head to the side, she stared up at the man beside her. What was he saying? Had he gone over the edge like Cybil?

He looked down at her, a slow grin spreading. "You don't believe me."

"Of course not!" she snapped, taking a couple of steps away from him at the same time.

"Then what're you afraid of?"

She stopped. "I'm not afraid. Just shocked that you would make such an awful claim, that's all."

He turned around to face her straight on. Leaning against the tall armoire beside the doors, he propped an arm on the top, the gun dangling from his fingers. "Well, little lady, I'm afraid I've got another shock or two in store for you. I'm not out of my mind with grief like you're thinking, and I'm not just making wild claims here. I offed those two FBI agents. Wasn't looking to. Shit, no one could've been more surprised than I was to find out Clay Waters was a Feebie. Him and this other agent was out there in the brush behind the bunkhouse talking when I came up on 'em. They didn't hear me, so I stood there a couple of minutes listening. Didn't take long to put what they were talking about all together.

"Waters was here to keep an eye on you; find out what you'd done with all the money you stole from your old man, Sammy Wyatt. The other one had just arrived last night. Seems they were onto the fact that Wyatt had hired a hit on you, and he'd shown up to help Waters find out who it was."

He laughed as he watched her blanch pale as a plucked goose. "Know what the funny thing is? They would never have put two and two together if not for that hit-and-run out in California."

Dawning was slow in coming, but once it settled it took her breath as surely as a fist just slammed into her stomach. "You?"

Dillon raised an eyebrow. "What? You asking if I'm the one who ran you down with a car out there in Hollywood? No way, lady. I don't work like that. I'm in this strictly for the money, not to cause suffering. When I'm paid to off someone, it's pure D professionalism all the way. I do good, clean work. A single bullet to the base of the skull, and they never know what hit 'em. Painless as a shot of Novocaine."

Lacy covered her mouth with her hand. "You . . . you really murder people?"

"Well, not just people. Only folks I'm paid to kill and only if the money's good enough."

Lacy laughed at that, but it had an unnatural, tinny sound to it. The sound of hysteria. She had to clamp down on herself. Get a grip. Find a way to save herself. "How much money is 'good enough' to salve a conscience for taking a life?"

Dillon twirled the gun as he thought over the question.

Lacy began to tremble. Dillon was performing gun tricks for her! It was only noon, yet the day had grown so dark, she could hardly make out his features. Could only stare at the place where silver flashed as the gun whirled. She jumped when he suddenly spoke.

"Sometimes as little as ten gees. Fifty in your case, you being a real prize and all."

He *was* crazy! Lacy didn't wait to hear more. She turned and started to run. She got only ten or twelve feet before she heard a click as the hammer was pulled back.

"Where you running off to, sweet cakes?" Dillon asked.

She froze. Caught up short as a deer pinioned by the beam of headlights.

"Please," she whispered so quietly she wasn't sure she hadn't merely uttered the plea in her mind.

"Dying ain't hard, Lacy, girl. It's the living that's hell."

She started to turn, ready to fall on her knees and beg if that's what it took. She screamed as Dillon raised the gun and pulled the trigger.

Jesse shook his head in disbelief as the sheriff ended his conversation with his deputy in Rooster Corner, cut the connection, and folded up the compact cellular phone he'd held to his ear.

"Well, you both heard," Doug Fenton said, blowing out a mighty gust of breath and focusing somewhere between Jesse and the Los Angeles FBI bureau chief who'd arrived some twenty-odd minutes earlier.

They'd heard, all right. Not only had Rose and Cybil Pryde both died horribly, violently, two federal agents been shot—one mortally, the other perhaps as well—and it seemed someone had gunned down Liberty Ambrose earlier that morning. She was doing well, the bullet fired by an unknown assailant only creasing her shoulder ... still, what the hell was going on? Three seemingly unconnected incidents of phenomenal proportions and that wasn't counting Raul Trajillo's murder just two days before.

The sheriff shook his head. "Hellfire, we've had more violence in the past forty-eight hours than I've experienced in my thirty-four years as a law officer! Will someone please tell me if the whole world is suddenly unraveling at the seams or has hell merely been moved to Rooster Corner?" He spat, shifted his weight to one foot, and rested a hand on the butt of his firearm holstered on his hip as he directed his gaze at Jesse. "They haven't found your mother's body yet, son. Two of my boys have followed the river as far as Kenny Dalton's spread. Don't worry, they'll find her. They're gonna stay with it all the way to the gulf, if needs be."

Jesse nodded, cleared a sudden lump from his throat.

Doug's eyes couldn't stay there focused on the other man's pain like that. He coughed and averted his gaze to Chief Anderson. "Got a message for you, sir. From the deputy chief in L.A. Says you're to contact him or Agent Gary Maltz ASAP. Says to tell you he might know the identity of the person who shot your men. May have been the same one who murdered two women in L.A. yesterday, then caught a plane for Dallas last night."

"Use your phone?" Warren Anderson asked.

Sheriff Fenton watched the man unfold the wallet cellular and begin punching in numbers. He was impressed, mildly intimidated even. The FBI man was something to watch, though he couldn't quite pin it down. There were the extraordinary good looks—early Hollywood movie star handsome à la Grant, Peck, or Gable—but there was more, a distinction in his presence as well. In the way he carried himself, the way he dressed, the way he spoke. He was a man one listened to and no doubt more often than not found himself agreeing with. Then Doug nailed it. The man was a born leader, oozing charisma and inspiring trust. A rare combination these days.

Jesse had been watching Chief Anderson as well, but his thoughts had been in a darker place, with the tragedies that had befallen the Southern Star and questions about what the FBI had been doing working undercover on his spread.

He swept his Stetson from his head, shook off the rain that had gathered in the brim, and brushed his thick hair back before settling his hat in place again. Then he looked at the sheriff. He was just about to suggest that they give Chief Anderson some privacy when he heard Lacy scream. The sound was swallowed up by the loud pop that followed it.

"Gunshot," he said as his heart slammed against his chest.

The three men along with four or five other local and state officers all darted for the house at the same time.

Jesse reached it first.

Chapter Thirty-six

The woman moved with care toward the hacienda. She wore a heavy frown, and her clothes were soaking wet. She was tired and damned sick of waiting for the cloud of hornets that had settled over the Southern Star to scatter so she could go home.

Now they were leaving. A few at a time, but thinning out just the same.

She'd been watching the goings-on from inside a dense thicket of prickly raspberry vines. Besides having to worry about snakes that liked to hide there as well, she'd had a poor view and had been pricked several times by the spiny vines. She scratched her arms and the backs of her hands as she stopped behind a heavy hydrangea shrub at the far northwest corner of the house and peered through the petals of huge white blooms assessing her chances of making it undetected to the front door.

It was getting late. Exactly how late, she wasn't sure. She'd lost her watch and with the day dark and dreary with cloud cover and rain since morning, it was hard to gauge how far away nightfall was. She hoped sooner rather than later. Otherwise, she might well be found out before she was ready.

In spite of her weariness and irritation, she had to smile at the prospect of the stir it would cause if she was discovered before she was ready. Might be worth it just to see the look on Jesse's face, not to mention that stupid sheriff.

The smile fell away at once. Might be fun, but she hadn't risked everything for a few minutes of amusement. She'd almost lost it all. Had come within a hair's breadth of it.

She squared her shoulders, pushing the thought away. She'd survived . . . against all odds . . . and she was home.

Jesse sat at his desk in his office. For the first time since awakening to Luz's screams that morning, he was alone. Alone with the horror of the day's events. Alone with his grief and anger. Alone with the insurmountable responsibility of putting his life back together.

Outside, he could hear an occasional voice raised to another as a few last stragglers from the local, state, and federal law enforcement agencies wrapped up their work for the day. Tomorrow they'd be back, putting the last pieces of a convoluted puzzle together. But for now, he'd been left to search for reason in all the madness, and though proof that life continued could be heard outside the hacienda walls, inside it was quiet as a tomb.

Jesse laid his arms on his desk and lowered his head, squeezing his eyes shut against the burning of tears that were just beneath the surface, refusing yet to be shed.

He heard a noise like a door creaking and jumped with surprise. His chair scraped against the oak planks of flooring as he rose heavily to his feet. No doubt one of the sheriff's men had come to announce their imminent departure. He stopped at the door of his office. Maybe if he stayed put, they'd go away, leave him to his suffering. He listened a few minutes. Heard nothing other than the loud, rhythmic ticking of the clock in the foyer. He started back toward his desk.

There. He heard it again. Definitely someone at one of the doors.

Annoyed, he strode toward the foyer, the *click, click, click* of his booted heels sounding more like loud bangs against the unnatural quiet of the house. For the first time, the weight of all he'd lost that day threatened to bring him down with it. He stopped, leaning against the wall, and took a couple of deep stabilizing breaths. He recovered enough to straighten, but this time the tears had come too near the surface to be held back. They slipped from the corners of his eyes, barely getting a start before he brushed them away, then pinched the bridge of his nose to stifle more. He couldn't fall apart now.

The back door creaked on its hinges and a faint

scratching noise provoked a frown to Jesse's brow. It cleared in the next instant, replaced by a wide disbelieving grin as he heard the feeble canine whine that followed.

Thorn!

Jesse threw open the back door, falling to his knees as he gathered the giant dog to him. The cur was a matted mess of mud and blood-soaked fur. One of his eyes was cut and swollen shut, and he held his right front paw tucked protectively under him. Still his tail and tongue worked as he wagged his back end effusively and lavished Jesse with hot, dry kisses.

The dog had done the impossible, surviving the falls and the river currents, and for just an instant, Jesse felt hope for his mother leap in his chest. But that was asinine. She'd not only been sent crashing over the falls, she'd been shot. Besides, after all the harm she'd caused—Jesse couldn't think about that, all that had been lost. Instead, he concentrated on the miracle that he was holding.

"Come on, boy," he said, slipping his arms around the dog and lifting him carefully to carry him to one of the stainless-steel sinks in the laundry room downstairs. "Let's get you washed off so I can assess the damage. We'll have to get the vet out here to see you. Your tongue feels like you might be running a fever. Nose is hot, too. But don't you worry, you didn't make it all the way back not to be rewarded. Soon as we're done down here, I'm going to find you a juicy T-bone."

Jesse didn't stop talking until the last of the mud and grime and blood had disappeared down the tub's drain.

An hour later, satisfied that the dog needed rest more than anything else, he found an old blanket and made a bed for him in the corner of the kitchen. Hunkering down in front of the animal, he patted his head and wished him a good night. "You were very brave today, Thorn. I'm proud of you. Lacy was, too. She told me how you jumped between her and Mother to save her."

Thorn lifted his tail a couple of times in polite acknowledgment, then closed his eyes and sighed mightily.

Jesse managed the first grin of the day. Thin, tight, but a genuine, honest-to-goodness, bona fide smile, all the same.

"Sleep well, boy," he said, and headed for bed.

He was more than halfway up the stairs when she called his name. He turned around, searching the dimly lit foyer for her. He found her standing in the portico that led to the living room.

"What are you doing down here, Lace?" he asked, his tone gentle. "I thought I gave you strict orders to stay in bed."

She shrugged, smiling up at him. "I wanted to be with you."

This time the grin that spread across his face was wide, unrestrained. "God, woman, I'm glad I have you," he said as he stepped from the bottom stair and crossed the foyer in a couple long strides to gather her into his arms. He held her tightly, his face buried in the sweetly scented softness of her hair. "I swear to God, my heart stopped today when I heard that gun fire and thought it was you that had been shot."

"Don't think about it," she said, pulling him closer so that every inch of her was pressed against him.

She wore only a sheer satin gown and Jesse could feel her nakedness beneath it. He groaned. "Damn, you feel good."

"Take me right here, Jesse," she said, tilting her face up to kiss his throat.

He picked her up in his arms, carrying her toward the sofa, but she stopped him. "No, not there, lover. Here, on the floor like we did the night you brought me home from Mexico."

He fell to his knees, lowering her to the thick Persian rug that covered most of the living-room floor. "You remembered that?" he asked.

She ran her fingers through his hair, nodding as she smiled provocatively and ran her tongue over her lips. "Mmm," she purred. "How could I forget? We fucked so long and so hard I could hardly move for the next two days."

He pinned her face between his hands, his long fingers splayed over the sides of her head. Most of her—her body from her shoulders to her feet—was covered by a blanket of darkness. A single light shone from the foyer and its rays cut a slant into the room like a spotlight on her beautiful, perfect face.

She giggled and bit down on her bottom lip. "What? Why are you staring at me like that?"

He didn't answer. He couldn't. Emotion had balled in his throat, making words impossible. She was so damned beautiful, he could only stare. Her nightgown was red, a color she hadn't worn for the last few days; scarlet, actually, a color that was good for her, contrasted against the alabaster of her skin. He had to admit, though, he'd liked her in the softer pastels she'd chosen of late. The delicate tones seemed somehow more in sync with the woman he'd fallen in love with all over again.

"You're going to make me self-conscious staring at me like that," she said, slipping a hand beneath his to tuck her hair behind her ear. "Is something wrong?"

He didn't answer right off.

"Jesse, darling, are you all right?"

His sudden, unexpected laughter startled her. She pushed him away from her, rolling out from under him and scampering to her feet.

He got to his feet as well and, gripping her by the shoulders, turned her so that she stood bathed in the full light.

"What's the matter with you, honey? Why are you looking at me like that? And stop laughing. Have I said something funny?"

Instead of answering, he snapped his fingers as he remembered Thorn asleep in the kitchen. "I'm not laughing at you. Hell, the joke's on me, isn't it?"

"Sweetheart, what are you talking about?"

"Never mind. Just come with me." He took her hand and started from the room, but she put the brakes on. "Jesse, stop this! Where are you taking me?"

He stopped, turned to look at her, his eyes immediately going to the corner of her upper lip. "I was going to take you to the kitchen. Show you my surprise."

She canted her head just a bit. "You have a surprise for me?" she asked, her voice tinged with a hint of suspicion.

His shoulders sagged as he shook his head. "It's just the dog. He made it home, but that probably wouldn't mean much to you, would it? You never cared much for him anyway."

"Dog? You mean Thorn?" She was stalling, her mind

racing. Jesse could see the wheels spinning as she tried to get ahead of him, figure out what the hell he was talking about.

She flashed another of her gorgeous, disarming smiles. "Jesse, sweetheart, would you please stop staring at me like that." She wiped at the corner of her lips with her fingers, drawing his attention to her long, tapered nails that were painted crimson. "Is my lipstick smudged? Is that it?"

He shook his head. "No, your lipstick, your fingernails, everything about you is perfect as always."

"Then why are you looking at me like I have two heads?"

"Because you do, don't you?" he asked, the last of his amusement entirely faded from his tone. "One with a dimple on the right side of your cheek, the other with the dimple on the left."

It had been a long, emotionally taxing day for Chief Warren Anderson. He sat in the back seat of a black New Yorker with two Dallas-based FBI agents. One of them had just connected him with his office and handed him the telephone. It was the first opportunity he'd had to return his deputy chief's phone call. "You're being patched through to an American Dallas-bound flight, sir," the man said as Warren put the phone to his ear. "Agent Gary Maltz is en route and has some crucial information that bears on this case. He—"

Warren waved him to silence, then pressed a finger to his ear as Gary's voice came over the airwaves. The connection was grainy, choppy, and he struggled to hear what the man was saying.

"Slow up, Maltz. Go back. Start over. I'm hardly picking this up." Then to the driver of the car: "Pull over."

He was listening to the airborne agent again as he climbed out of the vehicle and began to pace along the shoulder of the road.

"Yeah, I got that," he replied when Agent Maltz asked if he'd heard everything he'd said about the two murdered women in California and about the videotape one of them had made the day before and left in the entranceway addressed to him in a padded manila envelope. "Cut to the chase, Gary. What was on it?"

"Her life ... shhh ... Had more money than ... shhh ... Was furious when her daughter ... shhh ... some dude in Topanga Canyon. Wrote the girl ... shhh ... will."

The conversation continued, Maltz repeating himself several times whenever the the static was too heavy for the chief to hang a hacked-up sentence together. Then all at once, Maltz was coming in loud and clear.

"You get that, sir?"

"No, run it again. Just the last part about the girl's death."

"Not just the old lady's daughter, Chief. The boy, too. Got ahold of some bad shit and were both dead before their pals in the commune could get them to the hospital. You get that?"

"Yeah, Gary. You're coming in loud and clear now. Just keep going before it breaks up again."

"Right. Well, this bitch, Charlotte—Lottie to her friends—went to the Canyon to pick up the babies."

"Did you say babies? Plural?"

"Yep!" Gary said on a triumphant note. "That's the whole point. There were two girls, sir. Twins. Old Lot brought them both home, but she claims she couldn't raise them both, so she gave one of them up for adoption. Said they were identical. Couldn't tell them apart except that they each had a single dimple. One on the left cheek, the other on the right."

"And our girl's the one she kept," Warren thought aloud.

"You got it. Unluckiest day of her life, you ask me. I don't know how the other one grew up, but it couldn't have been as horrible. This Lottie was one mean bitch," he paused before adding quietly, "though from what the LAPD boys tell me, our girl got even in spades."

Warren wasn't paying attention. He was thinking about the latents lifted from the burned-out car. One of them belonging to his witness, the other unidentified. He thought he had them now. "Charlotte Daniels have anything to say about the girls getting back together in the past few years?"

"Bingo! But listen, Chief, they've just advised us that we'll be landing in Dallas in the next few minutes. I have to hang up. An agent is waiting with a car to drive me down. I'll hook up with you in a couple of hours and you can see the tape for yourself."

"I'll be waiting, Gary. Safe landing."

"Yeah, thanks. Oh, Chief? One more thing, how's Mandell?"

"Gone, son," Warren answered quietly, though it wouldn't have mattered if he'd shouted the reply. Their connection had been broken. Just as well. The drive from Dallas wouldn't be as long this way.

He hung his head for a brief second before slapping the roof of the car and climbing back in the back seat. "Turn around, young man," he said to the agent behind the wheel. "We've got to get back to the Southern Star. And while you're going, let's do a test drive, see how fast this boat will move."

As the agent whipped the car around in a smart, tight U-turn, the FBI chief laid out what he expected to find when they arrived back at the ranch. In his precise, quiet way, he laid out the game plan, then sat back and stared out the tinted windows.

Twins! Son of a gun!

Lacy awakened with a start. The room was as black as pitch and she felt panic well inside her. She had always hated the dark, been afraid of the monsters that lurked in its secret corners. But today was worse than usual. Today the monsters had come out in the daylight.

She clamped a hand over her mouth as a cry bubbled to the surface.

Scampering from the bed, she groped her way to the door, the last ounce of restraint enabling her to tread slowly.

A light burned in the hallway, and she darted from the room only to be brought up short by the yellow CRIME SCENE tape on the door to the room next to hers.

Tears washed to her eyes at once, and shame tingled all the way to her fingertips.

Rose.

Cybil.

Dillon.

Thorn.

And those two FBI men.

All of them dead, and she'd taken a nap!

Jesse! Where was he? She started for his room, stopping when she heard the sound of his voice below. He was laughing ... unless she was dreaming. No, a body didn't ache like this in dreams.

She wore a T-shirt and sweatpants, no shoes. She padded soundlessly toward the stairs. She started down, stopping when she heard a second voice.

"You're crazy," Lacy heard a woman reply. She pressed her hand to her mouth. She recognized the voice. How could she not? It was her own.

Nausea washing over her, she grabbed the railing, steadying herself, as she gulped back bile and listened.

"It's over. Finished. I've figured it out," Jesse was saying. "You know, every time I looked at her, I kept wondering what it was that wasn't quite right. I almost had it this morning, when I faced her reflection in the mirror." There was a pause before he added, "Right after we made love."

"You bastard," the woman said, her voice a hiss.

"And then you smiled and it hit me right between the eyes. Your dimple is on the left. Wrong side. And the tiny crescent-shaped scar on the corner of her lip? Yours is missing. Dead giveaway. You're good, but this time you messed up. Should have done your homework better. Anyway, game's over and sorry, babe, you lose."

"No, Jesse, darling, she loses. I'm your wife."

Lacy had arrived downstairs and stood in the doorway now, though neither Jesse nor the woman—her clone— had noticed her yet.

Jesse's slow grin slid into place on his handsome face. "Yep, I figured that out, too. Thing is, honey, it doesn't matter. All you've got is a piece of paper. It doesn't mean squat. You may be my wife, but she's my heart."

"Her name's Sheila," his heart said from the doorway. "Sheila Daniels. And my real name is Shelby, Jesse. Shelby Sands. We're twins."

Sheila whirled around at the sound of her sister's voice. "So, the stories about your amnesia were phony, huh?"

"No, you're wrong. They were all too real. I didn't remember anything until yesterday when I ran into Alex. My adopted brother? You do recall meeting him, don't you? You were all over him."

Sheila's lazy grin arrived on cue. "Of course. A gorgeous bear. Football player, isn't he?"

Shelby ignored the question. Continued her account of regaining the memory that had been taken from her in a cruel murder attempt. "I didn't remember you at all. Not until just now when I saw you. Then it all came back to me. The first time we met when I went with my family to Vegas and saw you up there on that stage in the chorus line." She laughed though there wasn't a modicum of humor in the hollow sound. "I went home and made the dolls for us. Yours in pink, mine in blue. When Jesse brought me here after . . . I recognized the doll but the dress was wrong, and now I know why. It was your doll up there."

"Yeah, I was real touched," Sheila said.

"The next time I saw you, you were leaving for Texas; going to hook yourself a rich cowboy you said. I didn't hear from you again until you came to see me last month. Said your marriage was over." She looked from her sister to Jesse. "I told her how sorry I was. She'd been so sure you were the man she wanted, and that's when she said the words I remembered the day we flew home from L.A.: 'I thought so, too,' she said, 'Only I hadn't expected to be bored to death.' "

Shelby turned her gaze back to her twin, dashing away tears that were suddenly spilling over her lashes. "I hurt for you, but you just laughed, said I should forget it, that you were fine. Then you suggested we treat ourselves to a special day together. Even insisted on paying for everything." Her lip trembled and she had to stop for a minute as it all came flooding back, making sense for the first time.

Sheila laughed. "You make it sound like I dragged you off in handcuffs and leg irons. Jesus, you poor little mouse. I treated you to the best day of your dull, mundane life."

"You did that," Shelby agreed. "A massage, facial, manicure—the whole nine yards. Then shopping for a designer dress you insisted I wear to dinner that night even though I told you I had to get back to Laguna, to my work." She ran a hand over her hair and surprised herself by laughing. She looked at Jesse. "Do you get it yet?"

"Not all of it, no," he said, keeping his gaze focused on Sheila.

She shrugged, "Hey, let her tell you. I think she's really got it all figured out. I wouldn't deny her the opportunity to show off for you."

"Go on," Jesse told Shelby. He didn't need to hear any more. He thought he already knew the most important part of the story—who'd run her down on the pier—but they were buying time, so he encouraged her to continue.

"She took me to her hotel room and showed me a photo of Clay Waters. Said he was after her, had been hired to kill her. Of course that was a lie. As we all know now." For the first time, she frowned and confusion puckered her brow. "Why did you tell me he was a professional hit man?"

"So you'd tell me if he came around asking about me, of course. I didn't think he'd followed me from here, but I couldn't be sure."

"But if you'd already planned—"

"To kill you?" Sheila finished for her as twins are prone to do. "I couldn't know how cooperative you'd prove to be. Had to cover all the bases."

Shelby shivered with the chill inspired by her sister's cold confession. She felt Jesse step up beside her, was immediately warmed by the arm he wrapped around her shoulder, and continued on with her first journey down memory lane.

"I was exhausted, but I was worried about you, too, so even though it was late—almost ten—I went with you to Anthony's for dinner. Only when you dropped me off in front of the restaurant, you said you were going to park the car, make a quick phone call, then join me at our table."

Sheila laughed, shaking her head as she, too, remembered what had happened next, though from a vastly different slant. "Of course, I never had any intention of going into the restaurant. I'd made the reservation for two in my name, then parked down the road a ways so I could see the front door, but you couldn't see me." She rolled her eyes, then directed them at her husband. "It was a week night and late, as she said, so the pier was fairly empty. Still, I had no idea how well she'd cooperate. Poor dear sat in there until almost one o'clock before she gave up and came out looking for me."

"And then you ran her down, smashed her against a wall like the vicious bitch you are."

Tears streamed from Shelby's eyes now, but she met her sister's gaze unflinchingly. "And when they found me, I was dressed in designer clothes, my hair freshly styled, even my nails perfectly manicured, just so I'd fit the image of the beautiful, wealthy, pampered Lacy Pryde."

"Precisely, and you were fantastic. Cooperative to the last. Just stood there like the good little girl that she is, right against the wall where I left her." She laughed with the memory that was even sweeter in the telling. "She didn't move until the second she realized I was driving fast and aiming straight for her. Then she reacted exactly as I had choreographed it, dropping down and cowering while I smashed into her."

Shelby was trembling and trying hard not to show it. She knew Jesse felt it, for he'd tightened his hold on her. She forced a note of calm into her tone when she spoke. "But why? Couldn't you have just disappeared?"

"Oh, hell, yes! That way Sammy would never have stopped looking for me. With you dead—you were supposed to die, you know—I would have been home free. I had all his money. That's why the FBI sent Clay here. They wanted me to know that they knew. And then I got word that Sammy had contracted a hit." Sheila looked at her husband. "No offense, sweetheart, but I was getting bored playing little house on the prairie anyway."

"Then why are you back now?" he asked.

She laughed. "Well, I guess I could claim I came back because you're mine, and blame it on a definite aversion to sharing my toys." She looked around, then took a couple of steps backward and dropped into an easy chair. "You don't mind if we're comfortable while we have our little family reunion, do you?"

"Not at all," Jesse said, letting his arm drop from Shelby's shoulder and taking her hand to lead her with him to the sofa.

"But that's not the reason," Shelby said. "So why?

Are you planning to try again? Prove you're dead to your boyfriend?" Shelby asked.

"Exactamundo, sis."

"So what's with the sexy nightgown and the come-on? Was I going to be so besotted, I'd just sit by while you killed your sister, then run away with you?" Jesse asked, his sarcasm as sharp as a razor.

Sheila had crossed her legs. One of them swung impatiently now. "Why, that would have been nice, but no, I don't expect that would have ever happened." She laughed. "Never was much of a believer in fairy tales. I just wanted one last fuck. One for the road, you might say."

"And then what? You were going to kill me, too?"

"Uh-huh. Besides, how could you live if I killed her? She's your heart, after all." She rolled her eyes. "Gag."

"Sorry to make you sick. But, hey, maybe this bit of information will put you back in form: Chief Warren Anderson's right here in Texas. He and La—ah, Shelby—were reunited today. At least, that's what they both believed was happening. Turns out they were meeting for the first time, but who knew? Anyway, he wasn't very pleasant to her. Seems he blames her for the murder of his two FBI agents early this morning. He was also trying to get back to his deputy chief in L.A. about a double homicide in a ritzy borough called Brentwood. You wouldn't know anything about that, would you?"

Sheila's face paled. "No! They couldn't have connected that to me. You're lying."

"No, Sheila, that's *your* specialty," her sister said.

"Then why me?"

"Maybe because all hell's broke loose—six people hurt here today, five of them dead and at least four of them connected to you—or maybe it's just the FBI chief's good instincts, I don't—"

"Wait a minute," Sheila said, uncrossing her legs and leaning forward. "What are you talking about, six? I heard about Waters and the other one on the radio on my way from Dallas this morning. Picked up the news about poor dear Mother Rose and my loony-tunes sister-in-law while I was hiding out on the range, waiting for a chance to sneak into the house. But where do you get six?"

"Someone shot Libby while she was out riding this morning," Jesse told her, his tone cold. "We suspect it was

Dillon. We're guessing he mistook her for Lacy ... for you, that is, though we won't know till they can find the bullet and do a comparison with bullets from his shotgun."

Sheila shook her head. "Well, I'm confused. Not overly upset about our beauty queen's mishap, but definitely confused about your brother's part in all this. And how could anyone confuse that oversized Barbie doll with me? None of this makes sense."

"It does if you consider she was wearing a red T-shirt—your signature color, after all," he said, his gaze going to her crimson nightgown. "She was also riding your horse."

She shrugged. "Okay, so the man couldn't tell a broad rump like hers from a stop sign. That still doesn't explain why he shot her."

"Because he was a hired killer, Sheila," Shelby offered quietly. "He was paid fifty thousand dollars by Sammy Wyatt to kill you. He was the hit man you ran from."

"Dillon? I don't believe you!" She laughed at the wonder of it. "Where is he? I want to hear this from his own lips."

"He's dead," Jesse said flatly. "Killed himself this afternoon. Surprised you didn't hear all about that if you were hiding out there all the while."

Sheila hunched her shoulders. "Nope, missed that. Must have been when I was talking to a couple of state troopers. They were sweethearts, warning me about being out there with a killer on the loose. Even offered to escort me to the house. Cute boys, but denser than cow dung."

"You're a mean woman," Shelby said.

"Umm, yes, I suppose I am, though I prefer to think of myself as a survivor." She slipped a hand along the side of the chair cushion and pulled out a small handgun. "Which reminds me, I'd better be getting to business."

Jesse felt Shelby stiffen beside him and increased the pressure on her hand, signaling her to relax, to trust him.

"Well, I see you kept something I gave you," he said, referring to the .22 she held in her hand.

"Actually, not," she said on a thin smile. "I merely found it upstairs in my bedroom when I was changing. It was right there tucked beneath my lingerie where I'd left it. Thoughtful of you not to move my things," she said to her sister.

"You were in there while I was sleeping?"

"Stood right over you, sweetie, wishing I'd brought a knife up to cut your pretty throat."

Shelby gasped and Jesse used her fear as an opportunity to gather her into her arms and whisper a two-word order, "Start screaming."

She didn't question him, just opened her mouth and screamed with terror that wasn't difficult to simulate.

Sheila bounded to her feet, spreading her legs wide and gripping the gun with both hands, ironically just as Jesse had taught her, and aiming it at her sister's head.

Jesse shoved Shelby to the floor, then rolled after her, covering her body with his own.

The front door crashed open, but not before a whir of black crashed into the woman, sending her backward against the wall. Her head hit the windowsill with a sickening thud, and she didn't move. Neither did Thorn. Not even when the FBI agents attempted to pull him away. He backed them off with a low, rumbling growl.

He didn't budge until Shelby called him. After all, it was her scream that had brought him running to her defense.

Several minutes later she still knelt in the middle of the living-room floor, her arms still wrapped around the giant dog's neck, and her tears falling into his thick, woolly coat.

Jesse was crouched at her side. "That makes two times I owe him for today. He's proven quite the hero."

Shelby managed a weak laugh that came out sounding more like a sob. "She didn't get it, but then maybe she never had anyone to teach her," she said, her tear-blurred eyes fastened on the place where her sister's body was being covered with a sheet of green tarp. She'd known she was dead the instant she heard her head crack and saw the blue eyes turn to glass.

"About what, darlin'?" Jesse asked softly, pulling her toward him and forcing her eyes away from the sight of her sister's body.

"Fairy tales and heroes."

She hugged both of her heroes and smiled.

Chapter Thirty-seven

Shelby and Jesse sat in his office on the sofa as the videotape Chief Anderson had left behind for them to watch. "Might answer a few questions," he'd said as he handed it to her.

The tape had been playing for a little over six minutes when it ended, and the screen turned to snow. Six minutes to explain away the lives and deaths of her natural parents, and a decision that had had such a profound impact on so many lives.

Jesse reached for the remote control to turn it off, but she stopped him, taking it from his hand and depressing the REWIND button. She let it go only for a few seconds. "I just want to see the end one more time," she offered in way of an explanation.

The telephone rang and Jesse got up to answer it. "It's Joey," he said. "I'll take it out here and talk to him so you can finish up in here."

"Tell him I send my love and am keeping Libby and the baby in my prayers."

As soon as he disappeared, she pushed PLAY.

The grandmother she'd never known appeared on the screen once again. Her gnarled fingers nervously brought a cigarette back and forth from her thin, shriveled lips, followed every few seconds by great gusts of smoke. But Shelby stared at the woman's eyes and focused on the voice that was as hard and cold as ice chips.

"—Didn't have to take either of them. But half the blood that ran through their veins was my daughter's. She'd defied me by running off with their scumbag father, but I sort of figured she'd made up for it by giving me another chance. So, I played Solomon, you might say. Except instead of a sword, I used a line from a nursery rhyme. Eeny, meeny, miney, moe, and I split the baby. Adopted little Sheila so there wouldn't be any record of the other one on the birth certificate. The other one—"

Shelby pressed the OFF button, dropped the remote control, and scooted off the couch. She walked to the window and stared out at the land she'd come to love in such a short span of time. Thorn was at her side.

Jesse came to stand behind her, circling her waist with his arms. "See, you haven't lost your shadow," he said.

She smiled as she laid her head back on his chest. "I wish he'd relax. I know he's still hurting from the injuries he sustained in the river."

"In time. He's got to learn that the villains are all gone."

"Me, too. Might take some time."

"Well, if nothing else, we have that." He nudged her away from the window. "Let's go."

They stopped in the foyer to pick up the bags they'd packed the evening before after returning from the family cemetery where four of their family members—even the sister she'd never known except as an enemy—had been laid to rest.

They were leaving the Southern Star, maybe forever, maybe just until the house had been razed per Jesse's instructions, and until the wounds inflicted on their souls had healed.

"Are you all right? About leaving your home, I mean?"

"As long as I have you, I'm good."

She smiled and turned away, meeting her reflection in the mirror. She remembered the line from her favorite childhood fairy tale. "Mirror, mirror, on the wall, who's the fairest of them all?" Just like in the story, the wicked witch was dead and the question no longer begged an answer.

She shuddered.

"What's wrong?" Jesse asked.

She hesitated. No, she wouldn't give up her faith in the most important lessons learned in fairy tales. "Nothing," she said truthfully. "I was just thinking about happily ever after."

He grinned as he craned his neck to peck her lips. "Well, then, darlin', we'd better get going, 'cause we might already have the happy, but we sure ain't gonna find the ever after till we've made an honest woman of you."

She laughed and foolishly glanced around for Thorn. He sat only inches from her heels.

"We'll solve another problem by getting married, too."

Jesse raised a brow in question as he held open the door with his shoulder and let her pass by.

"My name, silly. I'm no longer sure who I am. I feel like Shelby, but I feel like Lacy, too. After we're legal man and wife, you can resolve that by just calling me Mrs. Pryde."

"Hey, I can fix the problem sooner than that. I'll just go on calling you darlin'."

"Yep, that'll work."

SIGNET ONYX

PASSIONATE SECRETS, SCANDALOUS SINS

☐ **BLISS by Claudia Crawford.** Rachel Lawrence seeks to mold her beautiful great-granddaughter Bliss in her image despite the objections of her entire family. Then comes the riveting revelation of the shocking deception that Bliss's mother and aunt can no longer hide . . . as four generations of women come together to relive their lives and love, and face the truth that will shatter their illusions and threaten to doom their dreams for the future. (179374—$5.50)

☐ **NOW AND FOREVER by Claudia Crawford.** Nick Albert was the type of man no woman could resist. Georgina, Mona, and Amy were all caught in a web of deceit and betrayal—and their irresistible passion for that man that only one of them could have—for better or for worse. (175212—$5.50)

☐ **NIGHT SHALL OVERTAKE US by Kate Saunders.** Four young girls make a blood vow of eternal friendship at an English boarding school. Through all the time and distance that separates them, they are bound together by a shared past . . . until one of them betrays their secret vow. "A triumph."—*People* (179773—$5.99)

☐ **BELOVED STRANGER/SUMMER STORM by Joan Wolf. With an Introduction by Catherine Coulter.** Bestselling author Joan Wolf has received both critical and popular acclaim for her compelling romances many of which have become collectors' items. Now, this exclusive dual collection brings back two of her long out of print contemporary love stories. (182510—$3.99)

*Prices slightly higher in Canada